The Love Lie

MONICA MCCALLAN

D1525664

The Love Lie

© 2024 By Monica McCallan. All Rights Reserved.

First Edition: December 2024

By The Author

Acknowledgments

My life has changed a lot since the release of my last novel almost two years ago. I married my soulmate. I lost my mom to cancer. I moved hundreds of miles and settled into a new life.

In spite of everything that's happened, I've always known that I didn't want my writing days to be over. So with this newest book, I can officially say that they're not.

Dedication

To Haley - The person who made me believe in soulmates. Who loved all the things about me that I didn't always love about myself. Who gave me the truest place in the world, which is by your side.

Synopsis

A year ago, Sydney King was a successful pro tennis player with a long-term boyfriend, a plan for the future, and a shot at fulfilling all her dreams.

Now, she has a cheating ex-boyfriend and a career-ending injury, and—quite frankly—things could not be going worse for her.

She hopes that returning home to Stoneport, Massachusetts will be the reset her life needs—until she finds out her ex's wedding to the woman he cheated with is the social event of the season.

The last person Sydney expects to find camaraderie with is her former fiancé's sister, Reese Devereux. Back home after the purchase of a local inn, Reese has wounds of her own and seems even less enthused about her brother's wedding than Sydney.

When an unexpected mix-up creates the perfect story that she and Reese are dating, shockingly, Reese runs with it. Sydney knows it's a bad idea, but being on Reese's arm gives her the chance to pretend life is just a little bit more in her control than it feels.

Both women are coming home to their pasts, but it's up to them to decide what they want their futures to look like.

One

SYDNEY KING, formerly the nineteenth best women's tennis player in the world, sat with her body curled up on the sofa at The Stone's Throw Inn. A plush blanket covered her bare legs, and she snuggled in deeper until it enveloped her completely.

Nothing but her head poked out, which was a shame since her blonde hair, tied up in a messy bun, had seen much better days.

She liked the feeling of being hidden right now, not even the writing across her shirt visible. She loved this shirt—soft after hundreds of washes, a reminder of how far she'd come. It was from her first professional tennis tournament, the letters spelling "Puerto Vallarta Open" all but faded into obscurity.

Just like her career.

Her muscles twitched from disuse in a way that she tried not to let gnaw at her. The television across from her played a talk show, but it couldn't drown out the noise in her head. She could still smell the faint scent of the lobster roll that had been delivered from the kitchen thirty minutes ago. She took in a shallow breath as her stomach roiled, nauseous from all the fried food she'd consumed in the last few days.

How the mighty had fallen.

She rolled her neck and stretched her arms to alleviate the

energy pent up inside of her, fingers snagging on something sharp, stuck on the blanket, as she did. Without looking down, she flicked a leftover piece of last night's tortilla chips away from her.

Guess she hadn't eaten the whole bag after all.

Since returning to her hometown of Stoneport, Massachusetts, three days ago, she'd rarely ventured out of The Stone's Throw, a charmingly outdated inn right next to downtown. This was her trip to do with as she wished. And right now, she wanted to pretend like the outside world didn't exist.

Which was why, as her phone vibrated somewhere underneath the blanket, she let the call go to voicemail.

Her lips twitched as she considered standing up, but she found the option overwhelming enough that she ended up sinking deeper into the sofa.

She let out a frustrated groan into the empty room.

Where had it all gone so wrong?

It was a question Sydney had spent the last few months thinking about tirelessly.

On paper, everything should have worked out. It felt like she was staring at a perfectly executed rally, yet she'd still lost the point. The match, really.

Stretching out her knee along the couch, she felt a phantom twinge. After months of rehab, she knew it wasn't real. It still hurt, though. All of the rehab had hurt, too, and, ultimately, it had been a lot of pain for nothing.

Professional tennis had been her dream for the last fifteen years—the pursuit of it all she'd ever known, really—and now she was staring down the barrel of what came next.

She'd attended her dream college on a full ride to play tennis after dedicating her adolescence to thousands of hours training at a local academy. It had meant forsaking her junior and senior years of high school in person in favor of two years of homeschool classes, but at the time, it hadn't felt like she was giving anything up.

For years, she'd slogged through the lower circuits before

finally getting a wildcard entry into the pro tour four years ago. She'd been twenty-four. Young, in the scheme of life, but she was up against women who'd started playing professionally at fourteen, with already a decade of experience in major tournaments under their belts by her age.

Still, she'd finally been making her mark.

Last year, she'd made it to the quarterfinals of the Australian Open and then the semifinals at the US Open in the fall. She'd lost both matches, but she'd never forget the high that came with entering the stadium, under bright lights and a sold-out crowd.

She flexed her bare, extended foot, missing how the different surfaces she'd played on felt beneath her sneakers.

Until a few weeks ago, she *was* tennis. Her lifestyle, diet, training regimen, and the place she'd called home were all oriented around a simple, singular goal: to see how far her career could take her.

And now, with a stupid series of decisions made because she couldn't keep her emotions in check, she'd lost everything.

What's it that they say? Love means nothing in tennis? She'd sure proved that right.

"Idiot." Frustration was laced through her voice as she searched for the bag of M&M's she'd placed somewhere within reach earlier.

Whether she was talking about herself or Grant, she didn't know.

"Hey! Are you about done with your pity party this morning?"

Hallie Thatcher, her childhood best friend, stared at her from the door to the hallway. Wisps of Hallie's dark hair haloed her temples, her face flushed. She'd already accomplished more in the morning than Sydney had in the last few days since she'd arrived back in Stoneport. Sydney was at least five inches taller than Hallie, not that anyone in the inn would know, given that she had spent most of her time glued to this spot on the couch. She and the furniture had become one. Where she ended and it started was really no one's business these days.

Hallie's voice cut through the, to quote her friend, 'pity party' she'd *maybe* been throwing herself. "I've been standing here for like a minute. Don't think I didn't see what you did with that tortilla chip."

Sydney pitched her body forward over the sofa in a fluid movement, her fingers sliding along the carpet until she found a sharp edge.

"Gotcha," she said, holding the chip up in triumph like she'd just accomplished something.

Hallie only lifted her eyebrows and stepped farther into the shared living room, their respective bedrooms flanking both sides.

Hallie had taken over day-to-day operations of the inn from her parents two years ago. She worked possibly even more hours than Sydney had—back when she'd still had a career.

And since Hallie lived on-site that meant that, in a way, Sydney did now, too. At least, she did while she figured out what came next.

Which she would do. As soon as she managed to separate herself from the couch.

She could always go back to Florida and live in the house she'd purchased for her parents a few years ago. But when she'd finally accepted that continuing the tour this year wasn't possible, it hadn't taken long to realize that being enveloped in her parents' sympathetic yet mildly concerned hovering wasn't what she needed.

She'd needed a reset, and coming back to the place where she'd fallen in love with tennis—coming *home*—while maybe a touch masochistic, felt like the right next step.

She was grateful that her friend, with very few questions asked, had offered her a place to stay. Sydney had tried to make it work on the tour for as long as she could, but as the days wore on and her ranking continued to plummet, she'd been caught in a vicious cycle that had chewed her up and spat her out in no more than a few months.

"I'm sorry, Hal," she said when she placed the chip on the end table, promising herself she'd throw it away when she got up.

And truly, she was. Sorry, that is. It was terrifying how easy it'd been to fall apart when it felt like there was nothing anchoring her to the world and her place in it anymore.

Hallie was already moving toward the small kitchen nestled along the wall to dig for her midday smoothie ingredients when she finally threw Sydney a bone. "You're fine, Syd. I know this year hasn't been easy for you. Plus," she said, leveling a smirk in Sydney's direction, "you've always been the messy one."

"Messy, not dirty. There's a huge difference," she muttered back, but it was drowned out by the sound of the blender.

And truly, there was. Clothes strewn about her bedroom after a shower and deprioritizing weekly deep cleans in favor of hitting a few extra balls on the court were far different than living in the detritus of sparkling water cans, chip crumbs, and stray M&M's that had overtaken her life recently.

She couldn't seem to pull herself out of the rut that deepened by the day.

When she'd been injured during last year's final pro tournament of the season, it had been a blow... to put it mildly.

She'd done everything they'd said she should. Rehab. Rest. Okay, she likely could have done that one better, but she couldn't stand the idea of coming back this season in anything less than peak physical form.

But when she'd hit the court for what she hadn't known would be her final year, she could feel her body still wasn't right. Her knee's range of movement was still too limited, exacerbated by her preference for hard surfaces and quick hits.

She'd lost during the first round of the Australian Open, and it had only gone downhill from there.

If the body keeps the score, hers was looking to take her out without allowing a single point.

Her serve was weaker. She couldn't cover the court as easily, even at a few inches shy of six feet. The nail in the coffin was that she was afraid to make the quick adjustments that were crucial to her almost imperceptible edge in reaction time, something she'd been honing for years as she'd reached the next levels of play.

The end came not with a bang, but with a whimper. There was no singular moment, no reopening of her ACL tear that had forced her to be carried off the court. Just a slow degradation of stamina, focus, and confidence in her game.

She didn't trust herself—and that was the worst thing that could happen to an athlete at the professional level.

Finally, at her coach's recommendation, if not downright insistence, she'd retired from the tour a week ago, officially rescinding her spot in the next open, which she'd originally been set to fly out for in a few days.

Wimbledon, which had made the knife twist in a little harder.

And then she'd accepted—still hoping this was all a bad dream—that her career was over.

It felt like she was proving everyone right.

Her sponsors, who always seemed more interested in her staying conventionally attractive than whether she won matches.

Her coach, who'd already moved on to working with the next sixteen-year-old phenom who'd had a tennis racket in hand before they could walk.

Her long-term ex-boyfriend—that one still stung.

After six years, he hadn't even had the decency to break up with her. She'd walked in on him accidentally, in the apartment in Boston where he resided and where she spent as much time as she could, given her busy tour schedule.

She tried not to think about how happy she'd been a year ago, when the steps of her future seemed to be falling in line. At the time, it had felt more like a ladder she was methodically climbing than a row of dominoes, just waiting to be toppled.

Her plan had been to give tennis her all for the next three

years, after which she'd retire from the pro circuit and move back to Boston to be with Grant full-time.

They'd start trying for a family, and eventually, she wanted them to move back to Stoneport.

It was easier not to think about when life had been going well, when her ex's betrayal had felt like a survivable blip on her way to something greater.

Now, with her life in shambles, it had seeped into the edges of her consciousness, her mind picking at it like a scab she couldn't let heal.

"I can see it on your face," Hallie said. "You're spiraling."

It was only then Sydney became aware of how hard her fingertips were digging into the back of her neck, like she was trying to massage the thoughts out of her.

She dropped her hand back into her lap. "I'm not spiraling."

Top professional athletes with years of mental conditioning didn't *spiral*. They formulated a plan and then got back to work.

So why, *why*, couldn't she make herself do just that?

Professional tennis was done. Grant was definitely done. There was nothing for her in Boston or Florida.

Her parents, well intentioned though they were, had started to give her a *look*, like they were growing concerned about her mental health.

Well, they could join the club.

So she'd packed a bag and bought a one-way ticket to New England, intent on staying for at least a few weeks.

It's not like she had anywhere else to be.

Everything in Florida reminded her of the life she'd lost. She'd wake up in her bed, muscles already stretching out in anticipation of her morning workout, only to realize there was no reason to head to the court.

And her specialized diet? Now pointless. At least her second-chance romance with M&M's was a bright spot on an otherwise bleak horizon.

She'd let Sara, her agent, know that she was going

incommunicado, with the promise she wouldn't be caught in any compromising positions. Sara seemed to believe that there would be life after professional tennis, in terms of possible sponsorships and job opportunities, but Sydney didn't have the mental fortitude to consider that right now.

Even if she could conceive of her new reality, it felt almost impossible to feel excited about it.

"You can stay here as long as you need. Coming back here to reset was the right choice. It's a good plan," Hallie stressed.

Sydney pulled her blanket more tightly around her. "That was something day-one me told you. I'm now day-four me, and things are different. I'm a woman changed by the brutality of the world." But she had to give her friend credit for being such an active listener this past week.

Hallie lifted an eyebrow. "Three days to complete defeat, King? That doesn't sound like the person I used to know. You competed in our final tennis match of the sophomore season when you had that horrible flu." It was the last match she'd competed in at the high school level before starting full-time, private training at the Manhaven Tennis Center.

She shuddered, feeling like she could still taste the awful tinge in her mouth from all those years ago.

"And how'd that go?" Hallie pushed, ignoring Sydney's obvious unwillingness to participate in this pep talk.

Sydney muttered something unintelligible, sinking impossibly lower into the couch.

Hallie moved closer to her, standing above Sydney with her hands on her hips. "What's that again?"

When the *incident* in question had happened, she'd been starting to get interest in colleges, and clinching the top spot and an undefeated season at a school like Stoneport was exactly the feather in her cap that she needed to start realizing her dreams.

"I won," she admitted, loud enough for Hallie to hear this time.

"Hell yeah, you won! And then you went and barfed your brains out in the bathroom. Like the champion you are."

That earned a laugh from Sydney, though she refused to acknowledge the high five Hallie was leveling in her direction. "I think that was more than the flu."

"Who gets stressed after the competition is over?" Hallie protested.

"Someone with a ten-step life plan. That was step two, with step three happening imminently."

Hallie put her hand down, finally accepting defeat. "What was step three?"

"Training at Manhaven Tennis Center before getting a full ride to Walker College."

"Which, again, you succeeded at." Hallie smiled, a comforting gesture that the dimple in her right cheek pop.

"A lot of good that did me," she lamented, hating the irritation in her own voice.

"Sydney."

She looked up to find her friend's smile gone.

"Hallie." Sydney stretched her arms over her head, her forearms prickling with the sudden exposure to the air conditioning.

"You need to leave this room. It's been a week, and I'm starting to get concerned about a vitamin D deficiency."

"I drank that smoothie you made me yesterday," Sydney countered. She unfolded her leg and placed both bare feet on the floor before she stood up slowly, giving her muscles time to acclimate to the severe change of—yeah—a standing position. How the mighty had fallen. "And to be fair, it's only been four days."

"Your life isn't over, Syd."

"Well, it definitely doesn't feel like it's starting." Petulance, party of one.

"You're only twenty-eight."

"With no prospects," Sydney said in her best impression of an upper-class English accent. She knew she wasn't winning any awards for it.

"Better none than the one you had," Hallie volleyed back.

Sydney winced. That one was fair, even if it hurt.

"I just don't want to be the hot tennis player who peaked too soon." It had always been a fear in the back of her mind. Her game spoke for itself, but she knew that sponsorships had been more plentiful and post-match attention more common because of her face and her body. At five-ten, she'd filled out in the hips and the chest in a way that earned her appreciative glances. It couldn't be avoided, and while she tried to use her looks responsibly, sometimes it felt like they were more important than her talent.

Hallie walked across the room and stood in front of Sydney. She reached her hands up and pinched her best friend's cheeks. "I'm sorry that your injury didn't come with the doubly emotional turmoil of disfigurement. You should have gotten hurt trying to save a litter of kittens from a burning building or something. And, in focusing on the positives," Hallie continued, "you get to stay in this beautiful house on the water."

"It's a hotel room."

"First of all, it's a suite. And it's free."

Sydney cupped her hands around Hallie's and sighed. She'd missed her best friend, especially these last few years when it had felt like everything was falling apart around her. "I'm sorry I'm being such a baby."

The always understanding Hallie squeezed her fingers. "You've had a hell of a year."

She stepped away from her friend, over to the window that looked out toward the beautiful, rocky shoreline she'd once called home. "Nothing is the way I thought it'd be. And, on top of that, I'm frustrated with myself for how poorly I'm adapting."

"Again I will reiterate: You've been through a lot. Tennis." A punctuated silence, one that Sydney knew would be filled with something else she didn't want to discuss. "Grant."

Still, she blanched at his name. "Don't remind me about the last one. I cannot believe I was so *stupid*."

Hallie's tone matched her own. "He's the stupid one. He threw away an amazing partner and person. People like him are very good at keeping everyone in the dark."

Hallie grew quiet for so long that Sydney wondered if her friend had left her to wallow.

Pulling herself away from the lull of the waves as they crashed against the short cliff at the edge of the property, she turned to face her.

"Hallie, are you okay?" Sydney knew that she'd been a lot the past few days, but she'd be fine. This was just a difficult time. "Really, I'm going to be—"

"I need to tell you something."

She hated the look on Hallie's face, hands clasped together in front of her. It was the same stance she'd had when they were growing up and she knew her parents were going to be mad about whatever she'd done. Or, more accurately, whatever they'd done.

Trying to hide a kitten in Hallie's bedroom when they'd been ten, for example. Not the best idea, considering she'd grown up sharing this two-bedroom suite with her parents when they'd managed the inn. They'd named him Stoner, missing the accidental joke by a mile until they were both older.

Then there was the time they'd tried to pierce one another's ears. Sydney's scream was so loud it had caused a guest walking through the hallway to go to the front desk in concern.

In retrospect, that should have been Sydney's first clue that she didn't exactly take difficult situations in stride.

They'd always been in trouble *together*, so it felt strange for Sydney to be standing on the outside of whatever tumult was coursing through Hallie, unable to read her mind.

Her body buzzed. "What is it?"

"My parents sold the inn." Hallie blurted the words out, her cheeks going bright red.

Relief coursed through Sydney, even as she tried to make sense of everything. In the seconds that Hallie had made her wait, Sydney had considered what felt like every possibility—from a terminal illness to, well, a faster-moving terminal illness.

She sighed deeply before sucking in a much-needed breath. "I mean, that sucks, Hal. Why didn't you tell me?"

The flush on Hallie's cheeks softened but didn't disappear. "I know you're going through a lot."

"But that doesn't mean I don't want to be here for you."

Sydney gestured for Hallie to come join her near the window. When she was close enough, Sydney looped her longer arm over Hallie's shoulders. They stared out at the water, a ritual they'd had since childhood.

"So, tell me about it. What made your parents decide to sell?"

She felt Hallie roll her shoulders against her. "They've been spending more and more time in Colorado since Mason and Claire had the twins. They're going to buy a house near them, but all of their money's tied up in the inn."

Sydney nodded. Mason was Hallie's older brother, who'd moved out to Colorado for college, where he had met his wife, Claire. The twins, if Sydney remembered correctly, had just turned one. It made a lot of sense, even if Sydney hated the idea of the Thatcher family no longer owning The Stone's Throw.

Everything really was changing.

Still, she shoved her disappointment down. "Those kiddos are cute. I'll give them that."

"Aren't they," Hallie admitted with a glum laugh. "Finicky vacationers and hardcore antiques shoppers were no competition when it came down to it."

"So, what will you do?" Suddenly, Sydney looked around the room. "Are we even supposed to be here?"

"It's fine," Hallie said, though her reassurance didn't quell the unease building in Sydney's stomach.

"Wait. How are *you* doing?" She could feel her adrenaline picking up. "I mean, this is big. Life-changingly big. For your family and for you. What are you going to do? Am I back here so we can do some sort of goodbye tour?"

"Syd." Hallie laid a gentling hand on her arm. Sydney had always been the one to get keyed up faster. "First of all, it was your idea to come back to Stoneport."

Sydney acquiesced with a quick nod, the most she could manage at the moment. Tennis had been the only thing her brain worked through quickly. Everything else needed time to marinate and roll around in her mind before it made sense.

While she was toying with what all this new information meant, Hallie spoke again. "I'm staying on for six months to help with the transition. Hence our access to the finest of accommodations."

"Who are the new owners?" Along with staying in dozens of hotels during her tennis career, Sydney had stayed in even more by virtue of her ex, Grant, whose family was in the hotel business. Add in that her best friend's family had up till recently owned an inn, and she knew far more about the hotel business than the average person.

"About that..." Hallie stilled next to her, staring so hard at the water it was like she was looking for a drowning body in the choppy waves.

Sydney's thoughts immediately went to Grant and his family's business, which was, coincidentally, a New England–based hotel chain that would absolutely love The Stone's Throw Inn as one of its coastal properties. Her blood ran cold. "Oh."

"No, no," Hallie said after uncomfortable seconds, finally turning to her. "It's not that bad."

"But it's... bad?"

"It's... um... well, it's... you know..." Hallie wasn't usually at a loss for words, having spent the majority of her life defusing scheduling snafus, customer complaints, and guest relations issues.

"Hallie, just say it—"

"It's a Devereux, but not Grant."

Sydney's brows lifted. Grant's father, Tripp, was the head of The Devereux Group, and Grant had worked at his side since graduation. His mom, Sharon, was a Stoneport socialite who had little to do with the business except, according to Grant, spending the money it made. And Grant had an older sister, Reese, who had been out on the West Coast since she'd gone to college, but Sydney was sure she'd started some software company.

"Reese does... What does she do again?" Sydney snapped her fingers, trying to remember as she ignored the unsettled feeling in the pit of her stomach. Of all the Devereuxs, she'd spent the least time with Reese by a wide mile. Sydney had stayed in Florida with her parents for holidays while Grant had come home to Stoneport. She and Reese's paths had crossed maybe once in the last six years.

"She created a hotel management software for smaller properties. We use it here. Though, now that it's been sold, I'm not sure if it'll be phased out."

Sydney was still trying to make sense of things as the words started clicking. Her spine snapped up straight. Hotel management. Small properties. Reese had sold her company.

"Your parents sold the inn to Reese Devereux? But—she's not working with her family?"

Hallie quickly held her hands up, eyes wide. "She's not associated with them, best I could tell. She seems to have very little to do with her family, actually."

Sydney waved her finger in the air, feeling like she was finally getting up to speed. "So... my ex-boyfriend's sister bought your family's inn?"

"Small towns?" Sydney started to laugh at Hallie's weak shrug, but the laughter died on her lips when Hallie added, "So, anyway, she'll be arriving tomorrow. To officially start working with me on the transition."

Cool, cool, cool.

It didn't *matter.* That's what Sydney repeated to herself, even as her stomach churned.

She didn't even know Reese. And Reese and Grant had never been close. Returning to Stoneport or, at the very least, shacking up with Hallie, wasn't a permanent life plan anyway. Reese would be so busy taking over operations, their paths would probably never cross.

"I mean, that's fine," Sydney said, unable to come up with a better word for the situation. Only, it didn't feel fine. It felt like another slap in the face; a continuation of the last year, as she'd been scrambling—and failing—to find solid footing underneath her.

Clearly, that fight wasn't over yet.

"It's weird," Hallie said.

Relief at Hallie's willingness to have an honest conversation about the absurdity of this situation flowed through Sydney. "It is weird! I'm glad you said it first!"

Hallie warmed to her theme. "My parents started this process a while ago, and there was significant interest from The Devereux Group."

That perked Sydney up. She never pretended she was a great person. "Which means that Grant and his dad didn't get the property?"

"No. My parents have never liked Tripp. I mean, what adult man goes by Tripp after twenty?"

Sydney finally laughed, a genuine sound that broke the tension. "Well, with a family name, there are only so many variations to tell them apart."

As far as Sydney was concerned, Grant Devereux IV had lucked out. His grandfather, who Sydney hadn't met before his death, went by Junior. Grant's dad went by Tripp. She didn't know if she could have stomached calling someone she was in a relationship with Junior or Tripp, even just to other people.

God, one generation earlier, and maybe this could have all been avoided.

"So this isn't that bad," Sydney said, psyching herself up for some slight awkwardness in the coming weeks, now that Reese would be around more. And it sounded like Reese wouldn't be having her family over for Sunday lunches. "Grant doesn't even live in Stoneport, so at least that's a consolation."

"Eh…"

Her head snapped toward Hallie, and she mimicked her friend's shrinking shoulders. "What do you mean, 'Eh'?"

"That's the other thing."

"There's another thing?" Sydney felt her relaxing summer, the one she was finally settling into for a reset and recalibration, quickly evaporating before her eyes.

Hallie began talking so quickly the words would have been unintelligible to Sydney if not for their twenty years of friendship. "I really think Stoneport will be good for you, but I knew that if the situation was complicated, you wouldn't want to come. But, so, anyway, Grant is back." She made a manic, frazzled noise in the back of her throat. "He's getting married this summer and the town is acting like the prodigal son has returned and I'm so sorry I didn't tell you sooner, but, well, like I said, I really think Stoneport will be good for you," Hallie said, starting to repeat herself like she was stuck on a loop.

The words struck Sydney, the sentences falling into place at the same time she pressed her head against the cool glass of the suite's patio door. "Well, shit."

Two

NOTHING HAD PREPARED Reese Devereux for the
reality of taking over management of The Stone's Throw Inn.

It was only ten a.m., and she'd already watched Hallie, her
guide during the transition period, put out more fires than she
could fathom a business sustaining.

And Hallie had told her this was a light morning!

Reese had done her research. Pored over every how-to guide
on management best practices. Hell, she'd built an app that
helped small hotels and inns manage their day-to-day operations
seamlessly.

Building a website. Accepting and managing reservations.
Check-ins. Cleaning. Dining Room reservations. Special requests.
Guest engagement.

Reese was realizing—with stomach-churning clarity as she
watched Hallie's fingers move more quickly across the front desk's
keyboard than seemed possible—that she only understood these
things in theory.

The practical application was, however, a completely different
story.

Even when they were building her app, she and her ex-partner,
Megan, had visited dozens of properties to ensure they

understood the nuances of the trade. The difference was, they got to leave at the end of the day with a significant amount of insight but no real responsibility on paper except to fix any bugs in the software.

She wasn't prepared for Greg and Candace, both employees, to be in a lovers' spat, Candace refusing to work a shift if Greg was scheduled, too.

And how did one person use twelve towels in a single night? They were probably better off being burned than put through the industrial-size washers that lived in the basement.

Let her not forget Mr. Ketterman, who, apparently, always stayed with his wife in a specific room, the name of which escaped Reese at the moment. Only, he'd forgotten to book the room for his anniversary next weekend, and now it was suddenly Hallie's—and, by extension, Reese's—problem that it wasn't available.

"I understand, Mr. Ketterman," she heard Hallie say with a calmness in her voice that was hypnotizing, nodding along as she added, "I don't want you to be in hot water with the missus either."

Sympathy for someone's poor planning had not been on Reese's bingo card today. She was all about operational efficiency but hadn't considered that it would be the guest at fault, which didn't feel like their problem to fix.

Still, The Stone's Throw was a small location, with loyal guests who had come back year after year. She knew from Hallie pulling up Mr. Ketterman's customer profile that he and his wife had stayed here on their anniversary for the last twenty-nine years, like clockwork.

Reese should really add a repeat booking feature to the software.

Stop it, she chided herself, looking again at Bruce Ketterman's profile, which she'd already scanned a half-dozen times.

The hotel management software that she'd spent years pouring her heart into was no longer hers. Instead, she now had what may be a multimillion-dollar mistake on her hands.

Hallie continued to give affirmative sounds as Mr. Ketterman prattled on. "How about this, Mr. Ketterman?"

Blessed, blessed silence through the phone, for the first time in minutes.

"It's your thirtieth anniversary, right?" Hallie nodded when his voice filtered through the receiver, but Reese already knew she wasn't wrong. Scanning the screen, Hallie pointed to a room that wasn't blacked out as already reserved. "We have a nicer suite available next weekend. I'll give it to you at the same rate as your usual room. We'll make sure it's decked out beautifully when you arrive. You can let Mrs. Ketterman know that life with her is always new and exciting, and you wanted to give her an experience that signals a positive start to the next thirty years."

Hallie hummed again, nodding along, a smile blooming as she listened to him. "Yes, exactly. Traditions are amazing, but show her that you still want to woo her! That you're not a man who's going to rest on your laurels when it comes to love!"

Less than a minute later, Hallie had his information updated into the reservation for the suite, had applied a promo code to give him the other room's rate, and she'd added a note for housekeeping regarding the special occasion.

Reese was beyond impressed.

"I'm thinking a charcuterie board and a bottle of champagne for next week," she said to herself as much as to Reese when she hung up the phone.

"You're good," Reese said. "More than good. I'm a little intimidated right now, and that doesn't usually happen."

Hallie laughed and adjusted the metal name tag attached to her chest so that it was perfectly straight. "Here at The Stone's Throw Inn, we aim to please." She looked back down at her computer. "Let me just finalize this reservation, and we can keep going."

Reese had arrived late the night before. Her flight from San Francisco had been delayed, but she'd made it to the inn just as the summer sun was setting. This morning, after far too little sleep, she'd made sure to pad over to her window to watch the sun rise across the Atlantic Ocean, a sight she had sorely missed in her twelve years on the West Coast.

Northern California, at least along the shore, had its many charms—progressiveness, inclusivity, a bustling tech scene—but it was never a substitute for how captivated she felt by New England. The West Coast was bold and vivid and jarring in its expanse. Her little slice of Massachusetts, which she'd called home for the first eighteen years of her life, was defined by small communities littered along the coast, with lobster shacks and town squares and more antique shops than a person here for a weekend trip could ever hope to visit.

The Stone's Throw Inn was a perfect encapsulation of all the things she had loved about growing up in Stoneport. Set at the edge of town against the rocky shoreline, the main building was situated far enough back from the sea that the Thatcher family had created an outdoor oasis of adirondack chairs and firepits to enjoy the view.

And the sounds. God, she'd missed the sounds.

The gentle lapping of the waves as they reached the coastline. She'd always loved how they lulled her, better than any sleep meditation app she'd found since. The seagulls, possessing more confidence than was probably safe for them as they made their presence known with low, piercing keows. They bobbed and weaved and shot up high in the sky, circling for fish below or an errant french fry dropped by a tourist.

"Okay, where were we?" Reese looked up to find Hallie flipping through a three-ring binder on the concierge desk. It seemed like she was looking for something specific, though what that was, Reese had no idea.

Reese had liked Hallie immediately. She was focused, thoughtful, and had a knack for problem-solving. She wondered how Hallie felt about her parents selling the inn, if she was really as amenable about the situation as she seemed. Basically, Hallie was training her own replacement, and, in the process, giving up a family legacy that must have defined her entire life.

Reese knew a little something about that—about feeling like decisions were made around her instead of with her and that, in the grand scheme of things, what she wanted didn't matter all that much.

But she wouldn't repeat the same mistakes. The Stone's Throw Inn was 100 percent hers. Hers to help thrive. To accidentally tank into the pits of despair. To plod along in survival mode as she went prematurely gray from the stress of what she was realizing was a far more difficult and nuanced job than she'd given hotel owners and managers credit for.

She touched her dark hair, paranoid that it was already happening.

Even if it were, she told herself she didn't care. The most important thing was that not her father nor Grant nor Megan were involved in this venture. And, gray hair or not, it was a small price to pay for autonomy and control.

"So, how do you go from successful tech entrepreneur to the owner of a forty-year-old inn? Your family's in hotels, right?"

Reese scrunched up her face before she realized she was doing it. She hated being compared to—or contrasted with, for that matter—her family, but Devereux was a big name in a small town.

Hallie closed the binder in front of her and folded her hands on top of it. Maybe she hadn't found whatever she was looking for. "Touchy subject?"

She liked how forthright Hallie was. Clearly a person who'd grown up dealing with people her entire life, she wore her ability to navigate conversations like a second skin.

Reese was trying to soak in the unspoken teachings Hallie could provide just as much as the litany of lists and tasks that she was working to memorize.

She ran her finger across the shiny surface of the front desk, which stood chest high and provided a much-needed barrier between herself and the rest of the world. "I'm not sure if you like or dislike my father's hotel group, but I can say with absolute confidence that he has nothing to do with me purchasing The Stone's Throw."

The Thatcher family knew that she was the one purchasing the inn, but she'd come in with an all-cash offer. She knew they'd appreciated that she wasn't part of a large conglomeration, and it was her goal to maintain the charm of a place that had become a part of the town's fabric over the last four decades.

As far as business transactions went, it had been fairly straightforward. No board. No investors. No percentages of ownership. She ponied up the cash, and then the proverbial—and literal—keys were in her hands.

Hallie had agreed to stay on for six months. Reese would keep her on forever if she wanted to, but she had no idea what Hallie's long-term goals were. Sooner than later, she may find herself hiring a new manager, someone who'd never know the inn the way Hallie did.

God... what in the ever-loving hell had she gotten herself into?

In the last few years at her company, she'd been relatively insulated from all the 'people-ling' aspects of her role. That was a technical term she'd learned about at business school, clearly.

Megan had been the one who'd schmoozed with investors and still networked with their business school alumni while Reese had tucked herself away to tweak the software functionality and run the numbers on profitability and do any myriad of things that an early-stage founder did daily to ensure their dream could continue to exist.

Maybe if she'd been a little more dialed in on the people aspect of things, she wouldn't have been so shocked by everything that had happened back in San Francisco.

"I assumed you weren't working with them, given that they'd already made an offer," Hallie said, studying her.

Reese pursed her lips. "Oh?"

"About a year ago, before my parents were seriously considering selling."

"Why didn't it work out?" She tried to sound casual, but she'd at least admit to herself that she was wildly curious. She was pleased, at least, to realize she was taking another page out of Hallie's playbook on forthrightness.

Her father had made it clear years ago that she was never the sibling who was being groomed to take over The Devereux Group, and since then, she'd tried to put anything business-related to the side. It was the only way she'd be able to have a productive relationship with her family.

"It was a good offer. Not as good as yours," Hallie said with an impish smile, "but my parents had actually started the process of selling to them at the time. The financing fell through, though I don't know a ton more than that. Our lawyers said that deals fall apart all the time before they ever reach the finish line."

Reese nodded in agreement. There were hundreds of moving parts on mergers and acquisitions that could cause something to not work out.

"Anyway," Hallie continued, "my brother and his wife had just had twins, but they live in Colorado. Once my parents got the idea in their head that they could spend more time out there, they started to seriously consider selling, even after that original deal fell through."

So maybe, in some small way, Reese had her family to thank for The Stone's Throw becoming available after decades of ownership by the Thatcher family.

She scoffed.

Hallie looked at her strangely.

Reese's hand flew up to her mouth, heat rising on her cheeks. "Sorry. That had nothing to do with your story. I was just thinking about how The Devereux Group is the reason this whole thing kicked off. And look at us now."

The large clock in the entry hall chimed, and Hallie looked at the computer screen, panicked.

"Only about half of the guests checking out today have already done so. It's going to be nonstop for the next thirty minutes, and I need to find a replacement for Candace. She's on the cleaning rotation today."

Ah, yes. Candace, and her Shakespearean-level lovers' quarrel with her paramour, Greg.

"What can I do to help?" Reese asked, just as the first set of guests came into view on the steps with their suitcases. She tightened her dark ponytail and smoothed her button-down shirt to gather herself.

"I'll send a text out to the other staff to see who can cover her shift."

"Are you going to fire Candace?" Reese asked seriously.

Hallie shook her head. "She's nineteen and in the throes of young love. They'll work it out, like they always do, and then beg to be on the schedule together. Plus, when she's here, she's the best we've got."

Reese scrunched up her forehead. "Okay."

"If you want to overrule that, it's your prerogative," Hallie added, though both of them knew it wasn't likely. Reese was a newborn baby right now in terms of hotel management experience, and they both knew it.

"We'll have to get a late start on cleaning the rooms for the guests checking out, but use that tablet." Hallie pointed at a shelf only visible if you were standing at the back of the desk.

"Okay," Reese said, grabbing the iPad and hitting the home button. The screen for her software popped up, and she immediately felt the twinge of sadness that happened whenever she saw it.

"Look at all the occupied rooms that don't have checkouts today. We can worry about cleaning them later, but please stop by and restock the toiletries."

"Which toiletries?"

Hallie nodded, like she wasn't at all annoyed with the idiocy of Reese's question. "New towels, two per person. New bottles of shampoo, conditioner, and bodywash. A new bar of soap. There's a cart in the cleaning closet on each floor. It should be well stocked, and there's a list of what each room gets."

Reese scanned the app and looked at the list of rooms that had guests staying through at least the weekend. Of the twenty rooms, eight had checkouts today.

Which meant... "Okay. I'll stop by these twelve rooms and make sure they have the daily amenities, using the list on the cleaning cart."

"Perfect," Hallie said, like a parent using positive reinforcement for even the smallest of wins. "Skip the ones that have a 'Do Not Disturb' tag on the door, but mark it on the app."

Reese nodded again.

The two guests who had been coming down the stairs at the far end of the hall finally made their way over, coffees from the drink station in hand. Reese could see two more couples meandering in their direction, one from the dining area, where breakfast was available until ten a.m. but where stragglers loved to sit afterward, and another from the staircase.

"And so it begins," Hallie said with a wide smile. "You good?"

Was she? "Sure. I'll get started now."

Reese disappeared just as she heard Hallie's chipper voice asking the first guests if they'd had a good stay.

Her phone buzzed in her pocket, and she quickly checked to make sure it wasn't Hallie with a last-minute instruction. It was her mom—for the second time this morning—who'd somehow found out she was back in town. That was the only possibility as far as Reese was concerned, since the Devereuxs weren't known for idle chitchat.

Eventually, her parents would find out that she'd purchased the inn, but she was trying to avoid that for as long as possible.

Being back for her idiot baby brother's wedding was going to be enough family-imposed torture for the summer. She didn't know what the fallout would be when they found out that not only did she own The Stone's Throw, but that she'd unknowingly undercut The Devereux Group in some way.

Right now, though, she had bigger fish to fry. Namely, not walking in on any naked guests who didn't hear her knock.

She took a staircase off to the side that Hallie had told her most of the staff used while working. It went up to the third floor, which had fewer rooms than the other two floors. Starting there was probably a good bet.

They'd taken a tour earlier this morning to help Reese get a better sense of the inn. While she was a whiz with almost anything technical or business-related, spatial and directional awareness weren't skills she possessed. Add in multiple staircases, and she was lucky she even found the cleaning closet.

Even then, the giant 'Cleaning Closet' label on the door did help. A lot.

True to Hallie's word, when Reese unlocked the door, she found a small, well-stocked cart that would see her through her newest task.

Reese had been putting effort into her life for as long as she could remember, but that effort very rarely included any type of physical labor.

Still, she knew all the work it took to be good at most types of jobs, and as the new owner of the inn, it was important that she knew how to do them all.

She pushed the cart to the end of the hallway and flipped her focus to the iPad nestled on top of a set of plush, white towels.

"Looks like three out of five rooms on this floor are staying," Reese said to herself.

The rooms on the third floor were all suites, doors widely spaced apart to make room for the one-bedroom or two-bedroom configurations.

The Stone's Throw had originally been an Art Deco mansion, built in the 1920s but unused for a large portion of the twentieth century.

Hallie's parents had purchased the building in the mid-eighties and added this floor about twenty years ago, so they were the newest rooms in the inn by a wide margin.

After knocking, Reese stepped into the first suite, a one-bedroom with a living room that had a gorgeous view out across the Atlantic Ocean. People flocked to Stoneport for a variety of reasons, but Reese knew that even if the inn was a little dated, it still pulled in strong occupancy numbers because it was set on a breathtakingly scenic overlook.

Only, Reese didn't want people to accept whatever room they booked because it was in close proximity to what they really wanted. She wanted The Stone's Throw to be an inn that people would still flock to even if it was located inside of a city dump because of how it made them feel at home. Because of the ambiance. Because of a certain je ne sais quoi that made them want more—to sort through every small detail and figure out *why* they loved it so much.

And she wanted to be the one to give that to them.

With her renewed vigor, she finished the third floor. After the cart was back in the closet and safely locked, she traversed the main staircase down to the second floor of the inn. This one boasted the most rooms, nine in total, all standard kings or double queens. Each room she serviced had slightly different decorative touches. She made note of this as, during her previous visits for the purchase, she hadn't been able to view every single room.

She didn't stop at her own room on the second floor, but she gave her current home a nod as she passed by.

By the first floor, she felt like she was hitting her stride.

The ground floor was bustling with early afternoon activity. She could smell the limited lunch menu being prepared: casual fare including a lobster roll, clam chowder that made Reese's mouth water, and a bevy of other seafood dishes that rotated weekly.

She was wondering if she'd have time to grab something as she worked through her list of rooms, drawing closer to the scents infiltrating her nostrils and making her stomach gurgle. She'd been so on edge this morning before meeting Hallie at seven that she hadn't eaten yet.

A few feet back, she'd dropped the first-floor cleaning cart back in its space. The cleaner who'd come in at the last minute, Brittany, had given her an appreciative nod as she'd pulled the cart right back out and headed toward the other end of the hallway to start the full cleanings for checkouts.

"One more," she coached herself, the door to the kitchen within sight.

She knocked, loudly enough that someone still in the room would hear her. Double-checking to make sure there was no 'Do Not Disturb' sign, she used her master key to unlock the door and let herself inside.

She'd taken to keeping the doors open when she serviced them, just to make sure guests weren't concerned about a non-uniformed woman without a name tag traipsing through their rooms.

This room, she noted, was configured differently than any of the others she'd been inside, with additional touches to make it more like an apartment than the suites on the third floor. It was almost as if three normal rooms had been fused together, the doors on the left and right in the hallway that should be there having been removed.

These must be Hallie's owner's quarters—at least for the next six months. When Reese had purchased the inn, she hadn't been very concerned with what would be her future accommodations if she'd wanted them.

Hallie's willingness to stay on in a managerial capacity had meant that of all the things Reese needed to concern herself with to get oriented to hotel ownership, where she slept for a few hours a night wasn't one of them.

The room she'd walked into was a living room, with a kitchenette built along one of the side walls. There were art prints on the walls that weren't the hotel's aesthetic, along with furniture that didn't match the other rooms. The back wall boasted a beautiful glass door that overlooked a small, private patio. Beyond that, the ocean was visible as the edge of the property dropped off at a small cliff butted up against the sea.

On each side of the living room were what appeared to be bedrooms, each of which likely had its own bathroom.

Reese moved to the left and found a well-lived-in room that must have been Hallie's. She quietly placed the new towels in the bathroom.

The door to the other bedroom was closed, likely unoccupied unless Hallie had it decked out as some type of office. Any guests of Hallie's probably used that bathroom, which was how Reese decided to close out her task strong and replenish the soaps, at the very least.

Reese opened the door, noticing the clothing strewn across the floor first.

Her confusion ratcheted up a notch when it sounded like a shower was running behind the closed bathroom door, but it took a back seat in her brain when a woman's scream pierced the room.

She froze, her stomach plummeting from the sound as she quickly glanced up and then immediately back down.

The ground was her best friend right now. She studied it like an artist studying a landscape before painting it.

She knew from her brief glimpse that a woman stood in front of her at the foot of the bed, decked out in nothing but a pair of teeny-tiny boy shorts. Reese's mind tried to catch up, seeing in her peripheral vision as the woman pulled her earbuds out of her ears before using her arms to cover her chest.

"I'm so sorry," Reese said when she found her voice, speaking to the floor. "I didn't know anyone was in here."

On reflex, she handed the woman one of the towels she was holding in her arms like a security blanket.

It felt hot in here. Why was it so hot?

Reese knew that she should flee the room as quickly as possible, but she was equally mortified and transfixed.

Also, she needed to save this train wreck of an interaction.

Was this Hallie's friend? Girlfriend?

"Ugh," Reese groaned, covering her eyes with a hand and pitching her view into darkness.

"I know I haven't been working out lately, but I didn't think it was that bad."

The teasing voice, sweet but with a bite of sarcasm, made her drop her hand, pulling her eyes toward a body she knew looked sculpted out of marble.

"No. It's not that," Reese said once she'd made it to the woman's left shoulder, which was tan. Smooth. And looked incredibly soft.

She cleared her throat. She'd been out of the game since her business and personal relationships with Megan had imploded. That was proving to be a mistake right now.

No. She was Reese Devereux, and she needed to start acting like it. She'd graduated from Stanford undergrad and Stanford business school at the top of her class. She'd built and sold—begrudgingly—a multimillion-dollar software company. She'd just launched her newest venture with the acquisition of The Stone's Throw Inn.

Unexpectedly seeing a beautiful woman in nothing but her underwear was just another day at the office—which made a lot of sense given that her office was now a hotel.

"Reese."

The sound of her name was like a lightning bolt through her chest, and she finally inched her eyes over to meet vibrant green, like a lush, tropical forest after a rain.

It couldn't be.

Holy shit. "Sydney? Sydney King?" She tried to find the right words but failed. "What are you doing here?"

She unconsciously took a small step forward, trying to get a better look at her brother's ex-girlfriend—respectfully, of course. It had been years since they'd seen one another in person, not that she hadn't seen Sydney splashed across magazine covers or on gossip websites over the last half-decade.

Even though her outfit now wasn't dissimilar to the one she'd worn on the cover of *Sports Illustrated* a few years ago, it was still hard to accept that Sydney was standing here, in front of her. It was like seeing a teacher out in the wild: unexpected because it wasn't their natural habitat.

Time had been good to Sydney. Reese could happily admit that. Her long, blonde hair was tied up in a high ponytail, her body all lines of sinewy muscle that ran across her limbs.

Sydney hadn't bothered to wrap the towel around her; instead she was holding it against her chest as she looked at Reese with less confusion than Reese had expected, given the situation.

"Hallie's my best friend," Sydney finally answered, her gaze flicking across Reese's face like she was looking for something.

What it was, Reese didn't know.

Reese released a deep breath, struggling to maintain eye contact. "I'm still so sorry. Hallie didn't mention you were staying here with her. I knocked on the door, and no one responded."

Sydney pointed to the earbuds that now rested on a dresser. "Was sort of in my own world. Trying to pump myself up for a midday jog. It should have been a morning jog, but..." The words trailed off, a soft, embarrassed smile flashing across Sydney's full lips. Her white teeth popped against her perpetually tan skin, which made sense given that, if Reese remembered correctly, Sydney spent most of her time in between tournaments in Florida.

Oh god, did Sydney know that Grant was getting married this summer?

Grant, from where Reese was standing, was a fucking idiot for letting Sydney get away. Or breaking up with her and falling head-over-heels in love with Brynn Fitzpatrick soon after—if she believed the official version being peddled by the rest of the Devereux family.

Thinking about him, it was like she could hear Grant's stupid voice inside her head. "Reese?" he was saying. "Why haven't you answered any of Mom's calls? She's been trying to get a hold of you all day, and I'm not the family's errand boy, you know."

Why was Sydney looking at her like that? Head cocked to the side, straining her ear toward the open door. Almost like she could hear Grant's annoying voice, too.

Oh.

Oh no.

It happened quickly, as she heard his decisive footsteps in the living room before she saw him come into view. Two years younger than she was, he'd been taller by the time they were teenagers. Add an extra inch for his stupid pompadour hairstyle. Now, as a man in his late twenties, his frame took up most of the doorway to the owner's quarters second bedroom.

Reese instinctively moved in front of Sydney, who was still very much unclothed and shrinking backward so that her legs bumped against the edge of the bed. Reese heard the soft sounds of the sheets moving and ignored a fleetingly intrusive thought about how Sydney's tanned skin must look against the crisp, white linens.

"Why is your door open?" Grant demanded. "No one was even at the front desk, unsurprisingly. I'm forced to wander around like an idiot. At least your voice carries—" He stopped fully once he entered the bedroom, his eyes bouncing back and forth between Sydney and Reese, trying to figure out what was going on.

He sure had the idiot part right, regardless of the situation.

It was unlikely he'd guess that Reese had bought the inn and she'd just had a hell of a first day unexpectedly walking in on Sydney naked. It was a hard guess on the best of days, and she didn't think he possessed even a molecule of that level of critical thinking.

His forehead was scrunched in obvious confusion. "What's going on?"

It reminded her of when they were teenagers, and he'd miss the point of movies entirely. When Reese would try to explain the plot, he'd stand up, scoff, and call the film 'stupid' to further illustrate whatever point he thought he was making.

Life had been hell on earth when he'd learned the word 'reductive' while studying for his SATs with his hundred-dollar-an-hour tutor and applied it to every single thing he didn't like.

Strangely, Reese found it comforting that he hadn't changed all that much since birth. Still petulant. Still whiny. Still thought the sun shone out of his ass.

And now, he was planning to further enshrine himself as the family's golden child by marrying Brynn Fitzpatrick, daughter of one of the largest real estate investors on the East Coast.

It must have been her father's wet dream when he'd found out they were engaged. Gross but apt, as far as descriptions went.

She needed to remind herself that Grant was on her turf now. In her inn. He wasn't the one calling the shots, even if he didn't know it yet.

"Nothing that's any of your business," Reese finally answered, inching over to fully obstruct Sydney from his view.

She'd waited until she could see the vein in his forehead bulging with frustration at being so far out of the loop he didn't know it existed.

She didn't think Grant was that smart, but he was persistent. And that could be a problem at this moment.

"I think I deserve an explanation about why my sister and my ex are naked in a hotel room together."

Reese pursed her lips. Yep, he was still as idiotic as she remembered. Luckily, they saw one another infrequently, and only with the buffer of their parents between them. But their interactions didn't feel infrequent enough at this moment.

It wasn't an unfair question, but it was so classically Grant that she wanted to laugh. Sydney wasn't his girlfriend, and Reese barely had a relationship with her brother. Why he felt like he could waltz into someone else's hotel room and demand answers only reinforced her disdain for him.

"Technically only one of us is naked, Grant." Sydney's voice floated from behind her, and as Reese shifted her body sideways, Sydney's head peeked around her to look Grant in the eye.

Sydney stood up then, towel held across her chest, before she took a step closer to Reese, staying slightly behind her. Their bodies were almost touching, and the warmth of Sydney's naked skin pushed insistently against Reese's shirt. Sydney smelled like coconut and something floral, and it set Reese's synapses on fire.

Grant, to his credit, stood frozen, except for his eyes pinging back and forth between them, like he couldn't process what was happening.

With a quick half-step, Sydney now stood right next to Reese, their arms brushing and that heat threatening to engulf Reese again, when Sydney added with a widening smile, "And it's still none of your business."

Three

SYDNEY DIDN'T HAVE Reese and Grant Devereux shooting daggers at one another in her bedroom on her bingo card today. In this lifetime, actually.

Hallie was going to lose her mind when she found out what was transpiring in their shared suite—not to mention that she was missing it.

"I'm not leaving here until I get some answers." Grant crossed his arms across his chest and leaned against the doorframe.

Sydney gave him an appraising stare, still not moving. "Guess you should order room service because you'll be waiting a while," she said flippantly, even if it felt like her world had been turned upside down in the last few minutes.

He looked the same, definitely no worse for the wear given what he'd put Sydney through. His hair was still coiffed. His skin was tanned from weekends at the golf course. Even his outfit, khakis and a polo shirt in the summer months, hadn't changed.

It was like, so easily, he'd just moved on, that nothing for him had really changed.

She'd hoped that she'd never have to see Grant again, let alone during one of the hardest periods of her life. It was adding insult to injury that he was gallivanting around Stoneport while he prepared for his wedding, something that, a year ago, they'd been discussing as a couple.

But seeing him again had sparked something in her, a fire that she hadn't felt in months. It was the same sensation she'd gotten before a big match, and it flared through her veins, waking her up from the inside out. She felt alive when she saw the confusion written across his face, very similar to how she'd felt last year when she'd walked into his condo in Boston.

The moment she had caught him cheating still didn't feel real, even today. When she remembered it, the scene felt removed, like she was watching a movie instead of having lived it herself.

Grant had been with her for the first week of the French Open, where she'd never placed higher than the second round. By the time he left on Sunday to be back for work on Monday, she'd secured a place in the fourth round, her best showing on the clay courts that she'd always struggled with.

All year, she'd been focusing on her slide across the surface along with better timing for the ball's change in pace. The bounce was higher on clay and became more inconsistent with the divots on the court. An extra two hours a day of practice at her training center's clay courts had helped make her game formidable.

When she'd lost in the fourth round on Tuesday, instead of heading straight back to Florida, she'd grabbed a direct flight to Boston.

Knowing that she'd been absent more often in the months leading up to Roland-Garros, she wanted to show Grant how much she'd appreciated his support.

So she'd decided to surprise him.

Because she'd *missed* him.

Her stomach roiled at the memory.

Like an idiot, she'd misunderstood all of his flexibility when it came to her career. She'd believed he wanted her to focus on tennis because he was supporting her. Instead, her career had conveniently kept her out of his way for extended periods of time so that he could have an affair.

Or multiple.

She hadn't stayed long enough to get all the details.

Still, he'd done an impressively good job of playing the doting boyfriend up until the moment it had all fallen apart.

Maybe that's why the breakup had hurt so badly. Because she was still having trouble reconciling the person who'd lived a double life with the man she'd once loved.

Because the partner he'd been to her for the six years they'd been together hadn't been a partner who'd seemed prone to cheating. They had nightly phone calls when she was in Florida for training. He sent flowers to her at every tournament he couldn't attend. They'd talked about what their future would be like when she retired in a few years, with plans for marriage and children and a life that Sydney was excited to live.

She still felt robbed of the life she'd been building. Resentful that he'd walked away scot-free. Infuriated that he was getting married this summer, like his life hadn't skipped a beat while hers had been shaken to the core.

Until this moment, she hadn't realized how angry she was. She hadn't let herself *accept* how angry she was.

The three of them still stood around her room, saying nothing, but she knew Grant would fold first. He wanted to be the loudest voice in the room, and he never understood the power of silence, in letting your opponent fall on their own. You don't need to beat someone if they beat themself.

So, just like clockwork...

"Is that why you're staying in this dumpy inn, Reese? So you and my sloppy seconds can sneak around together?" Grant scoffed, like the idea was ludicrous, even as the supposed evidence stood side by side in front of him.

She'd have given Grant a point in the invisible tennis match she was watching play out if he hadn't done exactly what she'd anticipated.

Sydney didn't know who should be more offended: herself, on behalf of Hallie and their entire childhood of great memories, or Reese, who'd just become the owner of said inn. She wasn't even going to touch the 'sloppy seconds' comment with a ten-foot pole.

All her disgust did was make Sydney want to dig her heels in and commit to the act further.

Asshole.

But it was Reese who got to him first. "You mean the inn you and Dad couldn't afford to buy?"

Well, well, well. Point to Reese.

Grant squinted at her. "How do you know that?"

Another point to Reese. Grant wasn't quick on his feet and missed the hit by showing his surprise.

"So it is true," Reese said, her teeth flashing in a way that made Sydney melt from the pure enjoyment. "I'd love to hear more about that."

Grant's face grew red. "The family business isn't really any concern of yours, now, is it?" he said, trying to rein in his breathing.

The situation had quickly escalated from a four to a solid nine, and she wondered what Grant would do when he didn't get what he wanted. Not that she knew exactly what he wanted right now, but he was clearly infuriated at the idea of Sydney and Reese being an item.

Though she'd been with Grant since college, she'd always been open about her bisexuality.

And he was actually starting to believe that they were a couple, Sydney realized as his gaze darted between them, his fists clenching. She'd unexpectedly found herself on a speeding train that she didn't want to slow down.

She felt invigorated, even as he took a step through the doorway.

Her whole body pulsed, little vibrations zinging across her skin, her arm hairs practically electric with the buzz moving through her.

For the last year, she'd felt like she hadn't had any power, and now that she was given a little dose, she was heady with the weight of it.

She placed her hand on Reese's elbow. "I didn't know that Grant was stopping by today," she said honestly, squeezing Reese's arm and giving her a puzzled look.

Sydney loved the heat coming off of Reese's skin, and she fed off it as she flexed her fingers.

Reese's tight smile was its own answer before she said, "I didn't either."

Grant threw up his hands and took another step closer. "Are you two seriously together? This isn't some sort of joke?"

She could see the spittle at the edge of his lips.

"Contrary to popular belief," Reese said before leveling her brother with a gaze that Sydney thought could melt metal, "not everything is about you."

Sydney didn't know why Reese was still going along with this, but she was grateful, satiating herself on the extra moments of excitement.

"In what world is the fact that my ex-girlfriend and my sister are dating not about me?"

Sydney bit back a laugh. Grant had always had a high opinion of himself, and that seemingly hadn't changed over the last year.

Regardless, for the thrill of satisfaction that she was getting out of this whole situation, a perfectly executed role reversal that rivaled the feeling of a great shot down the line, Grant no longer got to see her in various states of undress.

"Get out of my bedroom, Grant," she said, glancing at him and then the door.

She tapped her foot in a steady rhythm until he finally started turning around at a snail's pace, like he was waiting for camera people to pop out of the closet and tell him he'd been *Punk'd*.

Reese started following her brother to the door.

"You should stay," Sydney said in a soft, coaxing voice, grabbing onto Reese's hand.

"What the hell, Syd?" Grant bellowed, even as he complied

with her request. At least he wasn't stupid enough to stay in a woman's room against her will.

Sydney could see him glowering at Reese as he stomped away, sulking like a child.

She loved it.

She knew it was wrong, but she fucking loved every second of it as Grant made frustrated sounds with every step he took.

"And you don't get to call me Syd," she yelled at his back as the door shut behind him.

She dropped Reese's hand and started rummaging through her suitcase.

"I just need to throw on some clothing," Sydney said. She was more invigorated for that run than she'd been fifteen minutes ago. Maybe at any point since her injury.

Her limbs still buzzed as she picked up a sports bra that was hanging over her chair and slid it over her head.

Sydney was comfortable with nudity, having lived the last decade of her life in locker rooms. Not to mention the saunas, ice baths, and any myriad of physical therapy techniques that could give an athlete an edge.

So, even as her skin prickled with awareness that Reese Devereux was only a few feet away from her, respectfully looking out the large window toward the ocean, she moved her focus to finding a pair of running shorts and a tank top in the suitcase she hadn't unpacked yet.

She could say goodbye to all the free swag from her sponsors now that her retirement had officially been announced. It wasn't like she couldn't afford to buy her own clothing, but she loved packages showing up on her doorstep, perfectly fitted to her long frame.

Her agent had been giving her space since her retirement, though she was sure that Sara was squaring away any clauses related to her not fulfilling the terms of her existing contracts: Wilson for her rackets and Nike for her clothing and footwear. God, she hoped that Rolex let her keep the beautiful watch they'd gifted her from their Datejust collection last year, when she'd moved into the top twenty.

"Are you sure you don't want me to go?" Reese asked, pulling Sydney's attention to the window where The Stone's Throw's new owner stood, still looking out at the shoreline.

Reese Devereux, a woman she'd only met once—maybe twice —before today, was now going to be a very present fixture in Sydney's life.

And Sydney, in that moment, realized that she knew very little about Reese. What she did know had come secondhand from Grant and wasn't exactly flattering. Which, on principle, made Sydney like Reese all the more.

Reese's dark hair flowed in soft waves as she looked out toward the ocean, her shoulders straight. Even at this moment, she was all business. Sydney caught the contour of her cheeks, soft and round, that made Reese look younger than she actually was. Even from feet away, she could see the light color splashed across those cheeks.

The new owner of The Stone's Throw Inn, the sister of her ex-boyfriend and, if you asked Grant, Sydney's new girlfriend.

Things were really changing, in every facet of her life. She couldn't imagine the Thatchers not owning the inn, a place she'd spent countless days throughout her childhood.

Sydney took a deep breath, her energy starting to even out. Sometimes after a big match, it would take her hours to come back down to any sort of stasis.

"Oh my god," Reese said, her hand lifting to her forehead so forcefully she almost slapped it. "Hallie is going to think I've abandoned her. That I saw ghosts and ran screaming off the cliff."

Sydney smiled at the visual as she pulled on a pair of running shorts. "I feel pretty haunted by ghosts of the past today, so that's not far out of left field."

Reese groaned, and Sydney tried not to be endeared by her embarrassed smile, so different from her posturing moments ago with Grant.

From where Sydney was standing, Reese and her brother couldn't have been more different. She could practically see Grant seething as he paced back and forth in the living room. Meanwhile, Reese was contrite, if not a little shy, as she stood in the confined space with her brother's ex-girlfriend.

Reese's soft, brown eyes lifted up to meet hers. "I am so sorry about that. I didn't know he'd show up here."

"I didn't think you two were close."

Reese scrunched her nose. "We're not. My mother probably sicced him on me when she found out I was back in town."

Sydney pulled her ponytail out of the tank top she'd just thrown on before cocking her head to the side. "So they don't know that you bought the inn?"

She was surprised by Reese's sheepish expression. "No. And I'm not exactly champing at the bit to tell them."

"Why not? Seems like there's no love lost between you and Grant. It must feel good to get the best of him," Sydney said as she felt the flicker of exhilaration rush through her.

Reese looked back out at the choppy waves. "My relationship with my family is complicated. It always has been."

Sydney felt lucky that she couldn't commiserate. Her parents were her rocks. They'd been so supportive that she felt the need to flee their love to wallow in self-pity instead of meeting their well-intentioned eyes at every turn around her house in Florida.

Sydney had only talked to them once since arriving, so she made a mental note to call them soon.

Sydney cleared her throat as she sat down to put on her slim, top-of-the-line knee brace. "Thanks, by the way."

"For what? Walking in on you naked? Bringing my brother into your bedroom? I can't wait to see the review you leave for the inn," Reese finished wryly.

"No." Sydney laughed. "For letting me have a little fun at your brother's expense. I don't think I realized how mad I still was about him cheating until I saw him again. A lot of pent-up energy, ya know?" She extended her leg once the brace was snug around her knee, flexing the joint to make sure it was positioned correctly.

Clearing her throat, Reese took a step closer to where Sydney sat on the bed, a strange look on Reese's face. "I didn't realize he cheated."

Of course Grant would manage to push through his infidelity with him still smelling like a dozen red roses.

"With Brynn?" Reese added. "I mean, if that's not too intrusive of a question. I fear I've already spent too long with Hallie this morning."

Sydney laughed and started putting on her sneakers. "She's definitely a straight shooter."

"Understatement of the year. But she's amazing with this place."

After she tightened her shoelaces in a ritualistic way that had morphed into her pre-run routine at some point in the fifteen years, Sydney stood up and slapped her palms against her thighs.

"Yes, with Brynn. I caught them together—came home early from a tournament to visit Grant in Boston, and I walked into some alternate universe where they weren't just having an affair, but completely playing house."

She appreciated how wide Reese's eyes went. "That must have been a total mindfuck."

Sydney nodded. "Even as I watched them from the door, moving around the kitchen as they cooked dinner together, I still couldn't quite believe it."

"I am the last person who wants to hear anything positive about my brother, but are you sure you didn't misinterpret it?"

The sound out of her throat was somewhere between a laugh and a scoff. "I wish. I would have gone in less 'guns ablaze' until I saw him lift her onto the countertop and make it very clear that this was not two friends hanging out together for the evening."

Reese made a gagging sound, which Sydney valued immensely.

"And then about a month later, one of my opponents told me

she saw on Facebook that he'd gotten engaged." Sydney paused for emphasis. "Right before we were playing a match against one another."

Sydney ran her hand through her ponytail, feeling surprisingly vulnerable. Of all the people she'd ever expected to have this conversation with, Reese Devereux was not one of them. "I've spent the last year wondering whether I could have been more present in our relationship. If I was somehow emotionally absent in my quest to be successful. If I checked out on him before he checked out on me, you know?"

"Soul-searching is always a good thing," Reese answered diplomatically. Sydney didn't know her, not really, so it wasn't a fair question for Reese to answer.

"I probably wouldn't be so upset if I was on my way to a Grand Slam title right now, but retiring a few weeks ago has really given me time to think in a way that, to be honest, I fucking hate." Sydney wrapped her arms around herself, goosebumps prickling her skin in the air-conditioned room now that her adrenaline had worn off.

As she came down from her high, she just felt tired.

Reese, however, seemed like she was finally ramping up. "I didn't know you retired. Why?" She waved her hand apologetically. "Again, sorry for the intrusive question."

With Reese's hands on her hips, staring intently at Sydney, she looked every bit like a formidable businessperson.

And, more than that, Sydney found herself *wanting* to answer.

"My fault," she said with a shrug, pretending like it didn't hurt as much as it did. "I threw myself into tennis, literally and figuratively, after the breakup, and it worked until it didn't. I partially tore my ACL in November. At a stupid, meaningless tournament because I just couldn't stop. Couldn't stop pushing. Couldn't stop training. Couldn't stop trying to do anything to escape the way I was feeling. I opted to forgo surgery and start the tour this year, but I wasn't ready."

Reese glanced down at her knee. "Did you hurt yourself again?"

Sydney winced and reflexively stretched her knee. She still had better mobility than the average person, but that was no match for the professional level at which she used to operate. "I wish there was at least a good story. It was death by a thousand cuts— bad match after bad match. I got in my head more and more until I was basically useless. There was no way I could even qualify for the last Grand Slam tournament of the year. My coach thought it would be helpful for me to take some time. Decide what comes next."

Reese nodded sympathetically. "I'm also going through a transitional period in my life, so I understand. I felt like a lot of what I worked for was taken away when the bottom dropped out of my life. The Stone's Throw Inn is my chance to recapture a little bit of the feeling that I'm in control."

This was, by a wide mile, the longest conversation she'd had with Reese, and still, she was finding that she didn't want it to end.

"Interesting place you picked," Sydney teased, her hand lightly touching Reese's forearm. "Where the guests are as fickle as the weather. Have you met the 'too many towels' guy?"

Sydney's stomach flip-flopped at Reese's vibrant smile

"I call him Mr. Cheaper by the Dozen. I had to drop twelve towels in his room earlier. What is he doing with them? I'm dying to know."

"Hallie and I brainstormed it, but the best we could come up with is that he uses a new towel for each part of his body," Sydney guessed.

Reese had a thoughtful look on her face. "Showers four times a day?"

"What the hell is taking so long?" Grant's voice cut through the wall separating them. Sydney had actually forgotten he was waiting in the living room.

"I forgot about him," Reese admitted, clearly sharing in her surprise.

Sydney laughed. "It's good for his ego." She looked toward the door, assuming their moment of fun was winding to a close. "Are you going to put him out of his misery?"

Reese looked at her seriously. "Why would I do that? I mean, I'm happy to correct the situation, but I don't think I owe Grant anything, especially answers about my love life."

Love life.

Sydney hadn't had one of those in a year, even the fake kind.

Hell, probably longer, given the side game Grant had been running for who knows how long.

This was a horrible idea. Bound to blow up in their faces. She didn't even *know* Reese.

But when she thought of Grant's smarmy face on the other side of the door, she didn't want Reese to correct him. She wanted him to squirm. Really, their breakup had been his choice, and with his impending marriage, he shouldn't even be thinking about what was going on with Sydney.

"So you're really down to keep this lie going? All to piss your brother off?"

Reese nodded resolutely before she looked around the room, gesturing to the inn. "I feel like my life is getting a little too boring, you know?"

Sydney was quickly finding that smile disarming in the best possible way.

"Shake on it?" Sydney asked, extending her hand.

Reese met her in the middle, and when their hands connected, she felt warmth and those little zigs and zags of electricity that made her feel alive again. She wanted to chase that feeling.

"Can we work out the details later?" Reese asked, slipping into business mode. "I'll see what Grant wants, and you can go on your run?"

"Thank you for running interference."

They walked toward the living room together, and Reese poked her head out first.

Sydney braced for impact.

But Grant was nowhere to be found.

Instead, Hallie stood in the kitchen, making her daily smoothie.

She looked up at the sound of the door, her gaze flitting from Sydney to Reese and then back again.

Sydney felt like she'd been caught with her hand in the cookie jar, even though nothing had happened.

"I wondered where you'd gotten off to," Hallie said to Reese as she dumped her frozen fruit into the blender, then started to chop her kale.

Reese stepped forward and ran her hands down her shirt. "This morning really went sideways. I'm sorry."

Hallie waved her off. "I saw Grant skulking around here. I assumed something was going on, though I didn't expect it to involve you two locking yourselves in Sydney's room," she finished, lifting an inquisitive brow at her best friend.

"The door wasn't locked," Sydney argued, not that that was really the point.

"Glad to see you're going out. I was worried the sofa would be permanently indented with your languishing outline."

Sydney's cheeks flamed. "Hallie."

Her friend was having a little too much fun at her expense.

"I joke, I joke. Anyway... what have you two crazy kids been up to?" Hallie looked expectantly between them.

"So here's the thing, Hal."

Hallie threw her kale in the blender and placed the lid on it, waiting. "Hit me."

"I'm going to need you to get on board with the story that Reese and I are dating."

"You're dating? God, woman, she's only been here for a day," Hallie said, half disbelieving and half impressed.

Sydney rolled her eyes. "If anyone asks, we're madly in love.

Can't live without one another. Life and poems and songs all finally made sense. Got it?"

"Who would ask?" Hallie practically screamed over the blender she'd just started. The dark red liquid from the crushed strawberries was slowly giving way to a light green as the kale began to work into the mixture.

Sydney loved when Hallie was intentionally obtuse, even if she'd never admit it. "Probably a Devereux, if you happen to see one of them slinking around the inn again."

"Are we in a throuple? I'm getting throuple energy," Hallie said as she turned off the blender, her too-loud voice echoing off the walls.

Reese laughed from next to her. "It's a tempting proposition, but I should probably crawl before I walk."

Sydney bit down the unexpected flare of jealousy that Reese was considering the idea.

"I'll play tennis with you soon if you go along with it," Sydney offered. As always, Hallie had somehow become the linchpin of her scheme, and Sydney needed her best friend's buy-in if this shtick was ever going to have a modicum of believability.

"Bestie, I was always going to go along with it. But I would love to play tennis," Hallie said gleefully. "Almost as much as I love a good bit of subterfuge."

Sydney looked at Reese, who seemed like she was suddenly wondering if they were in over their heads.

"We need her," she pointed out. "She knows everyone. By tomorrow morning, the whole town will believe we're madly in love."

Reese looked at her skeptically. "Depends on the story."

Sydney grew confident again. She'd dated Grant for over half a decade, and she knew exactly how to push his buttons.

She flashed Reese a winsome smile, loving the feeling of anticipation that came with a new challenge that stirred in her belly. "Leave that to me."

Four

REESE *ACHED.*

Her back.

Her butt.

Her feet.

As she made the fifteen-minute drive to her parents' house, she was aware of muscle groups in her body that, until today, she hadn't known existed.

She leaned forward and touched her tailbone, rubbing it gingerly as she tried to keep her eyes on the winding road.

The scenic highway that took her out of town was vibrant with summer foliage, and she kept her windows rolled down, inhaling the smell of salt water and fresh air.

The drive was good for her. Calming.

After the events of today, both physical and mental, she felt wrung out.

What had she gotten herself into?

The inn. That was its own conversation, one that made her stomach churn uncomfortably when she thought about it for too long. Her fingers wrapped more tightly around the wheel, and she took a few deep breaths to keep herself centered.

It would get easier.

It *had* to get easier.

She would hit her stride. Beg Hallie to stay on full-time or start the search immediately for someone else to manage the day-to-day. Read every book known to humankind on effective management techniques.

But no, apparently she wasn't busy enough, so she'd decided to take on a pet project to antagonize Grant.

And because she just couldn't let sleeping dogs lie—namely, her already shitty relationship with her brother—she'd had to rile him up.

At this point, it seemed like a character defect that she wasn't able to step away gracefully and accept reality.

Grant could have been the least competent person in the world, and it still wouldn't have changed the fact that her father didn't see her as the future face of The Devereux Group.

"It's nothing personal, honey," she said, mocking his deep voice as she took a curve and the expansiveness of the ocean came into view.

Boats dotted the horizon, the summer sun still high as she navigated the rental car's quirks. She really needed to have her car shipped from California.

Add it to her already dizzying to-do list.

She had so much to accomplish, but instead of getting her bearings at The Stone's Throw and closing out her life in San Francisco, she...

A strange sound bubbled out from her throat.

What had she done?

Gotten caught up with Sydney in some zany idea to torture her brother as he prepared for his wedding? She wouldn't pretend she was a saint, but even on her worst days, this still felt like a lot of energy to waste on a fruitless endeavor.

Grant would never change.

His wedding would go off without a hitch.

He'd ascend to his rightful place in the world as the head of The Devereux Group once their father retired.

No thirty-minute brainstorm about her and Sydney's fabricated meet-cute and no well-earned jabs at Grant's expense would change things.

She looked down at the dashboard clock. Ten minutes until she was late. It didn't matter that she'd finally returned her mother's calls this afternoon, after all new check-ins had been completed and the request—or, more accurately, the summons—for dinner had only been three hours away.

She wondered what Grant had already said to their parents. He'd probably run straight back to their too-big house and told a story of woe, about how she was back in town and already trying to ruin his life.

He'd always been good at playing the victim, even as life was served to him on a literal silver spoon.

Beyond the practicalities of whether it was a bad idea or not (it was), uneasiness had settled over Reese as she'd worked through the litany of tasks that helped The Stone's Throw function each day.

She'd gone to the kitchen with Sydney and Hallie to grab lunch and hatch their ill-conceived plan. The kitchen was chaos personified, even with the small lunch menu the inn had available on weekends for guests and visitors.

Then she'd gone down to the laundry, where she'd strained to heave dozens of pounds of towels and linens into the industrial machines, watching them spin and gurgle and remove any traces of the guests that had used them.

When the sun was high in the sky, she'd shadowed a member of the waitstaff, who served drinks on the patio that overlooked the rocky shoreline.

It had been the only time she'd been outside today. She wanted to spend the upcoming week, when things were hopefully a little slower, familiarizing herself with the property's grounds, which included a pool and a tennis court that had seen better days.

As she took another curve, the sun glinting off the waves like diamonds, she let the anxious thoughts that had been whirring inside of her take root.

Five months ago, she'd been blindsided.

Megan had been more than her business partner; Reese had thought they were building a life together.

In their second year of business school, Reese had pitched an idea for a hotel management software for one of their projects. Megan, social and affable and vibrant, had given Reese the confidence that the idea had viability.

They'd worked on the project tirelessly, eventually taking it into Stanford's incubator program for startups and securing their seed funding before graduating.

Megan was the front woman and had happily taken center stage everywhere from TED conferences to meetings with angel investors, a place where Reese had never felt entirely comfortable.

After being told her entire life that she didn't have the type of main character energy it took to be at the helm of a company, she'd started to believe it.

So while she worked on the engineering and financial sides of things, Megan was focused on getting their name out there and connecting with the right types of properties, the ones who'd be great customers for Checked.

Reese had built the software, one painstaking line of code at a time, tweaking and improving and updating the product until they were ready to go live six months after graduation.

She'd never wanted it to be all hers, but she loved that it was something she'd built, a testament to her hard work and determination.

And in the midst of it all, she'd found more than just a business partner. Megan had kissed her at their business school graduation, and from that moment on, they had become a team, in every sense of the word.

Which was why, even though her company had been ripped away from her, it hadn't hurt half as much as Megan's betrayal.

Reese's skin still felt hot and itchy whenever she thought

about the conversation in which Megan had told her that they were selling the company whether she was on board or not.

With their last round of funding, a little over two years ago, they'd owned fifty-one percent of the company between them. If they'd voted as a team, the company was in their hands. Reese had always believed that would be the case. But when Megan put her shares in with the investors, who were eager to see their return realized as soon as possible, it had tipped the scales.

It hadn't mattered what she wanted because she didn't have the power to stop what was happening.

Reese didn't trust herself.

She'd been so blind. So stupid. So trusting.

She'd lost her company. Gotten her heart broken. And then, to prove some sort of misguided point, she'd dumped millions of dollars into a seaside inn, though she had zero practical, day-to-day knowledge of the realities of running a hotel.

So, was throwing herself into this convoluted situation for nothing more than a little ill-advised gratification at her brother's expense really the right path for her?

By the time her parents' veritable mansion on the water came into view, she'd talked herself out of the insane plan.

She didn't need to add this heaping dash of chaos to her life when it was already verging on unsustainable all on its own

After dinner, she'd go home and let Sydney and Hallie know that she'd made a mistake.

They'd understand. With everything going on, it didn't make sense.

Easy.

* * *

Reese had been inside her parents' house for fifteen minutes, and already, she was looking around for sharp objects with which to put herself out of her misery.

The fire poker she'd passed when she'd moved through the

living room had been a suitable option. Too bad she'd been ushered past too quickly to grab it.

She sat across from Grant, who'd been glaring at her since they'd first made eye contact, stabbing at his salad like he wanted the arugula to be her.

"Reese," her mom said casually, like it hadn't been a year since they'd seen one another in person, "I'm shocked you didn't tell us you'd be in town."

Last summer, she'd taken a weeklong trip to Stoneport, during which she'd made the ultimate mistake of staying with her parents. Her mom hadn't understood the concept of remote work, her dad was barely home before sunrise, and the few dinners he'd had with Grant had been just as painful as the present one.

But instead of mentioning any of that, Reese smiled broadly. "Luckily, good news travels fast."

Grant scoffed.

Her mom delicately picked at a cranberry in her salad, like she could hardly stomach the idea of consuming so much food. "Will you be summering in Stoneport?"

Sharon Devereux was the quintessential 'almond mom,' something she hadn't given up with age. At fifty-six, she looked like she was in her mid-forties. Reese truly didn't know who'd win in a footrace between the two of them, and hopefully she'd never have to find out.

Reese took a sip of her wine, wondering if this was the right time to tell them she'd purchased the inn. She hadn't done it in opposition to her family, not even close. Until today, she'd had no idea they'd even been interested in the property.

For her first venture, she'd wanted a place she was comfortable in, where she understood the people and the town. The mechanics of ownership were all foreign to her, but she *knew* Stoneport.

"Yes. I'm going to be here through the summer."

Understatement of the year, but they didn't need to know that.

"Shacking up with her new girlfriend," Grant added, the whites of his teeth gleaming against his already summer-tanned skin.

Her mother's eyes lifted. "Oh?"

She'd felt Grant circling as soon as she'd walked in the door. It became clear he hadn't yet told their parents about their earlier run-in. He was waiting. For what, she didn't know. Maybe just to see the conversation play out in real time.

"Did Grant not mention that he stopped by The Stone's Throw today?" Reese asked, gently veering away from the subject of her fake girlfriend.

"You're staying there?" her father asked, suddenly taking interest in the conversation. "Your mother didn't mention it."

Reese nodded. "It's got great bones. Needs a little updating, but what doesn't."

Her father put his evening newspaper down, shifting his focus to Grant. "I'd have to agree with your sister on this one."

Something passed between them, and Reese desperately wished she knew what it was.

She also wished that, even after thirty-one years, her father's approval didn't matter to her so much.

He'd built The Devereux Group from the ground up, starting with a single property in the early nineties. Since then, the group had grown to a portfolio of fifteen mostly coastal hotels that dotted the New England seaboard.

She was proud of what her father had accomplished, for both himself and his family, even if it was hard to reconcile that with the fact that he refused to see her as part of the company's future.

Reese turned her attention back to her mom. "How did you know I was staying there?"

Sharon continued to look at her cranberry with suspicion. "Steve and Joyce Dyson were driving by and swore they saw you in the parking lot."

Of course. Of all the wonderful things about Stoneport, living under a microscope wasn't one of them.

Honestly, it was shocking that her family didn't yet know she'd purchased the inn. Her parents had never been close with the Thatchers, but still, it must have been common knowledge that the inn had been sold.

"So, Reese," Grant cut in, dangling his fork from his manicured fingers and letting it fall in lazy circles above his salad plate like it was a scrying stick. "Seems like you've been busy."

She squinted at her brother. Did he know?

No, she decided; he was still mad about what had happened earlier.

Of all the things she'd learned today, Grant's infidelity had been the least surprising. He wasn't overly chauvinistic in public, but his access and means had always given him a sense that he could do whatever he wanted.

Clearly, he'd taken that to heart.

Reese batted the loaded question away. "What millennial isn't?"

He put his fork down before edging his elbows onto the table. Hands clasped in front of him, he made sure that his obscenely expensive watch glinted off the light. "I'm surprised you didn't call to share the good news that you'd sold your software."

Maybe because she hadn't qualified it as *good news* to her.

Reese flashed a smile. "I figured this was a nice dinner for us to celebrate your upcoming wedding. I didn't want to steal the spotlight."

Grant scowled.

Now, that was the most interesting thing that had happened yet tonight.

The tension was put aside as the kitchen staff brought out the main course. Reese had made it a point to learn how to cook in adulthood, given that it was a skill that hadn't ever been taught in their family.

But god, had she missed the seafood in New England. The scent of pan-seared scallops enveloped her as the plate was put down.

After the day she'd had, she was starving.

Her mom, blessedly, continued the conversation, discussing the latest comings-and-goings of the town, what her charitable organizations were up to, and dropping subtle jabs at any of their long-time neighbors, who'd done something to get in her crosshairs.

The offenses ranged from hiring a new landscaping company that didn't create the perfect crisscross design in the Miller's front yard to Mrs. Gordon announcing her own son's engagement a week after Grant's.

Reese, halfway through her scallops, put her fork down. "So, Mom, you must be excited that your only son is getting married."

She wondered if Grant would lunge across the table and strangle her. If his looks were any indication, the odds were about fifty-fifty.

And then her mother, in a move that was so uncharacteristically excited that it left Reese wondering if she'd been possessed, clapped her hands together. "Oh, yes! Brynn is such a sweetheart."

"I'm excited to meet her," Reese lied.

"Why? Angling to date her, too?" Grant muttered.

Sharon, who'd almost been ready to finish her first scallop, put her fork back down on her plate. "What was that, Grant?"

Grant cleared his throat, waiting until all eyes were on him. "I was asking whether Reese wanted to date Brynn, too. Considering that she and Sydney are an item, it's not that unbelievable."

"Reese and Sydney?" Sharon said the words like she was rolling them around, trying to make sense of them. "*Your* Sydney?"

Gross. As if Sydney belonged to anyone, especially someone like Grant.

Grant nodded vehemently, grateful their mother saw his side of things. "She couldn't keep her own girlfriend, so she had to go and find my leftovers. Really, where did you two even meet? Did you seek her out when Morgan broke up with you?"

Reese's lip curled. "You know that her name is Megan. And why do you keep referring to a woman you once professed to love as different versions of uneaten food? You know, I read a very interesting book discussing how masculine language always reduces women to food—"

Grant cut her off. "Why won't you answer the question?"

Because she was buying time, deciding how she wanted this conversation to go.

"I didn't know that you were keeping such in-depth tabs on my comings-and-goings, Grant. Don't have enough at work to keep you busy? Dad just sit you in an empty office to twiddle your thumbs?"

"Reese." Her father's voice was sharp, but she didn't spare him a glance.

She could see the vein in Grant's forehead again.

Frustrating him was... euphoric.

She felt alive. More alive than she'd been since she'd lost her company. Lost Megan. Purchased the inn.

Years of discontent were bubbling up to the surface, and her body was alight with the back-and-forth.

"No, Grant, please. Explain to me how you cheating on your ex-girlfriend and immediately getting engaged to your affair partner is somehow my problem?"

"That can't be true," Sharon protested.

God, sometimes Reese envied her mom's obliviousness.

Reese frowned; saying the next words gave her no pleasure. "The Venn diagram between his relationships with Sydney and Brynn is simply a circle. I'm not saying these two crazy kids won't make it work, but it's not like they're starting their life together on the most solid foundation."

"You don't know anything about my life," Grant spat back.

What, was he going to tell her next that she wasn't the boss of him? It was a rich comment, given how much he thought he knew about both her personal and professional lives.

Reese picked her wineglass up and twirled it absently. "Then what makes you think you have any right to speak on mine?"

She'd walked into this house, so sure that she was going to drop the charade she'd spent the afternoon orchestrating with Sydney, but now, with adrenaline coursing through her veins, it felt like the best idea she'd had in a long time.

"Are you dating her just to get a rise out of me?" Self-involved as always, but hey, a broken clock was right twice a day.

On her best days, she didn't hate Grant, but she still couldn't muster up a modicum of respect for him. Especially right now.

"My relationship with Sydney is none of your business." Stick to the party line, and she'd get through this.

In spite of the chaos surrounding her, as Grant looked ready to blow a gasket, Reese found herself smiling.

Today had been... surprising. Sydney was funny and interesting, and she'd been through a hell of a lot the last year, hopefully only to come out stronger on the other side.

Reese had always believed that karma came around eventually, but she was realizing that people like Grant, who were insulated from the unjustness of the world—not that she wasn't aware of her own privilege—didn't suffer consequences unless people imposed them.

Now here she was, dropped into a fortuitous situation, almost divine in its invention while Grant, led by his own assumptions, was stuck in a hell of his own making.

Maybe that was true karma, and who was Reese to stop whatever was coming next?

Grant moved to stand up. "I cannot believe you think that you can—"

She felt her father's strong hands pound against the table before she heard them. "That's enough."

Silence cut through the dining room.

Reese was ready for the dressing-down of her life until she realized that her father was looking directly at Grant.

"You are lucky that Brynn Fitzpatrick accepted your marriage proposal. And you're even luckier that Sydney made no waves last year." He looked at Reese then. "If your sister's future is with Sydney, it's irrelevant to you."

Reese held her breath until her father looked back at Grant, who was sitting down again, visibly seething in his chair.

"Your future is with Brynn. Her family is coming tomorrow for a small get-together, and you will be the fiancé that I know you can be. Anything less will not be tolerated. You are the one who mixed business with pleasure where the Fitzpatrick family is concerned, and now it's your business to make her the happiest woman on earth. And you will not do anything to disrupt their investment in The Devereux Group. " The silence was deafening. "Do I make myself clear?"

Grant cleared his throat before looking down at his empty plate. "Understood."

Their father cut into a scallop before continuing, seemingly intent on continuing his monologue. "Sydney was a good match for you. Her publicity was good for the company, and being attached to her worked at the time. Marrying Brynn is a better match," Tripp said, nodding toward Grant.

She hated her brother's smarmy grin at the praise he got for acting like a dog.

"Are you kidding me?" Reese couldn't hide the bite in her words. Her father was fine with Grant being a philandering asshole as long as he, and The Devereux Group, came out better at the end of it.

Tripp pointed his knife at Reese. "You'll bring Sydney tomorrow. We've hardly spent enough time with her over the years, what with her busy travel schedule. She's retired from tennis now, I think I heard?"

Reese wiped her mouth with a linen napkin. A date to a wedding was one thing, but forced attendance at a myriad of Devereux family events wasn't the outcome either of them had been searching for when this particular wheel had started spinning.

Karma really was working in mysterious ways.

Reese nodded. "I'll see if she's available."

"Perfect," Tripp said, smiling broadly before he turned his focus to Grant. "You will be cordial as the son of the host. I will not hear a single negative word out of your mouth about your sister or her girlfriend."

He didn't ask if Grant understood this time. In their father's eyes, it was a requirement, not a request.

"Anyway," Sharon said in a voice that was artificially high, trying to course-correct from whatever turn their dinner had taken, "hors d'oeuvres will be served on the patio at three p.m. sharp, and the dress code is coastal cocktail."

Of course the dress code was 'coastal cocktail.' As if her family wasn't already pretentious enough. It wasn't like they were the Rockefellers. The Devereux family owned fifteen properties in the New England region, though they'd never expanded outside of the area. Whether that was intentional or not, Reese didn't know, given that she had never been privy to that type of business information.

The reality was, for her pride in her father's accomplishments with The Devereux Group, he'd been given his start by Grant Devereux II, who'd made his millions as an investment banker. Failure would have been unlikely, if not downright impressive.

The housekeeper came to take away their plates, at which point Tripp stood and picked up his newly refilled glass of wine. "Grant, care to join me in my office? I'd like to discuss a few things with you ahead of tomorrow."

Over the last forty-five minutes, all of the wind from Grant's sails had deflated.

Tripp walked around the table and placed a quick kiss on Reese's head. "It's always good to see you, honey. Congrats on the acquisition by the way."

Her father was a real Sourpatch Kid as far as Reese was concerned, which was the most euphemistic descriptor she could find, and still, she hated the way she preened at the praise.

What Reese wouldn't have given to be the one asked to go into his office and talk shop. To discuss the intricacies of the hotel world in general, the changing markets and the influx of foreign money that had been littering the space for the last five years.

All she'd ever wanted was to learn from him, to sit at his feet, work by his side, and understand how to build something that would last.

But it hadn't happened up until this point, and it sure wasn't going to happen now. Not when her father was dead set on The Devereux Group's future riding on the back of a man who Reese knew for a fact had gotten a tribal tattoo across his shoulder blades at the age of twenty, something he'd somehow managed to keep from their parents all these years.

Her mother poured herself another glass of wine, and Reese held her hand over the top of hers. "Your father's under a lot of stress, Reese."

"*Life* is a lot of stress, Mom. For everyone. I don't think he should be given a special award for wanting to be in a position of power and then taking the responsibility out on other people."

Her mother leaned closer, like she was sharing a secret. "You know your brother is challenging."

"Yeah, and water's wet," Reese said with a sarcastic laugh. "It was his choice to groom Grant as his successor. This was the future *he* wanted."

"Your father's just old-fashioned."

As if that made it any better. Tripp Devereux wasn't too old-fashioned to keep up with the changes in technology and travel expectations, but ask him to support a woman in a position of power and suddenly he was Barney Fife, looking down at his shoes all 'golly wiz, shucks.'

"But you'll come tomorrow?" Sharon asked, squeezing Reese's hand.

For the first time that night, Reese really looked at her mom. She seemed... tired. Her makeup was done flawlessly, but her shoulders sagged now that they were alone, and there was a dullness in her eyes that tugged uncomfortably at Reese's heart.

For all the difficulties with her family, Reese was the one who'd stepped away from her mother, not the other way around. "Are you doing okay, Mom? I'm sorry that Grant and I got into it at dinner. I didn't mean to upset you."

Sharon waved her off and stood up, breaking the intimacy of the moment. "You know me, sweetie. Always another event to chair or fundraiser to organize. Add in Grant's wedding, and there aren't enough hours in the day."

Reese cocked her head to the side. "Why are we hosting the wedding events? Doesn't the bride usually do that?"

"Your father insisted." Sharon rolled her eyes as if to say, 'You know men.' "He wants to make a good impression on Stan Fitzpatrick."

"If it's his choice, why are you doing all the work?" Reese asked.

Another wave from her mother's perfectly manicured hand was the only answer she was going to get.

Reese stood up, too. It looked like the night was going to be blessedly short, though tomorrow was going to come too soon. "Well, just make sure you're taking time for yourself."

"I will." Her mother walked her to the door. "You were always so driven. I'm sorry that your father doesn't look at it the same because you're his daughter."

"Too much business is done in cigar bars and on golf courses," Reese said, mocking her dad's matter-of-fact tone when he said misogynistic statements like they were facts instead of opinions.

Her mother took both of Reese's hands within her own. There was a whole extra level of physical closeness in the Devereux household tonight. "I'm proud of you. I know I don't say it enough, and god knows I don't understand half of what your software did, but I'm really proud of you, honey. And it'll be nice to see Sydney again. I'm glad you're bringing her tomorrow."

There it was again, that invisible hand that seemed to wrap itself around Reese's heart and squeeze.

She gave her mother a soft kiss on the cheek. "Thanks, Mom. I'll see you tomorrow."

"On your best behavior," Sharon said in a no-nonsense tone, slipping back into the person Reese had come to know over the last thirty-one years.

Reese waved back at her mom as she reached her car, not answering.

Five

"YOU CRAZY KIDS HAVE FUN!" Hallie yelled from the front porch as she pretended to snap a photo with her hands.

Sydney knew that her best friend was living with the chaos of the last twenty-four hours. Two days ago, Hallie had been trying to coax her out of their shared living space. Now, with the wind at her back and an axe to grind, Sydney was decked out in a soft, olive-colored dress that came to mid-thigh, ready to take on the world. The elastic waist didn't hurt, hidden as it was by an adjustable, woven belt in a sand color that, she thought, accented the dress nicely. She'd worn her blonde hair down, flowy and softly curled so that it cascaded in waves around her shoulders.

Sydney knew that she looked good, and she knew that everyone at the party would know it, too.

Eat your heart out, Grant Devereux IV.

She didn't want him back, not by a long shot, but after months of focusing on nothing but tennis, then weeks of wallowing in misery, it was nice to get dressed up, regardless of the occasion.

A pair of strappy, open-toed heels in the same color as the belt completed her look, and she focused on keeping one foot in front of the other as she navigated the gravel driveway.

Reese walked slightly in front of Sydney over to the passenger side door. They both reached the door, and Reese opened it and gestured for Sydney to get in. "I'm creating an ambiance," she said with a rueful grin that Sydney found herself matching.

The rest of the day was likely to be nightmarish, so why shouldn't they soak up the last moments of fun before entering into the belly of the beast?

Reese turned to face the inn entrance and slipped her sunglasses on. "You're seriously the best, Hallie. I'm sorry I'm already flaking out on day two."

"Perks of being the owner," Hallie said, zero judgment in her voice. "Just know that if I meet someone beautiful who wants to whisk me away on their sailboat for a few days, I will be calling in sick." She fake-coughed for good measure.

Reese laughed, and it made Sydney go a little soft inside at how well Reese and Hallie were getting along. She wanted Hallie to be happy. To be excited about whatever it was that would come next for her.

And she liked that Reese seemed so calm, like maybe this day was going to go better than Sydney anticipated.

Plus, to Reese's credit, Sydney knew that she'd been up since six a.m., doing work to get up to speed on the management of the inn. Hallie had told her during her daily return to the room for her smoothie, impressed with the information Reese had absorbed as she'd sat out in the check-in area, poring over a binder that Hallie had prepared for training.

Sydney eased her long legs into the car as Reese and Hallie finished their conversation, waiting a few seconds before Reese shut the door for her.

It was a gorgeous day. White, puffy clouds were splattered across a vibrantly blue sky, and dozens of sailboats dotted the horizon.

Reese had texted her last night, asking if she was free for a Devereux family event today, and Sydney, still keyed up from the endorphins that had come from her run a few hours earlier, responded without thinking twice.

She'd never really understood people who made poor choices for the thrill until now. Inserting herself back into Grant's life was one of the top most idiotic things she'd ever done, and still, she relished the chance to take back the narrative.

Grant wasn't some person she'd dated for a few months who'd blown her off because her travel schedule was too much for them to handle or because they were jealous of the attention her celebrity status afforded her.

He'd been her partner for six years. Her cheerleader. The person who'd always supported her pushing herself to get to the next level. The one she'd been making plans with for a life after tennis.

A marriage. A home. A family.

And now, even though Sydney knew it was a special level of masochistic, she was going to put herself right in his crosshairs and watch him move down that path with someone else.

Maybe it would help things make sense. There was a part of her that wanted to see them together. To see what they had. To see how it *felt* to see Grant again.

Their breakup had happened quickly, all things considered.

She'd caught him with Brynn, and once her brain had caught up to speed and she understood what was happening, she'd turned around and walked right back out. No overdrawn conversations. No excuses as to how she'd 'misinterpreted' what she'd seen.

It had all happened in seconds, in an apartment she'd tried to visit as often as possible but that, for the first few years of their relationship, they'd called home together. It wasn't until she'd joined the women's pro tour that she'd bought her house in Florida and moved down there full-time.

She'd asked Grant to go with her, but he'd said that it wasn't the right time. He was gaining more seniority within The Devereux Group and was responsible for more hands-on management within their portfolio, along with spearheading the expansion opportunities they'd been pursuing in surrounding regions and states, like New York.

Given the way he'd supported her dreams, she'd wanted to do the same for him.

So together, as a team—the same way they'd picked out the bed he'd slept with Brynn in, the artwork that adorned the walls, the way the spice rack Brynn casually selected oregano from in the kitchen was organized—they'd made the decision to do long-distance.

He'd never given her any indication that he hadn't wanted to make it work.

She still felt so mind-fucked by the entire situation.

There hadn't been signs except that they weren't together every second of the day.

And if that was a requirement for fidelity, she didn't know how any couple had ever made it work.

"How are you feeling?" Reese asked from the driver's seat as they rolled along the coast. "You're awfully quiet. Regretting your decision?"

Sydney understood that if things imploded, it would be far worse for Reese's day-to-day life than her own. What Reese was really asking Sydney was if she'd be able to keep it together at the event and beyond; to really go through with this.

"I want answers," Sydney said, staring out the window. "I just felt so blindsided by the whole situation."

Reese made the turn onto the private road that would lead them to the Devereux home. "Do you think you'll be able to get them?"

"I—" Sydney turned and looked at Reese, who was already focused on her. "I want to know if any of it was real. Did I waste six years of my life on someone who only saw me as a way to pass the time, only when it was convenient?"

She appreciated the strained sound that Reese made, like maybe she understood that sentiment herself.

"I don't know if you'll get those answers with my brother. I've never thought very highly of him, but you're a capable, talented, beautiful woman, Sydney. There must have been something that kept you with him for six years."

Lips pursed, Reese shifted her focus back to the road, looking intently at it even though she knew exactly where they were going.

"Just say it," Sydney urged.

She could see Reese chewing on the inside of her lip, mulling over what to say. Finally she broke the silence with, "Even if that something was him intentionally misleading you."

Sydney uncrossed and recrossed her legs. "You may be right, but still, what does that say about me? That I didn't see it for so long? Am I delusional? Or just an idiot?"

She hated the insecurity in her voice, that she was letting someone like Grant make her feel this way.

They pulled into the cul-de-sac five minutes early. The driveway was already filled with at least a dozen vehicles of varying degrees of wealth and obnoxiousness.

Reese parked the car and pushed her sunglasses onto her forehead. Honey-brown eyes bore into Sydney's. "It says that Grant was really good at hiding it."

Sydney chose not to respond to that. "I thought this was a small get-together?" she asked, changing the subject as Reese cut the ignition.

Reese rolled her eyes in response. "I'm sure my father can't help using Grant's wedding as a business opportunity."

"Ah, yes... Tripp Devereux. Not my favorite person I've ever met." She cut her eyes to Reese. "No offense."

"None taken. I have my own issues with the man, so let's just add that to the list of our current commonalities."

Reese got out of the car and walked around quickly, opening Sydney's door again.

It gave Sydney a chance to admire Reese's outfit. She was wearing silky palazzo pants in a gorgeous dark cyan. A white-and-magenta pattern was woven throughout, giving the illusion that the shapes were flowers. Reese had gone simple on her top, a similarly silky, fitted white button-down with the top three buttons undone, tucked into the high waist of her pants.

Reese's dark hair was voluminous, a perfect abundance of tresses that flowed from her side part and cascaded around her cheeks and jawline before resting below her shoulders. Sydney wondered if it felt as soft as it looked; her attention was momentarily distracted by the strands of auburn and gold glinting throughout.

If that hair was natural, Reese had won the genetic lottery.

Reese cleaned up exceptionally well, and Sydney knew that the two of them together would turn heads today.

"You look—great," Sydney said when she accepted Reese's hand, changing course at the last second, even as the word 'beautiful' had pushed into the forefront of her mind.

Was that a faint blush on the elder Devereux's high cheekbones?

Sydney's grin grew impossibly wider.

The Cape Cod mansion loomed before them, and Sydney waited for Reese's cue to head in.

"Now it's my turn to ask," she said, her forearm brushing against Reese's warm skin when the brunette didn't take a step forward. "Regretting your decision?"

She didn't push but rather waited as the silence stretched out between them. It wasn't uncomfortable as they stood next to one another, sharing what felt like a bubble of safety for the next few moments.

Reese stared up at the house, where Sydney—by way of Grant—knew she'd spent her childhood. It was hard to fathom growing up in such a massive compound, six or seven bedrooms along with a pool house that was at least the size of an apartment.

She wondered what Reese saw when she looked at the house. A childhood home filled with love and support? A too-big, artificially curated compound where the family lived separate lives? Something in between, good memories mingled with bad that made Reese's return all the more complicated?

Grant had always been very focused in the present. What was happening with the business. Where they'd go for dinner. How Sydney's promotional deals were coming along. He discussed his father with regards to his management of The Devereux Group. He ignored his mom's seemingly well-intentioned check-ins on the sparing weekends when Sydney was with him in Boston.

"I was thinking about it on the way over," Reese finally said, shifting her focus to meet Sydney's.

"And where have you landed?"

Reese slipped her hand inside Sydney's. "We've gotta be able to sell it. Are you okay with that?"

She liked how Reese's slightly smaller hand felt in her own, warm and soft. She gave it a light squeeze. "United front?"

Reese nodded, an errant strand of that gorgeous hair dropping across her forehead. She quickly tucked it behind her ear before giving Sydney a surprisingly charming smile. "United front."

And then, hand in hand, they walked into the house together.

* * *

Blessedly, they made it to the backyard without running into anyone except a member of the house staff, who opened the front door.

Once they'd passed through the French doors that led to the immaculately decorated patio area, Sydney's limbs started buzzing.

This was getting real.

The backyard, which included the patio, pool, and a flat, meticulously manicured grassy area, was decked out in blooming flowers; linen-covered tables with a smattering of serving platters holding food that, even from afar, made Sydney's mouth water; and, to top the ambiance off, an abundance of well-dressed, middle-aged members of the New England upper crust that Sydney spared no more than a passing glance.

She'd lived her life in the world of professional tennis. There was very little these people could do that would make them more pretentious than anything or anyone she'd seen up until this point.

Beyond the landscaping, which created a beautiful backdrop for an afternoon outdoors, the yard sloped down until it reached the ocean. At the shoreline, a wide dock that could handle at least a small yacht was set.

Reese kept their hands entangled, giving Sydney's a quick squeeze as they approached her mother.

"Hey, Mom." Reese leaned forward and kissed her mother's cheek. Sydney preemptively tensed her shoulders, watching curiously to see what Sharon Devereux's response would be.

"Darling! You made it," Sharon said, already gesturing for a server to bring them drinks. "It's nice to see you again, Sydney."

And it seemed like Sharon... meant it?

Sydney wasn't sure of the narrative Grant had hawked to his family, but she had no false ideations that she'd come out looking like the scorned party.

Sharon seemed to hold no grudges. Or else she was toeing a diplomatic party line between both of her children.

"It's nice to see you again, too, Mrs. Devereux," Sydney said, tipping her head down in acknowledgment. She'd give Sharon credit for Reese, at least.

The few times she'd interacted with Reese and Grant's mom before now, Sharon had always been relatively meek, aware of the conversations in a room but generally content to let them play out around her. Sydney was sure she was an astute woman, but she gave very little away.

"Have you said hello to Grant yet?" Sharon asked Reese.

She watched as Reese scanned the crowd of about two dozen people. "We just arrived. I thought you said the party started at three?"

"Some of your father's associates have to leave by four p.m., so they arrived about an hour ago."

Sydney would have killed someone if she was hosting a party and guests showed up that early. She assumed Reese felt the same way, given how her posture straightened, eyes narrowing as she scanned the party.

Though Sydney knew the party was likely to be more of an affair than Reese had let on, her date seemed genuinely surprised at the number of people already milling about, patting one another on the back as plumes of cigar smoke wafted into the sky.

"Are you ready to do this?" She felt Reese's soft breath against the shell of her ear; an involuntary shiver worked its way down her spine.

"Now or never." She couldn't even manage to be embarrassed at the throaty whisper of her voice as the remnants of the unexpected touch dissipated.

Reese led her through the crowd and over to where Grant was standing with a group of a few people within their age range.

Eyes were on them immediately, the men giving them both a once-over before zeroing in on their clasped hands.

Sydney looked down at their interlocked hands once more, finding it a source of both comfort and strength.

When she took a deep breath and looked up, scanning the group, she recognized Adam Moore. He was one of Grant's friends she'd met in Boston. They'd done dinner and drinks a few times, Adam always with a different woman on his arm.

There was only one other woman in the group, whom Sydney had seen in person once before. She wouldn't qualify the interaction as 'having met' her.

"Hi, Grant," Reese said as she stepped into the circle, the half-dozen bodies parting to make room for her and Sydney.

"Reese." Grant offered her a minimal greeting, but it seemed like they'd all silently agreed to move on from the theatrics of yesterday. He swiped a lock of hair from his forehead before slotting his hand into the front pocket of his khaki trousers.

Then, like he'd thought better of it, he dug his hand out so that he could place it on the small of Brynn's back.

In spite of feeling like she'd just stumbled into a meat market, Sydney liked that there'd be an audience. She hoped it would keep everyone, including herself, on their best behavior.

"And you must be Brynn," Reese said, stepping forward again and extending her free hand. "I'm sorry it's taken this long for us to meet, but let me officially say congratulations in person."

"It's nice to meet you, Reese." Brynn was soft-spoken, far quieter than Sydney had expected.

"And this is my girlfriend, Sydney," Reese added, like Brynn may not know.

She may not have.

But what Grant lacked in scruples, he did make up for in partners with impeccable fashion sense, at least.

Seemingly disinterested in following the status quo of wearing the traditional white, Brynn was dressed in an expertly fitted navy dress with gold buttons running down the center. Her blonde hair was tousled but loose, falling about an inch above her shoulders.

Quieter *and* more understated.

Was this what Grant was after? A Stepford wife who'd better fit into the WASPy New England scene?

Sydney shook the thought away. While she knew what Grant had done and the full extent of his culpability, she wasn't going to make any assumptions about Brynn's involvement in the affair. Not without more information.

The fateful day in Boston, when everything had changed, Sydney hadn't actually looked at Brynn closely. She'd been too focused on Grant, on how he was touching her so intimately.

All of her brain power had gone toward trying to find any reasonable explanation for what she was looking at.

Now she was at this moment, almost exactly a year later, at her ex-boyfriend's sister's side, about to meet the new fiancée over canapés and obscenely overpriced champagne.

What a difference a year could make.

Truly, she wasn't even sure if Brynn had seen her. Especially since Brynn was looking at her now, more curious than bitter, like she was wondering how Sydney fit into everything.

Brynn extended her hand, still speaking quietly when she said, "To be honest, I'm not sure what the protocol is for meeting my fiancé's ex, but you look beautiful."

Sydney gave Reese a moony smile before shifting her attention back to Brynn. "Thank you; so do you. And my past with Grant is water under the bridge as far as I'm concerned."

She didn't spare Grant a look as she spoke, knowing he'd hate that.

"It's been a minute, Sydney," Adam said, pulling the conversation back to the correct side of just-shy-of-awkward.

"Nice to see you again, Adam." He wasn't even in the top one hundred people she'd be excited to see out on the street, but at this moment, he was Jesus performing a miracle as far as she was concerned.

Adam looked between Sydney and Reese. "How'd you two link up?"

Scratch that. Clearly, he wasn't wasting any time today ferreting out information for Grant.

She and Reese had already had this conversation, the story of how they'd fallen into one another's lives at just the right time.

Sadly—for Hallie, at least—her best friend's suggestions had all been vetoed, including Sydney knocking Reese out with a tennis ball and running to her rescue to revive her, Reese knocking Sydney out with a tennis ball and running to her rescue to revive her, and, Sydney's personal favorite, Hallie knocking both of them out with tennis balls and upon them waking with amnesia, Hallie allowing them to believe that they were deeply in love.

There was a smile on Reese's lips when she finally answered. "I was in Indian Wells for a little R&R, and the Paribas Open was happening. I almost went to Palm Springs instead. Can you believe that?" Reese's eyes went wide at the possibility of their missed meeting, and Sydney had to stifle a laugh. "Sydney and I ended up staying at the same hotel and ran into each other at the bar. I almost didn't recognize her; it'd been so long since we'd seen one another."

"Small world," Grant deadpanned. He looked around the group to take stock of their responses, but they all seemed enraptured by the story.

Perfect.

Sydney moved a little closer and slipped her arm around Reese's back, enjoying the softness of her shirt as her fingers toyed with the fabric.

"I lost in the first round," Sydney said, picking up where Reese had left off like a well-oiled machine, further selling the story with a hint of self-deprecation and a winsome smile. "And I was planning on taking the red-eye back to Miami but decided to stay for the night."

She felt how Reese's body had melted against hers. It was one of the most enjoyable feelings she'd had in months.

"Best decision I ever made," they said in unison. It was perfectly unscripted, and they both burst into laughter and drew closer.

Reese looked at her then, their eyes locking. Sydney felt that little spark again, like life was happening to her instead of around her.

The prying eyes of the crowd floated away as Sydney enjoyed the attention of a beautiful woman who was putting on the show of her life.

"I can't pretend like life doesn't work in strange ways," Sydney said, acknowledging at least part of the truth of the situation.

Reese held her gaze for a beat longer, rewarding her with a smile before shifting her focus back to Brynn and Grant. "So, I'm dying to know, how did *you two* meet?"

Six

"I FEEL like this could be going a lot worse," Sydney said, leaning down the few inches that it took to whisper in Reese's ear.

Reese tilted her chin up, appreciating the cadence of Sydney's voice, how her eyes sparkled with mischief once they were alone.

They'd survived another twenty minutes in the small group before excusing themselves to refill their drinks.

Sydney had been asked inane questions about professional tennis along with stupidly personal ones about her injury and retirement from the tour, but she'd handled it all gracefully, her touch never straying from Reese's back as she fielded the questions like she was attending a post-match press conference.

"Grant and I were both told to behave today," Reese admitted as they grabbed two glasses of champagne from a waiter passing by.

They stopped by a side entrance to the house, and Sydney leaned back against the stone that cut across the home's ground-floor exterior.

Her brow lifted before she took a small sip of her drink. "Really?"

Reese nodded. "Dinner last night was eventful. I'm not sure whether Grant was more upset at the possibility of his engagement being overshadowed or because I'm dating you, but I didn't exactly do my best to quell his concerns."

"Atta girl." Sydney extended her drink to toast Reese.

Reese met her in the middle, the soft clink of their glasses audible in the privacy of the alcove.

It was a moment of quiet, and Reese relished it until Sydney's smile dipped. "It almost seemed like Brynn didn't know? About the cheating at least. Did you get that sense?"

Reese considered the question, shooting a glance to the patio area to make sure no one was eavesdropping. "Unless she's a psychopath, I don't think she'd have been able to tell that story about the two of them meeting at a hotel event two years ago without giving something away. It's one thing to tell a lie. It's another to tell it directly to the face of the person who knows it's a lie."

"You're probably right."

Lifting an eyebrow, Reese caught Sydney's gaze again. "Are you trying to talk yourself out of your own theory when I'm agreeing with you?"

Sydney ignored the question. "I guess it's better that he wasn't just trolling dating apps."

"So because it wasn't premeditated, the damage he inflicted doesn't mean as much? And I don't know if I'm in agreement about the dating app thing. I think he has it in him." Reese wasn't going to give her brother an inch right now, even if Sydney's conviction, for whatever reason, was wavering. "Either way, he started an entirely separate relationship with someone while you two were planning a future together."

"I just..." Sydney's words faltered before she found them again. "It seemed like Brynn really doesn't know, and that makes me feel badly for her."

It was impressive that even within their current situation, Sydney could maintain this level of empathy for Brynn. It was a virtue that Reese didn't know if she herself possessed.

She placed a gentle hand on Sydney's forearm. "I know what

you mean, but I don't know if you or I are the best people to make waves. I agree with you, though; Brynn seems sweet. Definitely too good for my brother." She realized her misstep when Sydney arched a brow. "You were *also* too good for my brother, clearly. I thought that was already implied."

"Damn, right," Sydney said, her face a little flushed from the champagne and the warmth of the summer day.

Reese watched as Sydney took a few deep breaths, seemingly allowing the stress of the last thirty minutes and the new information they'd discovered to settle in.

Despite the fact that they were surrounded by at least three dozen people now, the moment felt intimate.

It felt good to be on the same team as someone again, to anticipate one another's moves. She hadn't had anything close to it since Megan, and even then, as she looked back on their relationship, things had been strained for years.

She could acknowledge that now.

They'd settled into their sides of the company, their lives revolving more around their business partnership than their relationship as lovers.

But Reese had been happy. Building their product. Supporting one another. Sharing the same goal.

It had been safe, if not exhilarating.

Comfortable.

Sydney King seemed like the opposite of everything in Reese's sterile life.

She was surprising in the best ways, headstrong and full of possibilities, like a match just waiting to be struck.

Reese had never been the type of person to play with fire, but she'd found herself in a controlled burn, the parameters of their situation clearly laid out between them. They'd play at affection and infatuation, with no real risk to Reese's heart.

Reese would have someone to help her not lose her mind during what was to become a full docket of Devereux family events this summer while she focused on settling in at The Stone's Throw.

In turn, Sydney would get her answers. She would find a way to make sense of the awful things Grant had done to her. And if Reese had her brother pegged accurately—which she knew she did—Sydney would realize that Grant was good at putting on a show but was too selfish and indulgent to ever give enough of himself to be a truly good partner.

Once Sydney accepted that she had never been the problem, she'd stop hiding in Stoneport and get back to living a life that was full enough for her vibrance.

Reese loved a good plan, and as long as she remembered what this was, there was no risk involved.

But remembering the plan grew more difficult as she looked down at Sydney's long legs, one of them bent up against the wall. "Is your knee okay?"

Sydney nodded and stretched her right leg out, balancing on her left heel. The long, lean muscles popped against her skin.

It took an embarrassing amount of effort for Reese to pull her gaze away.

Pushing herself fluidly off the wall, Sydney stood up straight. It brought them closer, and Reese sucked in her breath like it would stop their dresses from touching. She was already anticipating the little jolt before it happened. "One-hundred-percent fine, at least for frolicking among the New England elite."

She had no problem admitting that Sydney was attractive. Especially when she was being playful, her lips eased into a teasing grin.

It was infectious.

Reese met her stare, her body trembling in anticipation. "Good. I'd hate to have to carry you out of here, even though it would make for a good story."

Sydney placed her hand on Reese's shoulder, pretending like she was going to jump into her arms.

The warmth of Sydney's touch was immediate. Reese could

feel its imprint soaking through to her skin, the small hairs on the back of her neck standing up like she was electrified.

Control the burn.

"Thank you, by the way," Sydney said, her green eyes intent and searching, "for going along with this."

"Are you finding what you're looking for?" Reese held her breath.

She watched Sydney bite at the bottom of her lip, gently tugging it between her teeth. "I thought I wanted answers, but now I think I'm just trying to find my way back."

Reese reached up and placed her hand over Sydney's, allowing herself to indulge in how good the weight felt on her shoulder. "You will. I promise."

And then Sydney decided to throw a piece of kindling on Reese's fire by licking her lips, their faces now inches apart.

Reese took a deep breath, trying to steel her fluttering stomach, wondering if this was how wildfires burned down entire forests—a single ember with no real intention of causing mayhem engulfing everything in its path.

"Reese! There you are."

Her mother came into sight just as Sydney's free hand reached around to rest on Reese's hip, further igniting the heat in Reese's veins.

They both jumped at the intrusion, like they'd been caught doing something wrong.

What they had been caught doing, Reese didn't want to think about.

"Just taking a minute, Mom," Reese answered quickly, shaking the hazy, foggy feeling that had settled through her limbs.

"Your father wants to introduce you to the Fitzpatrick family."

And he needed you to come fetch us like his assistant? Reese resisted saying the words out loud, though her father was quickly dropping in her favor for a number of reasons.

But the interruption was good.

Necessary.

Attraction was one thing, but she and Sydney didn't need the added complication of acting on anything.

Sydney shrugged, dropping her hands down to her sides.

Reese could feel the last wisps of whatever had been happening floating away on the gentle breeze.

As she moved to follow her mom, she almost tripped when Sydney's fingers interlaced with her own.

"You've got this," Sydney said quietly, placing the hand holding her champagne glass against Reese's back to steady her. They made their way over to where two people, presumably Mr. and Mrs. Fitzpatrick, stood, along with Brynn, Grant, and Reese's father.

"Ah, yes," her dad said loudly, ushering them into the circle. "This is my daughter, Reese, and her girlfriend, Sydney."

"Wonderful to meet you both. I'm Margie," Brynn's mom said as she moved in decisively for a hug.

Margie Fitzpatrick immediately felt more motherly to Reese than most of the women she'd grown up with. Her shorter stature and fuller figure gave her a soft look, her eyes and smile battling for brightness against her vibrantly orange-and-blue dress.

Reese stiffened at the unexpected affection, but she quickly accepted what was actually a really good hug. Margie even went for a quick rub on her back before releasing her.

Sydney was given the same treatment, though she smiled and hammed it up, giving back the affection just as good as she got.

"You look beautiful, Margie. And you must be Stan." Sydney extended her hand, shaking it more confidently than a woman who hadn't been staring at Reese all wide eyes and parted lips only moments ago.

Reese needed to take a page out of Sydney's book.

She shifted her focus to the present, offering her own hand to Stan Fitzpatrick. "Great to meet you, Mr. and Mrs. Fitzpatrick. I've heard so much about you," she lied, pasting on her most affable smile.

"Reese's been out in San Francisco, making her mark on the startup world," her father said. "Her hotel management app was just acquired."

Mixed emotions swirled through Reese, her chest involuntarily filling with pride even as a scowl worked its way across her features.

Her father hadn't so much as congratulated her in person before last night, and here he was, touting her achievements like some kind of prized pony for the illustrious Fitzpatrick family.

She smoothed the look quickly and took another sip of champagne.

"Daughters," Stan said, genuine wonderment breaking into his voice as he looked at Brynn like she'd hung the moon.

Ah, so that was her father's angle. Stan Fitzpatrick was a true family man, and Tripp would gladly play the part to look more favorable in his eyes.

Reese wondered what it would have been like to grow up with a father like that, one who genuinely supported her and looked at having a daughter as a gift, not a consolation prize.

Tripp laughed good-naturedly. "You're telling me. Grant went into the family business, but Reese wanted to chart her own path in the world. Stanford undergrad and business school, co-founder of her own app—with funding—by the time she earned her MBA and set up shop in San Francisco."

Not rolling her eyes was one of the hardest things Reese had ever done. She was almost impressed, as low as the bar was, that her father could repeat those factoids about her last decade of life considering the lack of interest he'd shown in the milestones as they'd been happening.

Stan slapped Tripp on the back, clearly drunk with love for his wife and daughter. "Women. Marvelous."

The never-ending champagne flutes circling the party probably didn't hurt either.

"And you," Stan said, turning his attention to Sydney.

Reese stiffened, ready to place herself between them depending on the next words out of Stan's mouth.

"I watched you play at the US Open last year. Brilliant performance. I was sorry to hear about your retirement, but it sounds like you've landed on your feet," Stan said as he looked happily between Reese and Sydney. "You two make a striking pair."

Reese lifted an eyebrow even as she said, "Thank you," as gracefully as she could manage.

She let the disappointment roll off of her. She'd really liked Stan until two seconds ago.

Stan waved his hand, realizing he may have been misunderstood. "You're like the new Serena Williams and Alexis Ohanian. A professional athlete and a tech founder. And the fact that it's two women carving their way in this world together... brilliant."

Apparently, Grant had somehow found himself in the most feminist-forward home in all of New England. She smiled, knowing how much he probably hated that.

"Only, Sydney is retired and I'm not currently a founder," she batted back, curious what Stan's response would be.

Mr. Fitzpatrick didn't miss a beat. He was positively gleeful when he said, "And look at what you've both accomplished before meeting—and so young! Imagine what you'll be able to do together."

It was a sweet sentiment, but Reese didn't let herself get lost in thinking about it like it was reality. They'd survive the summer, and then they'd go their separate ways.

She felt Sydney's hand encircle her own, and she looked over at Sydney's green eyes, which were already on her. "My future trajectory is different than I ever expected, but I can honestly say that I'm a changed—and better—person by having the chance to be with Reese."

"Beautiful," Stan said, and Reese honestly wondered if that was a tear she saw in his eye. All six-plus-feet of this man, with his closely shorn salt-and-pepper hair and linebacker shoulders, were very in touch with his emotions.

Reese smiled back at Sydney, catching the soft smirk on her face as she disentangled their fingers so that she could run her thumb gently along the corner of Sydney's lips. "We're very excited about whatever comes next."

"Money, prestige, power, those things all come and go. It's family that's important. That's all we've ever wanted for Brynn."

Reese pulled her attention back to the conversation as Tripp added, "I couldn't have said it better myself."

It took a lot not for her to roll her eyes. Honestly, she wasn't sure if she had succeeded, judging by the way Sydney's fingers began tapping into her back like she was trying to communicate in Morse code.

"My wife and I play doubles at the club occasionally. Nothing like having my favorite partner in life as my partner on the court, too. Sydney and Reese, do you play doubles?"

Reese clocked Grant bristling, and she wondered what Sydney would say. More time with the Fitzpatricks, especially one-on-one, had definitely not been on the agenda today.

"You know, I've been taking it easy with my knee recovery, but we've gotten on the court a few times," Sydney fibbed, shooting Reese a grin. "I much prefer having Reese as a teammate than as an opponent."

Sydney slid her hand flush against Reese's back again and pulled her close.

It was like Sydney had been born to play this role.

Reese relished the return of that hand. It was like a micro-massage, how Sydney's strong fingers pressed but didn't poke as she ran her fingertips along her spine.

Margie clapped her hands together. "Then we must play sometime. Stan and I are at the summerhouse through September." Margie put her hand on Stan's arm. "Honey, it would be lovely to have the whole Devereux family down."

"Incredible idea," Stan said, wrapping his large arm around

her shoulder and pulling her close. "We take summer seriously, so feel free to let us know what works with your schedule. We can make ourselves available. Nothing like a morning match followed by lunch."

Tripp was practically salivating. It seemed like he hadn't been invited to ye old Fitzpatrick summer compound until now. "Why wait? How's next weekend for everyone?"

Reese considered stepping back so her shoes weren't splashed by his drool.

"I'll have to check my schedule," Sydney cut in before Reese had to come up with an excuse. Neither of them wanted to leave Hallie in a lurch. "We haven't been back in Stoneport long, and it's been a while since we've both been back. The dance card's become a little unwieldy already."

Stan looked positively euphoric in the glow of a possible weekend together. "Well, let us know. Margie manages our schedule, and I don't know what I'd do without her."

He kissed the top of his wife's head, beaming, as she pulled business cards out of her clutch before handing one to Reese and one to Sharon.

The conversation veered to Tripp asking questions about the club in Bingham where the Fitzpatricks were members, about thirty minutes south of Boston.

Reese didn't care about whatever her father was saying, except that it gave her time to absorb her surroundings.

The juxtaposition between the Fitzpatricks and the Devereuxs, standing across the circle from one another, was obvious. Stan and Margie were a fluid pair, holding a conversation together, true partners, it seemed, in whatever endeavor they took on.

Her own parents couldn't have looked more different when held up in comparison, her father like a chameleon, adopting whatever temperament was needed to fit the group he found himself in.

Right now, he was playing the doting, interested family man, who wanted to shepherd the unification of two families as their children planned to be wed.

Reese found the whole act to be rather embarrassing; it was certainly a role she'd never thought of him inhabiting before.

But she'd need to unpack that another time.

Because it was her mom, for the first time, who'd really captured her attention.

Given that Grant was getting married, Reese had expected a little more excitement from her mother, regardless of her own personal feelings on the matter.

But besides her mom coming to find them, she'd stood quietly by Tripp's side once they'd joined the group, then watched the scene play out around her.

Reese made a mental note to check in on her mom more often, especially now that she was back in town.

Growing up, Reese had always felt that she had far more in common with her father than her mother. She'd wanted to follow him everywhere. Her days off school were spent sitting on the floor of his office when he'd been home, absorbing the conversations he had on the phone or just listening to the clack of his computer keys at all hours of the day.

Some kids got up to watch Saturday morning cartoons, but Reese got up with the sole purpose of wandering down to her father's office to see if he was there, already working.

Many mornings he wasn't, having stayed over in Boston the night before or already at the golf club to hit a few balls.

She wondered now if she should have spent more time with her mom. Some of the fundraisers and groups her mother chaired were no more than vanity projects in Reese's mind, but she'd gotten postcards over the years of events that her mother had worked on, inviting her to attend.

Some of them, as Reese thought back, were for projects that she also very much believed in.

Coastal conservation. Fundraisers for children in impoverished areas to access summer camps and enrichment programs. Book drives to support literacy among both the youth and adult populations.

Reese hadn't attended any of the events when she'd lived in California, though she'd always sent a check to support whatever was deemed the cause of the month.

Something that felt a lot like guilt churned uncomfortably in her gut, but she pushed the thought away.

"You doing okay?" Sydney murmured beside her, fingers still tracing that soft, soothing pattern along her back. "You look like you're about to chew off your lip."

It wasn't until she let it go with a gentle 'pop' that she realized Sydney was right. The edge of her mouth stung.

Not knowing what to say, she felt a wave of relief when Margie's voice cut through the moment.

"Any of you, all of you. The more the merrier," Margie said before she turned to Brynn and Grant. She looked back at Sydney when she said, "We've been trying to get these two on the court for ages."

Stan placed his hand on Grant's shoulder. "You work your son pretty hard in Boston. Hard man to pin down for a weekend trip. Such a shame."

"Isn't it?" Tripp answered, a look similar to the one Reese had seen at dinner last night passing between father and son. "We'll have to make sure we remedy that. I don't want Grant to miss spending time with his fiancée's family. Work can wait."

Reese bit back a scoff, which was luckily drowned out as Stan made an affirmative grunt at the same time he picked up a glass of champagne from a passing waiter's tray.

She wasn't sure how much more of her father's theatrics she could take today, but there was no polite way for her and Sydney to excuse themselves.

To make matters worse, as the next words left Tripp Devereux's mouth, she wished she'd spent her formative years building a time machine.

"You know, I have a thought…"

Reese had been distracted. Thinking about her mom. Shooting subtle looks at Grant to gauge his temperament. Relishing the casual touches that Sydney seemed insistent on making to sell their story.

It had caused her to underestimate her father, a man who, in her experience, generally got what he wanted.

She was already gritting her teeth when he said, "We hadn't expected Reese to be able to join us for so long this summer, but it would be fantastic if she was more involved in the wedding."

Sydney's hand stilled on Reese's back as she straightened to her full height. She could feel that her eyes were wide.

It was a reaction she couldn't hide, though she did manage to quell the scream that was happening on the inside.

Grant wouldn't want this either. Surely he'd find some smarmy way to backpedal their father's words. Right on time, her brother said, "I don't know if that's—"

But Margie Fitzpatrick was not of the same mind. "What a lovely idea. Stan, wouldn't that be great?"

Stan looked like a bobblehead, given how quickly he nodded. "I couldn't imagine a better way to celebrate the unification of our two families, making sure that Reese is involved as well."

Reese was growing desperate, her stomach churning uneasily as she ran down the list of people who could stop this out-of-control train. Sweat broke out on the small of her back.

Putting the screws to Grant was one thing, but becoming a participant instead of an observer in the Devereux-Fitzpatrick wedding? That was definitely not on her list of things to do this summer.

Between getting up to speed at the inn and the already numerous occasions that she'd have to play loving couple with Sydney, she was trying to think through any way she could gently nudge this in the direction of having someone else think it was a bad idea.

Sydney shot her a quick glance, shrugging like she was at a loss, too.

Flicking her gaze around the circle, Reese settled on her future sister-in-law.

Brynn couldn't want this. The situation was already strange enough, what with Reese dating her fiancé's ex-girlfriend. She probably wanted as little contact with them as possible.

"I'm sure that Brynn already has her bridesmaids," she ventured. "I don't want to impose. I'm just happy that I'm able to be in town to attend all of the events."

"It's up to you, honey," Sharon said to Brynn with a soft smile, picking the world's worst time to join the conversation, "but there is an uneven number of bridesmaids and groomsmen. It could round things out nicely."

Her own mother, Judas.

From her interactions with Brynn that afternoon, Reese had started putting together that she was an introvert in a sea of gregarious social butterflies.

It was clear that she deferred to her parents, and though the circumstances couldn't be worse for Reese to be using this as a science experiment, she was curious if Brynn would fall in line with her parents or go to bat for herself and her future husband.

An important rite of passage for any child, standing up to their family.

Grant's meek rejection of the idea had been surprising given how quickly he'd dropped it, their father seemingly controlling him by some invisible string.

"I think..." Brynn began. She looked at Reese for a few seconds before a gentle, genuine smile broke out across her face. "I think that it would be a nice way for us to spend more time together. I'd like to come to think of Reese as a sister, and this is a great place to start."

Well, fuck.

The coffin had been nailed. Then superglued. Then duct-taped. Then wrapped in tamper-resistant packaging. Then put in the world's most secure vault.

There was that damn tear in Stan's eye again.

With a single sentence, Brynn had made it impossible for Reese to worm her way out of this without looking like the world's worst sister-in-law.

Grant's slumped shoulders and persistent glare in her direction told her he knew the same thing, even if he'd hold it against Reese forever anyway.

Reese forced a smile onto her face and met Brynn's stare. "I feel the same way," she croaked. "Can't wait!"

Seven

"AND WHAT DO WE HAVE HERE?" Hallie raised her voice and let out a whistle as Sydney reached the front lobby of the inn, attracting the attention of a younger couple grabbing coffee from the drinks station.

Sydney rolled her eyes but gave the two guests a small wave. Even if her professional career was over, she still had a little decorum in the event that she was recognized. She was best known within the tennis world, but some of her endorsements, along with magazine and commercial exposure, had made her more of a household name than she'd expected, so she'd learned to be mindful.

It was Tuesday morning, and Sydney was up at the crack of ten, dressed in a casual tennis outfit, her bag slung over her shoulder.

She felt good, her leg in a snug brace, her muscles loose from an hour of stretching that showed her just how out of shape she'd grown over the past month.

Sydney stopped at the desk Hallie was positioned behind, leaning on her forearm. "Are you trying to wake the whole neighborhood?"

Hallie took a sip of coffee and peered over the cup, looking at

Sydney intently. "It's closer to noon than sunrise, my sweet summer child."

"Can you blame me for taking advantage of the first time in my life that I don't have to be up at six a.m. every day?" She inhaled a deep breath, savoring the scent of the clean, fresh air that seemed to infuse the inn.

Hallie gestured broadly, almost knocking over her coffee. "We aim to please here at The Stone's Throw Inn. Early mornings. Late nights," she said with a wink. "We've got you covered."

Upon her exhale, Sydney's deep breath morphed into a sigh. "You know it's not like that. I've been taking walks around town in the evenings."

"You're no fun," Hallie pouted, eyes searching Sydney's for any sign of deceit. "I'm trying to live vicariously through you. I at least thought this little pep in your step was because you got laid or something."

Sydney shook her head. "I assume you mean with Reese, but no, I haven't seen her."

She wasn't lying to her best friend. She hadn't seen Reese since Sunday, when they'd gone their separate ways after the party.

She tried not to dwell on that. Their agreement didn't involve any non-family functions, or even an expectation of friendship, which Sydney was in no position to push.

"She's been squirreled away in the office this week, reviewing all of the financials and the operating reports for the last..." Hallie started counting on her fingers. "Oh, forty years."

"Is she finding anything good?" Sydney asked, leaning forward. "Maybe receipts on flooded bathrooms from that private swimming pool we tried to make?"

Hallie waved her off. "That's water under the bridge—or, carpet, I guess," she finished with a laugh.

Sydney laughed, too, thinking through the weekly torture they had accidentally enacted on the Thatchers. "God, we put your parents through it."

"They loved it."

"Did they? Trying to make a family-owned business work while we were playing *Eloise at the Plaza*?"

Hallie looked around, a softness in her eyes. "Seems like it all netted out on the positive side for them. Their retirement is well funded, and they're sitting pretty on a patio in Boulder with their grandbabies."

Sydney followed Hallie's gaze to a doorway where they'd marked their heights every year in childhood. "And what about you? Are you netting out where you want?"

Hallie was one of those unflappably buoyant people who seemed to let life roll off their backs like water off a duck.

She'd never complained once about losing her best friend beginning junior year so that Sydney could train full-time. And when her parents had started traveling to Colorado more, she'd happily stayed behind to keep the inn going.

Sydney was realizing that she'd taken Hallie's positivity for granted. She saw her as a best friend who'd always been her rock, seemingly without her own choppy seas ever throwing them off course.

Sydney finally allowed herself to relax when she saw a genuine smile flit across Hallie's lips. "I am. If I stay at the inn, it's because I want to, not out of some familial obligation. I think that's pretty positive."

She made a mental note to have a more serious conversation with Hallie soon, about how her friend was feeling with so many big changes in her life.

"So, what are you getting up to?" Hallie asked, deftly changing the subject as she looked at the racket bag still slung across Sydney's shoulder.

"I was thinking of heading over to Manhaven."

"Wow, you're a real glutton for punishment lately," Hallie said with a light laugh as she plucked at the sweatband Sydney wore on her right wrist. "Honestly, I'm just glad you weren't planning to go out to our court. It's definitely in need of some sprucing up."

Sydney winced. That was putting it mildly. She'd walked by the tennis court last night, near the edge of the property. It wasn't unsalvageable, but there were cracks in the court, and the net was sagging in the middle like someone had spent a few hours—or years—using it as a hammock.

"Well, until Reese decides to focus on the finer amenities of this establishment, Manhaven it is."

Manhaven Tennis Center, where she'd spent more hours than she did at home growing up, was one of fewer than ten full-time, high-performance training programs in the United States that catered to taking young athletes to the next level of play.

By the age of twelve, Sydney was taking private lessons at the center four times a week. Instead of completing her last two years of high school at Stoneport, she'd switched to virtual learning and started training six hours a day, five days a week.

She had been lucky to live less than a twenty-minute drive from a place that had the coaches and experience needed to help shape her into the player she'd become.

Unlike a few other full-time program participants she'd trained with, she'd still been able to live at home in Stoneport, so her life had been minimally disrupted.

She still got to see Hallie in the evenings and on weekends, and the Thatcher family had allowed her to use the tennis court at the inn for a few hours every Saturday and in the evenings when it was closed to the guests.

Her success was partially a result of hard work and dedication, but it wouldn't have been possible without people who'd believed in her, supported her, and allowed her to become the best version of herself—professionally-speaking, at least.

Apparently she'd missed the lesson where she picked better partners, but she shrugged the thought off as quickly as it flitted through her mind.

When she'd gone to Walker College, lured by the promise of a full-ride—and at the significant pushing of her parents to get a four-year degree instead of heading right to the pro circuit—their tennis regimen had seemed like a breeze.

Sydney looked at the clock, double-checking the time. "I've gotta get going."

Hallie looked toward the door that led to the small office where she sometimes worked. "Not going to say bye to your girlfriend?"

A dead-eyed stare was the first response her best friend got before Sydney finally added, "I know that my life is a comedy of errors right now."

"At least it's not a tragedy," Hallie said with a nonplussed shrug.

"Verdict's still out."

On Sunday night, she'd come back and regaled Hallie with the highlights of the day, including Tripp offering Reese up on a platter as a bridesmaid to the wedding gods, a pathetic attempt to curry favor with Stan Fitzpatrick, whom Sydney had liked immediately.

She'd held back in her retelling, though, wondering if the thoughts unsaid had only been in her own mind. She'd liked spending time with Reese. Had enjoyed their closeness, had loved the softness of her skin and how comfortable it had felt to have a protective arm draped around her waist during the party.

Maybe she would have mentioned those things to Hallie, but the ride back from the party had been quiet, Reese more withdrawn than she'd been earlier in the day.

For whatever thrill Sydney was getting from this situation, complicating things by pushing the boundaries of a woman she actually knew very little about probably wasn't a smart decision.

They'd parted ways with a promise from Reese to let her know about this weekend. Sydney's calendar was wide open, as it usually was these days, but she hadn't heard from Reese yet. She made a mental note to text her later and confirm whether they'd be making the trek to an even more well-to-do part of the coast.

Sydney wrapped her knuckles on the smooth wood. "I'll see you later?"

Hallie, who'd started focusing intently on something happening on her laptop, spared her a glance before looking back down at the screen in front of her. "Count on it, bestie."

And with that, Sydney walked out to her car and began the short drive to a place that had become a second home.

* * *

Sydney inhaled deeply as she stepped into the Manhaven Tennis Center. There was a distinct smell in tennis complexes that never changed over time: a mix of rubber from the tennis balls, disinfectant to keep the courts clean, and a light combination of antiperspirant and sweat that mingled into a smell sort of like the coast on a slightly cold day.

She loved it.

When she set foot on a court, it was like the scent triggered her body to relax, her muscles already starting to anticipate moving with the rhythm of play.

She could hear the *pop* of the balls as they released from the tennis ball launcher, her ears tuning into the difference between some players connecting their racket with the ball outside of the sweet spot and those who were able to hit in the perfect center, a melodious *thwack* that was one of her favorite sounds.

Her fingers twitched against her sides, already anticipating holding her racket; the way her fingers would wrap around the grip, shifting her hand's placement millimeters at a time to execute the perfect hit.

She prided herself on being a great all-court player, shifting seamlessly between dominating serves and strong baseline ground strokes, between thoughtful net attacks and relentless defense.

Sydney was surprised to see that, late in the morning on a weekday, all of the tennis courts were in use. Closest to the entrance, kids no older than six or seven were spread across two courts, hitting balls with varying degrees of success. Deeper into the center, there were juniors running sprints, practicing their footwork as they maneuvered with agility around a set of cones.

On the five courts that mirrored the ones she was closest to, small groups of adults looked like they were in lessons, practicing ground strokes, playing doubles, and volleying back and forth.

She noticed then, on the farthest court back, on the side where the juniors played, her old instructor, Brian Chester. It was easy to spot him, even though it had been five years since the last time she'd seen him. He always covered his gray hair with a tennis-ball-colored hat, and at five-foot-eight, he stood only slightly taller than the girl he was talking to at the net.

Sydney was far away, but she clocked the young player at fourteen or fifteen years old, racket slung across her shoulder as she listened intently to Brian's feedback.

Her curiosity was piqued, seeing Brian in a one-on-one session when the center was obviously bustling, and she headed for the walkway behind the baselines.

Even with more than two million Instagram followers, it wasn't like she got stopped daily, but it did happen enough that she was conscious of her public image.

Her agent had posted a message on Instagram that Sydney had written regarding her retirement, including that she'd be taking some time off to rest and decide what would come next.

Sara, almost true to her word to give Sydney space, had only reached out once so far, earlier this morning.

Fans are gutted, disappointed to say the least, and they already miss your glowing face and winsome personality. Not to mention that talent! Just thought you'd like to know that everyone wants to know what comes next!

Well, wasn't that the million-dollar question.

She hadn't posted since her retirement announcement; hadn't even looked at the comments. What anyone else thought about it wasn't her business.

But at Manhaven, where casual tennis players mingled with

young hopefuls who ate, slept, and breathed the sport, she knew she'd attract more attention.

Securing the baseball cap she'd donned before walking into the center, she only looked toward the courts to make sure she wasn't walking past them while a point was in play.

Once she reached the last court, she dropped her bag and leaned against the wall.

Brian walked back to about half-court, and instead of using the ball machine, he began to hand-feed tennis balls across the net.

They were practicing slices. His student was positioned at the baseline, but she hadn't yet looked in Sydney's direction.

Sydney remembered having that kind of focus, being like a dog with a bone, nothing distracting her from the next hit that was coming her way.

Sydney watched intently. The girl had raw talent, even if she was still rough around the edges. She sometimes moved from the baseline, depending on where Brian hit the ball. Her intuition was spot-on though, always anticipating where the ball was going but lacking the finer skill of returning it perfectly, a thousand tiny variations of every hit that would become second nature with, oh, ten thousand or so more serves.

"You'll be there soon enough, Jenna. You have the time. Set yourself up for success," Brian said as his student—Jenna, it would seem—moved toward the net and sliced, though her ball extended beyond the far baseline, out of bounds.

"Got it," Jenna said, her voice a little winded as she moved back toward the baseline, then turned around and got in her stance again.

"Sydney, what is Jenna doing wrong?" Brian's eyes had shifted to her, though she was now realizing he'd known for much longer that she was standing there.

Brian's skill as a coach was that he didn't miss a thing, on or off the courts. It was hell for a teenager, but it'd made her a better tennis player.

"What, you didn't think I spotted you the second you stepped into the center?" he said with a vibrant smile. "Especially when you're one of the best players I've ever had the opportunity to coach?"

Jenna turned around then, her eyes going wide, and her racket almost slipped from her hands.

Sydney gave her a small wave and stepped up to the baseline. She looked down at the familiar sight of the white line millimeters from her sneakers, being careful not to touch it. She loved the rituals of tennis, and even though she wasn't serving, she still treated that line like it was electrified.

"Okay with you?" she asked, looking at Jenna.

She'd been used to reverence from younger players who met her, hoping they would become one of the only hundreds out of tens of thousands in their age range who had the skill for professional play.

Now it felt a little strange, given her unceremonious retirement and, for the first time in her life, a lack of confidence regarding what would come next.

Jenna's head bobbed up and down quickly as she stepped behind the baseline. "Yes. Do you want to use my racket?"

"Sure," Sydney said, taking the racket that Jenna had already offered her. At least if she did terribly, she could blame it on not schlepping a few extra feet to get her own from her bag.

Sydney bent her knees slightly and let the weight of the racket move between her hands.

She'd missed it, how everything around her stopped while she was waiting for the ball, anticipating what would happen.

Grant and his betrayal were so far from her mind she'd need a passport to get there. Her career, or lack thereof, filtered into the background, unimportant as she felt the court beneath her feet.

And Reese? Well, that one was still hanging around at her periphery, but she made the intentional decision to push her further into the din.

"Your knee okay for this?" Brian asked, expressing genuine concern.

Sydney nodded, settling the grip in her right hand, her left one gently braced on top of it.

Brian bounced a ball. "Ready to show 'em how it's done, kid?"

After another nod, the ball was careening in her direction. She stepped forward deftly, muscle memory taking over as her arm formed into an L-shape. She felt the racket make contact with the ball in a high-to-low swing path, keeping her wrist in a neutral position even upon impact. She threw her right shoulder into her movement to put power into the motion, her racket moving across her body but slowing down after contact.

She came back to a standing position, watching the ball as it landed on the two white lines that intersected to form the back left corner of the court.

Brian was already moving toward the net. "Beautiful shot, but I expected nothing less. You can take a breather, Jenna," he added a little louder for his student's benefit, given how she looked adorably starstruck.

"Thanks," Sydney said, turning to Jenna to return the racket before she jogged to center court.

"I wondered if I'd see you around here again." Brian extended his arms across the net for a hug.

He smelled the same as ever as she leaned into his chest, like a clean aftershave and the shea butter he'd always worn religiously.

"No place like home," Sydney said as she disentangled herself to look at her old coach fully. "You look good. I thought I'd be coming home to an old man."

"These knees aren't what they used to be," he said as he knocked his racket against his leg and looked down at her own braced knee. "Seems like we have that in common."

Sydney shrugged. "I've had better years."

"It's true? You're officially retired?"

"I hope so because otherwise, I'm overdue at Wimbledon about now," she deflected.

In her mind, she still told herself that she was on an extended break, that her return to pro tennis was inevitable. But at least a year of surgery and rehab to fully correct her knee injuries would put her at well past thirty before a return would even be possible, and the same amount of time without full-time practice and training would have passed, too.

It was an impossible dream that would only end in her slogging her way through first-round losses and failing to qualify for the tournaments she used to have a chance of winning.

Brian leaned in closer, clocking the look on her face. "You doing okay? I know the transition can be hard. We feel like we're invincible when we're young, like we can go on forever." He placed his hand on Sydney's shoulder, squeezing it gently. "I'm here for whatever you need. A hitting partner. A friend. A drinking buddy," he finished with a laugh.

"God," Sydney said, smiling, "I can't believe I haven't seen you in so long."

She'd missed Brian. He seemed to be able to slip between coach and friend and confidant in a matter of seconds, and at the heart of it all, he'd genuinely wanted to help her succeed.

"You're evading the question." He was also famously forthright, she was being forced to remember.

Sydney bit the inside of her lip, trying to find the right words. She wished she had her racket to swing back and forth to distract herself. Instead, she placed her hands against the white of the net and squeezed. "I'm managing. I thought I had another couple of good years in me, but life had other plans."

"All of our careers end one way or another, and you've already had an impressive one."

That meant a lot, coming from Brian. He'd watched her go from a gangly kid to a formidable contender as she'd gone off to college, and he'd continued to coach her during summers when she was home. No amount of career wins, endorsement deals, or social media followers could take the place of the approval of someone she deeply respected.

"Do you ever miss it, playing professionally?"

"Every day," he said seriously. "But I love coaching, too. It's something I always felt you would be great at."

"Are you trying to recruit me for a job?" she joked.

"If I thought I could get you, absolutely." That same serious tone was back in his voice. "You have your whole life ahead of you, Syd. I'm excited to see what you do with it, just as much as I loved watching your matches on TV over the last few years and seeing you learn new skills when you were just a kid."

His words affected her, deeply, and she started to feel her eyes prickle with tears.

"To be honest, I'm not sure what comes next," she admitted, working to talk around the lump in her throat.

"How long are you in town?"

It was a great question. "I'm not sure, honestly. I came back to relax and get my bearings for a little bit. Definitely through the summer." She'd committed to attending Grant's wedding in early September with Reese, which was still months away. Sure, she could fly back and forth from Florida, but there was this feeling she had, like Stoneport was where she needed to be.

Brian tapped at his temple. "I've always found that life, just like tennis, is a mental game."

Sydney groaned, remembering the countless hours of drills she'd been put through, the exhaustive self-regulation to stay calm under pressure, the visualization of the possibilities she could find herself in during a big match. "Don't I know it, sensei."

"How's the knee, all things considered?"

"It's decent. Fine for casual play. I'd need a full surgery and recovery if I wanted to get back to the professional level, if the doctors are right." She paused before adding, "And there's the lack of trust in myself to contend with, if the sports therapists are right."

Brian considered her words, then his focus shifted to Jenna, who'd appeared back at the edge of the court.

"Well then," he said, as Jenna picked up her racket and began taking practice swings, "you want to make this kid's year and force her to play doubles against us?"

* * *

Sydney locked her car and headed into The Stone's Throw.

She and Brian had won, unsurprisingly, but Jenna had put up a good fight.

After Jenna's private instruction had ended, she and Brian had gone to a restaurant and grabbed a late lunch, along with a drink, something they'd never done before.

And the whole day had felt... good.

Comforting and normal in some ways. She'd gotten back on the court. Brian's laughter boomed loudly whenever he missed a shot.

But it was also strange and foreign. Brian wasn't coaching her; his tips were directed at Jenna on the other side of the net. And Sydney had still been tentative with some of her movements, not wanting to put too much pressure on her knee once they'd gotten into the match.

When she ambled into the lobby, limbs loose from a day of exercise, she noticed Reese sitting at the check-in desk.

Her hair was up, with tendrils framing her face as she looked down at a printed stack of papers.

Sydney stopped at the front desk just as Reese looked up, surprise written across her face.

"Don't worry, I'm not a check-in," Sydney said, putting her hands up. "But I was starting to wonder if you'd absconded back to the West Coast."

Reese blushed, and it made Sydney wonder if she'd actually been avoiding her. "Sorry, it's been a busy week."

"Hallie said you were deep in financials," Sydney supplied, suddenly feeling awkward when Reese didn't seem to want to meet her eyes.

Reese gestured vaguely at the papers still in front of her. "Yeah, I'm trying to wrap my head around everything."

"So you aren't ignoring me?" Sydney let the surge of adrenaline from her day of activity pull the words from her before she could second-guess them. "A girl sort of expects a call after a date where she meets the parents."

And suddenly, Reese looked absolutely apologetic. She pinched the bridge of her nose and shut her eyes. After a moment, she opened them to look at Sydney. "I'm sorry about that. It had nothing to do with you, honestly. I'm a little bit stressed about this whole bridesmaid thing with Brynn, and I throw myself into projects when I'm stressed," Reese said, gesturing at the multiple colored highlighters and sticky tabs that were affixed to different pages in the pile.

Sydney held her hands up to her chest, trying her best to embody the spirit of a Disney princess. "So the date went well then? Do you think there's a second in our future?"

She resisted the urge to twirl to really sell it.

"You were perfect," Reese said, with an almost wistful quality that Sydney knew she must be misinterpreting.

"Any feedback from the parents? Grant?" Sydney was only half joking, wondering how the day had gone from Reese's perspective.

She thought she saw Reese's eye twitch when she said, "Grant and I haven't spoken, though I'm sure he's about as happy about it as I am."

"Given what you know, I'm sure he's not thrilled that you and Brynn will be spending more one-on-one time together."

"Honestly, I can't even figure out who knows what at this point, if it even matters." Reese ran her hand over her hair, like she was collecting herself before she made a sound caught somewhere between a scoff and disgust. "And my dad was such a bootlicker at the party. I haven't even given myself time to get wrapped up in that."

Sydney laughed, mostly to hide her shock at the words

coming out of Reese's mouth. "Wow, yeah. I mean, I don't disagree. Stan and Margie were really the MVPs of the day, if I get a vote."

"And you," Reese said earnestly. Sydney's cheeks warmed at the compliment.

"Hey," she chastised, waiting for Reese to look at her, needing her to *really* understand her. "You held your own. Absolutely."

She could tell that Reese wanted to dismiss her words, but she didn't want to let her. After the day Sydney had had, she wanted Reese to feel that same sense of possibility.

Reese had moved away from the clout of her family to create her own future. She'd successfully built and sold an app that helped thousands of small businesses. Now she was back in her hometown, taking ownership of the inn and working tirelessly to make sure she was doing a good job at it.

"It's nice of you to say," Reese finally relented.

Sydney leveled a charming smile in her direction. "I only speak the truth."

Reese finally clocked the way Sydney was dressed, leaning over the desk to get a full look at her outfit. "Did you play tennis today?"

"What gave it away?" Sydney asked as she felt Reese's gaze continue to scan her body.

And just like that, it was back, the spark that she'd felt with Reese last weekend. It was impossible to ignore, with them so close. Reese was leaning over the check-in desk, and Sydney's long arm rested on the counter so that Reese's chest almost brushed against it.

Want, surprising in its intensity, curled low in her stomach, and she enjoyed the heat it spread through her body.

In a different world, if Grant wasn't her ex-boyfriend, and Reese had actually been a beautiful woman she'd met somewhere outside of all of this, things would be very different.

But they weren't, and a large part of today had been about Sydney accepting reality.

So that's what she tried to do when she willed her body to calm down, orienting herself back to the task at hand. "I was wondering if this weekend was still happening. With the Fitzpatricks, I mean," she clarified.

Knowing they had a public event together in just a few days would help dump a little more cold water on any of her confusion about what this was. And wasn't.

Reese sighed, looking at her intently. "I know it's a lot to ask, but I think my dad is hell-bent on making it happen. Are you willing to come?"

Their situation—their *act*—was complicated, but Sydney couldn't deny the little thrill that ran through her body at the idea of them spending the weekend together. All she needed to do was maintain perspective, to keep any of her own confusion simmering enough to not be noticeable.

She beamed a megawatt smile in Reese's direction, hopefully allaying any of the fear Reese had about them pulling this ruse off for longer than an afternoon. "Can't wait."

Eight

WHEN REESE HAD TOLD Sydney earlier this week that her dad was hell-bent on making this weekend happen, she hadn't been lying, let alone exaggerating.

It was Thursday morning, and she'd already received at least a dozen texts from her father about the upcoming event.

What to bring. How to behave. Not to paint her brother in a bad light.

She'd laughed at the last one. As if Grant needed any help from her on that front.

Taking a drink of her almost empty coffee, she squinted at her laptop screen, scrutinizing the financials more closely now that she was into the inn's most recent decade of operations.

The only thing she'd put her foot down about with her father was that she couldn't head to Bingham on Friday, given that she was already going to be missing another weekend day at the inn so soon after coming on board.

She'd confirmed with him on Tuesday night, after running into Sydney in the lobby, that the two of them would arrive on Saturday. She'd also agreed to play nice with the Fitzpatrick family.

Messy. It was all so messy.

Reese hadn't been *avoiding* Sydney. She was just stressed out. Which is what she repeated to herself for the hundredth time.

The way Sydney had looked at her on Sunday hadn't helped, given all her soft eyes and sweet smiles.

Coupled with the way Sydney had looked on Tuesday, filling out her tennis outfit as she practically bounded walking into the lobby... yeah, that was a memory that Reese wouldn't soon forget.

Since Megan, she hadn't even looked at another woman with appreciation or interest, and now she was going to spend the weekend in close confines with *People* Magazine's Sexiest Female Athlete of the Year.

2022, in case anyone was wondering. And yes, Reese had googled the specific year for the sake of accuracy.

Groaning, she put her head in her hands.

Having Sydney by her side would make these wedding events better, not worse, she reminded herself.

Deep breaths, she encouraged herself as she visualized the mounting pile of complications, trying to allay her own fears.

The wedding would be fine, even if she had to be a bridesmaid.

Grant was a menace, and he more than deserved to be put through the ringer.

Her mom was being weird, but given how little she actually knew her mom, maybe she'd always been like this.

Finally, there was her dad. She'd started to give up any false ideations about what kind of man he really was.

When she'd been younger, she'd thought he was a titan of industry, with a portfolio of properties in the double digits that at the time was as significant in Reese's mind as if he'd built the pyramids.

Now, she was spending time with him as a true adult, and she couldn't say she was especially impressed.

Not with how he treated his wife, only acknowledging her mother when it benefitted him. Not with how he ran his business, intent on ushering Grant in as the future of The Devereux Group because of genitalia instead of talent or effort. And certainly not with how he kowtowed to the Fitzpatricks, willing to say or do whatever he needed to get their investment money.

Maybe if it had been something else he'd embellished, she'd have cared less. He could have pretended that he loved polo or that his passion was wildlife conservation. Those things wouldn't have worked their way under her skin.

But no, he had to pretend to be dedicated to his family, and worse than that, he had to pretend that he was proud of Reese and the life she'd built. A life that he'd conveniently forgotten to mention had only been necessary because he'd made it clear she'd never be seen like Grant in his eyes.

Reese would have loved to one day take over The Devereux Group, but even by the end of high school, she knew that it was never going to be her future. If her father had given even a whisper of suggestion in the opposite direction, she'd have gone to a school on the East Coast with a stellar hospitality and tourism management major, aligning all of her focus into becoming a worthy successor when he decided to retire.

Instead, she'd moved across the country to start on her own track, one that would ultimately put her at the hands of her own destiny—or so she'd thought.

She frowned as she lifted her cup to her lips, only to find it empty.

A knock on the doorframe pulled her attention to where Hallie stood, a fresh cup of coffee in hand.

"How did you know?" Reese asked, genuinely baffled as she accepted the cup, which was fixed just the way she liked it.

"You walk by the front desk to get coffee," Hallie said, pointing down the short hallway that connected to the lobby. "You've been on a pretty consistent schedule this week. Once you hit fifteen minutes late, I took a chance."

"I appreciate it." She reminded herself that she really needed to find a way to get Hallie to stay on board.

"How are things going in here?" Hallie gestured toward the

paperwork on the desk. "Finding any good skeletons in the cleaning closets?"

Reese shook her head. "Nothing that's giving me heart palpitations or making me wonder what I've gotten myself into."

For the most part, that was true. While there were a few more projects and areas of upkeep that had been left to languish than she'd expected, the inn turned a modest profit every year after its operating budget, which stayed relatively close to accurate, was spent. There were a few bigger projects that she'd want to handle over time—improving the pool area, updating the guest rooms, and installing some more permanent outdoor event spaces—but overall, things could be a lot worse.

"Coastal erosion is a serious issue," Hallie deadpanned. "In another two hundred or so years, this place could fall off the side of the cliff."

"I'll keep that in mind." Reese shuffled her papers together, looking for something to keep her fidgeting fingers occupied.

"Knowledge is power." Hallie lingered in the doorway.

"Did you want to chat about something?" Reese was starting to feel a little claustrophobic in the small office, even though Hallie's diminutive frame only took up about half of the entrance.

She'd never been great with confrontation, unless it was with Grant. Megan had always been the person who dealt with employee issues.

Hallie cleared her throat, growing serious as she stretched to her full, albeit short, height. "I want to know what your intentions are with my best friend."

Reese's heart beat uncomfortably in her chest before she found words to drown out the blood rushing through her ears. "My intentions are to help Sydney get closure."

It's what Sydney, herself, had professed to want, so she figured it was a safe answer.

"And what's in it for you?" Hallie asked, crossing one leg over the other and leaning against the doorframe, signaling a move into a more casual chat.

Reese remained on high alert.

"To torture my baby brother, for a multitude of reasons," she answered honestly, thumbing across the stack of papers.

Hallie's shoulders slumped, and she ran a hand through her hair. "Sydney would kill me if she knew I was talking to you about this, but I feel like I have some responsibility here."

Reese lifted a quizzical brow. "Why are you responsible?"

As far as Reese had seen, Hallie was about the best friend a person could ask for.

"I let her come back to Stoneport, knowing that you'd bought the inn and that Grant was getting married. I put her directly in the Devereux family path because I missed my best friend and wanted to spend time with her."

"I don't think that makes you culpable in what, colloquially, I think many people would refer to as 'a harebrained scheme.'" Reese made air quotes around the phrase, which earned a grin from Hallie. "That was all me and Sydney, and I don't think anyone on the planet would put that on you."

"Yeah, what's that even about? You two were literally alone for five minutes," Hallie said, more puzzled than anything. "Sydney is not what I'd call an impetuous person."

Reese shrugged, her face scrunching up. "My brother brings out the worst in both of us?"

Hallie laughed. "That's putting it mildly."

"You're a good friend, Hallie. I'm grateful that Sydney is willing to go to these events with me and provide a buffer from my family. I hope that in return, like I already said, I can help her get some sort of closure."

"What, she needs confirmation that Grant's a complete asshole? I could have told her that."

Reese held up her hands and didn't allow her smile to become a laugh. Hallie really hit the nail on the head with that one.

"No argument here. But someone telling you something and

you learning and accepting something for yourself are different. I think Sydney just wants to make it make sense."

Hallie scowled. "I always thought she was too good for him."

"Again, no argument," Reese said, her interest piqued.

"Sydney didn't go to high school with Grant and me the last two years. She was already training full-time. I've never liked him. And when I found out they were dating toward the end of her junior year of college, right when he was graduating, I about fell off my beanbag chair."

Reese could see it clearly, Hallie sitting on a beanbag chair that took up the majority of her dorm room floor, sprawled out within its massiveness as she tried to hold on to her flip phone in her surprise.

"I was a little surprised myself," she admitted, "but Sydney wasn't successful or famous in the way she is now. I mostly just couldn't figure out why someone like Grant, who seemed to be the epitome of a young bachelor, would enter into a serious relationship right after college."

"He probably saw what we all saw, that Sydney was going to be a major contender in the world of tennis. Her star was on the rise, and he wanted to go along for that ride. She's smart. Gorgeous. Talented. He could do far worse."

Reese nodded in agreement. Hallie definitely wasn't getting any argument from her there either.

"And still, he threw it all away." A lump formed in Reese's throat as she forced out the words. It was guilt, that she was happy that Sydney was out of Grant's clutches, even if it had come with considerable hurt.

"Exactly. Which brings me back to my central point," Hallie said, growing serious again. "Sydney King is my best friend and the best person I know. If you do anything to put her in harm's way, let alone hurt her yourself, there will be hell to pay."

"Erm... got it."

Then Hallie smiled brightly, and it was the strangest thing to see, juxtaposed with her threatening demeanor mere seconds ago.

"Okay, good. I've never done the whole 'threatening someone' thing, but I feel like it went well. You agree?"

Reese shut her eyes and nodded, pinching the bridge of her nose. "Yeah, Hallie. You did great, though I don't know if it always includes a request for feedback from the person you're intimidating."

"Always room for improvement, I guess." Hallie rapped on the doorframe. "Okay, well, your coffee's getting cold. You'd better drink up. We have a busy afternoon of check-ins for the long weekend. See you in the lobby in twenty?"

Reese leaned back in her chair, letting the soft movement soothe her. "I'll be there."

Hallie bounded out of the office, treating threats and intimidation the same way she treated a pep talk, and maybe to her, they were the same.

Yet again, though, the idea had been reinforced, by someone other than herself this time, that her situation with Sydney wasn't something she should take lightly.

* * *

Later Thursday night, Reese was dragging herself back to her room when her cell phone rang.

She answered the unknown number. It could be any of about a half-dozen vendors she'd called earlier that morning regarding quotes for some of the bigger projects she was considering at the inn.

"Reese speaking."

"Hey, Reese. This is Brynn." There was a pause before Brynn unnecessarily added, "Fitzpatrick. Grant's fiancée. Your mom gave me your cell number; I hope that's okay."

All she wanted to do was shed her clothes and take a long, luxurious bath, but instead, she let herself into her room and plopped down on top of her unmade bed, where Reese pursed her lips. "Sure thing, Brynn. What's up?"

"So my mom let me know that you'll be joining us this weekend, which is great," she said, like she genuinely meant it, her voice taking on that airy, excited quality Reese had become familiar with the weekend before. "I wanted to get your dress size so that I could bring a bridesmaid dress for you to try on."

Reese stifled a groan. She'd been trying so hard not to think about her upcoming inclusion in the wedding event of the season.

Instead, she pasted on a smile she hoped came through in her voice. "That's so thoughtful. I'm a six or an eight, depending on the brand."

She could hear Brynn scribbling on a piece of paper. "Got it. I'll see if I can get one of each for you to try on, just to make sure you like it. It's this local dress shop, so I can swing by tomorrow."

Brynn was already being extremely thoughtful, and Reese was suddenly steeped in guilt at her complete ambivalence to the woman's existence.

It wasn't Brynn's fault that Grant was good at hiding who he was. If Reese used dating her brother as a litmus test for how much she respected someone, she'd have run the other way from Sydney. Probably screaming.

"I really appreciate it, Brynn. Thank you."

"Reese?" Brynn said quietly, then was silent as she waited for acknowledgement.

Reese had placed her phone on the end table before getting up and starting to undress, the call of a hot bath becoming too much to resist.

"What's up?" she asked, distracted at the fact that her pants wouldn't cooperate.

"I want Sydney to know, I hope there are no hard feelings. You two are lovely together, and I hope Grant breaking up with her is all water under the bridge. I'm just excited to have a relationship with you, maybe even with Sydney if she's open to it."

Reese stopped, falling over sideways on her bed when she misjudged how far she'd gotten her pants off. "Wait, what?"

115

She could hear the uncomfortable catch in Brynn's voice. "Oh, um... just that I know things are complicated, and I wanted to make sure everything was good between the four of us."

"Yeah, right." Reese was trying to catch up with what Brynn was saying while trying to shimmy out of her pants, which she'd gotten down to mid-thigh.

Why were they so damn tight?

Reese cleared her throat, realizing she hadn't actually given Brynn an answer. "It's all good with Sydney and me," she half lied.

"Okay, great," Brynn said, relief evident in her tone. "I'm really excited for us all to spend more time together. Grant works so much, and it will be nice to have more people that I consider family around."

Working hard? That didn't sound like her brother. At all.

But maybe, even if she didn't truly believe it, Grant had found his one in a billion with Brynn, the person who was worth throwing it all away to lead a happy life together.

In spite of all she'd learned about the business world, she'd never had her father's willingness to do whatever it took to close the deal. Right now, he would want her to say whatever she needed to keep Brynn excited about her impending nuptials.

But that wasn't who she was, and it wasn't who she wanted to be. Still, even for the sake of peace, she couldn't get close to promising that they'd all be one big, happy family one day.

Brynn was sweet, but she doubted that her future sister-in-law would be the glue that mended a lifetime of brewing resentment between Reese and the rest of her family.

Beyond that, it wasn't fair to expect Brynn to be responsible for something of that magnitude. Hell, Reese didn't even know where she'd start, if she wanted to fix it on her own.

So instead, she was stuck playing a part, biding her time until she could once again extricate herself from the Devereux family drama, something she'd successfully avoided for the last twelve years.

"It'll be good for us to get to spend more time together," Reese said sincerely, echoing Brynn's words. She wasn't going to sing her brother's praises. She wasn't going to lie and tell Brynn that she and her brother had a great relationship.

What she could do was promise that she'd be kind to Brynn, and until she knew what Brynn knew, which she wasn't going to ask because she wasn't a complete idiot, she'd keep her cards close to her chest.

"It means a lot to hear you say that, Reese. All right, I'll let you go."

"See you Saturday, Brynn," Reese said as she hopped over to the end table and hit 'End' on her phone.

She looked down at her pants then, a still-tangled jumble of fabric that she hadn't managed to get off.

With focus, she finally extricated herself from the tapered legs and let out a huff.

As she walked over to the bathroom, her phone began to ring again. She ignored it, set on running her bath, which was already long overdue.

Once she started the water, she checked her missed calls. It was her mom, but she didn't have the energy to call her back right then. It would probably be more about what her father had been insisting, with firm directives to make sure this weekend went off without a hitch.

How had she suddenly become responsible for the emotional well-being of so many people? She'd found herself at a nexus of conflict with the lie that she and Sydney had spun, and she was wondering if the two of them had what it took to see things through to the finish line.

And what was that line, anyway?

When Sydney got her answers? When she realized that getting any type of closure from Grant was a fruitless endeavor?

When Brynn successfully made it down the aisle and became Mrs. Devereux?

When her dad found out she'd purchased the inn and officially disowned her?

As the days wore on, she was sort of looking forward to that last one. To forcing her father to finally say that he didn't deem her worthy. Maybe this time, she'd actually do something to deserve it.

She willed her thoughts to float away as she dipped a toe into the hot water before lowering her entire body in. She leaned her head back against the edge and let out a calming breath, enjoying the gentle sloshing sound of the bath flowing around her.

Everything was going to be fine. Her dad would do most of the talking this weekend, Brynn seemed like she just wanted a friend, and she and Sydney would rarely be alone together.

It was all going to work out.

Her phone rang from the bedroom again, and instead of listening to it ring, she slipped under the water and let it envelope her senses.

Nine

"WHEN I WAS A KID, Bingham felt like a world away," Sydney said as Reese's car meandered along the coastline.

They'd been driving for over an hour, and they were about halfway to their destination.

It was a slightly chilly Saturday morning, but the weather would warm up in a few hours, when they were slated to arrive at the Fitzpatricks' seaside mansion, just 'a hop, skip, and a jump away'—they'd been told, according to the text that Stan Fitzpatrick had sent Reese's entire family—from the country club where they'd be spending the day.

Sydney had snuck little glances at Reese, conversation light as the radio played instead.

Reese was dressed more casually today than she had been last weekend, in an airy linen shirt that was half tucked into her white, high-waisted, wide-legged pants.

"Is it okay that I'm taking the scenic route?" Reese asked, her eyes staying on the road. "I figured you weren't champing at the bit to get there any earlier than necessary."

They'd had a quiet send-off early this morning, at least between the two of them. Hallie, the jubilant ray of sunshine that she was, had cups of coffee ready for them and a few good-natured jabs about what their sleeping situation would be tonight.

Sydney had waved her best friend off, but it was something she'd thought about more than once over the last couple of days.

Reese, however, hadn't seemed to give it much consideration. She was clearly distracted as they'd thrown their weekend bags in the car and started their Saturday morning drive.

Sydney took in Reese's posture, which hadn't relaxed since they'd gotten in the car. "Are we taking the long way for me or for you?"

She watched as Reese's shoulders sagged. "I've interacted with my father more this week than I have in the last ten years. Apparently, the possibility of currying favor with the Fitzpatricks has gotten me off the bench and back on the starting team for children who have value to him."

"We don't have to go," Sydney said, meaning it. "I saw a lobster shack a few miles back. We can sit in the parking lot until it opens and then gorge ourselves on a morning lobster roll."

"I don't know that 'morning lobster rolls' are a thing."

Sydney looked at her, aghast. "There is *never* a bad time for a lobster roll."

Reese glanced over at her, still clearly lost in her own thoughts. "He called me on the phone this morning. *To check in.*"

It took Sydney a few seconds to realize they were still talking about Tripp.

"Is that not something you two do? Like, ever?" Sydney, in contrast, talked to her parents multiple times a week on the phone. When she was in Florida, they lived together. Being surprised to see one of her parents' names flash across her phone screen was an alien concept to her.

"Let me put it this way: I think he would have had my mom send a card for my college and business school graduations if he could have gotten away with it. You've probably spent more time with my father in the last couple of years than I have."

Reese was probably right, Sydney acknowledged with a wince.

She'd had dinner with Tripp, Grant, and varying groups of business associates and friends of theirs over the last half decade when she was in town in Boston.

And yet, she'd never liked Grant Devereux III, colloquially known as 'Tripp' to anyone from their dinner companions to the female waitstaff he stared at for a few beats longer than Sydney had ever been comfortable with.

When she'd been with Grant, she'd made an effort, truly. They'd gone to dinner at dozens of places over the years during Sydney's visits to Boston.

And his father had always come off as... smarmy, for lack of a better word.

It felt strange and a little embarrassing to accept that Grant was just a Mini Tripp, which she'd never let herself acknowledge before.

Settling down with Grant once she retired from the tour had always been the plan, so if she'd needed to put some blinders on to stay the course, she'd done it. Unthinkingly at the time, honestly, but the signs were obvious in retrospect—at least where his self-important personality was concerned.

On some level, though, she understood how Reese was feeling.

"I used to think that it was sweet that Grant wanted me to spend time with your dad," she said, "that he wanted to make sure I was ingratiated into his world."

Reese looked briefly at Sydney. "And now?"

"Now, I feel like I was just a prop for them to parade around at dinner with people Tripp wanted to impress," Sydney admitted.

It was something she was only recently coming to terms with.

She'd liked going out to dinner with Grant, but when she was back in Boston for such limited periods, spending time with other people meant they had less time to reconnect and focus on themselves as a couple.

Sometimes, she'd just wanted to cuddle up on the sofa with a glass of wine and a romcom, her partner's head resting on her chest as she played with their hair.

Grant had never let her do that.

And now, given all she knew, she wondered if all of their evenings out had been a way for him to keep things superficial, not giving them much time to dig into serious conversations or make space for them to be vulnerable with one another.

On top of it all, going out with him often had made it feel even more unlikely that he was carrying on an affair, not that she'd really given it much thought. It was just another data point that likely flitted through the back of her mind over the years, that if he had been up to something, he'd have wanted to squirrel her away in the apartment, away from prying eyes or someone who could catch them.

It'd been well orchestrated, so much so that Sydney had never consciously thought about the possibility at the time. It was only in retrospect, when she understood the full extent of Grant's duplicity, that she saw her former life through a clearer lens.

"No one wants to feel like a means to an end," Sydney continued. Their eyes connected before they both looked away.

Maybe it made Sydney's stomach churn uncomfortably because, on some level, that's what she and Reese were doing to one another, the only difference being they both knew the score.

"He's going to be insufferable this weekend," Reese said.

"Which one?" Sydney asked honestly.

Reese laughed. "Both, I'm sure, but Grant seems to have his tail between his legs most of the time when my dad and Stan are around."

Sydney crossed her fingers. "Here's to hoping that streak continues."

"Is this weird for you?" Reese asked, meeting Sydney's gaze for a second before she returned her attention to the road. "We didn't really talk about it after the party."

Sydney chewed on her lip, considering the question. "I'm

definitely thinking about things differently than I used to, especially where Grant and I were concerned."

"Are you finding that path forward?" Reese asked, referencing their conversation from the previous weekend, the one in which Sydney had thought she needed answers, but now was looking for a way to move on.

"One step forward, two steps back," Sydney lamented. "I just keep thinking I should have known, but the more I think about it, there's still nothing that jumps out and screams, 'He was cheating on you.'"

They'd reached Boston, and Reese eased the car onto the highway and accelerated so they could get around the city quickly. "Like what?"

Sydney pretended to be interested in a piece of lint on her navy-colored linen pants.

She tried to hide the vulnerability in her tone, but she knew the crack in her voice spoke volumes. "He'd come to some of my matches, when he could fit them into his schedule, and he'd always sit in the section for coaches and family."

Reese lifted a sculpted eyebrow but kept her eyes on the road. "Well, he was your boyfriend."

"Yeah, but, like... a lot of those matches were televised, especially as I got into the deeper rounds. And gossip sites loved picking apart my comings and goings. Wasn't he worried about Brynn catching him? Did she know?"

It was the million-dollar question, and maybe they'd get the answer this weekend.

"I'm not sure," Reese offered. "I talked to Brynn earlier this week, about my bridesmaid dress. She seems like she genuinely wants to be friends with us."

Sydney almost choked on the to-go coffee she'd plucked out of the car's center console and pointed between them. "Us? As in you and me? You can't be serious."

"She said 'us,'" Reese repeated. "She said she knew the

situation was complicated, whatever that means, but she was excited for us to all spend time together."

"It just doesn't make sense. We weren't the most high-profile couple in the grand scheme of things, but paparazzi were normal, especially at tournaments. And you know Grant. He loves to go out and be the center of attention. And sometimes," Sydney said with a hint of loss in her voice, "he'd plan these really romantic dates for us after matches, whether I won or lost."

Reese gave her a side-eyed glance. "Grant doesn't strike me as the romantic type."

"He'd call me, just to check in. Every day, without fail."

Reese pursed her lips. "I feel like that should be the baseline for a serious relationship, not the goal."

And maybe that was true, but, "It's just difficult to accept. Not the breakup, I mean," Sydney clarified, "but that I was so wrong. You were right. I think he was intentionally misleading me. He had to be."

She'd run it around and around in her mind over the last week until she'd accepted the truth. Grant had always been cocky, if not a little conceited, but they'd gotten together before she'd been famous. When there were no endorsement deals and Sydney had had to take multiple layovers to reach her tournament destinations.

It was for that reason, she'd realized, that he'd snuck past the bullshit meter she'd honed as her celebrity status had grown. He was Grant, a boy she'd grown up with, while she was still on the sidelines. A young adult she'd gone to college with, who'd started showing up to her matches junior year, when he'd been a senior and probably had a million other things he could be doing that would be more fun. Finally, he was a man she'd had plans to build a life with, who'd prioritized staying in Boston to help continue his family's legacy.

He'd always seemed more than happy to accommodate holding off on marriage and children and integrating their lives in any meaningful way because he was doing it for *her*.

What a pile of horseshit.

"I hope you know that gives me no pleasure," Reese finally responded, saying the words like they were physically painful for her.

Sydney brushed off her concern. "Grant has always been indulgent. Fast cars. Nice things. A certain lifestyle. He's used to getting what he wants, and he likes to feel important. I don't know why I thought those traits wouldn't extend to women or that he wouldn't find someone else to make him feel important in my absence."

"Knowing that still doesn't make what he's done okay. Or make it somehow your fault because you trusted him. Again, something like trust is the baseline to me, not the goal. If someone abuses that, it's entirely on them."

"Spoken like a woman with some experience in this area. Left a bad breakup in San Francisco?" Sydney tilted her head toward Reese, who wouldn't quite meet her stare.

"I'm sorry, by the way. Spending so much time with my family has been weird for me, too," Reese said, avoiding Sydney's question entirely. "I feel like I've been dropped into the plot of a soap opera and that I'm always a half step away from breaking down in laughter or tears at the ridiculousness of the whole situation."

"We're not exactly helping the melodrama," Sydney acknowledged, even though her heart still thrummed with awareness, wanting to know what, or who, had helped fuel Reese's desire to leave California.

She knew that Reese didn't have a great relationship with her family. That she'd moved out to California for college and business school and then stayed there when she'd started her company. She knew that she was intelligent, and even though she could likely do anything she set her mind to, she'd decided to come back to Stoneport and build a life here, complete with an out-of-date inn to run.

Beyond that, Sydney didn't know much.

She didn't know the little things like Reese's favorite movie. Or what her comfort snack was when she was PMS-ing.

And she definitely didn't know the big things, like who'd broken her heart. Or why coming back to a place that clearly caused her so much turmoil had seemed like a better alternative than staying where she was.

Sydney reached her arm across the console and rested her fingers lightly on Reese's leg, her stomach fluttering when Reese's thigh tensed under her hand.

"Why don't we focus on having fun this weekend?" she suggested. "No scheming to make Grant's life more difficult as punishment for his shitty behavior. No worrying about anything except having a good time in whatever moment we find ourselves in."

Giving Grant this much of her energy was just giving him more power, and he didn't deserve that.

"Is it that simple?" Reese asked, a slight raggedness in her breath when Sydney pushed her fingertips into her soft skin.

"I don't have a lot to worry about except you, so I think the ball's in your court as to whether you think it's possible."

Reese looked contemplative. "So we're putting a pause on things a week in? Are we really that weak?" she asked, but her voice had gone soft, like maybe it was an idea she'd been considering, too.

"As fun as torturing Grant is," Sydney said with a mischievous smile, "it's already losing its luster. I've never been great at being vindictive."

Reese glanced at her, tugging her lip between her teeth. "Me neither."

And the idea of spending the day with Reese, having fun as a 'couple,' was more enticing than Sydney would admit to anyone, including herself.

"So we're going to be on our best behavior?"

"Kill 'em with kindness," Reese said as she flashed Sydney a broad smile.

"Think we can manage it?" Sydney realized she'd still been tapping her fingers gently against Reese's thigh, so she removed her hand and placed it in her lap.

Reese made a sound, and she wrapped her knuckles more tightly around the steering wheel. "Guess we'll find out."

* * *

The Fitzpatricks' coastal hideaway was more understated than Sydney had expected, she noted as they stepped through the doorway and placed their bags near the entrance. Don't get her wrong; it was still a mansion, but she hadn't expected it to feel so... homey.

"Come in, come in," Margie said excitedly, ushering them into the entryway.

The house was decorated in soft, neutral hues that were common in New England, ones that mimicked the water along the coast, but there were photos of the Fitzpatrick family plastered on almost every available surface. A variety of books, face down to keep the page open, were set on the coffee table farther into the living room, which opened onto the kitchen, and Sydney noted the half-empty coffee cups on the kitchen island.

She liked the home's lived-in quality immediately, and some of her tension eased away at the sight.

She'd played in televised tennis tournaments where thousands of eyes watched her every move. Had done photo shoots for magazines with millions of readers. She'd honed her public speaking skills after hundreds of post-match interviews and even the few TV commercials she'd done. Luckily, perfume and watch commercials didn't want her to speak as much as they wanted her to walk purposefully or hit the ball in what would become slow motion by the time the editors were done with the shots.

But, somehow, none of that stood up to the scrutiny of an intimate family weekend as Reese's girlfriend.

"We're so happy you're here," Margie said, enveloping her in another encompassing hug once they'd set their bags down.

"We are, too," Reese beamed as she casually interlaced her fingers through Sydney's, looking around the open downstairs area. "Where's everyone else?"

"Stan, Tripp, and Grant headed to the club early this morning, after your dad and brother arrived from Boston, to play a quick round of golf. I believe your mother is meeting us directly there, and Brynn is..." Margie looked around before she called out, "Brynn, hon? Reese and Sydney are here."

Within seconds, Sydney could hear the padding of feet on the hardwood stairs, and then Brynn came into view.

"Morning," Brynn said exuberantly as she hit the ground floor, court-ready in a tennis skirt and a polo shirt.

To Reese's credit, she'd been telling the truth on the drive here. Brynn did seem genuinely excited to spend time with them. Weirdly, so, if she was honest, but Sydney had already made the decision to roll with whatever happened in the next twenty-four hours.

She got the sense that maybe Brynn was a little naive, given her doting parents, and it made something protective swell inside of Sydney. Pushing it down, she smiled brightly, hoping that Brynn knew what she was getting into by marrying Grant. "Morning, Brynn."

Never in a million years would she have thought she'd be hoping that the person Grant had cheated on her with was a party to the infidelity, but here she was, wishing it were true just so she didn't have to wonder if sweet, friendly Brynn was also a victim in all of this.

This weekend is supposed to be fun, Sydney reminded herself.

Margie ushered them over to the kitchen island, thankfully providing cover in the form of chitchat to help Sydney extricate herself from her thoughts. "Coffee? Tea? How was the drive? It's such a pretty day already."

Since they'd arrived, Margie hadn't stopped moving, seemingly boundless energy contained in her short frame.

"Will you be playing today?" Sydney asked, noticing that Margie was wearing a pair of tapered white jeans, a dark, billowy button-down, and a pair of sandals.

"Hah! I'm more of a 'have a glass of wine on the patio' kind of gal, if you know what I mean," she said, winking in a way that only middle-aged women seemed to be able to pull off. "I love to get out in nature, but anything that involves coordination is dangerous for me—and everyone in the general vicinity."

Brynn nodded in agreement, maybe more than a little firsthand experience written across her face. "Mom once fractured Dad's hand when she accidentally hit him with a tennis racket."

Sydney's eyebrows lifted in surprise, though it wasn't the strangest tennis injury she'd ever heard of.

"They weren't playing doubles," Brynn added.

"I ran to the net to return a shot. Stan had also moved forward on his side, and well," Margie explained, "I accidentally smashed down on him when I misjudged how far out I needed to put my racket."

Sydney tried to envision the mechanics of how something like that would play out.

Brynn focused on the look on Sydney's face. "I know, it seems improbable, but it's true. My mother," Brynn said, wrapping her arm around Margie, "defies convention."

The affection between Brynn and her mom was palpable as Margie managed a half-hearted embarrassed look and leaned into Brynn's embrace.

Feeling Reese stiffen next to her, Sydney disentangled their hands so that she could slip her arm around Reese's back.

"Stan took it in stride, as usual. I swear I could leave that man tied to a pole, naked in the desert, and he'd thank me for giving him the chance to get a little sun," Margie said, with what was clearly love in her eyes.

Sydney found that she genuinely liked the Fitzpatricks. Their warmth. Their hospitality. It was refreshing, and as she continued to feel Reese's uncomfortable posture beside her, she realized it was clearly a juxtaposition to the Devereux family, no matter how you sliced, diced, or minced it.

"Sounds like he's a keeper," Sydney joked, happy to carry the conversation, though, strangely, it only felt like she could take a solid breath when she felt Reese relax into her.

"When do we need to head to the club?" Reese asked, shifting her focus down to the weekend bags they'd deposited on the ground. "Should we get ready?"

Margie checked her watch. "Sure. I'll show you two to your room so you can get changed."

And at those words, Sydney's stomach fluttered with anticipation.

Fun or not, this weekend was going to be... something.

Ten

REESE COULD GET on board with playing tennis every day if it meant that she could watch Sydney move around the court, long limbs sprinting gracefully as she hit seemingly impossible shots.

It was one thing to watch a professional tennis player on television, when the camera was zoomed out and the whole court was visible, two opponents battling back and forth with commentators explaining the hits and volleys.

This was something else. Like magic, Sydney seemed to anticipate the ball before their opponents, Brynn and Stan— unluckily for them—had even finished the follow-through on their racket.

"I'm starting to regret telling you that I didn't want you to take it easy," Stan said as he missed a shot down the doubles line, the ball skittering off and across the court where Grant, much to his obvious chagrin, and Reese's dad, were playing a half-hearted singles match.

Sydney laughed, animated and light, as she spun her racket in her hand.

Sydney looked so free, her skirt billowing around her as she covered her half of their side of the court nimbly, her leg brace looking more like a decoration than a necessity for her safety.

This was Sydney King in her element, laughing and letting out little puffs of sound when she hit a shot, practically skipping when she returned to her position before the next point.

It was infectious, the lightness that permeated the match, fun and exciting and good-natured, like all Sydney was thinking about was the next shot.

Not their scheme.

Not how Grant had betrayed her trust.

Not how Sydney was playing against her ex-boyfriend's new fiancée.

Reese wished that she could let go to that degree and just experience the thrill of an enjoyable game without all of her baggage seeping into her consciousness.

It didn't help that she couldn't miss how her father kept looking over at their court, like missing an hour of networking with Stan would somehow send his whole life toppling into disrepair.

So, maybe it was a little more obnoxious than intended, when she laughed, too.

"You're pretty good, Reese. Does Sydney give you lessons?" Brynn asked as Reese stepped back to the serving line. Brynn dropped into a low stance diagonally across the court from her, ready to receive the serve on their new game.

Reese shot an amused grin at Sydney, wondering if she'd take credit for Reese's passable serve, which was rusty after years of disuse.

Sydney winked at her, doing a trick where she spun the bottom of her racket on her index finger. "I take zero credit for Reese's impressive athletic abilities. If anything, I feel like she's been holding out on me. Competitive much, babe?" she asked as she lined up at the edge of her service box to await Brynn's return, looking over her shoulder and smirking.

Beyond Sydney, who'd trained professionally, both the

Devereuxs and the Fitzpatricks had grown up in the world of country clubs, where a weekend of tennis was as normal as seeing a movie or going shopping.

In Stoneport, her parents were members at the local country club, and she'd spent summers on the courts, having taken lessons when she was younger to learn the fundamentals.

Honestly, she preferred golf, but that was because she'd spent years working to get better at it, hoping she'd be able to tag along with her dad on the weekends when he'd headed to the course.

By the time she was a teenager, she'd given up asking, knowing that he would come up with some variation of the same excuse.

That she'd get bored.

That the course was no place for his young daughter.

Maybe that was why it hurt all the more when, at the same age she'd wanted to start joining him, Grant had started going with him instead.

"A boy needs to learn about the finer things in life. Deals are closed on the course, not in the boardroom," he'd said. Reese remembered the way he'd ruffled Grant's hair, her brother looking so disinterested that she wondered if he'd even heard Tripp.

And then, Reese had thought to herself, at the age of twelve, that The Devereux Group didn't have a board. They had an executive team of men who looked and acted and thought just like her father, the same men with whom he spent weekends on the golf course.

But at the head of the pyramid was Grant Devereux III, and at the end of the day, he was the gatekeeper.

At some point, he'd deemed Reese unworthy of seeing behind the curtain.

It didn't stop her from spending her adolescence trying to prove it to him. To be smarter, more successful than her brother.

Along with playing tennis at the club, she'd taken private golf lessons, like a minor league baseball player, just waiting for her chance to be called up to the majors.

When it happened, she wanted to be ready.

And when she'd finally accepted that it wouldn't happen, she knew, deep down, that there was a small part of her that still held out hope. It was where the resentment festered, tucked away from the light but finding a way to bloom in the darkness, fed with a lifetime of unresolved wounds that she hadn't found a way to heal.

Reese looked over at her father, who only acknowledged the conversation happening on her court if it was Stan's voice echoing across the net.

She held the tennis ball in her fingertips, launching it precisely above her, right arm coming down to connect her racket and hit it across the court to where Brynn waited to return it.

The serve was hard but inaccurate, hitting the court outside of the service box.

She appreciated that Brynn didn't yell 'fault,' the two feet beyond the white line where the ball touched down making it obvious the serve was no good.

"Quick timeout," Sydney said, throwing her hands up into the 'T' symbol and already jogging back toward Reese. Quickly, she was at her side, and she wiped a stray tendril from her ponytail. "Mind if I give you a piece of advice?"

Reese nodded, trying to quell the frustration that was bubbling up. "Yeah, go for it."

"Strength is good. Anger, not so much," Sydney said, sympathy written across her features. "You look like you want to murder the ball right now."

"I'm pretending it's my father," Reese responded seriously as she pulled a new ball from the pocket in her skirt.

Sydney turned away from the Fitzpatricks so that she was standing between their view of the conversation and Reese. "Did he flip you the bird or something when you were serving?" she asked, joking but tentatively concerned.

Reese wasn't in the mood for it, but she also wasn't going to take her frustration out on Sydney, who she knew was just trying to help calm her down.

"Weird time to have this conversation," Reese said as she nodded past Sydney, acknowledging they were in the middle of a match, "but I'm realizing I'm not as over all of my family stuff as I may have believed."

Soft, searching eyes met hers. "In my experience, things like that come in waves. I've thought at least a dozen times during this match about my retirement and how my best tennis days are behind me."

Reese's eyebrows drifted upward in surprise. "I'd never have known that. You look so... free."

Sydney shrugged, but she reached out and put her hand on Reese's forearm, her fingertips warm from their game. "Tennis is ninety percent a mental game. I'm free when I focus on what's right in front of me. On how the ball feels in my hand. How the court smells. How the sun feels against my skin. How enjoyable it is to watch you hit an impressive shot. I make myself believe that nothing else exists except what's happening at this moment."

"So you're avoiding reality?" Reese said sarcastically.

But Sydney only smiled. "Maybe. But I can either have a shitty game and then be in a bad mood after it, along with also having the same problems I already had before, or I can enjoy myself and then decide when I want to handle the other things that were throwing my concentration."

Reese looked at her dubiously, but instead of focusing on her anger, she focused on enjoying the softness of Sydney's hand, how its warmth permeated into her own skin and calmed her racing nerves.

"When it comes down to it, humans are both incredibly complex and incredibly simple. We have these big brains, but at the end of the day, we mostly use them to fight or fuck or feel."

She could categorically say that she hadn't expected Sydney to say that, so she let out a surprised laugh, her eyes going wide.

"So, what do you say?" Sydney coaxed, her earnest stare mapping across Reese's features like she was trying to anticipate Reese's response.

And Reese herself didn't know what it would be until she leaned her shoulder into Sydney's, bumping gently against her as she rolled her eyes good-naturedly. "You make a compelling case, King."

"Damn straight," Sydney said, her eyes alight as she beamed a bright smile in Reese's direction. Leaning down, she whispered to Reese, and her lips sent chills running up her spine when they grazed the edge of her ear. "Now, let's go show them who's in charge, babe."

* * *

They'd won the match, unsurprisingly.

Reese had held her own, but Sydney, even playing at half-speed, was a force to be reckoned with.

And she'd given Reese a pep talk that was both comforting and electrifying, which had been sorely needed.

They wrapped up by shaking hands at the net before Stan clapped everyone on the back and pulled them in for what Reese could only describe as a 'group hug.'

"What a match," he said, seemingly thrilled to have lost. "I'd love to do that again sometime soon."

"Sounds like a plan," Sydney said excitedly, moving toward the side of the court, where she placed her racket back in her bag.

Tripp was already on their court, heading for Stan like there was an invisible string pulling him over. Reese could practically see his tail wagging.

Grant sat glumly on one of the benches at the edge of the playing area, under an awning, but he sprang to attention when Tripp gave him a sharp nod to join them.

And Sydney? Well, Sydney was trying to torture Reese, standing at the edge of the court stretching, her long, lithe limbs accentuated as she extended and contorted her body into various extremely visual positions.

"I'm going to head to the locker room. Either of you want to join?" Brynn said as she finished packing her bag.

That got Sydney's attention, and she sprang back to a standing position. "I'd love to grab a quick shower and change." She looked toward Reese. "You coming, babe?"

Heading to the locker room with Sydney was a level of masochism she wasn't prepared for. Instead of meeting Sydney's welcoming smile, she glanced down at her watch. "I think I'm going to head to our lunch reservation."

"Margie and Sharon are at one of the outdoor tables, off to the side of the club restaurant," Stan supplied, cutting off whatever Tripp had been in the middle of saying.

When she reached the edge of the court, Reese handed Sydney one of the rackets she'd let her borrow. "Thank you."

"You did great," Sydney said as she leaned forward to take the racket, giving Reese a soft kiss on the cheek.

Reese's body responded immediately to the light contact, her skin buzzy where Sydney's lips had touched it.

It was the second time in as many hours that Sydney had somehow managed to have her lips on some part of Reese's face—or head, depending on how you defined the ears as a part of the body—but regardless, Reese wondered what it meant.

But she was trying to take a page out of Sydney's book, even off the court.

They'd promised to have fun this weekend, and waiting with anticipation for the next time Sydney would touch some part of her *was* fun. And exhilarating. And exciting. And tingle-inducing.

It was with that in mind that she grabbed Sydney's hand and pulled her close, their bodies touching from hip to chest. "Thank you," she said, nuzzling her face into Sydney's neck, which was slightly salty Reese discovered as she inhaled lightly.

She felt as much as she heard Sydney's sharp intake of breath; it only lasted for a second before Sydney melted into the touch.

The scoff she heard a few feet away, undeniably from her brother, only made her lean into the moment more. She ran her hand down Sydney's arm until she found her hand, their fingers intertwining as she finally took a small step back.

A moment passed between them as Sydney looked at her openly, like she was, just as much as Reese, wondering what this meant.

"Excuse me?" A younger teenager had moved toward them, unbeknownst to Reese, and was now fidgeting a few feet away. "Are you Sydney King?"

Sydney looked at Reese quickly, biting her lip. "We'll continue this later? Or, at the very least, talk about it?"

Reese nodded, worried her voice would betray her.

"I am," Sydney said, turning her attention to the girl and returning her smile.

The girl's hands were so fidgety that Reese wondered if she'd drop the phone she was holding. "I'm sorry to bother you. I waited until you were done playing, but I didn't want to miss having the chance to talk to you. You're my favorite player."

"I love that," Sydney said genuinely, taking a step toward the girl. "What's your name?"

"Maddie," the girl said breathlessly, like she'd been waiting her whole life for this moment.

"Well, Maddie, I was about to hit the locker room, but did you want to grab a picture before I go?" Sydney asked, glancing down at the phone.

"I'll take it," Brynn said almost as excitedly as Maddie. She reached forward to grab the device out of Maddie's still-shaky hands.

Reese could commiserate. Sydney was currently inspiring a consuming, jittery feeling in her as well.

"Go rest up," Sydney said in Reese's direction, tilting her head toward the clubhouse beyond the courts. "I'll be there soon."

It was while Reese was walking along the edge of the courts and through the gate that exited the tennis area that she realized how she was feeling.

She *missed* Sydney, and it became punctuated as she moved farther away.

She hadn't wanted to leave the comfort of Sydney's sphere, of how she made Reese feel: like anything was possible, like everything would be okay.

When she reached the table to find her mother sitting alone, she was still mulling over the distracting idea.

She plopped down unceremoniously into the seat next to her mom. "Hey."

Sharon was sipping on a glass of iced tea, sunglasses taking up almost half her face. "Hi, honey. How was your match?"

"We won, but some of the pride is taken out knowing that I brought a ringer," Reese said wryly as she clocked her mom's sunglasses. "What's with the new look? Going incognito today?"

Be in the moment, she promised herself, even if that meant pulling her thoughts—not an easy task—from Sydney and the last, lingering glance she'd given Reese as she'd walked away.

"Allergies," her mom said, waving her off as she set her glass down on the round table.

Reese looked around to the patio that was half full with lunch patrons. "Where'd Margie go?"

"She's hosting a fundraiser at the club next month, and the manager asked for her sign-off on the menu."

It was then that Reese stopped the conversation and took a closer look at her mom. "That sounds like your dream day coming true. Why didn't you join her?"

Her mom shrugged, her hands still grasping her glass of iced tea. "I'm a little distracted today. Didn't think I'd be much help."

"What's got you distracted?" Reese asked, continuing to focus on what was right in front of her, on how her mom's posture was a little off, and how, even under the sunglasses, she could see how her eyes darted around.

"It's nothing, honey. We can talk about it some other time."

Only, the way her mom said it, voice shaking with a light

tremble, made the hair on Reese's neck stand up, made her stomach do a swift somersault.

Reese scooted her chair sideways so that she could touch her mom's knee, and the anxious, whirring feeling inside of her picked up momentum. "Mom? Is everything okay? What's going on?"

It was probably nothing; she just needed her mom to confirm that, in fact, it *was* nothing.

So, why wasn't her mom doing that?

The silence stretched out between them, causing Reese to hold her breath.

"I'm fine, honey," Sharon finally said, breaking the tension but doing nothing to allay Reese's fears. "I'm just waiting for some test results, and I guess I'm a little nervous."

Reese sat up ramrod straight. "What test results?"

Why hadn't she known? Granted, she and her mom didn't talk often, but this wasn't a casual check-in call or an invitation to one of her fundraisers. This was *serious*.

And, for whatever reason, her mom hadn't told her.

"I had to have a procedure about a month ago. It went well, but they needed to run tests yesterday afternoon to confirm that they got everything. I should have the results back early next week to give me the all-clear." Sharon smiled weakly, poorly selling the confidence she was trying to project.

It was like time had stopped, and Reese really did have no option except to be excruciatingly present in the moment, trying to make sense of her mom's words.

She rolled the words around in her mouth. They tasted bitter before she forced herself to say them out loud. "Mom, are you telling me you have cancer?"

"No, no," Sharon said, placing her hand on Reese's. "I *had* cancer. They caught it very early. Stage 1. They're confident they got it all, but they want to make sure. I'm just, well, you never know..." Her mom trailed off, her fingers absently stroking Reese's knuckles.

"I'm sorry I didn't know," Reese said before thoughts came tumbling into her mind that she couldn't help voicing. "Did Dad go with you yesterday? Is this why you called me Thursday? Mom, why didn't you tell me?"

Shame flooded through her like a dam had broken, more potent than the fear she'd felt moments ago.

"I didn't want you to worry, honey. Until a week ago, I didn't even know you'd be in town so soon. I was planning to let you know when the post-op check-up results came back."

"But you had a surgery," Reese argued.

"A minor procedure," her mom corrected her, missing the point by a mile.

Reese had always felt like an outsider in her own family, but this really took the cake.

She shook her head, pushing the thoughts away. Whatever feelings she had about the situation, she needed to be here for her mom, who was obviously scared about whatever was happening.

"You're worried, though."

The words hung between them, and she watched her mom's shoulders deflate. "I probably shouldn't be, but I've just had weeks to worry at this point. I think I got a little carried away. But I promise," she said, squeezing Reese's hand, "that no matter what, it's going to be fine. Even if I'd have to do radiation or something, they really did catch it *so* early."

"Who took you to your appointment yesterday?" Reese asked, the guilt continuing to gnaw at her.

Suddenly, she wanted to know every piece of information related to her mom's health, from how she'd discovered something was wrong to this current moment, where a literal piece of her mother was off in some petri dish, probably, awaiting a litany of tests that would hopefully come back with clear and conclusive results.

For whatever issues she and her mom had, Sharon Devereux had been there for every scraped knee, every school project, and every milestone in Reese's life. In adulthood, it had been Reese's choice to keep her mom at arm's length. She'd taken her mom's unwillingness to stand up to her dad on her behalf as her tacit approval of his behavior, and when she'd realized that, stepping away from her family as a whole had become much easier.

But she'd known, on some level, that her parents' relationship wasn't as simple as that.

It was just easier to *believe* it was that simple.

"I drove myself. I'm not an invalid, you know." Her mom smiled then, chiding Reese like she'd done when Reese was a little girl.

"That's not the point! Why didn't Grant or Dad take you? Do they know what's going on? You were obviously worried. You needed support."

"Yes, your dad and brother are aware of what's going on," her mom admitted before adding, "It was a routine check-up, even if I was nervous about it. I drove myself, and everything was fine."

Reese looked at her skeptically, frustration blooming hotly in her chest. Guilt warred with anger so that neither had a place to dissipate.

"I want to know when you get the results. Please."

"Yes, honey. I promise I'll keep you updated. Are you going to be around for a while?"

Reese nodded emphatically. "Yes, I'm moving back to Stoneport. I've *moved* back to Stoneport already, actually."

In her mom's defense, it seemed like there was a lot they didn't tell one another, and Reese was just as culpable.

"Reese, that makes me so happy." Her mom's voice choked up with sincerity, and a rogue tear streamed out from under her sunglasses.

Outward emotion wasn't especially common in their family, but Reese attributed it to the health scare her mother was reaching the tail end of, hopefully with a positive (or negative, as the case may be) conclusion.

But the way her mom said it, the way she let out a deep exhale when Reese told her, made her feel like she'd made the right decision to come home.

"Apologies that we're a few minutes late," Stan said as he, Tripp, and Grant approached the table, paying no attention to the fact that they were the first ones there besides Reese and Sharon.

The Devereux men did not have the same apologetic nature. Tripp took the seat right next to Stan when he sat down, and Grant sat on the other side of Tripp.

As Reese looked across the table at Grant and Tripp, she felt like she was at a middle school dance, where the boys and girls flocked to separate sides of the school gymnasium. Did her dad and brother think she had cooties or something?

The hot, overwhelming feeling that had been simmering below the surface reared up again.

Her dad hadn't even talked to her mom yet, hadn't even *seen* her since her appointment yesterday. He'd spent the night in Boston, Margie had mentioned, choosing to stay in the city instead of comforting his wife.

Disgust, she finally identified, was the feeling welling up inside of her by the time Margie, Brynn, and Sydney approached the table.

Sydney clocked the look on her face immediately, mouthing a 'you okay?' as she sat down in the open seat between Reese and Stan.

Reese nodded but clenched her fists under the table.

She felt Sydney's hand enveloping her own, and it allayed the roiling in her stomach until her father spoke.

"I'm starving," Tripp said as he leaned back in his chair, perusing the menu. "What do you recommend here, Stan?"

Stan was contemplative, really giving the question a degree of thought that Reese didn't think it warranted. "The turkey club is great, but you can never go wrong with a lobster roll."

But oh, what it must be like to be Tripp Devereux, with not a care in the world except his next meal. Either he was the master of compartmentalization, or Reese had been giving him too much credit throughout her life—which was really saying something, since she'd never had a strong positive opinion of him outside anything related to business.

"Oh," Brynn said, her attention turned toward Reese. "The store didn't have the dresses available for pickup yesterday, but they overnighted them. If you're up for it, we can head over after lunch and try them on."

The idea of even a small respite from her father was like music to Reese's ears. "That sounds great," she said, meaning it.

"Mom and Sharon, you're both welcome to join if you'd like," Brynn added effusively, her big eyes looking pointedly back and forth between them to really sell the invitation.

Sharon spoke first. "Oh, I'm not sure..."

"You should come along, Mom." Reese leveled a soft smile in her direction. "It'll be nice to have you there."

Reese wanted to keep her mom close right now, to let her know that she wasn't alone. It was a feeling that Reese understood all too well, like the world was on her shoulders and asking for help would only be a bother to other people.

"What about me?" Stan asked, surprisingly glum.

Brynn rolled her eyes good-naturedly. "Dad, you already came to *my* dress fitting. Maybe we give Reese a little space today, yeah?"

Stan tilted his chin up, a surprisingly childish look that he wore well, and again, it made Reese soften slightly. He relented. "Well, I suppose that I can be convinced to go home and start prepping dinner while you all are out having fun. Those steaks aren't going to marinade themselves."

"Exactly, honey," Margie said to mollify him, smiling broadly. Reese expected this wasn't the first time they'd had a variation of this charming domestic conversation.

What would that be like? Having a father that wanted to do even stereotypically feminine things with you just to spend time together? To not want to miss a moment of the person you were becoming?

Reese had spent her life fitting into the mold of her father's world, and it still hadn't granted her entry.

Sydney's thigh was resting against her own, like she was willing Reese to calm down.

It was a whole special level of frustration that she couldn't even enjoy a beautiful woman wanting to casually touch her as they enjoyed lunch together!

And, really, she was trying.

Trying to calm her racing mind. Trying to not think the worst of her father's behavior, trying to tell herself that maybe she didn't have the whole story.

Trying, trying, trying...

...and failing, evidenced by the fact that by the time their meals arrived, her eyes had narrowed into slits. It was almost physically impossible for them not to, given the way her father was bloviating at length on The Devereux Group and his plans for their future expansion into the mid-Atlantic region.

"It's an ambitious plan, Tripp, but you know I don't generally discuss business during family time," Stan said before taking a bite of his lobster roll.

Tripp nodded and cut into his salmon. "Right, right. But since we're becoming family, the two are blending together, no? When would we ever talk shop?" he asked, letting out a forceful laugh.

Margie placed her napkin back on her lap, having used it to wipe off an especially creamy-looking spot of sauce from her seafood pasta. "Stan has dedicated working hours when we're at home together. Unless one of his investment properties is actively burning down, we've learned over the years that it can wait."

"Absolutely, my dear," Stan agreed. "There will always be another deal. Another cocktail hour. Another young upstart looking to earn their piece of the pie."

Reese wasn't sure, but she felt like Stan's gaze lingered on her brother for an extra half second longer than was normal as he'd said the words. Probably wishful thinking on her part.

Was it so wrong to want everyone to dislike the same people you disliked?

She didn't think so.

"That's why it's so great to work with family." Tripp wrapped his arm around Grant's shoulders and squeezed firmly.

Gross.

"Managing director is an ambitious undertaking for someone so young," Stan said, his fork pointed in Grant's general direction, like he was daring her brother to disagree.

Tripp was quick with a response, cutting any retort Grant could possibly have off at the knees. "Promoted last year, but the business is in his blood. I have no doubt he'll make a fine president of The Devereux Group one day."

"The lady doth protest too much, methinks," Sydney whispered, leaning in close before she gave Reese's thigh an affectionate squeeze.

"Understatement of the year," Reese whispered back before Sydney returned to sitting fully in her own chair, taking another bite of her poke bowl as she tried to hide her smile.

"Around the time Brynn and Grant were engaged, if I remember correctly." Stan polished off his lobster role in an impressive last bite.

Reese knew that tone, and she knew that Stan knew that he was remembering correctly. It was impossible to rise to his level of success without a decent bullshit detector. Reese was starting to get the sense that maybe Stan still had some questions about the pending nuptials and his upcoming union with the Devereux family.

There was a decent chance that Tripp was playing checkers while Stan was playing chess.

God, she hoped so.

"We finalized it in the middle of last year, but the plans were well underway already," Tripp deflected. "With our mid-Atlantic expansion goal, it made sense to have someone of Grant's caliber leading our existing operations, keeping the ship on course while I focus on the future of the business."

"I thought you'd mentioned working on the expansion, Grant?" Brynn asked from her seat next to him.

Instead of answering immediately, Grant cut forcefully into his yellowfin tuna steak, practically mashing it into pieces. "I'm helping out wherever I can be of assistance."

Reese had never loved an awkward silence so much.

Stan, still intent on being a good host, stepped in. "And Reese, when we met last, your father had mentioned you wanted to chart your own path. Never considered going into the family business?"

She could feel her father's eyes boring into her.

Telling Stan that she could have had a role at The Devereux Group if she wanted to be her brother's assistant would likely cause Tripp to flip a table, which is why she *did* consider saying it, however briefly.

"I saw a need that wasn't being met in the boutique hotel and inn space, and I felt like I could do something positive. So I did," she finished with a minimizing shrug.

"Reese is being modest," Sydney chimed in next to her, taking her hand on top of the table. "She grew her company into the most successful hotel management software for small businesses in the market. It's no wonder Checked was made an offer they couldn't refuse."

Reese's eyebrow lifted as she turned toward Sydney in surprise. She wasn't aware that her fake girlfriend had done additional research into her company.

But the true story, the one that would never appear online, painted the acquisition in a much dimmer light.

Reese worked to not let it cloud her mood—at least, anymore than it already was.

Stan nodded emphatically. "You obviously love the hotel

space, given the company you started, but you're a free agent now? No plans to join the family business?"

Out of the corner of her eye, she could see her father stiffen.

"No, not at the moment," she said diplomatically, mostly to keep the peace during what was becoming a decently enjoyable lunch. After all, her fingers were still entangled with Sydney's.

Stan slapped his hand down on the table. "I can't believe it. Tripp, you're going to let her get away? You're a veritable gold mine of information and talent, Reese. The whole package. Business knowledge. Technical prowess. Persistence," he said, looking at her with true appreciation for what she'd accomplished.

The praise felt good, and she allowed that feeling to percolate for a few seconds, at least until her father joined back in. "Well, we were trying to keep things close to the vest, but there have been conversations. Now that Reese is open to new roles, it may make sense for her to join us at The Devereux Group."

Tripp nodded solemnly in her direction, like he was giving her the opportunity of a lifetime. Like perhaps now she was ready to ascend to a meaningful role that he'd finally deemed appropriate for her.

Reese blanched.

Sydney choked on her water.

Grant's jaw went slack.

She didn't have the energy to look at anyone else; loathing caused bile to rise in the back of her throat.

In this moment, more than her father's rejection had ever hurt, his ability to so easily use her as a pawn was somehow worse.

And it was that feeling that propelled her forward as she said, "Actually, in the spirit of *charting my own path*," she said, parroting his tone, "I purchased The Stone's Throw Inn in Stoneport recently. It's my first acquisition, and I'm spending some time getting my bearings before considering any additional growth."

Her father's face twisted into an ugly snarl, which Reese

caught clearly before he could wipe the traces of it away. It was poorly executed, though, as what he'd managed to morph his features into made him look like he was having stomach issues.

Good.

"And we're so thrilled for her," Sydney said to likely cut off any surprised outbursts from the rest of the Devereux family. "She's really an incredible woman."

"That she is," Stan said, raising his glass up to hers in cheers.

Reese met Sydney's stare, a radiant smile smoothing all the rough edges of her thoughts. She pretended that her girlfriend was her biggest advocate, working in tandem with her instead of in opposition, and that Stan's praise canceled out her own dismissal of her father—not that she should need anyone's 'atta boy' to feel good about what she'd accomplished.

"I'm so proud of you, honey," her mom said in spite of the glower her father leveled at his wife's response.

For a second, the scraping silverware was the only sound at their table as the moment wound down from its crescendo.

Her purchase of The Stone's Throw was bound to come out sooner or later, and if it had an adverse impact on her father's well-being, then who was she to deny herself the pleasure?

"Reese?" Sydney asked, pulling her attention. "Since we're done with lunch, did you want to grab a shower before we head to the dress fitting?"

There Sydney was again saving her again, this time from what could become a prolonged, unbearable silence.

She stood up from the table but made sure to bend down and give Sydney a kiss on the cheek. "Great idea. Don't know what I'd do without you, babe," she said, wondering how much truth was baked into those words.

"Thank you for inviting us to lunch," she said, looking at Margie and then Stan.

Sydney grabbed her hand. "We should be wrapping up here by the time you're ready. I'll text you and we can meet at the car?"

Reese nodded. "Perfect."

And with that, Reese left the table and, in the process, left varying degrees of confusion, shock, excitement, and anger written across the faces of everyone present.

The cat was out of the bag, but she had a feeling the impact of her revelation was only just beginning.

Eleven

SYDNEY SAT in a comfortable waiting area, about the size of a living room, at Marcella's Bridal Boutique. The room, unsurprisingly, was bathed in whites and soft pinks, juxtaposed with touches of gold accenting the mirrors, furniture, and decorative throw pillows that dotted the love seat where Margie and Sharon sat together.

Across from the sofa, she and Brynn sat in chairs that were undeniably comfortable, and Sydney eased back against the plush cushion, flexing her legs.

Reese had been whisked away upon arrival into the fitting area, separated from the private viewing room by a large curtain. Marcella herself, at no more than five feet tall and with shock-white hair, had commanded the situation with ease, picking Reese out as the Cinderella for her dresses before they'd all finished entering the building.

"Wait here," was all she had said to them before disappearing behind the curtains with Reese a few minutes ago.

This group was more intimate, and somehow, more intimidating to Sydney than the group at lunch. Given that her ex-boyfriend's mother, his new fiancée, and *her* mother made up the party of the people she could have a conversation with, this was little surprise.

Even so, she decided to bite the bullet. "So, Brynn, you didn't want to get a dress in Boston? You live there, right?"

That should be safe enough, in terms of conversation topics.

"I've gotten all of my dresses from Marcella over the years. I think of Bingham as much more of a home than Boston will ever be." Brynn looked around fondly at the decorative drapery on the walls, her fingers fiddling with a pendant on her neck. "Grant and I are still discussing where we want to call home once we're married."

Margie smiled lovingly at her daughter. "We have a house in Boston where we all lived when Brynn was growing up, but summers in Bingham were always sacred, along with any weekends we could make work. When Brynn graduated high school, Stan and I began spending more time at our house on the coast, and it really stuck for both of us."

Brynn nodded in agreement. "And what about your parents, Sydney? Are they in Stoneport? You grew up there, right?"

She needed to find time to call her mom tonight, she reminded herself, along with responding to Hallie's dozen unanswered messages regarding the 'vibes' of the weekend.

"I lived in Boston for a few years after college." *With Grant, in the apartment I discovered you two in*, she added silently. "But when I moved to Florida after I joined the pro tour, my parents moved down there to be closer to me."

Sydney watched Brynn closely then, to see if any sense of awareness flicked across her features. But there was none to be found; Brynn was seemingly oblivious to how intertwined her and Grant's lives used to be.

"I love that," Margie chimed in. "We're fortunate enough that Brynn hasn't had wings that seem to want to carry her too far from home."

Brynn looked both bashful and embarrassed, making her face

appear much younger than her twenty-seven years. "I like New England," she said with a shrug.

"There's really no substitute," Sydney agreed. "I've lived in Florida long-term and traveled the world for tournaments, but it's still the place I love the most."

Sharon cleared her throat, quiet until now. She'd been quiet all day, really, but Sydney hadn't had the courage to strike up a casual conversation with her. Maybe ex-boyfriend's new fiancée and future mother-in-law, at the end of the day, had felt safer than ex-boyfriend and fake girlfriend's mother.

Wow, she needed to draw herself a chart.

"Reese mentioned earlier today, which makes a lot more sense given that she's purchased The Stone's Throw Inn, that she's officially relocated back to Stoneport," Sharon said.

Sydney had wondered when the questions would come from Sharon, and now the hairs on her neck started to prickle. Her own mother would have already asked Reese for a five-year plan on their relationship, especially after everything that had happened with Grant.

"Are you moving back then? Or will you two make long distance work in some capacity? If you're going back to Florida, that is?" There was a hopefulness in Sharon's voice that Sydney didn't want to dim with an honest answer.

She wasn't going to admit that she had no idea what the future held for her. Not professionally. Not personally. She barely knew what each day would hold.

But that wasn't a bad thing, she'd accepted over the last few weeks.

For the last fifteen years, her life had been so regimented that her day was planned down to the minute. With training, meal prepping—and, well, more training—she could function on autopilot instead of focusing on making decisions about her life.

Her life since coming back to Stoneport had become a veritable 'choose your own adventure' novel, with exhilaration and excitement—and *possibilities* that she'd only found before in the confines of big matches.

Was this what it meant to make your own fun?

Still... she was conscious not to put Reese in the hot seat, accidentally planning their fake life out together if she'd told Sharon something different. "My retirement was announced about three weeks ago, so I'm happy to be wherever it makes sense to spend time with Reese for the foreseeable future. I do have to head back to Florida in about a week to tie up some loose ends with sponsorships and the business side of things, but as much as possible, I want to be back home in Stoneport for the summer."

Sharon's shoulders relaxed, and Sydney felt a genuine smile widen across her own face. She liked the answer she'd given. Even though she'd lived in Florida for the past four years, she'd always seen it as *traveling* there and coming *home* to Stoneport.

Margie nodded sagely, moving her hands like an ocean wave as she said, "Compromise is the key to any good relationship. Sometimes you're the one ebbing, and sometimes you're the one flowing."

Sydney made a mental note to start keeping track of Margie's ocean metaphors.

"And Reese is getting everything settled at the inn, so I'm sure some time to focus her attention without me bothering her won't be a bad thing," Sydney joked.

"You two seem to have a really good thing going," Brynn said with an almost wistful sigh. "I'm really happy for you both."

Sydney was getting glimmers from Brynn's behavior and language that maybe all that glittered wasn't gold between the happy couple. She'd barely seen Brynn and Grant speak to one another, let alone engage in any private conversations or moments that helped Sydney understand how throwing it all away with Brynn had been worth it to her ex.

And trust, she had been watching.

There were no light touches. No soft looks. There was no

awareness of the other person, like no matter where the other was in the room, they were attuned.

When she and Reese weren't actively engaged in conversation, Sydney could feel her presence, keyed into Reese's moods almost as if they were becoming her own. She attributed it to the charade of keeping their lies together; yes, that was the reason she was always so mentally present wherever Reese was concerned.

The most present relationship she'd seen Grant engaging in was being called to Tripp, who was always hot on the heels of Stan.

"Grant seems to be traveling so much for work—" Brynn's words were cut off as Reese stepped out of the fitting room area.

"I did the pinning already," Marcella said, ushering Reese farther into the center of the room.

Reese's hair was pulled up into a messy updo, framing her high cheekbones and lush lips. Having her shoulders exposed highlighted the features of the bridesmaid dress, the silky, sage-green fabric draped expertly across her body like she'd been poured into it.

Sydney sat up quickly, shifting uncomfortably at the butterflies that had erupted in her stomach. "You look beautiful," she said before she could even process that she was going to speak.

It felt almost inappropriate, how her eyes couldn't seem to pull themselves away from the soft curve of Reese's hip, from the swell of her chest and how her cleavage just kissed together in the middle. Sydney knew how soft it would be to rest her head there, to nuzzle against the warmth and softness of Reese, who always seemed to smell so good.

They hadn't talked much on the drive to the dress shop, so Sydney hadn't mentioned that even with the club shampoo and conditioner, Reese had still smelled divine, like it was more than just what she wore, but rather a scent she produced that, to Sydney, was akin to ambrosia.

When Sydney finally met her stare, a flush dotted Reese's

cheeks and chest. Had she noticed the way Sydney had been mapping her body, appreciating every swell and curve?

"Sydney's right. You look beautiful," Sharon chimed in, standing up to get a better view.

Sydney very much considered doing the same, but she wondered if her legs would betray her.

Brynn moved over toward Reese, looking the dress up and down. "Do you like it?"

"Of course she likes it," Marcella said obstinately, fretting around Reese's legs and checking the angles on the dress. "She looks gorgeous."

There was no world in which Sydney—or any person with eyes—could disagree. The soft green of the dress complimented Reese's fair skin tone, and her dark hair with its errant auburn and russet strands positively popped.

And for as good as this feeling was, like Sydney was a puppy dog who just wanted to throw herself into Reese and beg for attention and affection, it made her nervous, too.

Amping up their fake romance was throwing Sydney off, she decided. Coupled with her lack of physical contact with anyone in, oh, close to a year, and she was wound tighter than she would be during a finals match.

Relax, she coaxed herself, releasing a deep, calming breath.

She stood up then, straightening her legs on the exhale and moving around to where the rest of the group was still admiring Reese's dress.

After Grant, she'd gone through what many would call a "post-breakup phase." There had been a men's player she knew peripherally on the tour, who'd looked like he'd won the lottery when they'd run into one another in Italy, late at night on the courts, and Sydney had made her intentions clear. There had been a woman she'd met in a bar in Prague after losing her third round match, who seemed to have zero interest in tennis but had talked nonstop about her love of old movies.

But they had been an escape, a chance to get out of her own head and use her body more than her brain.

She'd stopped going down that path because it hadn't made her feel better after, the fact that she was using a warm body to quell the falling, floundering feeling that persisted whenever she'd stepped off the court.

So she'd stepped off the court less and less, throwing all of her focus and energy into training.

It had worked. Until it hadn't.

And now here she was, with no tennis career and no love life, staring longingly at a woman she was playing pretend with, in a situation that made *Romeo and Juliet* feel like a very straightforward love story.

"You really like it?" Reese asked, and Sydney already knew before looking up that the question was directed at her.

She could feel her own flush now. She could do nothing but answer honestly when their eyes met, Reese looking at her with genuine curiosity.

"You look incredible," she said, appreciation bordering on reverence on full display in her tone.

She cleared her throat, her blush deepening. It was almost difficult to look at Reese, who was staring at her in this adorably innocent way, like she truly held Sydney's opinion in the highest regard.

Unable to lean into the moment or run fleeing from it, she turned her attention to Brynn instead. "Thank you for not being one of those women who insists on putting their bridesmaids in hideous dresses so they don't take away from their *special day.*"

Brynn, to her credit, looked horrified. "People do that?"

What a sweet, simple woman. Sydney truly couldn't understand how she'd wound up with someone like Grant, given it was becoming clear that her guileless demeanor wasn't an act.

And though Sydney may not have moved through adulthood with a traditional set of female friends, she'd seen firsthand what women could be like, especially on the tour.

Psychological warfare was real.

Once her sponsorship attention had exceeded her skill level—a fact that she was honest enough with herself to admit—she'd basically been iced out of any chance at real friendships. Regardless of what her magazine interviews led people to believe, she wasn't exactly popular with the other competitors.

It had made her all the more willing to fall back into the comfort of Grant, to focus on doing what she could on the courts, knowing that her future after her career ended was already secured.

But it had been lonely, and she'd missed having a friend like Hallie in close proximity every single day.

She reminded herself, yet again, to return her friend's text messages, the count of which, the last time she'd checked her phone, was now up to about two dozen.

"Good, yes?" Marcella said, cutting through the din of Sydney's thoughts and the light chatter that was happening around her.

Everyone nodded in unison.

"Margie, do you want to meet me out front?" Marcella asked, presumably to settle up the bill.

"I'll come, too," Brynn said, picking up her small clutch from the coffee table set between the loveseat and chairs.

Margie put her arm on Sharon's shoulder to get her attention. "Sharon, they have some lovely dresses on display out front. Do you want to peruse them before we head out?"

"Sure," Sharon agreed before turning to her daughter. "You really do look incredible, Reese."

"Thanks, Mom." Finally, Reese looked back up at Sydney as the last footsteps disappeared out of earshot and the dressing area's door closed behind them. "Mind helping me out of this?" she asked, already moving back toward the fitting room.

Sydney needed to shake herself out of her stupor. Like, immediately.

All she could hear was the rustle of the curtain that separated the fitting room from the small area in front of it, which Reese left open as she stepped inside to where her clothing was carefully folded on a small chair.

Oh, and the sound of her own heart, beating a wildly unhealthy staccato.

Reese pulled the few locks of hair that had escaped off the nape of her neck, exposing the dress's gold zipper. "Unzip me?" she asked, her voice a little more breathy than Sydney had expected.

It sent a shiver down her spine as she glided her hands up and gently encircled the small, gold piece of metal. The zipper moved like butter, and though she tried to go slowly, so as to not plunge Reese unexpectedly into nudity, the zipper teeth were unfastened within a second.

"Done," she said. She stepped back to give Reese space. Reese's hand was wrapped around the front of the dress to hold it up. "Do you want me to wait outside?"

Reese let her dress drop, and it pillowed into a gentle pile at her feet as she stepped away from it. "I've seen you almost naked, so it seems only fair at this point."

Sydney nodded, unable to look away from Reese's soft back, which was dotted with light freckles that Sydney wanted to map into constellations.

"Fair," she repeated slowly, unable to come up with a coherent thought.

Reese continued to move around the small room, putting the clothing back on that she'd been wearing earlier this morning. When she'd successfully fastened her bra and slid on her pants, she turned to face Sydney, her face flushed.

Sydney's stare dropped lower than she was proud of, transfixed by the sight of Reese's nipples pebbled into little points, visible through the lace of the garment.

"Seems like everyone's officially bought it," Reese said, pulling her shirt over her head.

"Yeah," Sydney said dumbly. They weren't the only ones.

If Reese had pushed her against the wall, she'd have surrendered happily. And if Reese had wanted the same in return, Sydney could already anticipate how her fingers would trace the softness of Reese's thighs. How she'd work her arm around to Reese's back and push her fingers insistently into her skin to close the inches of space between them. Her long leg, sliding between Reese's, would provide just the right angle to push upward, and she was already imagining how Reese's head would keel back before thumping softly against the wall.

She wondered what it would feel like to have Reese's warm breath mingled with her own, how their bodies would fit together, developing a rhythm, the way they'd found one on the court earlier today.

Sydney wanted it. So much so that she hadn't realized she'd stepped forward, looking up to find Reese flush with the wall at the same time she registered her fingertips trailing gently along the small patch of bare skin between her pants and shirt.

"Sydney?" The soft, husky tone in Reese's voice caught her off guard, and she looked up to meet wide, brown eyes. Reese's chest was rising and falling deeply.

Sydney blinked once. Then twice, as her mind started to come back into her body.

"I'm sorry. I got caught up in the moment," she said honestly, shaking the wisps of desire from her thoughts, even if her body hadn't yet gotten the memo.

She took a step back, dropping her hand to her side.

Sure, they were both consenting adults who could do whatever they wanted. But if it happened, Sydney didn't want it to be like this, rushed and hurried in the fitting room of a dress shop. It made her feel like it was an illicit affair, and that wasn't what she wanted.

Especially not with Reese.

Reese used the room created when Sydney had moved back to shift sideways, creating even more space between them.

"Right, makes sense," Reese said before glancing around the

fitting room, no longer meeting Sydney's eyes. "Are you ready to head out front? We have the rest of what I'm sure will be an eventful day ahead of us—a guarantee if the Devereuxs are involved."

Sydney extended her arm. "Lead the way."

As she trailed behind Reese out of the fitting room, she wondered if she'd just made a huge mistake.

* * *

The rest of the day had been weird. It was the only way Sydney could describe it.

When they'd returned from the dress fitting, Tripp was nowhere to be found. He'd made up a flimsy excuse to Stan about an urgent issue with one of the properties, stating that it would be better if he went personally instead of sending Grant. He'd added that he wanted to make sure his son was able to enjoy his weekend with his fiancée's family, which is how Sydney had definitely known that he was lying.

She hadn't seen a single, altruistic deed from Tripp Devereux since she'd met him.

Interestingly enough, the facts of the story had all been relayed by Stan with gusto as he'd manned the grill, willing to replay the events in what she assumed was almost word-for-word detail. She loved a man who knew the power of good gossip, but she also sensed that he hadn't quite believed the story either.

Reese, to her credit, had seemed relieved, and the remaining group had all gone on to have a relatively enjoyable evening, which was, in Sydney's opinion, the weirdest part of the whole situation.

Sharon had opened up by dessert, discussing with Margie their respective philanthropic endeavors and laughing like old friends once the first bottle of wine they'd been sharing was empty.

As they'd all said good night in the living room, where Sydney,

Reese, and Stan had just finished performing a three-person massacre when they'd been teamed up in charades, Sydney was finding it difficult to remember a more enjoyable night in recent memory.

Sure, Grant was in attendance, but he'd mostly sulked in the corner, sitting on his phone and making the uneven teams irrelevant.

She followed Reese upstairs as Margie and Sharon settled in with another bottle of wine on the sofa. Stan had headed to bed, and Grant and Brynn had already disappeared, though she didn't much care where.

It wasn't until they reached the landing that Sydney's trepidation flared up, her footsteps leading her closer and closer to the bedroom where she and Reese would be sleeping tonight.

First and foremost, she needed to apologize to Reese for whatever had happened earlier today.

The desire she'd felt had been all-consuming, swirling around in her body and propelling her forward before she'd understood what was happening. It wasn't like she'd never seen an attractive person before.

But Reese had been so unguarded and playful, and Sydney had gotten caught up in the moment.

She was still thinking about how she'd apologize when the door clicked closed behind her, something she'd apparently done when she felt the cold metal beneath her fingertips.

"I was going to get ready for bed," Reese said, already digging around in her weekend bag on top of the comforter. "Did you need to get into the en suite?"

"I'm sorry," Sydney said before she lost her nerve. She stepped over to the side of the bed where she'd be sleeping, plunging her hands into her bag to stop them from shaking. Or to, at least, stop Reese from seeing it.

"Sorry?" Reese repeated, her brows furrowing. "For what? I agreed with you that it was my fault during charades for not realizing when you stretched your arms out and pretended to fly that the answer was *Titanic*."

Exasperated, Sydney let out a strangled sound.

Why was this so hard? Maybe because she felt like an idiot, getting carried away like she had.

Sydney stood up to her full height and willed herself to continue. "I'm sorry about earlier today. In the fitting room."

Reese's eyebrow drew upward, and a look that Sydney couldn't decipher passed across her features. "Why are you apologizing? You didn't do anything wrong," Reese said matter-of-factly.

"I know that this situation is already complicated enough, and I'm sorry if I made you uncomfortable with anything I did." There. That was a passable apology, even if Sydney's insides wobbled like jelly while she waited for Reese's response.

Reese zipped up her bag and placed it on the floor before she started walking toward the bathroom. "You didn't make me uncomfortable, but you were probably right to stop things before they went too far."

Sydney clocked the 'probably,' her heart skittering as she wondered if there was a part of Reese that had wanted them to keep going.

But she didn't have time to dwell on that. Damage control was the name of the game. "So we're okay?"

At the doorway, Reese turned around, giving Sydney an appraising stare. "Yes, Sydney. I promise, we're okay."

Before she had time to respond, Reese shut the door into the bathroom.

Sydney flopped down on the bed forcefully, groaning into the mattress. "Get it together," she said into the pillow she'd found and shoved under her head, not that she deserved the extra comfort.

With Reese safely ensconced in the bathroom, those what-ifs had time to flit through Sydney's mind again.

Probably. What did *probably* mean?

Probably, as in things would have gotten weird if they'd kept going? Or probably, as in it would change everything, and maybe that wouldn't be the worst thing in the world?

Either way, that 'probably' signaled possibility, something that Sydney was already deep in her awareness of in the last few days.

A year ago, Sydney wouldn't have thought twice about going after what she wanted. Not in the relationship sense, since she and Grant were still together, but if there was something she wanted to achieve, she'd been unrelenting in her pursuit of it.

Three years ago, she'd gotten her parents the house they loved, even though it hadn't been on the market. Two years ago, she'd snagged one of the top coaches in Florida, intent on improving her game and making her name in the Grand Slam finals a common occurrence. Early last year, she'd won two smaller tournaments in the first three months of the tour, solidifying herself as a contender to be reckoned with.

It was like there was a massive line cleaved straight down the middle of her life, before and after she'd discovered Grant's infidelity. Now, she didn't know who—or what—to trust, especially not when her own judgment was concerned.

Sydney was attracted to Reese; that was just a statement of fact. And she felt more like herself whenever they spent time together. Alight. Curious. Playful.

But given her track record for the last year, she wasn't the best one to push anything between them. Reese was the one with complicated family dynamics on her side, and it wasn't fair for Sydney to muddle their agreement when any ensuing fallout would land more heavily on Reese's shoulders.

Which was a lot easier to convince herself of until Reese stepped out of the bathroom, dressed in boyshorts and a soft, almost threadbare T-shirt with the Stanford logo on it.

Sydney felt her pulse low in her stomach, a dull ache at the sight of her.

"All done?" she practically squeaked as she hopped up from the bed.

Reese nodded, and Sydney slipped quickly into the bathroom.

Just like they had in the bedroom, Sydney's thoughts warred within her, and it wasn't until she looked at her watch that she realized she'd been hiding out over the sink for almost half an hour.

After changing, brushing her teeth, and washing her face, she'd spent the other, oh, twenty-two minutes in various states of distress.

"Ugh. She's going to think I'm having a meltdown in here." Which wasn't that far from the truth.

Also, when had Sydney started talking to herself so much? She really needed to call Hallie, but at least she'd see her tomorrow to work through everything.

But she knew, if Hallie was here, she'd tell her to buck up and get her ass out there. Nothing good ever happened from sitting on the bench.

With that in mind, she opened the door and tried to summon courage she didn't feel to get into bed next to Reese and pretend like she wasn't a complete tongue-tied loser.

Reese, again, wasn't making it easy for her, lying as she was under the covers with her pillows propped behind her as she read a book.

Was being aroused from someone else looking comfortable a thing? It seemed plausible, if Sydney's bodily response was any indication.

"What are you reading?" she asked, slipping under the covers as unobtrusively as she could manage.

Reese rested the book on her stomach, and Sydney made sure not to think about how she'd touched that skin only hours ago. "A management book on best practices for integrating yourself with new teams."

"Very... specific." Sydney took a chance and snuggled a little farther under the covers. Stan and Margie had great taste in bedding.

"It's boring as all hell," Reese admitted with a wry grin, "but I'm committed to doing things right at The Stone's Throw."

And things like that! Why did Reese have to be genuinely kind and want to do a great job at her work, even if she was the owner and, in reality, could do whatever she wanted?

But instead of Reese picking her book back up and leaving the conversation there, she rubbed at the corner of it, staring at Sydney intently.

"What's on your mind?" Sydney finally asked, the not-knowing worse than whatever Reese would say. Probably.

"You didn't believe my father's story about an emergency at one of his properties, right?"

The tension evaporated from Sydney's body, and she let out a horse laugh. "No. Not in a million fucking years."

Reese's face grew serious then, and she shifted sideways to look directly at Sydney. "Which would make me assume that he was so infuriated with what I'd said at lunch that he couldn't stand to keep his composure for the rest of the day." Her voice was morose, like she hated what she was admitting.

Sydney hadn't thought of it like that, but Reese had a very genuine point. "It seems likely."

"Shocking that Grant isn't the biggest asshole in my family," Reese bit out, her words sharp.

"What's the deal there, if you don't mind me asking?" Sydney said softly, treading as lightly as she could. "Why wouldn't he be happy about your success?"

It was well and truly a foreign concept to Sydney, a parent who didn't want the absolute best for their children.

Reese grew contemplative, her lips twitching back and forth before she finally settled on her words. "I've always wanted my father's approval. He's known that, and no matter what I've done or achieved, he couldn't find the willingness to give it to me."

"So everything he said about wanting you to come work at The Devereux Group today?"

"He'll say whatever he needs to stay on Stan's good side. I wouldn't be surprised if he orchestrated the entire engagement between Brynn and Grant at this point."

That was a sobering thought for Sydney, not that it changed Grant's undeniable infidelity. But it was a level of malfeasance that was difficult to wrap her mind around.

"I'm sure it's hard," she said, "knowing what an amazing woman you are and still having someone like him refuse to celebrate it."

Reese pulled a face. "What does it all matter if the people around me don't love and support me? If I'm just moving from one business venture to the next, never feeling like I have a safe place to land?"

Sydney thought maybe this was about more than just family, but she stuck to the topic at hand.

"I don't think that's true," she said, grabbing Reese's hand from on top of the covers. "Your mom is so proud of you. You can't fake that."

And Sydney meant it. Sharon Devereux clearly loved her daughter, and in spite of Tripp's negative reaction, she'd looked at Reese like she'd never been more proud of her when Reese had made her announcement at lunch.

Except, as Sydney said the words, Reese's eyes welled up, and large, fat tears immediately streamed down her face. "I haven't been treating my mom well."

Sydney couldn't envision a world where Reese wasn't good to people, her mom especially. "You lived across the country until a few weeks ago. You're back, and your relationship seems like it's in a really positive place, at least from where I sit."

"She had cancer, and she didn't tell me," Reese choked out. "She already had the surgery and everything."

The words were like a gut punch to Sydney. All she wanted to do was draw Reese close and hold her tight, letting her work the sadness and frustration out of her through the tears that fell.

"Hey, come here. Can I give you a hug?" she asked, not worried about the implications or the confusion that had been running her ragged thirty minutes ago.

"I'm all snotty," Reese said in a half laugh, half sob as she wiped her hand across her face.

Sydney opened her arms. "I don't care."

She waited—and would wait as long as Reese needed—until Reese, with a sniffle and a hiccup, scooted the six inches across the bed to where Sydney lay.

"You don't have to do this," Reese said as she continued to soften against Sydney's frame, her hand coming to rest against Sydney's stomach.

"I want to do this." And Sydney meant it. Truly.

They lay there for a minute, Sydney stroking Reese's temple with her fingertips in a soothing pattern, silent except for an occasional sniffle from Reese.

"When did you find out?"

Reese nuzzled her face against Sydney's chest, leaving a tear streak across it. "Today before lunch."

Sydney hugged Reese more tightly against her. "I'm so sorry. I'm so fucking sorry, Reese."

"It was only stage 1, so they're pretty confident they got it all, but she had more tests on Friday, and she's waiting for the results," Reese informed her before she let out a scoff. "My *father* didn't even spend time with my mom today. Didn't help take her to the appointment yesterday. Didn't stay tonight, even though I'm sure my mom would have appreciated not going to bed alone, worrying about the results like she is."

Reese's words made Sydney feel sick, and she pulled her in even closer, intertwining their legs. "That's awful."

She could feel Reese nodding against her chest. "I know. I was trying to be on my best behavior today, but once I knew that, and then when my dad started pretending like he'd ever welcome me at The Devereux Group, I sort of lost it."

"I think it would have made complete sense if you'd flipped the table," Sydney said seriously. "I'm so sorry you have to deal with him."

"I'm more sorry this means that you have to deal with him," Reese responded before she let out another strangled sound. "I can't believe that I ever wanted to be like him. That I looked up to him growing up. God, I'm so stupid."

"No, you aren't," Sydney said. As she felt Reese starting to get worked up again, she ran a soothing hand up and down her arm. "You aren't. He's the stupid one. Throwing away an amazing daughter like you for some outdated gender roles and ideas about business? He may be the dumbest man on the planet."

They lay there quietly, with Sydney stroking Reese's temple again.

Finally, Reese's soft voice floated up from where Sydney had wondered if she'd fallen asleep against her. "I think I've seen too many 'Florida Man' articles to believe he's the *dumbest*."

Sydney's heart stuttered when she felt Reese smile against her chest, and without thinking, she leaned down and kissed the top of Reese's forehead.

"That was a friendly kiss, to be clear," she said quickly, hoping Reese didn't pull back into herself.

Reese nuzzled in closer, her voice sleepy when she said, "I don't care what kind of kiss it is. I just know that I appreciate it, and you."

In seconds, Sydney could feel the even rise and fall of Reese's chest.

Before she drifted off to sleep herself, she thought about how this was what she'd always wanted, to hold someone close, just two people finding comfort with one another in the world.

It wasn't how she'd expected to have it, but she wouldn't change a single thing.

Twelve

THE DAY before the Fourth of July was the busiest Reese had survived—or was trying to survive—yet.

More accurately, all week had been a slew of nonstop check-ins, checkouts, and problems with guests, staff, and vendors.

They were also, at Reese's insistence, opening their patio to the public to watch the fireworks show that the city would be setting off tomorrow at dusk.

The Stone's Throw Inn oozed charm and stayed busy during the summer, but after poring over the finances, her hope was to improve the property's visibility to encourage higher occupancy rates year-round.

The first step was getting more people in the door to test handling a bigger crowd, at which point she'd move on to planning specialty weekends to attract specific types of guests. Fall foliage tours. Whale watching. Microbrew tours. Gallery shows for local artists in the great room, set to the side of the lobby where guests generally had afternoon tea or read a book.

Everything was on the table, and even though they were in the throes of summer, she already had fall and beyond on the brain.

She was barely keeping her head above water responding to all the emails.

Which was why she didn't immediately look up when a shadow fell across her laptop, checking her schedule, as she was, for the dozent time that day to make sure that everything and everyone were where they were supposed to be.

"I did the whole speech and everything." It was Hallie, her voice a mix of confusion and frustration that was at odds with her usually bubbly demeanor.

Reese looked up then, giving the lobby a quick once-over to make sure they were alone. "What speech?"

She racked her brain, trying to remember what Hallie could have told her in the last few days. She knew how to use the software, blessedly. Candace and Greg had spent the first part of the week in another lovers' quarrel but as of this morning were back on the mend. And Reese had given up any false ideas about firing Candace, having seen her speed and efficiency firsthand. She'd pushed any vendors coming on-site back to the week after the Fourth, knowing she wouldn't have time to deal with them anyway.

Honestly, she thought she'd been killing it this week. Between spending time with her mom in the evenings, who, she'd learned, spent most of the week alone while her dad stayed in Boston, and staying on top of her first holiday week as owner, she'd barely slept more than six hours a night since coming back from Bingham.

Hallie looked down at her, lips pursed.

It sent a skittering, nervous feeling through Reese.

Her lifeline to running the inn leaned in closer, and the churning in Reese's stomach intensified.

"The intimidation speech." Hallie paused, ratcheting up the tension as she looked at Reese, like she was supposed to know what Hallie was talking about.

All Reese could manage was a wide-eyed stare back, her brain working double time, trying to catch up.

Finally, Hallie rolled her eyes, and she let out a deep, resigned breath at Reese's lack of understanding. "About not hurting my friend."

Reese jutted her chin up, their faces almost colliding. "What's wrong with Sydney? Is she okay?"

"It was a good speech," Hallie lamented, like she was talking to herself more than anything before adding, "and she's fine."

Only, she stressed the word 'fine' like it was not, in fact, fine at all.

"I saw her in the lobby yesterday on her way to the tennis center," Reese responded quickly.

She and Sydney had chatted briefly, though the embarrassment that had welled up inside her at the memory of the weekend had made it easier to acknowledge the family who'd walked into the inn, ready to check in for the holiday weekend.

Part of her wished that she could go back to the moments before she knew about her mom, before she'd told their lunch party that she owned The Stone's Throw. To when she and Sydney had agreed on a fun, carefree weekend with no ulterior motives.

She still remembered how it had felt to push her body against Sydney after their match, skin and softness and the way Sydney's breath had hitched when she'd leaned close.

And maybe the dressing room would have gone differently. Relaxed Reese would have melted against that wall as Sydney moved closer and let something happen between them, even if it had been fleeting.

They'd been so close, their bodies connected in all the right places, before Reese's brain had gotten the better of her. Then she'd frozen—panicked, if she was being honest—at adding another complicated layer to her life.

But still, Reese wasn't *avoiding* Sydney. She really was nonstop busy with everything going on this week.

So, yeah, she could admit that this past weekend had been intense, and Reese wasn't exactly sure where to go from there.

Both things could be true.

She'd left snot stains on Sydney's shirt, for god's sake.

There wasn't a single time she could remember even crying in front of Megan or anyone else for that matter.

Her anger and sadness and frustration had always been a solitary endeavor for her, turning inward and pushing through it.

All it had taken was a few supportive words and open arms, and Reese had cried like a baby for the first time in years.

So no, she didn't exactly have a playbook for breaking down in front of a woman who'd quickly been occupying more and more of her mental energy the same day she'd found out her mom had cancer and had then decided to implode whatever tentative sense of calm she'd been managing with her father.

Even if she could give herself a pass for the breakdown, that woman happened to be her brother's ex-girlfriend, whom she'd become embroiled in a fake relationship with to antagonize said brother for his lifetime of mediocrity, which he'd gleefully rubbed in her face every chance he got.

Recipe, meet disaster.

"Sydney does that, too. The whole spiraling thing," Hallie said knowingly, breaking into Reese's thoughts.

"You are a... very involved friend." Reese chose her words carefully, blinking to bring herself back to the present moment.

"I'm a very involved person. Period," Hallie answered with an unassuming smile. "It's a gift and a curse. Growing up surrounded by so many people coming and going in my life."

If anything, Reese could at least appreciate the self-awareness. "You still haven't answered my question. What's wrong with Sydney?"

"She really is fine. I promise. It's just, she's being surprisingly tight-lipped about your weekend, which isn't like her. And in my defense," Hallie said, some of her bravado slipping away, "I'm trying to adjust to this whole 'us being back in the same place again' thing, and I want to make sure I'm doing everything I can to help her."

Reese's insides softened. Hallie was a good friend, even if her prodding was sometimes misguided. And Sydney, very likely wanting to uphold Reese's privacy about what had transpired, had kept things to herself.

The weekend had been a veritable domino effect of situations boiling over into, well, *worse* situations, and mentioning any of them out of context wove a complicated web of half-truths and lies by omission.

"Hallie, the weekend was a little intense because of my family, and I'm sure that Sydney was just respecting my privacy." Reese's cheeks warmed with the admission, not realizing how much it meant to her until she'd laid it out.

Hallie nodded, absorbing the answer. "So you aren't avoiding my bestie? My other half? The sun around which my Earth spins?"

Reese tempered her smile at the colorful descriptors. "I have some stuff going on, which Sydney is aware of already. I promise."

"So... how was *your* weekend?" Hallie asked, before quickly adding, "I mean, outside of the crazy family stuff."

Reese found herself smiling in spite of all that had transpired and at odds with the confusion warring inside of her. Even though her brain had curated a list of all the reasons giving in with Sydney would be a bad idea, all she could see now when she thought about the weekend were those piercing green eyes and a contagious smile that she'd been missing this week.

"A lot better with Sydney there," she answered honestly.

"Sounds about right," Hallie agreed.

"My family is... dysfunctional," Reese settled on, watching as Hallie absorbed every single word. "It's really nice to have someone there to balance out the crazy, someone I know is in my corner."

"Sydney's one of the most loyal people I know. And, if you haven't noticed, she may be a bit too trusting."

As she had said before, she felt that Grant had abused Sydney's trust; their breakup was squarely on his shoulders. Reese understood all too well what it felt like to have your faith in someone broken.

And, for the last six months, that feeling had made it especially easy to keep everyone at arm's length.

Sydney King, in under two weeks, had broken through every safeguard she'd put in place.

More than that, she liked that even though she knew Sydney struggled with what it all meant—Grant's betrayal, the confusion about whatever they were doing—it hadn't changed who she seemed to be, which was someone who wanted to show up for people and do the right thing.

Really, though, she did owe Sydney more of an explanation, or even more of just a conversation, if Sydney wanted to have one.

It was clear that, after the weekend, she'd left the ball in Reese's court.

They'd driven back home to Stoneport early on Sunday morning, and Sydney had been gracious enough not to mention that they'd woken up the way they'd fallen asleep, with their legs intertwined and Reese pressed into Sydney's chest.

The whole night had been cathartic, to put it mildly. She'd slept like a baby, and though she'd been trying not to think about it, she was pretty sure when her alarm had gone off, she'd let out a frustrated groan and burrowed in deeper against Sydney's impossibly soft T-shirt.

Reese realized, as Hallie's watchful gaze still scanned her face, that the question wasn't rhetorical.

"I hope I haven't given Sydney any reason to feel like her trust in me is misplaced. I've moved back to Stoneport, and I'm going to be here." She ran her hands along the wooden check-in desk, anchoring herself to its solidity. "We both have our reasons for agreeing to our fake dating, but I think that out of the two of us…"

Reese's words trailed off, and Hallie leaned closer. "'Out of the two of you' what?"

Reese's lips pursed. She hadn't let herself think about it over the last few weeks, how Sydney's time in Stoneport was very likely a stopover onto her next adventure. She was a world-renowned athlete and a relatively well-known name even outside of the tennis world.

Sydney had come back home to lick her wounds and recalibrate her life. The loss of a long-term relationship and her career in the last year couldn't have been easy to manage.

Reese knew that firsthand.

Once Sydney decided what she wanted to do next—and Reese had no doubt that it would be a choice among many different things—she'd very likely leave Stoneport.

"I don't think we'll keep her," Reese admitted. "I know she's going to have opportunities coming her way soon, if they haven't already started. She mentioned that she's going back to Florida next week to meet with her agent."

"And to see her parents," Hallie countered.

It was something that Sydney had shared with her on the ride home from Bingham. She'd framed it casually, checking in about any upcoming events to make sure she wasn't going to miss them.

To Hallie's point, Sydney was incredibly dependable.

But there was another thought that kept niggling in the back of her brain. Reese had broken down, had unexpectedly leaned on Sydney, and less than twelve hours later, Sydney was reminding her that she wasn't always going to be here. That her life wasn't really in Stoneport.

Maybe it was a coincidence, but Reese was still on high alert, attuned to every possible worst-case scenario.

"Sydney's plan was always to move back to Stoneport eventually," Hallie answered, but it didn't even sound like she believed herself, given the way she wouldn't make eye contact with Reese.

Reese nodded. "I'm sure that was a prudent decision for after retirement, back when she had a long-term partner she wanted to settle down with. That's not Sydney's life anymore."

It wasn't like she was trying to argue, but she thought maybe wishful thinking was the driving force behind Hallie's words.

"Either way, Sydney's here now," Hallie said, "and all you're doing is wasting your own time avoiding her."

"I'm not avoiding her," Reese said, her voice falling away as she clocked Sydney walking into the lobby area, tennis bag hanging on her tanned shoulder.

Why did she have to look so good, like, all the time? It wasn't fair.

And then Sydney beamed a megawatt smile in their direction, one that had been captured many times before for literal magazine covers, and ambled over to the desk.

"Well, if it isn't my girlfriend and my best friend, together in one place."

Hallie's chest puffed out with pride, but Reese could feel her cheeks warming.

"I was just asking Reese for the details from this weekend," Hallie said, "since you've been less than forthcoming with information."

Sydney shot her best friend a look that made Reese, though she tried to hold it in, snort with laughter.

"Prying into people's personal lives feels like an HR violation, Hal."

Undeterred, Hallie pressed on. "Is that possible when she's the owner?" She shot a grin in Reese's direction. "Also, at this point, I think I am HR. At least for another few months."

Sydney lifted an eyebrow. "Then it's a fairly egregious abuse of power."

"Either way," Hallie said, waving them off, "Reese gave me the skinny."

It was interesting how color fanned across Sydney's face, blooming wild over her cheekbones.

Reese watched as Sydney tightened her fingers around the strap of her bag. "Be that as it may, I was hoping to talk to Reese for a second before I headed to the tennis center."

"Guess that's my cue," Hallie said, standing still for a few prolonged seconds. "I'm sure there's some sort of crisis I can find to manage effectively right now."

Sydney gave Hallie a stare that only worked between lifelong friends, her voice droll when she said, "I have no doubt."

Reese watched Hallie wander away, her pulse picking up as Sydney focused her attention across the desk, to where Reese sat as still as she could manage.

"Sorry for all the cloak-and-dagger," Sydney said with a sweet smile. "I just wanted to ask about how your mom was, and I didn't know if you'd shared that with Hallie."

Warmth spread through Reese for an abundance of reasons. "Her doctor's office called yesterday afternoon. Everything looks good."

Sydney's shoulders visibly relaxed, and she reached her hand across the table to hold Reese's. "I'm so happy to hear that."

The sincerity in Sydney's voice was like a warm blanket that Reese wrapped around herself.

Yesterday, when her mom had called with the news, the relieved whoosh of air she'd let out had been unlike anything else she'd ever experienced.

Their fingers were still intertwined when Sydney said, "I should also apologize in advance for anything that Hallie may have said to you. I think that throwing herself into my drama has been a bit of an escape for her the last few weeks."

Reese sat with that idea, even as she enjoyed how Sydney's fingers gently tapped against her hand. Hallie, like the two of them, was going through a significant amount of change, and she was glad that Sydney reminded her of it.

"To be fair, you've given her a lot of material to work with."

Sydney feigned shock as she held her free hand up to her heart. "I'd like to think it's been a team effort. Speaking of which, have you heard from your dad?"

Reese shook her head. Honestly, she hadn't thought of him much, except with respect to what a joke of a husband he was. "I have not, and he's not exactly at the top of my priority list these days."

"Well, we'll get to see him in..." She could see Sydney trying to remember when their next family event was happening.

"Next Saturday at the couple's shower," Reese supplied. She thought she did a great job of hiding the grimace in her voice.

"A celebration of love and joy in honor of the happy couple," Sydney teased.

Reese let out a deep breath. "The theme is 'Love you a brunch.'"

Sydney made a fake gagging sound before dissolving into a fit of laughter.

It felt good to see her so light. Reese hadn't known, as they'd gotten deeper into the bowels of wedding-related events, how Sydney would react. Maybe Sydney herself didn't even know, but Reese wanted her to have an ongoing opt-out clause in case anything became too much.

"And you're still okay with everything?" she asked. "I don't want to put you in any difficult situations."

Sydney waved her off readily. "Exposure therapy at its best. I figure by the time the wedding comes, I'll be in tip-top performance shape."

"To do what?" Reese asked, apprehension that she tried to bite back edging into her voice.

She didn't *really* think that Sydney would do anything, but with everything going on with her mom, she had to ask.

"Dance with my beautiful girlfriend and have an amazing time," Sydney said, her soft eyes giving no hint of teasing this time.

Reese's stomach swooped low, and she knew that she was blushing. "Kill 'em with kindness," she said when she recovered.

Before she lost her resolve, she pushed forward, speaking again. "I want to thank you again. For everything you're doing for me. For everything you did this weekend. It meant a lot, having you there."

Sydney stood up a little straighter, a tender smile on her face. "I'm glad I could be there."

Reese cleared her throat, intent on not getting lost in the moment or reading too much into it. Sydney had already done so much for her, and the one thing she had to offer was not blurring any lines.

Well—any more lines.

"Me too," Reese settled on, hoping she'd effectively conveyed her gratitude.

Sydney gave Reese's hand a squeeze, which she'd been holding for the last five minutes, and it sent another flutter of butterflies flapping through Reese's stomach. "I need to get going. I'm meeting Brian at the tennis center."

Reese nodded and pulled her hand away first, missing the contact immediately. "You'll have to let me know how that's going soon."

"I will," Sydney said softly as she hoisted her bag more tightly against her shoulder.

Reese watched her walk out of the inn, begging herself to keep it together for the next few months.

* * *

Reese was sweaty. Actually, that wasn't entirely accurate. That implied that she *had been* sweating. The reality was, she *was* sweating, little beads of heat running continually running down her back. She hadn't stopped moving in almost three hours as she'd worked to get everything together ahead of the fireworks show.

But now, there was nothing else to check on, no last-minute emergencies that required her attention. She stood, waiting, taking a few deep breaths to calm herself down.

Dozens of people milled around the outdoor patio space as the sun began to set, splashes of light reflecting off the waves in the gloom below.

The fireworks would be set off on a barge about a quarter-mile out to sea. Reese could already see dotting the horizon, and though it looked unimpressive right now, she knew it would elicit oohs and aahs in a few short hours.

Her mom had come early, and Reese had set her up in one of the dozen adirondack chairs that were always available for guests to relax on during their stay.

With her plan to open the inn to the public for the show, she'd worked with Hallie to secure a myriad of other seating options, along with encouraging guests to bring blankets and their own chairs.

The Stone's Throw Inn boasted one of the most beautiful, unencumbered views of the coastline, and she wanted to make sure that people knew it.

Kids of varying ages ran around on the grass, some with sparklers that they twirled with glee.

It was exactly what she'd hoped it would be.

She wiped her sweaty brow and glanced over to where her mom sat, unobtrusively checking in. Her lips tipped into a smile when she noticed Hallie sitting on the arm of her mother's chair, talking animatedly. God knows what Hallie was telling her, or vice versa.

Warmth radiated next to Reese, and the familiar scent of soft perfume enveloped her senses. "Don't worry," Sydney said quietly, leaning closer to Reese to be heard over the din of the crowd. "Hallie won't spill the beans, if that's what you're worried about."

Reese met her stare, and the buzzy feeling in her limbs that seemed to crop up whenever she was near Sydney reared to life. "I didn't think she would."

They stood, shoulder to shoulder, staring out at the expanse of grass before it fell away into the ocean below.

"I love what you've done with the place," Sydney commented as she turned her focus back toward the growing darkness.

The patio was bathed in fairy lights that would be turned off when the fireworks started. They were woven around the unused outdoor heaters and crisscrossed through the trellis that created a privacy wall on the right side of the brick-laid space.

It gave the patio a soft glow, complemented by laughter filling the yard as various configurations of people silhouetted in front of them waited for the show to start.

Reese had spotted Sydney the second she'd walked through the French doors and onto the patio about fifteen minutes ago. She'd come in with a group of people Reese didn't recognize.

Reese nodded toward them as they sat on a blanket in the middle of the crowd. "I see you brought friends."

Sydney nodded, a vibrant smile settling on her lips. "Jenna, one of the full-time students at the training center, and her parents. I also dragged Brian here," she added proudly, indicating her former coach.

Reese let the excitement flutter through her, knowing that she wanted Sydney to be impressed by her event.

She'd come to accept since they'd had their conversation yesterday that Sydney had that effect on her. The start of their friendship—if that was what it was—was beyond messy, but she wanted to be closer to Sydney, in whatever ways that meant.

"Are you excited for your trip back to Florida? You leave tomorrow, right?" Reese let the words hang between them, already knowing the answer to her second question. Sure, she wanted to spend more time with Sydney, but she was also intent on keeping her tethers to reality.

"Yep. I have an early flight out, and my parents are picking me up from the airport."

"Both of them?" Reese asked. She couldn't remember once in her life that both of her parents had come to pick her up from somewhere. On her few, sporadic trips home over the last decade, it had always been easier to get a car at the airport than to accept her mom's offer to drive into Boston and pick her up.

Sydney laughed. "They're, um... very hands-on parents. And

besides tournaments and when I moved to Florida initially, this is the longest I've gone without seeing them."

Reese honestly couldn't imagine that reality. "So do you just, like, show up at one another's houses? Have a standing weekly dinner when you're not away?"

She found herself wanting to know more about Sydney's life —her *real* life, the one that Reese would never experience.

"We live together," Sydney said, like it was the most normal thing in the world. "I used to be traveling at least half the year, and when I'm home, I have full training days. I like coming home to people."

That was an insane concept to her. Reese and Megan had lived together in San Francisco, but they'd spent long days in the office, with Reese mostly squirreled away working on the coding for the software. When they'd been home together, their life had consisted of takeout dinners and discussions about work before prepping for the next day.

Living with a partner had been fine, but living with her parents? Inconceivable.

Then again, she had to assume that she and Sydney had very different parents.

Reese tried to hide the disbelief she knew was etched across her face. "Not a solitary creature then?" was what she settled on.

Sydney shrugged. "My parents have always been my biggest champions, and life on the tour can get lonely. I wasn't exactly Miss Popularity, so it was really nice to come home to people who loved and supported me."

Reese's heart squeezed even though, again, she found Sydney's words hard to believe. "I can say, honestly, you're one of the most likable people I've ever met. Annoyingly so," she teased, gently elbowing Sydney's side.

She noted how Sydney grew still, wrapping her arms around her torso. "I appreciate you saying that, but it isn't a sentiment shared by everyone."

"Just don't go into the hotel business and we likely won't have an issue," Reese joked again, trying to ease the tension that had permeated the moment.

That made Sydney laugh, and Reese loved hearing the sound. "Don't worry. My experience is either staying in hotels or covering for Hallie so we wouldn't get in trouble in this one. No fear of competition *here*," Sydney said, the implication in her words clear.

"But my family is another story," Reese finished for her.

Sydney gave a slow nod. "In tennis, I've learned that focusing on what I'm doing instead of on anyone else is the most important thing. I'll give that same advice to you."

Reese brushed their shoulders together again, knocking gently into Sydney. "Sage wisdom, Ms. King. I'll file that away for a rainy day."

Their shoulders remained connected when Sydney said, "I've been thinking. If your mom is looking for something new to try, she should consider the tennis center. They have a ton of classes, and it could be a good way for her to meet people. I could introduce her to Brian after the fireworks if you think she'd be open to that."

Could a heart melt? Because that was what was happening to Reese's right then.

"I don't know how anyone wouldn't think the world of you, Sydney," she said. "You're probably the most thoughtful person I've ever met."

Sydney evaded the compliment but smiled anyway, a flush across her cheeks visible in the dim patio lighting. "So is that a yes?" she asked hopefully.

"I think my mom would really like that. And honestly, I'm starting to run out of stories about my life to keep her updated on."

Sydney lifted an eyebrow. "I find that hard to believe."

"Stories I can actually tell her," Reese corrected.

"It is a tangled web we weave."

Reese cleared her throat as she felt the moment growing serious again. "I don't regret it, though. Any of it."

The fairy lights, which had been set on a timer, turned off, signaling the fireworks would be starting soon.

Instead of heading back to find her group, Sydney slipped her fingers between Reese's and squeezed. "Me neither."

Within seconds, the first *boom* cracked loud above them, vibrant colors exploding across the sky.

Reese watched in awe, sneaking a glance at Sydney's features. As a roman candle illuminated the sharp planes of her cheekbones in the darkness, she found herself wondering what it would feel like to not lay eyes on her for an entire week.

* * *

"I am *exhausted*," Hallie said dramatically. "I'd throw myself down in a chair, but I don't know if I'd be able to get back up."

"I've got the rest of the cleanup covered, Hallie. Thank you for everything." Reese said the words as more of a statement than a request, hoping Hallie wouldn't feel obligated to help, then put her hands on her hips to show that she meant it. "I just need to do one more sweep for any trash, and I think we're good."

"You sure?" Hallie said in that same endlessly helpful way that Sydney had about her, though her voice was tinged with exhaustion.

Reese nodded. "I promise. This was my brainchild, and I take full responsibility for its management, including cleaning up."

"I am inclined to keep arguing about this, but I'm also worried that I'll fall asleep standing up," Hallie said. Her surrender seemed genuine; she was already making her way over to the patio doors.

"Good night, Hallie," Reese called out before Hallie disappeared inside, giving a half-hearted wave behind her.

The fireworks had ended more than half an hour ago, and the stragglers had finally made their way into the inn to head home.

Sydney, true to her word, had introduced Reese's mom to Brian, and she'd loved the excited, lit-up look that had overtaken her mom's face at the possibility of taking classes at the tennis center.

About ten minutes ago, Sydney had walked Jenna and her family, along with Brian and her mom, out to their cars. She lamented that she probably wouldn't see Sydney before she left tomorrow morning, but it was likely for the best. Her feelings were getting increasingly mixed up in her fake relationship with her brother's ex; she didn't need to add fuel to the fire.

The fairy lights were back on, casting a soft glow onto the trees that dotted the landscape. Reese scanned the grass, noting that all the guests had done a great job of depositing any trash they'd made in the large bins she'd placed outside near all the exits.

Organizing an event was similar to building software, at least in some respects. You had to give people choices but make it clear that there were desired and expected steps to follow for an optimum experience.

The tables on the patio were also cleared, though she'd have the morning staff wipe them down. The important thing was that any woodland creatures didn't smell a bag of potato chips or a candy bar and decide to come investigate if tonight was their lucky night. She didn't need 'Stone's Throw guest mauled by hungry bear' as a headline in tomorrow's *Stoneport Gazette*.

Contrary to popular belief, there was such a thing as bad publicity.

"You can't even tell this place was just crawling with people," Sydney said from behind her.

Reese's heart skipped a beat at the sound of her voice, and she busied herself with picking up an errant piece of trash on the ground.

She had to get her physical response to Sydney under control. Pronto.

"I figured you'd be getting your beauty sleep," Reese said, turning around to face Sydney who was only a few feet away.

Sydney didn't seem to have the same concern. "I can sleep on the plane. Honestly, I can sleep anywhere. It's a talent."

"One of many you seem to possess." Reese chided herself for what she had to accept was a flirty tone. Where had that come from? No one would ever accuse Reese Devereaux of being *flirty*. Practical, yes. Dedicated, sure. Flirty? It was incongruent with who she was as a person, but she watched as Sydney's brows lifted anyway, her lips teasing into a grin of their own.

"We never finished our conversation," Sydney said, stepping forward so they stood directly facing one another.

Awareness skittered across Reese's skin. "About what?"

Sydney's eyes were laser-focused on Reese. "On the tennis court, we had what I would call a *moment*," she said, enunciating the word before adding, "And then again in the dressing room. I'm just trying to figure out before I leave for a week and spin myself around in circles whether I was mistaken or not."

No one would ever argue that Sydney King was not forthright, and Reese was both turned on and intimated in equal measures.

Heat, and not from the balm of a warm summer night, spread across her skin, her spine tingling as Sydney continued to look at her intently.

Reese cleared her throat to buy herself a few useless seconds. Of course she was attracted to Sydney. Anyone with a pulse would be. Standing in front of Reese, dressed in a loose button-down that exposed her clavicle, tanned skin contrasting with the bright white of the fabric, Reese felt her resolve waning by the second.

Megan floated through her mind, not as a reminder of something she missed but as part of a realization that her feelings for Sydney were oh so different.

She and Megan had made sense. Two halves of a whole in how they'd run Checked. Comfortable together, even at the beginning.

Sydney was nothing like that. She was vibrant and fiery one moment, then soft and guileless the next. She was consistent in her support and attention, but she constantly kept Reese on her toes. There was raw attraction, something that had never kept her awake at night with Megan.

If Megan could hurt Reese so badly, what could someone like Sydney King do to her?

That was the real question, and it made Reese stay rooted in place, finding it impossible to close the slight distance between them.

Sydney held her hands in front of her, palms facing outward. "I'm not saying we need to do anything about it. I just need to know, for myself, whether it's all been part of the show for you. I haven't had the best track record this last year of knowing where people really stand," Sydney said with a self-deprecating smile.

"I got out of a bad breakup about five months ago," Reese said before she'd realized the words were coming out of her mouth. She found that she liked it, being honest with Sydney like she had last weekend, so she kept going. "We were business partners. We started Checked together in our last year of business school. I always thought that, even in spite of our differences, we were on the same page. That we wanted to see where the software could go."

"Sounds like you weren't?" Sydney asked tentatively, giving Reese physical space as she continued to stand still.

"Together, we had a majority share, so I never worried about the software being sold. But she sided with the board, and together, they had the shares to accept the offer from a larger competitor."

Sydney's whole face softened, her brows knitted in clear sympathy. "That sounds awful. Feeling betrayed by someone who was both your business partner and your girlfriend."

"I didn't realize she was going through with it until we were sitting in the board meeting and she cast her vote. I *felt* blindsided, but that was my fault. I knew she wanted to sell. Take the money and run. It's the dream in a start-up scenario, to be acquired once you build a great product."

"But you didn't want that."

"It's stupid," Reese said, running her hand through her hair. God, she must look like a mess.

Sydney took the smallest step forward. "I don't think it's stupid, if it's important to you."

"I *liked* what we were building. I didn't see the company as a means to an end, which maybe is silly given the industry I'm in. *Was* in. I wasn't ready to give it up, and I don't know why, but I thought that Megan would back me; it's not like we needed the money. We drew salaries from the company like employees. It could have really been something." Reese sighed, acceptance washing over her. "And now, I'll never know."

Sydney nodded, absorbing Reese's words seriously. "It's a hard thing to come back from, learning to trust people again."

"You seem to be doing okay with it," Reese countered, genuinely curious to know how Sydney managed it.

Sydney laughed then, running one of her hands against the back of her neck. "After Grant, I threw myself into tennis, and we all know how well that went. After tennis, I gave myself a few weeks to wallow, but I'm just not a pessimistic person by nature. I can be avoidant sometimes, sure, but I have parents who love me. I have a best friend who'd do anything for me. I'm lucky. And I don't ever want to stop thinking of myself that way.

"I was devastated by having to retire from the tour, but I have to believe that there's life after this. That it's amazing when things work out the way we want, but it can also be incredible when we have to chart new paths. I mean, otherwise, I wouldn't have ended up fake-dating my ex-boyfriend's sister. That'll be a story to tell the grandkids one day," Sydney finished with a wry, tentative smile.

"I'm not really sure what I can offer you," Reese said honestly. "Definitely not a better outlook on life than the one you already have."

Sydney took another small step forward then, grabbing Reese's hand with her own. "I *like* you. I think you're smart and interesting and brave and have done a whole hell of a lot in your life without very much support from the people who should have given it to you." Sydney's lips twitched. "And I think you're beautiful. That doesn't hurt either."

"You really know how to compliment a girl," Reese said lamely, still trying to catalog all of the things Sydney had said about her.

"Look, what I want—what I really want—is to be able to hold your hand or touch your face," she said, moving her other hand up to cup Reese's cheek, "and not have you think I'm doing it for any other reason than because I like to touch you. Because it feels good and I want it to make you feel good, too."

Reese leaned into the touch. Sydney's hand was warm and soft and comforting against her face, her thumb rubbing gently along Reese's cheekbone.

Sydney sucked in a deep breath, her hand stilling. "So if there's anything I can give you, I hope it's making it clear that I am attracted to you."

It was Reese who closed the space between them, finding Sydney's lips with her own. The kiss was tentative at first, and she wasn't sure she was breathing until Sydney sucked gently at her bottom lip, and a soft exhale of air rushed out of her, like she'd been holding her breath for weeks, waiting for this to happen.

She didn't want to be afraid. She didn't want to let her past define her future. She didn't want to stop herself because, even though Sydney's life wasn't set in stone, it felt safer to stop things before they ever got started than hurt later down the line.

Sydney's hand slotted down against her neck, adjusting them to get a better position, her tongue asking for entry against Reese's already wet lips.

When she granted it, thanked with a soft bite at the edge of her mouth, stars exploded behind her eyelids, and she wondered if the fireworks show was starting again.

Thirteen

SYDNEY HAD BEEN PRACTICALLY SKIPPING through the house since she'd returned to Florida on Friday morning. Unfortunately, the skipping wasn't easily hidden, and it was starting to lead to questions.

She bounced down the staircase before heading through the hallway and depositing herself in a seat at the kitchen island. By the time she'd hit the first floor, she'd tried to slow her steps, making sure her pace was leisurely and didn't earn her any more raised eyebrows.

"You used to bounce through the house like that after you'd won a match," her mom said from where she stood at the stove, stirring a pot of something that smelled delicious.

Rachel King was far less of a pushover than Sydney's father, who'd simply given her a kiss on the head after clocking her noticeably upbeat attitude since returning home, telling her that, "Stoneport seemed to have done her wonders."

In the three days she'd been home, she hadn't quite come up with an easy way to explain her newfound carefree nature, let alone the con—or whatever it had become—that she was running with Reese. Sydney was now an active participant in all of Grant's wedding events, something she knew her mom wouldn't approve of.

Which was fair, even if it meant she was constantly dodging questions.

Still, she was on cloud nine, and even a little subterfuge couldn't dampen her mood.

"What are you making?" Sydney asked, trying to change the subject.

"Gator gumbo," her mom supplied, stirring the pot before taking a deep inhale of the aroma.

Sydney blanched. "You're kidding me." She wouldn't call herself a picky eater, but she drew the line at anything that would be able to eat her back if they had the chance.

Her mom turned around, wiping her hands on a dish towel on the kitchen island. She had Sydney's green eyes and blonde hair, though her mom's face was sharper, a sort of 'no nonsense' look that had served her well in her previous life as a middle school teacher. "I thought we were all just saying whatever we wanted in this house now, regardless of whether it was the truth."

"Mom," Sydney whined, transported back to her childhood and the zero things she'd ever been away to get away with. That was why she and Hallie had always caused a ruckus at The Stone's Throw: Hallie's parents were much busier and less likely to catch onto their schemes until it was too late.

Rachel held her hands up. "I'm just saying. I've played good cop for the last couple of days, giving you space, but you left for Stoneport like a kicked puppy and now you're back, walking around with stars in your eyes. As a mother, am I wrong for being curious as to what's caused this sudden change in attitude?"

"Dad is 'good cop,'" Sydney argued. "You've been giving me those looks since I walked in the door."

"Because you didn't walk. You *floated*," her mom batted back.

"Have you gotten a hobby? Because I told you that hobbies would do you wonders. Great to keep the mind active and sharp."

"There are only so many games of pickleball a woman can

play, my dear. Not all of us have your zest for professional athletics."

Sydney tapped her finger on her chin, trying to remember what her mom had been up to lately. "How was that book club you joined?"

"A guise for afternoon drinking."

"Are we... against that?" Sydney asked, clocking the glass of wine her mom was now sipping.

"The cookbook said a South African shiraz paired nicely."

Sydney eyed the gumbo pot warily. "Have you tried it yet?"

"They could have at least bothered to read the book," her mom lamented, placing her wineglass back on the counter.

Sydney cocked her head to the side. "I thought you liked Florida."

Sydney had moved down to Florida four years ago. After her first two years of serious play on the pro circuit, knowing that she'd be living here for the foreseeable future, her parents had transitioned down to live with her full-time. Her mom had already retired, and her dad had gone remote for the bank he worked for in New England. It seemed like the perfect solution. She got roommates when she was home, and they got beautiful weather—with the occasional hurricane—and an idyllic way to spend their retirement.

"I like that *you* are in Florida, my darling daughter. Even when you are intentionally trying to change the subject at every turn."

"I'm not trying to change the subject. I was just checking in on how things have been going in my absence."

"Your father likes it here, though I have a suspicion that he could be happy anywhere," Rachel said with a loving smile. After the last few weeks Sydney had spent with the Devereux family, she didn't take a look like that for granted anymore.

"And you?" Sydney pushed again. She'd thought that her parents would like retiring to Florida. Everyone wanted that, didn't they?

"I've been... adjusting," her mom said after an uncomfortable silence. "Not having seasons is strange. Feels like Christmas in July every year."

"No shoveling, though. That's a plus."

"In your father's column," her mom said with a laugh.

"If you weren't happy here, why didn't you say something?" Sydney asked seriously. "I'm a big girl. I can take care of myself."

Did her parents not think that she could survive down here on her own? She used to be a professional athlete. She traversed the world to play in tournaments that required extensive physical and mental training, and as far as she knew, her living habits were up to acceptable standards, with the exception of her absolute refusal to separate lights and darks in the washing machine. That was just propaganda by Big Laundry™to convince her to do more loads.

"I know you're perfectly capable of handling your life, Sydney. I'm sorry if I implied otherwise."

Still, her mom wouldn't make eye contact with her.

"I don't believe you." Sydney picked up a banana off the counter and began unpeeling it, looking for something to do with her hands.

"It's not gator gumbo," her mom admitted. "You don't need to eat a banana. I promise you'll like it."

"Bananas are good for potassium intake," Sydney said before taking a bite. "And now who's trying to change the subject?"

"It's just not anything I want you to worry about."

Sydney's elation from only minutes ago had started to deflate, and she put her banana down on the table. She felt like a balloon inside of her had been punctured and was slowly leaking out as she flattened herself back against the chair.

"But you're okay, right?" What Reese had gone through with her own mother last week was a stark reminder of how quickly things could change.

"I promise I'm fine. You've just had such a rough run of things the last year, and I didn't want to add anything to it. And we've loved that we could be here for you with everything going on. Grant. Your career. I would have never forgiven myself if we weren't able to be by your side."

Sydney's shoulders softened, and for a moment, all she wanted was to be held again like she had been when she was little. Between her fanatical post-breakup focus on tennis and her injury and recovery, followed by her retirement from tennis, she hadn't given her mom and dad many bright spots in the last year. "I really appreciate that, Mom. I should have said that before."

"So," her mom said, meeting her stare, familiar eyes looking back at her. "I'm being so nosy because I see how much better you're doing, that there's a happiness in you that I haven't seen in a very long time."

Sydney rolled her eyes, mostly to temper the swell of teenage-level embarrassment she felt at being called out for her behavior. "It hasn't been *that* long," she said, picking her banana up again and taking a large bite.

Her mom studied her, watching Sydney thoughtfully chew her banana like it was a Michelin-starred meal. "Maybe since even before you and Grant broke up."

"Since he cheated on me," Sydney corrected once she'd swallowed, though there was no venom in her words. To her own surprise, he was barely more than a footnote in her thoughts these days, and she wouldn't have been thinking about him at all if not for all the time she was spending with Reese. "And, in retrospect, I don't know that I was all that happy with Grant anyway. It seems like things really worked out the way they should."

The look her mom was giving her was the same one she used to give her students when they were having a breakthrough. Sydney should have known; her mom had been her homeroom teacher. "That's an amazing outlook, Sydney. Any chance you're going to tell me what's helped you see things that way? Just some good old-fashioned bonding time with Hallie? How is she, by the way?"

Hallie, with her unflappable zeal for life, had gotten up at the crack of dawn, insistently, to drive Sydney to the airport. "Still raising a ruckus. She's been doing really well in spite of her parents selling the inn."

She realized her mistake after she was already careening down a slippery slope. Her mom looked at her in surprise. "The Thatchers sold the inn? Are you still staying there?"

Sydney nodded, trying to think around anything that could trip her up as they traversed this conversation, namely a serious brunette who'd thrown her whole life into the best kind of chaos over the last few weeks.

"Her parents moved to Colorado. They wanted to spend more time with their grandkids, and Hallie agreed to stay on for at least six months to help with the transition," she said carefully.

Still, her mom looked at her in confusion.

She studied her mother closely, but she could see no clear trap on the imminent horizon. "I told you that Mason and Claire had their twins last year."

"You did not. I would have sent the kids baby blankets." Her mom's confidence made her second-guess herself, and she thought back over the last year, when the twins were born. She'd just discovered Grant's infidelity, and though she'd returned to Florida after catching him, she'd gone directly to the tennis courts and hadn't left for what felt like days.

Things had changed, and tennis was the only thing she had to hold on to, gripping it more tightly than ever before.

"I'm sorry," she said, feeling guilt wash through her. She was finally coming up for air, and it didn't feel good to see the people she'd left behind.

She used to tell her mom these things. They'd eat dinner together most nights of the week unless she was away on tour, and they'd trade thrillers back and forth and discuss whether they'd guessed the ending before finishing the book.

The Thatchers and the Kings had never become friends outside of Hallie and Sydney's love for one another, but that was mostly by virtue of Hallie's parents' constant work at the inn. On the weekends, they'd deposit Sydney at The Stone's Throw, and in retrospect, she assumed the Thatchers were grateful to have someone to keep their precocious daughter occupied. Even if they tended to pay for it later.

"They're only a year old. I'm sure they still use blankets," Sydney said, joking to lessen the tightness that had taken up residence in her chest.

Now it was her mom's turn to roll her eyes. "That's not the point, and you know it."

"Well, I'll get their address from Hallie and make sure that you can send them along *as soon as possible*." This was good; they were navigating into safer territory on multiple fronts, giving Sydney time to polish off her banana and place the peel on the counter.

Her mom immediately scooped it up and threw it into the trash can at the end of the island. "So, what's happening with the inn? Seems like a big change for Hallie. Is she doing okay?"

Sydney rolled her shoulders, like she was readying herself for battle. Still, it was sweet that her mom was so concerned about Hallie. She'd had similar thoughts herself.

"The sale went through earlier this month. Luckily it's not a chain or something. Hallie seems happy to stay on for a while before figuring out what she wants to do next."

"That girl has always been so go with the flow. A teacher's dream, except for the—"

"Inability to sit still?" Sydney supplied with a laugh.

"Do you remember when you'd hit tennis balls on their court and she'd just run back and forth for hours picking them all up for you?" Her mom had a fondness in her voice that brought back so many good childhood memories.

"I haven't thought about that in years." Sydney watched as her mom turned back around to stir the pot of... "So, what are you *actually* making?"

She could see her mom's ears lifting, knowing that she was smiling. "It's a gumbo, but no alligator. I promise."

"I know New England has some dangerous animals, but none that will crawl out of the water and try to drag you back in."

Sydney wasn't exactly outdoorsy, but she knew enough to stay safe from bears on any hiking paths she'd found herself on. Alligators were a whole other story. She should have never read their Wikipedia article. They got points for their positive ecological impact, but other than that, no, thank you.

She made a mental note to text Reese about her opinions on alligators later, and a smile formed as she wondered what her response would be. Her fingers itched with the desire to pull her cell phone out, but she resisted the urge.

They'd texted sporadically over the past few days, with Sydney sending a few photos from her day-to-day life. A shot of the outside of the house in Florida. Her favorite orange tree in the backyard, which wouldn't bear fruit until later in the season. One of her lounging by their pool, which was maybe meant to make Reese miss her. Sydney's legs were on display in the photo, her toes dipping into the pristine blue water.

She hadn't expected how, even surrounded by a gorgeous view, she was still thinking about Stoneport, with its rocky shores and lush foliage, less muggy than the heat that permeated her neighborhood now.

"We may need to take a trip back to Stoneport soon," her mom mused, still stirring. "I'm curious about the changes the new owner has made to the inn. Have you met them?"

Sydney had never been a good liar, especially with her mom. Her skin prickled; that feeling like she was being led into a trap was back in full force.

But she also hadn't planned for her parents coming back for an impromptu visit.

"So... small world," she said, her breath catching in her throat. "Reese Devereux, Grant's older sister, bought the property." There. She'd said it, and the world hadn't fallen down around her. She was making too much out of nothing, and hopefully they could leave it there.

Her mom turned around. She clocked Sydney with obvious interest, mingled with a hint of disapproval that made Sydney's breathing pick up.

"And were you two... friendly, when you and Grant were together? That must be a strange situation for you," her mom hedged.

"I'd only met her a few times before now. She lived in California until she purchased the inn."

"Isn't that what the Devereux family does, owns hotels? Is Reese—Is that her name?—not working with them?"

Sydney shook her head forcefully, feeling the need to defend Reese. "No, they have nothing to do with it. Reese isn't exactly close with them."

Her mom lifted an eyebrow. "You know, I heard the most interesting thing the other week."

Now Sydney's stomach really did bottom out as she looked at her mom with confusion, wondering what would come next. "And what's that?"

"Your cousin Cade has been doing some work this summer. He got a catering job." Which didn't clarify the situation at all, but Sydney knew her mom had a point. She *always* had a point.

Sydney stayed the path, giving nothing away. "Good for him. He's going to college in the fall, right?"

Her mom was the oldest of four sisters, who all lived within an hour's drive of Stoneport. Sydney, content to wallow upon her arrival back in town, hadn't sought any of them out. Her aunt Beth, her mom's youngest sister, was Cade's mom, so he was a good decade younger than Sydney. She hadn't seen him in at least five years at this point. Didn't know if she'd recognize him if she did.

"He is," her mom said, beaming a smile before adding, offhandedly, "but he told Beth the most interesting thing a few weeks ago."

Sydney's body went cold as she started to connect the dots. Her mom, with incredible forethought, had been circling around her for the last twenty minutes, moving in closer and closer until Sydney was a sitting duck. It would have been impressive, honestly, if Sydney didn't feel like she was going to have a nervous breakdown. "Hmmm," she answered, not trusting her own words and, more importantly, refusing to participate in her own execution.

"He could have sworn he saw you at a party at the Devereux house, at some type of party to celebrate Grant's upcoming wedding." Her mom gave her a look that said, 'Can you believe that?'

"Crazy." Sydney felt like she couldn't catch her breath. Why was it so hot in here?

"But I told Beth that he must be mistaken. I mean, what would my daughter want at a party to celebrate her ex-boyfriend's impending marriage?" Her mom said the words so casually, in the way she'd always done when she wanted Sydney to admit something. The reality was, she knew that her mom already knew the answer.

"He should have said hi then, if he really thought it was me." Heat was rolling off Sydney now, like she was moving closer to the point of combustion.

Rachel clicked her tongue. "Well, you know, that's the thing. He said you looked pretty cozy with a woman there, and he didn't want to interrupt."

Sydney's stomach bottomed out, but her mom pressed on. "So now I'm thinking maybe that woman was Reese Devereux? I never had the pleasure of meeting her, so I wouldn't be able to know for certain."

"Interesting," was all that Sydney could come up with, the next in her line of one-word statements. Any lies or hedging were gone from her vocabulary with the irrefutable look her mom was leveling in her direction.

"Isn't it?" Rachel's voice was chipper as she busied herself cleaning off the island and placing the cutting board she'd used in the kitchen sink. "So then my daughter shows up here with a spring in her step but is surprisingly unforthcoming about the reasons for it. So I think to myself, it's been over a year since she and Grant split. Dating someone else wouldn't be strange. I'd be excited for her, that she's finding someone else to spend her time with, who will treat her the way she deserves."

"That is a good thing to want for your only child, whom you love dearly," Sydney agreed quickly, wishing she could melt into a puddle and escape onto the floor.

Regardless of how this conversation went, she was *not* admitting to her mom the harebrained scheme that she'd gotten herself into. Not in a million years. It was worse than any zany plan she and Hallie had dreamt up in childhood by a wide mile. She'd just spent minutes trying to convince her mom that she was doing okay, and confessing to her what she'd done would not give her mom confidence in her mental state.

But then her mom's stare softened, and she looked at Sydney like she could see all of her secrets, and, somehow, they only made her mom love her more. Unconditional support was the thing that had kept her grounded this past year, even if she'd eschewed her parents' well-meaning attempts to get her to open up, but now...

God, she was such a pushover.

"I'm dating Reese Devereux," she breathed out before she could stop herself. "It's new, but that's why Cade would have seen me at the party."

Her mom was nodding along, taking in Sydney's words with the utmost seriousness. She smiled softly, giving Sydney the space to continue.

"So, yeah. I don't know what else to say other than that. I didn't exactly go looking for her, but here we are," Sydney finished, looking up to meet her mom's stare again.

"And you like her? This isn't some type of strange transference thing because of Grant?"

Sydney grimaced at the idea. "No, I promise it's not. I really like her, Mom," she admitted bashfully, saying the words out loud for the first time, feeling the truth in them as they slipped off her tongue.

"Then I'm happy for you." After a reassuring smile, her mom turned back around and picked up the two bowls set next to the stove. "I'll get us some gumbo, and you can tell me all about it."

*　*　*

Sydney was just about to start her car when her phone vibrated from the passenger seat. She picked it up, smiling instinctively as she clocked the name on her screen.

REESE DEVEREUX - 11:43 A.M.

> You're meeting with your agent today, right?
> Good luck!

It wasn't surprising that Reese remembered that Sydney had mentioned her upcoming meeting. Sydney had told her Friday morning, when she'd arrived back in Florida safely, what her week was looking like so far.

They'd been texting more frequently as the days wore on, but it seemed like they'd both decided to stick to safe topics, like they'd tacitly agreed that whatever was happening between them deserved an in-person conversation and not confusing and fragmented texts between their—or, more realistically, Reese's— busy schedules.

So no, she hadn't told Reese how excited she was to see her again. No proclamations. No digging into her conversation with her mom and how she'd basically admitted how much she liked Reese. That was staying in the vault for the time being.

She was instead being casual. Cool, calm, and collected. Which maybe you could say was true about her on the tennis court, but her current personal life was another matter entirely.

Reese had burrowed inside her mind and wouldn't leave, and Sydney was counting down the days until she'd be back in Stoneport and they could pick up where they'd left off.

SYDNEY - 11:44 A.M.

Sure am :) We'll see what Sara has to say
about my life after professional tennis

REESE DEVEREUX - 11:44 A.M.

I'm sure it will be a good conversation. Great
at least to catch up with her.

SYDNEY - 11:45 A.M.

Fingers crossed! Heading there now

Sydney put her phone back on her seat and eased out of her driveway, heading toward the highway to Miami, where Sara Santiago's office was located.

It was a dreary Tuesday afternoon, the air so thick she could take a bite out of it. She cranked up the air conditioner and, for the first time in weeks, put on her pre-match playlist to get herself centered.

There was a storm predicted to make landfall later in the week, though she crossed her fingers that it would calm into little more than rain once it crossed east to west over the state.

With time on her hands on her almost hour-long drive down to Miami, and with thousands of other cars that seemed unencumbered by the impending storm, she took their cue and acted like this was any other day.

On any other day, at least for the last few weeks, she'd be pitching back and forth like a swaying palm tree, between thinking about her future and wondering what Reese Devereux was thinking about. Especially since their kiss. Double especially since she'd word-vomited to her mom yesterday. It had made everything feel more blindingly real, vocalizing it to someone on her side for the first time who didn't know about the ruse.

She'd told her mom the truth, at least as much as she could. Besides the nature of their real meeting, which *was* technically a meet-cute, with Reese accidentally walking in on Sydney half naked to give her towels, and the fact that Sydney had wanted to understand why Grant had done what he'd done, she'd tried to be as honest as possible.

So they hadn't actually met at the Paribas Open in California. That didn't change the truth of what she did tell her mom: that every moment she spent with Reese, she felt alight and free, like she was filled with possibility for the first time in months.

And even though it had started because of Grant, all Sydney could think about was how impressed she was with *Reese*. It was honestly insane to consider that she'd spent so many years focusing on the wrong Devereux.

In the early years of her relationship with Grant, she'd been charmed by him. She'd appreciated his confidence, that he seemed committed to taking on the reins of The Devereux Group and was willing to work to make that happen. She adored that even if it meant they needed to be separated—*hah!*—they shared common traits; namely, persistence and dedication to the things that were important to them.

Not that she had the siblings to look at in juxtaposition to one another, but with fresh eyes and a mending sense of confidence in herself, Sydney was realizing Grant didn't hold a candle to his older sister any way she sliced, diced, or minced it.

Reese was unstoppable, a force to be reckoned with, and it made Sydney like her all the more for it. Tackling ownership of the inn. Coming back to Stoneport in spite of her messy familial relationships. Pushing past Megan's betrayal.

When she and Grant had split, at least she'd had tennis to throw herself into. Reese, after Megan turned her back on their relationship, didn't even have her company any longer.

Reese was friendly but intensely private, and Sydney felt that she had somehow lucked into the chance of a lifetime, getting to know more about her. She didn't want it to stop, and as she meandered along with the always persistent traffic on I-95, her thoughts wandered.

Not to what had already happened, but to what *could* happen. To hypotheticals and wishful thinking and… daydreams…

that had started taking up residence in Sydney's mind more often than she'd admitted to herself since whatever was happening between them had started.

Sydney's past life hadn't had much time for daydreams. For what-ifs. In fact, thinking that way was antithetical and incongruent to achieving her goals. She didn't *wonder*. She manifested. She planned. She focused.

And now? Nothing about her future was a sure thing, and she was finding that she didn't really mind, especially as curiosity bloomed wild in her mind's eye, morphing into a million different questions she wanted to ask Reese when given the chance.

Did Reese like to sleep in late if given the choice?

What genre did she like to read? And would she laugh or gasp while sitting on the sofa, feet tucked underneath her, as something surprising happened in her book?

How did she like to be touched? Would Sydney's fingers ghost along Reese's body to pull her higher and higher, or would Reese reverse the roles, Sydney pinned underneath her as she made Sydney squirm with want?

For the first time in years, she wanted to know the answers to all of these questions. These *possibilities*.

She didn't care how it had started—as a chance to allay her own confusion, to see what she'd missed in her years with Grant and whether she should have suspected his infidelity—because Sydney was here now.

And she never missed a good shot when it dropped in front of her.

* * *

"Good to see you, Sydney. Give me just a second." Sara Santiago's assistant let Sydney into her almost entirely white office as Sara sat behind her desk, typing quickly on her laptop.

Sara's black hair was cropped short, and she wore a white pantsuit that made her blend in with the office decor. Her look was juxtaposed with a splash of color from her cherry-red shirt that perfectly matched her lipstick.

"You, too." And really, Sydney meant it. She'd always felt like Sara was in her corner. Realistic when needed. Shrewd when warranted. But always an advocate for Sydney's career.

As she waited for Sara to finish up, she scanned the curved window that made up most of the office, providing a panoramic view of the city below and of Biscayne Bay. Her skin prickled, and she wrapped the light jacket she'd brought in more tightly around her. Sara was notorious for the temperature of her office. She'd probably add an igloo if she could get away with it.

Sara shut her laptop and rocked back in her chair, studying Sydney. "You look good, King. Seems like your R&R's been having the desired effect?"

Sydney nodded as she eased into the chair on the opposite side of the desk. "I'd like to think so."

She watched as Sara's lips tipped into a smile. "So, tell me, what's new?"

"I've been up in Stoneport, my hometown, for the past few weeks. I've been playing casually at the tennis center I used to train at. I've been living in a hotel for the longest period to date, which I never thought would happen *after* retirement."

"That dreaded word: retirement. I wondered if you'd use it." Sara continued to study her, likely looking for any sign that she wasn't as okay as she seemed. In another life, she would have made one hell of a psychologist.

Sydney placed her palms down on her jogger-clad thighs and flexed her leg out straight. "I'd like to think of myself as a realist. Especially these days."

"Well then, realistically, how are you thinking about your future? Facets of your career don't need to stop just because you're not playing professional tennis anymore."

Sitting up straighter, Sydney tried to imagine what that meant. None of her prior brands had wanted to continue their relationship; they'd signed the termination paperwork weeks ago on those endorsement deals when her retirement had been finalized. It was hard to sell a racket or a nutritional supplement when she wasn't playing at the competitive level.

Still, her curiosity was piqued. "I assume you want me to ask what exactly those facets are?"

Sydney had enough money for a very comfortable life at this point, even if she never lifted a finger again, but sitting back and lounging all day wasn't ever going to make her truly happy. It was hard to envision a world where she didn't have a purpose, something that made her excited to get up every morning.

"I got an interesting call last week, from The Tennis Network." Sara paused, letting her words hang between them. "They wanted to discuss the possibility of you coming on board as a commentator."

A flood of excitement rushed through Sydney, though it was battling fiercely with other less positive emotions. "Is there a formal offer? Or are we just discussing hypotheticals and gauging interest?"

"I don't know if you've been keeping up with the news, but they've had some scandal recently," Sara said, lowering her voice even though they were alone. She was a professional through and through. "Dan Cody."

Sydney already had an idea where this was going. Cody was a player turned coach turned commentator who was a veritable energy generator for the rumor mill when it came to inappropriate relationships with the young female players whose careers he'd been helping to mold. It was a disgusting abuse of power, and more common than it should have been.

"So it's true then? About his relationships with players?" Sydney asked, a sickly feeling settling in the pit of her stomach. She couldn't imagine, at fifteen or sixteen, having someone she trusted with her life—someone like Brian, who'd been a father figure to her—abuse that power.

"Unfortunately." Sara's voice was laced with contempt, and it seemed like this was neither of the women's first point of exposure to the seedy underbelly of the tennis world. "Nothing can be done legally at this point, but he's out, and the network has deemed him persona non grata."

"Well, that's good at least."

"It's a small step in the right direction, though whether the network has always known remains to be seen."

Sydney had met Cody a few times at tournaments and social events over the years. She'd always gotten the feeling that he was smarmy, with his too-charming smile and offers to discuss her career and give her 'pointers.' Gross. She'd always stayed as far away from him as possible.

Good riddance. "So out with the old—"

"And in with the *you*, if you're interested," Sara said before adding, "There are three US-based tournaments coming up in the next few months. They'd like to try you out as a guest commentator in D.C. and Cleveland, and if all goes well, debut you on a wider scale at the US Open in September. Depending on the feedback as well as your ongoing interest, they'd make a formal offer to join the commentary team for next season."

Sydney let out a whoosh of air. Commentating and coaching were both possible trajectories she'd considered, but until a few weeks ago, it had felt like she was treading water, trying to make it day to day.

"It's a great offer, in my opinion. They love that you've been so recently in the mix, and you have an insider's perspective on the current landscape."

Sydney stood up and walked over to the window, staring out at the city and bay below. "When do you need an answer?"

"By the end of the week. I wanted to discuss the offer in person, but they need to get you prepped if you want to move forward. D.C. is coming up in less than three weeks." She noted the surprise in Sara's voice, that she wasn't jumping all over the offer.

And, really, it was strange that she wasn't. This was a dream job, dropped directly onto Sydney's lap. A true silver lining, happening because of her injury and at the hands of a predator being exposed in the industry.

But she'd never done a great job, she was realizing, at balancing her professional and personal lives. She thought she'd have more time to ease into something that felt right. That she'd have more time with Reese, to see what was blossoming between them, and she wanted to be there for Hallie, as she navigated this transitional period in her life. Let alone whatever was going on with her mom, which she still hadn't pinned down.

She took one little year off from being an active participant in her own life, and now, it had come calling, rife with people and decisions and, for the first time in a long time, the need to chart her own path forward.

Her life was back in full swing, whether she felt ready for it or not. She unzipped her jacket, ready to do battle with the Miami heat. "I'll let you know by Sunday."

Fourteen

REESE FELT like she had walked into the lion's den. If the lion was an almost six-foot-tall blonde who looked perfectly sun-kissed as she stepped into the inn lobby, wearing a bright purple romper that draped expertly across her body.

Awareness thrummed through Reese's veins at the sight of her, and she tamped down her visceral reaction as best she could. Reese wasn't usually someone who let her emotions, especially ones like these, get the best of her.

But Sydney looked beautiful. And when she leveled a smile in Reese's direction, Reese truly, *finally*, understood what it meant when someone's knees went weak.

"I'm sorry I'm running a few minutes late." Sydney smiled apologetically, running a hand through her hair.

"Ah yes, the couple's brunch," Hallie said knowingly, though what she knew wasn't clear to Reese.

Sydney shot her a look, though what it conveyed, Reese couldn't be sure. "Yes, bestie. The brunch you said you'd make sure I was up for when I texted you last night."

"Actually, you texted me *this morning*. And I *tried* to wake you up. Three times," Hallie emphasized before turning her attention to Reese, who'd been standing next to the check-in desk watching their back-and-forth. "Apparently, our girl had a hellish time getting back from Florida last night."

Reese leaned closer, looking for any sign of weariness on Sydney's face, but she looked flawless as ever. Still, Reese allowed herself a few indulgent seconds of just *looking* at Sydney before she asked, "What happened?"

"Well, first I tried—"

Sydney held her hand up. "Hallie, I'm pretty sure she was talking to me."

"Regardless, I thought my rendition of 'The Star-Spangled Banner' was pretty good." Hallie paused, sighing dramatically. "I guess it wasn't enough to get you to rise, though," she said as a broad smirk covered her face.

Sydney's own smile broadened. "There was something wrong with our plane. We boarded and then deplaned and then had to wait hours to find another one to fly out. My seven o'clock flight finally left around two a.m."

Her voice was casual and light as she described her travel woes. If the shoe was on the other foot, Reese would have still been a puddle of anxiety, recovering in bed.

Hallie nodded solemnly. "I think I heard her pour herself into bed around six a.m."

"At least there wasn't traffic getting out of the city," Sydney said earnestly.

Reese glanced at her watch, which showed it was about thirty minutes before eleven. She'd survived on as much sleep as Sydney had gotten last night, but she didn't wish it on anyone. She turned her attention to Sydney, who, when she'd thought that Reese wasn't looking, was shooting daggers at her best friend.

"Sydney, I could have gone without you. Seriously, it's not that big of a deal," Reese said, knowing that she could have survived without her for the day, though she'd absolutely have missed having Sydney at her side.

"I want to go." It was the softness of Sydney's words, along with the faint blush on her cheeks, that made Reese light up from the inside out.

It meant something—that Sydney had shown up, even when it wasn't easy. Reese didn't feel like a lot of people in her life did that for her, especially not if it was an inconvenience to them.

Reese looked down at her watch again. "All right. The sooner we arrive, the sooner we can leave." She shot Sydney a joking smile, hoping to convey that she didn't expect the day to be that awful. Who could be sure, though, when her family was around?

Hallie walked them to the door and waved them off, as she liked to do, before they slipped into Reese's car and started the short journey to Reese's parents' house.

Since their kiss and Reese's confession of how her last relationship had ended, they hadn't done a whole lot of talking about where they stood, even though things between them were getting more complicated. She'd missed Sydney while she'd been away in Florida, but their texting had been restrained to little updates and check-ins and, on Reese's side, a few anecdotes about Grant's idiocy.

Which meant that, unfortunately, their seeming goal of keeping things simpler had left Reese with a lot of blank space that she'd taken to filling in herself, whether accurate or not.

Even now, with the two of them alone for the first time in a week, neither seemed determined to push the conversation forward. The radio provided the only sound as they wound toward their destination.

Still, Reese couldn't stop *thinking* about what everything may mean, even if she couldn't quite voice her thoughts yet. She'd tried not to read too much into it when Sydney had sent back an entire row of emojis when she'd told—what she thought—was a great story relayed by her mom involving Grant forgetting their cake-tasting appointment last week and, after finally arriving fifty minutes late, scarfed down six types of cake within ten minutes. Which, because he hadn't looked at the options that Brynn had sent him beforehand, sent him into a mild allergic reaction to pistachios. He'd broken out in a vibrant, red rash across his neck and hands that Reese wondered if she'd get to see today.

She'd then gone on to replay how Brynn, in a panic, had called Sharon, who'd promptly informed her that, yes, Grant was aware of his allergy and had likely not looked at the list she'd sent him for consideration.

An unexpected boon for her was that now that she and her mom were on better terms, she was being given an inside look at Grant's day-to-day, which was... not great.

Reese flip-flopped between being embarrassed for Grant and distressed for Brynn, who, against all reason, seemed committed to moving forward with their impending nuptials.

Over the last few weeks, her anger at Grant had slowly started to dissipate, and it almost felt like punching down to try and interfere with his life, considering the job he did all on his own. He wasn't a great person by any stretch of the imagination, but her true ire, she could now acknowledge, was directed at her father.

On some level, she'd always known that. Only, she'd tucked it deep into a corner of her mind that she'd compartmentalized and pretended hadn't affected her, hadn't shaped her into the person she'd become. The difference, now, was that she was accepting how that bud of rejection had grown and festered and ensnared its tendrils into every facet of her life. That she wasn't the person she'd become in spite of it, but because of it.

Not that she was giving her father any credit for her success, if that's how financial freedom at the cost of personal relationships, family, and trust in herself and others could be defined. All it really meant was that she probably needed a lot of therapy.

Or, at the very least, to stop letting someone else's measure of her worthiness define her.

So she'd been thinking about that, too. How it had been easier to assume that her mom wasn't in her corner because it felt like a rejection every time she didn't stand up for Reese. The reality was that her father had never included her mom in business-related endeavors, and any insistence at Reese's inclusion would have fallen on deaf ears. In her own way, her mom had tried, but Reese hadn't been willing to see it.

Her mom had encouraged her to follow her passions. Every year, there was at least a box of items to be donated from whatever hobby or pursuit Reese had taken an interest in, and as she thought about it, her mom had always known about whatever she was learning in school, asking Reese thoughtful questions and making sure she had what she needed. A microscope from her stint as an amateur scientist. A telescope when Reese had developed an interest in astronomy. An abundance of specialized kitchen accessories from a short-lived dream to become a baker, the desire to name her future bakery Reese's Pieces a bigger draw than her actual interest in the complexities of recipes.

The reality of the situation was that it was Reese who hadn't wanted to have a relationship with her mom, not the other way around. Her single-mindedness and awe of her father had created a tunnel vision that made everything else seem like... less.

And it had meant, with a realization that had settled deep in her bones as she and her mom had shared a coffee earlier this week, that she'd become a lot more like her father than she wanted to admit, given how he treated others.

She'd held so tightly on to this idea that she could prove him wrong that all the best parts of her had crumbled in her hands.

She didn't want to be that person anymore.

But wanting something and doing it were orders of magnitude apart.

Because, she thought, as she snuck a glance at the woman next to her, who stared out at the passing homes, set back from the street in the way that only money could buy in a small town with so much coastal space, honesty and vulnerability seemed more difficult to achieve than any professional success she'd ever managed. She and Sydney had been thrown together by their mutual disdain for her brother, but now, they were in a place she'd never expected.

And that *scared* her.

After everything she'd learned about herself in the last few weeks, what else was lurking under the surface?

Sydney had been honest in her attraction, which was tingle-inducing to Reese, in the best possible way. It also meant that Sydney knew what she wanted.

But what did Reese want?

She cleared her throat as they rounded the corner, coming onto her parents' street. "I really appreciate this. You could have told me what a hellish time you had getting back from Florida. I hope you know that I'd have understood if you didn't come," she added, pushing down the disappointment she knew she'd have felt if she didn't get to see Sydney.

Because she wanted... she *wanted*.

"I wanted to see you," Sydney said, echoing the words that had flitted through Reese's mind seconds before.

Yes. She'd wanted to see Sydney. Not for their ruse. Not to put on a show for anyone. Sydney made her feel comfortable, like a version of herself that she was quite liking getting to know. Seen. It staggered her that, amidst the absolute chaos that was spending time with Reese's family, there was nowhere else Sydney would rather be than by Reese's side.

"I know we left things..."

"In your court?" Sydney supplied, though she didn't sound much like she minded. In fact, she seemed wildly at ease, relaxed against the passenger's seat, staring out the window.

Reese blushed, feeling the heat flood across her cheeks. "I've had a week to think about us. About you," she admitted.

Thoughts of Sydney had swirled around in her brain whenever she had a second to stop and think, and she didn't really know if there was anything to do about that anymore.

"And?"

She could feel Sydney's eyes on her as she stopped in front of the house, where cars were already lined almost completely around the semicircular driveway.

They were consenting adults who happened to be attracted to one another. They weren't doing anything wrong by acknowledging that. Sydney had already admitted as much, and now, it was Reese's turn.

Her focus dropped down to Sydney's lips, full and pursed ever so gently as she waited for an answer. She wasn't pushing, more so giving Reese the space to acknowledge whatever she was feeling in her own time.

It was the little rush of heat that slithered through her coupled with the strangest sense of feeling grounded and safe that made her lean in close, lips inches away from Sydney's when she said, "I was really hoping I could kiss you again."

So they had things to talk about. And Reese wasn't sure where all of this could lead.

But it felt *good,* in a way that nothing had in a long time, and it was that thought that pulled her closer, Sydney's breath ghosting across her lips, Sydney's own lips soft and close and begging to be covered.

The knock on the window shocked them both apart, and Reese took a long, steadying breath before she rolled down her window.

"Ma'am, I'll be happy to park your car," the valet said, single-minded in his job, oblivious to the way Reese clenched her fists to stop herself from strangling him. "We'd like to keep the flow of traffic moving as guests arrive."

She felt the steadying hand that Sydney placed on her thigh at the same time she heard Sydney's car door open.

"Don't shoot the messenger," Sydney whispered, a shiver running down Reese's spine at their closeness.

With another calming exhale, Reese pasted on a smile and exited the car, the moment broken.

* * *

Reese watched in awe as Sydney effortlessly worked the crowd. Hands were shaken. Air kisses were given. Laughter happened at the perfect moments, Sydney's eyes shining as she shot Reese a coy smile.

And Reese, like everyone else, was lapping it up.

This woman, who held any crowd in the palm of her hand, had very recently had those same hands on Reese's thigh, fingertips ghosting against the hem of her dress before they'd been interrupted.

It was heady, and Reese basked in her attraction as she observed Sydney, wondering where this thing between them would lead.

She was so lost in her own thoughts and fantasies that she didn't notice Brynn until she was at Reese's side. "It's so good to see you, Reese."

Brynn placed a tentative hand on Reese's forearm, and it wasn't without significant effort that she pulled her focus away from where Sydney was still holding court, regaling a small group of her father's business associates with a story about last year's French Open.

"You too," Reese said when she remembered her manners, stepping a few feet away from Sydney's admirers to have a private conversation with Brynn. This woman was the guest of honor, to be fair. She'd never give Grant the same respect, but Brynn had been nothing but sweet since they'd met, almost like a shy puppy that just wanted Reese's approval. And even if that felt *weird*, she didn't want to make Brynn feel like it was. It wasn't her future sister-in-law's fault that she had terrible taste in men, whether she knew it or not.

"Are you enjoying yourself?" Reese asked, finally giving Brynn her full attention. "Great party, by the way."

Brynn blushed. "Thanks. Our parents planned it, so I'm experiencing it all for the first time, too."

Like the engagement party, waiters roamed through the crowd dressed in all black, carrying trays of various brunch-related foods with an upscale twist. Smoked salmon crostinis with crème fraîche, smoked trout croquettes, figs with bacon and chile, and mini, messy cinnamon rolls with icing dripping down the edges that smelled divine.

Reese's brow lifted upward as she saw that one pass for the first time, her fingers already feeling sticky.

Brynn tracked Reese's gaze. "My dad insisted on those. He's also, unsurprisingly, responsible for the brunch theme."

Reese had wondered from where the 'Love You a Brunch' theme had materialized, given it wasn't her mom's style. She'd assumed it had been Margie's dream child, but when she really thought about it, Stan made a lot more sense.

"He always seems to be a man with a plan," Reese said before wondering, as she looked out at the bustling, well-oiled party, "And what, pray tell, did my father contribute to today's festivities?"

It wasn't fair, she realized, to put Brynn in this position. Her shoulders rounded inward, and her gaze flicked to the gold accent balloons arranged expertly to create an arch into the backyard, which was immaculately decorated in shades of rose gold.

"I think he offered up your family's home," Brynn answered honestly, a small quaver in her voice. This was surprising, considering this wasn't a party for Reese, and therefore, there was nothing for her to be disappointed about except that her father continued to be exactly the person she'd started accepting him as.

"Couldn't even spring to rent a Chili's?" Reese said more sardonically than she should have.

"Oh my god." Brynn giggled. "Now *my* dad would have loved that. He always said that you can have all the money in the world, but the things you thought were fancy as a kid will never truly change."

They shared a look, and Reese smiled as the soft beat passed between them. "I really like your dad. Your mom, too."

"Thanks, I think they're pretty great," Brynn said, genuine affection infusing her voice.

"Are you having fun?" Reese looked around, wondering where Grant was, not that she was even a little torn up about not having to deal with him at the moment.

"I swear I've met half of New England in the past few months," Brynn said as she let out a deep sigh. "It's been great, but it's a lot for me. I'm not exactly a people person."

Reese bumped their shoulders together, surprised at the little surge of protectiveness she felt. "Well, I'm a person, and you're doing great with me."

"You and Sydney are really easy to talk to."

"I'm going to give most of the credit to her," Reese said as her eyes flitted to Sydney, who was standing a few feet away.

When Sydney felt her stare and lifted her eyes to lock with hers, Reese felt it through her whole body. The feeling pulsed and buzzed and gave her a better high than any glass of champagne ever could—not that she hadn't already had one of those since arriving. An empty flute was now balanced between her fingers.

She let the feeling warm her from the inside out, indulgent and so not how she'd ever behaved. Sydney's eyes mapped her, those perfectly plump lips tipping into a knowing smile.

It was like she could feel Sydney's hand on her thigh again, inching it up in her mind, wondering what would have happened if they hadn't been interrupted. How soft Sydney's lips had looked, like they were made to be kissed.

Reese was wrapped up in the moment. Was Brynn still next to her? Unclear. What time was it? None of her business. Was her sycophantic father prowling about? She couldn't have cared less.

She was so completely trained on Sydney's face, on the line of her jaw and the colors in her cheeks, that Reese failed to notice what was happening around them. It was too late when she put all the pieces together; the scene playing out in slow motion.

Brynn was standing up straighter next to her. The waiter had moved into the periphery of Sydney's group to offer champagne refills. And finally, stumbling into Reese's view as she tore her stare away from Sydney...

...was Grant. The antithesis of nimble as he stumbled into the waiter. Time sped up, and it felt like everything was happening at once.

The champagne flutes were airborne for the briefest of seconds; then they shattered on the ground at the same time a dark purple stain spread outward from the side of Sydney's romper, like blood pooling after a gunshot. Sydney had made the mistake of being more aware of herself in the moments leading up to this disaster, and she'd turned her body briefly, her frame becoming a perfect target for the wasted champagne.

Reese was at her side in a second, the waiter already looking apologetic and trying to do damage control.

"I'm so sorry, miss. Truly," he said, offering the cloth on his arm to Sydney, who was already plucking the soaked material away from her skin. "Give me just a moment, and I'll be back to clean everything up."

He scurried away through the crowd as a few heads turned in their direction.

"Are you okay?" Reese's hand was already gentled against her back as she looked at Sydney for any signs she'd been cut with a stray piece from the broken flutes.

Reese held her hand out, which Sydney accepted as she stepped away from the pile of broken glass littering the stone patio. "Surprised more than anything else."

"But you're good?" Reese asked quickly, already onto her new most pressing matter, now that she'd realized Sydney was safe.

Sydney gave Reese's hand a squeeze, her eyes uncertain as she saw the look on her face. "I'm good. I'm going to head inside and clean up."

"You should go upstairs. Third door on the right. There's an en suite in that bathroom." She hadn't lived in this house in fifteen years, but she had no doubts that her mother kept every room meticulously maintained and stocked.

Reese disengaged their hands, though not before she ran her

fingers across Sydney's knuckles, their softness doing little to abate the fury rising inside of her. "I'll be up in a few minutes."

Seconds ago, the world had felt soft and hazy. Now it was sharp. Angry. *She* was angry.

Until this moment, with fire running through her veins, neither she nor Sydney had looked at Grant. Before he'd careened into the waiter, she hadn't even noticed him skulking about.

They'd been at the party for a little over an hour at this point, and except for seeing him on the sidelines of the heartfelt speech that Margie and Stan had given on behalf of the parents, she hadn't engaged with him. Thankfully.

But now, as she studied him more closely and tried to focus her rage, she could see the wrinkles in his half-untucked shirt, which had been obscured by his sportcoat until he started to turn around. His eyes were glassy but bloodshot, and he had a small stain on the knee of his khaki pants.

"You're drunk," Reese hissed. She stepped closer to him, separating him from the group he was trying to join.

Brynn stood behind Reese, more than willing to stay out of the fray. Reese couldn't blame her, but in her not-expert opinion on matrimony, it seemed like a bad start to things if the bride-to-be was already cowering in embarrassment.

"It's my couple's shower, Reese," Grant said with an exaggerated flick of his hand at the dozens of people milling about, though the party was thankfully large enough that only those in their immediate proximity knew anything had happened. Like good members of the upper crust, they were probably all still listening but had the courtesy of looking away to give the siblings the illusion of privacy.

"Don't you just *love it a brunch*?" Grant asked, the sarcasm dripping from his tone like venom, and Reese just... couldn't understand.

"Grant, this party is for you. Planned by your families. For a wedding that you wanted to have, after you asked Brynn to marry you." *After you betrayed Sydney, a woman you never deserved anyway, to live this life*, she added silently.

Nothing about it made sense.

Reese lowered her voice, realizing that Grant was even more drunk than she'd first thought. "Why are you acting like this?"

"Like you care," Grant scoffed. "The better child has returned to claim her rightful place. You already took my girlfriend. Coming after my job next?" The line would have been more impactful if Grant hadn't hiccuped, causing any viciousness he'd been going for to be cut off at the knees.

But even if Reese was calming down, now that Sydney was safely upstairs and Grant seemed willing to stand still for the moment, he was still so off base that it was hard to believe he wasn't minutes from passing out.

"You know our father has no interest in me joining the company. And I have no interest in joining it either." At first, she'd said the words to placate him, but it wasn't until she'd said them out loud that she knew it was the truth. As they rolled off her tongue and into the world, she felt them in her bones with staggering clarity.

There was nothing gained and everything lost by ever accepting a place with her family's business. Her sanity, for one, if Grant was any indication of what became of a Devereux child who followed in her father's footsteps. And, more importantly, her integrity, judging by how both Grant and her father had been behaving since she'd been back in town.

Grant scoffed again, like he couldn't believe it, his features pinching up in such an ugly way that Reese almost laughed.

But then she caught Brynn out of the corner of her eye, looking like she was going to burst into tears at any second. A part of her wanted to believe that Brynn had known what she was getting into, marrying Grant, but as the days wore on, it honestly seemed like that wasn't the case.

Which meant that, instead of tearing into Grant like she'd wanted to, she guided him by the arm, surprisingly compliant after his last outburst, over to a beverage station. She poured a glass of fresh cucumber water from the carafe set atop the table, waving a bartender off in the process.

"I've got this," Reese mouthed quietly across the few feet of space where Brynn looked adrift, breathing deeply to keep the tears at bay. She waited another beat, her attention focused on Brynn, until she saw her meander into the crowd.

She turned her attention back to her brother. "Drink this. Sober up. Get it together." She handed him the glass, which he immediately gulped down. "I have no idea what's going on with you, but you're at a party to celebrate your wedding, for god's sake. No one's forcing you to be here, so stop acting like it."

"Perfect Reese. Always doing the right thing," Grant said mockingly as he set his glass back on the table.

"What the fuck, Grant? I'm helping you, and you're still being an asshole. I don't know what you want me to say right now. Do you want me to leave you to keep embarrassing yourself? I'm sure that would go over well with Dad and all of his business associates. I'm sure it would go over even better with Stan and Margie, whose daughter you're marrying. Dad seems so far up Stan's ass that you, *the actual prodigal child*, may even suffer some consequences for once in your life if you don't stop acting like this right now."

Grant tried to speak, but Reese held her hand up, words already bubbling up in her throat. She was on a roll now, unable to stop herself. The picture of the last few weeks was coming together in startling clarity. "And Brynn. You know, your *fiancée*. The woman you proposed to, though you're acting like she's more of an inconvenience than anything else. You're more intent on talking about Sydney and refusing to accept that you fucked up and threw her away than on being embarrassed at what you're putting Brynn through. She looked like she was about to cry just now, and you couldn't give a shit if someone had pumped you full of laxatives."

Grant stared at her, slack-jawed, and Reese wondered if he was absorbing anything she was saying. Probably not, but it still felt good to voice these opinions. Really good.

Which was why she had one last piece to stay before she attended to more important things. "I'm going to give you the benefit of the doubt that spilling a drink all over Sydney was an accident, but I'm honestly still on the fence about it. I'd say it's too convenient, but I don't think you're sober enough right now to string a multistep plan together."

"Are you calling me stupid?" Grant finally responded, missing her point by a mile. God, he really was so fucking self-involved that it made Reese want to scream.

"Best-case scenario, I'm calling you drunk and a poor planner," she said decisively before adding, "Now, I have a girlfriend to attend to, and I'd encourage you to go see if Brynn is okay."

The dimness in Grant's eyes lit up, and especially in his drunken state, Reese knew that he wouldn't be able to stop himself from making a dig about her and Sydney. Whatever their plan had started as, it was clear that the idea of her and Sydney rankled Grant on a level even she couldn't have anticipated. Hard to imagine, considering he was the one who'd cheated.

Instead of waiting for whatever embarrassing—to him— comment he'd likely make, she moved the few feet back to the bartender. "He's cut off, and if it doesn't happen, it will be everyone's problem, especially yours. Got it?"

The bartender nodded at the same time he gulped, and Reese poured another cup of water from the carafe before she walked back over and handed it to her brother. "We're probably leaving. Have a good rest of your party."

And with that, she slipped through the crowd of people whose names she didn't know and whose lives she didn't care about, intent on finding Sydney and making sure that she was okay.

Fifteen

"I'M glad to see you're not worse for the wear." Reese's voice came from behind Sydney, standing in the doorway of what Sydney surmised had to be Reese's childhood bedroom.

Sydney turned around and leveled a smile in Reese's direction. "I'll survive."

It had only taken Sydney about five minutes to dab at the stain as best she could manage. Hopefully, a trip to the dry cleaner would do the rest.

She'd considered texting Reese, but her phone had died somewhere between canapés and shattered champagne flutes. When she'd poured herself into bed this morning, a full battery had been the last thing on her mind.

So while she waited, she'd decided to look around the room. In her defense, anyone would have done the same thing. When you were invited into your fake girlfriend's childhood bedroom, you didn't throw away that chance.

But she also wasn't going to lie about it.

"I feel like you knew that leaving me up here that long would give me more time to snoop," Sydney said with a grin as Reese stepped next to her, their arms brushing.

Sydney's stare was trained on a myriad of trophies and plaques covering most of one of the walls. Model UN. Debate team. Varsity swim team. Mathletes. National Honor Society. National *Business* Honor Society.

"I see you kept yourself busy," Sydney said, ghosting her hands along a plaque honoring Reese for her first-place finish in a Future Business Leaders' competition. "No wonder our paths never crossed in high school."

Reese smiled wryly. "I think that given the amount of time you spent on tennis, that's as much your fault as mine."

"Probably." The room made Sydney think of the one she used to have in Stoneport, with a very similar wall filled with tennis ribbons and trophies from her high school tournaments. She wondered what her mom had done with everything; only a small selection had been transported down to Florida when they'd moved.

Sydney traced her fingers around the edge of the plaque one last time before turning to face Reese. "So, how'd it go down there?"

She studied Reese then, trying to gauge her mood. When Sydney had left, the look in her eyes had been pure ice, directed at Grant. It was terrifying and incredibly sexy, in equal measures.

But now, Reese's stare was softer again, and her lips broke into a broad smile. "Grant is drunk as a skunk, to put it mildly."

The unexpected bark of laughter that pushed out of Sydney made her throw her hand up to her mouth to stifle it. "I'm sorry. That is not what I was expecting you to say."

"God, he is such a mess," Reese said, more like she was trying to figure something out than telling Sydney a fact.

But Sydney had been noticing the same thing. The Grant she'd always known was charming and witty and confident. This version of Grant she'd been confronted with all summer was like the shell of the person she'd known, not that it absolved him of any of the awful things he'd done to her.

"Do you, like, get the sense..." Sydney paused, trying to figure out the right words. "It seems like he doesn't even want to get married."

What Grant had done to her was inexcusable, no matter what the reason, but somehow, it had comforted Sydney that if he was going to do it, it was because Brynn was the love of his life and he couldn't live without her.

"It's like Brynn is just some sort of afterthought to him," Reese considered.

Sydney groaned. "Don't go making me feel badly for the woman my ex cheated on me with."

"I know," Reese lamented, her eyes apologetic. "But she's so sweet. Way too sweet for Grant. Maybe for this world entirely."

Sydney had been around long enough to know that suppressing feelings only worked for so long. "It's the quiet ones you've got to worry about."

Reese lifted a sculpted brow. "Guess that means I don't have to worry about you, at least."

"A magazine once published that the volume of my grunt on the tennis court was more decibels than a jackhammer," Sydney admitted, though she wasn't embarrassed about it. In fact, Hallie had framed the reference and mailed it to Sydney when she'd discovered the article and had barely gone a week in their friendship since without mentioning it.

Reese looked at her for a few contemplative moments before speaking. "Well, was it?"

"Colloquially, it's known as a grunt-o-meter during tournaments, and yes," Sydney added pointedly, "that's a real thing. They measured my sounds and then compared them. It wasn't as loud as fireworks or a gunshot, so I guess I've got that going for me."

Reese reached out to fidget with one of the trophies before straightening it. "Speaking of tennis, we haven't discussed how your trip home was. About the meeting with your agent. Good news, I hope?"

It was the way Reese looked at her then, a soft little furrow in her brow coupled with an endearing smile, that made Sydney herself question what qualified as *good* news.

Staring at Reese, it suddenly didn't feel like such a great opportunity to leave Stoneport for three upcoming tournaments, all in service of ultimately getting a contract next year that could keep her on the road more than she was home.

Home.

She thought of Hallie, a constantly perky ray of sunshine who knew her better than anyone in the world. Who was going through one of the biggest changes in her own life and still always had time and love and support for Sydney.

Her parents, who'd moved to Florida to be with her and who she was sure would be willing to come back to Stoneport if she decided to move back here full-time. Even if they never let her live it down.

And now, Reese. Who'd somehow slipped through the defenses she'd built up over the last year. Who was someone Sydney could see herself falling for. Really, truly falling for.

Would it be worth it to Reese to date someone who was in and out of her life?

That question boiled itself down into the sticky feeling that was lodged in her stomach. Up until now, her life had always been planned years in advance. Now that her plans had fallen apart, she'd been impulsive the last few weeks in a way she never had before.

It had brought her to Stoneport.

It had brought her to *Reese.*

Was she ready to walk away from all of that already?

And for what? A job she may be horrible at? That she may not even get? On top of what she'd be letting go of, could she take that rejection again, so soon?

She had to let Sara know about the announcer position by tomorrow, and refusing to think—seriously think—about her options until now meant that they were all swirling together, at the worst possible moment.

"Sydney?" Reese asked, apprehension in her voice as her smile faltered.

Sydney sighed, willing the confusing thoughts swirling around out of her body on the exhale. "She offered me a job. Or, more accurately, a tryout for a new job."

Really, the best thing to do was just *ask* Reese where she stood on everything instead of trying to draw up her own conclusions.

And, even more importantly, they needed to figure out what they *both* actually wanted.

Whatever was happening with Reese aside, Sydney needed to decide for herself what came next, too.

Reese tipped her head to the side and studied Sydney unnervingly, like she was trying to understand. Join the club. "And is that... not a good thing?"

Before answering, Sydney walked over to the bed. Her legs felt like jelly, and she sucked in a deep, calming breath before she sat down.

Why hadn't she given this more thought after talking to Sara?

Because maybe she wouldn't like the conclusion she came to, the truths it would force her to accept about herself.

"My agent, Sara, told me that The Tennis Network is considering me for a commentator position. I have to let her know by tomorrow."

Reese's eyes lit up before she saw the frown Sydney could feel on her own face, which prompted Reese's features to quickly return to neutral. "Okay, so... seems like we have mixed feelings?" she asked, coming to sit next to Sydney, who relished the current of warmth that flowed through her when Reese entangled their fingers together.

Reese ran her fingertips along Sydney's knuckles in a soothing pattern, and in spite of the tumult coursing through her, she almost purred like a cat.

"Talk to me about them," Reese encouraged softly, her fingers rubbing in small, focused circles as she moved from knuckle to knuckle.

"I've spent the last month mourning my relationship with professional tennis." She looked at Reese then, wondering if she understood. "Have you ever tried to get over something? Like, well and truly find closure and move on? Only, the idea of it keeps popping up. Keeps making you wonder if you made the right decision? Especially when whatever happened wasn't your decision in the first place. Tennis has been my whole life up until now. Am I just too afraid to give up the comfort of what I've known, even if it isn't a good idea to stay in this world?"

She appreciated Reese's thoughtful brow scrunch, which was more than a little endearing, while she considered Sydney's question. "I've spent my entire life wanting my father's approval. All those awards," Reese said, gesturing toward the wall, "were so that he'd notice that I was smart and capable and worthy of following in his footsteps."

When Reese's lips twitched, Sydney scooted a little closer, so that their thighs touched. She wanted to be physically connected for whatever Reese said next. It felt important.

This *moment* happening between them felt important.

"And then I got into a top college. And a top business school. And founded and sold a startup. And then bought a money pit worth a few million dollars." She looked at Sydney quickly, flashing her an embarrassed grin. "Respectfully."

Sydney held up her hands. "No offense taken."

"I think all of those things were reactive. I was reacting to what I thought would make other people happy, what would gain me their approval, when what I should have been looking for all along was my own."

"Too long for a T-shirt, but that's definitely the best inspirational quote I've heard in a while," Sydney said, pushing away the seriousness of Reese's words. They made her feel suddenly vulnerable.

The thing about honest conversations was that they had to go both ways.

And what Sydney knew, deep down—even if she tried to

pretend it was a million other reasons—was that she was scared. To fail. To hope. To make the wrong decisions.

"There are no wrong decisions," Reese said, like she was reading her mind. She squeezed Sydney's hand. "Only choices. And if you don't like the one you've made, you can make another."

It was the strangest feeling, butterflies erupting in her stomach at the same time it felt like there was a rock weighing it down. But Reese was giving her that look again, imploring and genuine in a way that made those butterflies flap even harder, like they were pushing the rock away.

"Everything fell apart this last year. I don't know if I have it in me to buck up and get back out there again," Sydney admitted, the words settling between them. "And I *hate* admitting that. To you, but especially to myself."

It felt good to say it out loud, even if it terrified her. She couldn't change something until she accepted the reality of it.

The softness in Reese's words made them come out as a whisper. "Are you excited about the commentary role? Is it something you'd like to try?"

"What if I'm not good at it?" Sydney asked with a shaky exhale. "I feel like I've been failing at an awful lot of things lately."

Her face turned reflectively to chase the warmth when Reese cupped her hand against Sydney's jaw. It was calming and electrifying at the same time.

"You haven't failed at showing up for me." It was the seriousness of Reese's words that captured Sydney most, like she was imploring Sydney to believe them. Fingers stroked against her skin when Reese added, "You showed up today after a hellish trip back to Stoneport. For me."

A beat passed between them before Reese pulled her lower lip between her teeth and added, "Looking insanely attractive, I may add." Her gaze dropped down Sydney's body before snaking back up to meet Sydney's stare.

And she felt it. *Everywhere.*

Where Reese was touching her face, which she knew was blooming wild with color from the heat. Curling through her stomach, where the butterflies had officially taken over. Snaking across her thigh, nestled against Reese's, before finding its way to her center, a deep, aching need pulsing outward and pushing her heart rate through the roof.

Reese leaned closer then, running her fingertips across Sydney's lips. Her breath followed a second later when she said, "I think you're probably good at a lot of things. And you don't strike me to be the type who's afraid to go after what you want."

Suddenly, the air was gone from the room, and every nerve ending in Sydney's body lit up, up, up as the feeling enveloped her.

Her lips met Reese's, both of them eager and searching as they came together.

Her hand quickly found Reese's thigh, just like when they'd been in the car earlier, and she was right back to wanting, to getting lost in how good Reese smelled, how her lips moved perfectly against Sydney's own. How it felt amazingly good to be able to touch Reese, heat sparking through her when squeezing Reese's thigh prompted a little moan that Sydney swallowed hungrily.

This wasn't like their first kiss, which had been soft and tentative. When Sydney had wanted Reese to know where she stood but not to push things too far.

Attraction mixed with a little vulnerability was a strong aphrodisiac, and all Sydney wanted was to chase this high, which was better than any win she'd ever had on a tennis court.

The moment was living, breathing and changing, as their tongues came together and explored. Sydney sucked Reese's bottom lip into her mouth, hoping to elicit another moan.

Which she received, and her fingers, which she hadn't realized had snaked into the hair at the back of Reese's neck, dug in harder, pulling Reese closer.

Months of frustration at the state of her life and weeks of arousal at Reese's capable hands, judging from how she'd managed to inch Sydney's romper up higher on her thighs, were coming to a head in an explosion of want that stole Sydney's breath.

"Oh—"

The sound of another voice shocked Sydney out of her haze. All the signs of her arousal—the aching between her legs and the insistent thrumming of her erratic heartbeat—were still present, but she used the small modicum of self-control she could find to go still and press her thighs together.

Reese blinked once, then twice, finally shaking her head. It seemed to do the trick to break herself out of the moment. "Mom," Reese finally responded, her voice full and throaty.

Sydney wanted to push her onto the bed, but she tamped down that desire and tried to find her focus, too.

Sharon cleared her throat, standing awkwardly—which was fair—in the doorway. "Brynn told me what happened, and when I didn't see you two back at the party, I wanted to make sure everything was okay. Seems like it is?" she asked, her cheeks the same shade of red as her daughter's.

Sydney had been privy to the evolving relationship between Reese and her mom over the past few weeks. She was a little charmed, and hoped that Reese was, too, that her mom was willing to come check on both of them amid what must be an incredibly busy day for her. Not only was she the host, but the party was taking place in her home. Sydney had seen at least a dozen waitstaff, bartenders, and caterers throughout the day. Except for the speeches, she hadn't seen Sharon stop moving.

Sydney stood up, sliding her romper down to its original position as she reached her full height. "I really appreciate you thinking of me, Sharon. It was just a little mishap, but all is well." She gestured to the almost imperceptible color change on the side of her outfit.

"I'm so happy to hear that." Sharon exhaled, genuinely relieved. "This day has been..." She stopped herself, her words trailing off while she pulled uncomfortably at her beautiful chiffon dress. "Well, I won't bore you with the details. But it's been a day."

Reese stood up then. She grabbed Sydney's hand, which was a welcome dose of contact after their minute apart, and led them closer to Sharon. "Is everything okay with you? Can we do anything?"

Sharon waved them off. "It's fine. Your brother's just in a bit of a mood, as is your father. Probably because of your brother."

She felt Reese stiffen next to her, thankful she didn't unclasp their hands. "They're grown men, Mom. Their inability to deal with their feelings shouldn't be your problem."

"It's a party, darling. I'm just trying to make sure that everyone has a great time," Sharon said diplomatically, a smile that almost seemed sincere on her face. She placed a hand on Reese's shoulder and gave her an affectionate squeeze.

"This is Dad's party, too," Reese pushed, taking a small step forward.

Sydney stayed quiet, wondering if they were headed into dangerous territory. She knew how Reese felt about her father, but she didn't quite know how Sharon felt about her husband.

Honestly, she didn't know very much about Sharon Devereux, now that she was thinking about it. As far as Sydney's relationship with the Devereux family had gone when she'd dated Grant, Sharon had been, even if it pained Sydney to remember, out of respect for Sharon, more of a side character than anything.

"Honey, I don't disagree with you, but I'm just trying to make it through the party. The most helpful thing that *you* can do for me is support my decisions in how to handle doing that. Does that seem fair?"

Reese softened then, and it was almost like Sydney could see her as a little child, the way she looked at her mom with such a repentant stare. "I'm sorry, you're right," Reese acquiesced.

Sharon smiled then, a genuine one this time. "Nothing to be sorry about, Reese. I'm just glad that you two are okay."

For everything going on in Reese's life, it made Sydney's heart a little lighter to see that she and her mom seemed to be mending fences.

"In the spirit of honesty, I may have given Grant a few choice words, though I doubt he'll remember them," Reese said with a rueful smile.

"And he probably needed to hear them." Sharon squeezed Reese's shoulder again before letting go and then checking her watch. "Dessert is coming out in ten minutes. I have to get back downstairs."

Sydney wondered if they'd follow, but a heated stare stopped her in her tracks. Sharon was already turning around, and Reese nailed her with a look that made all the heat from moments ago flair back to life, her stomach coiling tight.

"I was figuring we'd head out?" Reese said to Sydney, eyes searching.

If the look from Reese was any indication—the intensity of it made Sydney's stomach swoop low—then their moment was far from over.

A dumb nod was all she could manage as they followed Sharon down the staircase to the ground floor before parting ways at the foyer.

Waiting for the valet to bring their car around was excruciating, and Sydney kept her thighs pressed together to contain the want settling deep inside of her.

Because, yes, she wanted Reese. More than she'd wanted anything in a long time. The excitement. The comfort. The desire. It was all rolled up in a powerful combination of anticipation for what would happen next.

Mostly, she wanted to chase that feeling.

When they finally got into the car, Sydney's hand was right back on Reese's thigh, drawing little patterns while she tried to keep the buzz of excitement at a survivable level.

"Is Hallie expecting you for anything today?" Sydney hedged, trying to make sure they were on the same page.

If they weren't, she needed to start some deep breathing exercises and throw herself into the pool, pronto.

Reese shot her a disarming glance before her face grew more serious. "I just want to make sure that..."

Sydney's fingers stilled against Reese's leg, wondering what she'd say next.

Make sure this isn't a bad idea?

Make sure their expectations align?

Make sure Sydney was going to melt into a puddle with how much she wanted this?

"I want to make sure this isn't to avoid any decisions you're putting off making," Reese finished with another look thrown in Sydney's direction.

She shook her head quickly. "No, this is not that."

"But you do need to let your agent know by tomorrow, right?"

Sydney didn't appreciate how the question was shifting her back into reality. To decisions and insecurity and confusion about what came next.

So maybe she had wanted to avoid it a little bit.

And she didn't know if it made it better or worse that Reese Devereux so clearly had her number.

Reese turned her blinker on before turning onto the road that would take them back to The Stone's Throw. "And I'm not trying to be pushy. Honestly. I just..."

Sydney's heart beat a little faster when Reese reached down and entangled their fingers. "I don't want to be something that's an escape for you, Sydney. I know that much." And that same heart skipped at least a full beat when Reese's words sank in, when she let the softness of Reese's voice melt through her veins.

This wasn't an escape. It was *so* far from that.

It was just easier to pretend that along with everything else going on in her life, this didn't have the ability to send her life careening if it imploded.

But it was Reese she'd confided her deepest insecurities in, who'd given her the space but also built the trust to talk about and work through her messy feelings.

And it was Reese...

It was Reese.

"I have feelings for you," Sydney blurted out, surprising them both, the words hanging like a living, breathing thing between them. But once she admitted it, she found that she wanted to keep going. "It's not just attraction, though I do recognize that's a very, very real feeling that I have, too," she said with a shy smile.

Reese's stare turned toward her again, her own face dusted with a soft blush, though Sydney couldn't tell how she was feeling.

Was it a blush indicating that she felt the same way? Or was it that Sydney had embarrassed herself and Reese had secondhand embarrassment for her?

They pulled into the lot at the inn, Reese still silent. For seconds that felt like excruciating minutes, Sydney waited for whatever would come next.

How had she not noticed it happening? That all the confusion swirling around in her life was taking a back seat to her growing feelings for Reese. That, in spite of the tumult, it was *because* of Reese that she felt more like herself than she had in years. That, maybe, she was even becoming a better version of herself because of it.

She didn't want to lose that.

And she didn't want to lose the way it felt to hold Reese in her arms, to give her the same comfort and security that was given back to her in spades.

But, the reality was, it wasn't her decision to make.

That, truly, was the hardest thing about putting her heart in someone else's hands.

Reese turned her full attention toward Sydney then, eyes deep and magnetic, and Sydney just wanted to fall into them. Into her. "Cards on the table?"

Sydney nodded but didn't speak, afraid to breathe.

"I am insanely attracted to you. And I cannot believe how you can calm me down so easily, help me feel centered in spite of everything going on in my life."

"That's—"

"Let me finish," Reese said, squeezing Sydney's hand.

She gulped back her words and took a steadying breath instead.

"But we're both in crazy places in our lives, and I *do* worry that once you find your center again, this place—this life—won't be enough for you. And this thing between us is so new that I don't want to hold you back. "

"Is this about the commentator job?" Sydney asked, trying to make sense of everything Reese was saying. It did make sense, in a way, but it also felt like an excuse, even if that wasn't fair.

"Partly," Reese said, her eyes locked on Sydney. "I think you should give it a try. Your relationship with tennis has changed, but it doesn't need to end. Not unless you really, truly want it to be over." Sydney was considering Reese's words when she spoke again, imploringly. "I don't want you to be afraid to try things. To live your life."

"In case you've forgotten, I was cheated on a year ago and left to pick up the pieces of my romantic life. Wanting this—wanting *you*—isn't some easy thing for me. It's hard and scary and makes me shift between wanting to jump up and down and pass out."

"I want this, too, Sydney. And I'll be here. But I want to take things slowly to make sure you have the time and space to explore all your options. I don't want to be the thing you pick because it's the safe bet."

Was Reese not hearing her? Sydney felt the blood rushing through her ears, her heart thumping hard against her chest.

"Reese, I need you to really look at me," she said, and Reese's eyes lifted back upward to meet her own.

Suddenly, now that it was Reese in the hot seat, the penetrating stare from moments ago had been replaced with Reese's desire to look anywhere else.

"You would never be some consolation prize. You are exciting and terrifying and tingle-inducing in all the best ways." Sydney placed her finger under Reese's chin and lifted it gently upward, her voice soft. "But I am going to tell Sara yes because you're right, though not for the reason you think. I have been afraid of what comes after tennis, but me wanting you has nothing to do with running away from that. So I'll do both."

"Both?" Reese asked, looking dazed from the last minute of conversation.

"I'll do the commentator tryout–"

"Which you'll be amazing at," Reese said, blinking the haze away, finding her footing in the conversation again as she nodded along with her own words.

Sydney flashed her a self-deprecating grin. "Sure."

"You will be. The way you were holding court today with the party guests was... it was something else," Reese said, awe soaked into her voice in a way that lit Sydney up from the inside out.

She wanted Reese to feel that way about her. Always.

"So you'll try this? With me?" Sydney asked, anticipation bubbling up inside.

"Yes, Sydney. I want to do this," Reese said with impossible softness in her voice as she dissolved the space between them and kissed Sydney.

It was slow and sweet, but it ignited the desire from earlier, magnified now that there was no confusion standing between them.

The kiss wound through her body, settling deeply inside of her, beginning to fill in the cracks that the last year had left.

"We should really get you out of that. Make sure it didn't

stain, and all that," Reese said. When she finally pulled away, Sydney was so wound up she felt like she may burst into flames.

Sydney nodded. "Yes. Good idea."

They were out of the car within seconds, Reese finding Sydney's hand as she led her toward the inn.

If Hallie was at the front desk, she'd give a half-hearted wave and blow past her best friend, her singular focus now on getting her and Reese behind closed doors as soon as humanly possible.

And just like she'd expected when they entered the doors, Hallie was standing at the counter. She moved to wave but Hallie's hands were already up in the air, frantically trying to get her attention. Her mouth was moving, but no words were coming out, and her eyes looked slightly wild.

"What?" she said, going back on her own promise as she, with her hand still in Reese's, walked closer to where Hallie stood behind the counter.

This was weird, even for Hallie.

"Why didn't you answer my texts?" Hallie was already saying when they reached her.

Sydney pulled her phone out of her pocket and held it up, confused. If something was wrong at the inn, Reese would have been Hallie's first call.

"My phone died. I forgot to charge it last night. But Hal, I've got to, um... Reese and I need to discuss something right now. We were just heading to my room." Sydney looked at Reese then, and Reese's lips tipped into an amused smile that made Sydney's stomach flutter.

"Her room," Sydney corrected quickly, realizing her mistake. This was never about her outfit. And they'd have much more privacy there.

It was all that Sydney could think about right now.

Hallie looked past Sydney's shoulder to the sitting room, just off the inn's lobby. "Your parents are here."

Sydney's head whipped around so fast she was afraid she was

going to have whiplash, and Reese's hand in hers suddenly grew clammy. "What? I just saw them yesterday."

"And what a nice trip it was," her mom said from behind her.

"I swear that woman has a stealth mode," Hallie said underneath her breath at the same time Sydney shot her a side-eye.

"So much so," her mom continued, "that we decided to make a trip up to Stoneport."

Sydney's face scrunched, wondering what her mom was up to right now. "Because you missed me?"

"Well, how long has it been since we were all back here together? Since well before we moved, I think?" Her mom said it like it was a question, but Sydney knew that she was aware of everything at all times, including when they'd last been all here together.

"And, well, talking about Hallie and all the big changes at the inn, and your new relationship," her mom dropped in casually, like it didn't sound like a bomb in Sydney's ears, "we figured this would be a great time to surprise you and visit."

She shot Hallie a critical stare implying, 'Did you have something to do with this?'

Hallie shook her head forcefully and glared before lifting her hand up as if to say, 'Absolutely not. And how dare you ask me that.'

"Where are my manners!" her mom continued, hopefully oblivious to their silent exchange. She extended her hand toward Reese. "I'm Rachel King, Sydney's mom. I've heard so much about you."

Up until thirty seconds ago, Sydney had thought she was minutes away from being wrapped up in Reese and wherever the rest of the day would take them.

It physically hurt that she could still taste Reese on her lips, and she licked them instinctively, hoping this was all just a weird dream.

But, she realized when Reese let go of her hand—she missed the warmth immediately— today was apparently going to be the day of parental interruptions. So when Reese moved to return her mom's gesture, shooting Sydney a small smile, Sydney already had her hand at the small of Reese's back, tracing a soothing pattern there.

Even if she was missing out on what could be happening between them if her parents hadn't shown up, she still wanted it all with Reese.

Sixteen

REESE SUDDENLY FELT CLAUSTROPHOBIC. She'd met parents before, so she couldn't understand why she was freaking out.

Well, partially understand, at least.

It was hard to calm the blood pumping through her body when she was still aware of the ghost of Sydney's hands on her. Still *acutely* aware of Sydney's fingers playing against her back, which should probably have been calming but was having the opposite effect instead.

Physically, all they'd been doing was holding hands, but emotionally... She already had Sydney undressed in her mind's eye, eager to map the divots and contours and soft skin that she'd only seen hints of this summer. She bet that Sydney had an amazing back. Was it weird that Reese wanted to lick it?

She felt the heat fan across her cheeks at the thought. "Mrs. King, it's so nice to meet you, too," she said quickly, extending her hand for a shake. God, she hoped Sydney's mom didn't notice her sweaty palms.

Rachel cast a long look around the lobby, which now felt muted and shabby under her observant stare. "How are you liking owning the inn, Reese? Hallie and Sydney spent most of their youth here."

It would be a lie to say she didn't find Rachel King intimidating. She had Sydney's same tall stature, along with beauty that hadn't faded with age.

"It's been an adventure, to say the least," Reese admitted, knowing that lying would likely do her no good. She was a horrible liar, anyway. "And Hallie has been a godsend. I couldn't do anything without her."

Hallie smiled brightly and stood up a little straighter. Reese made a note to tell her more often because, truly, she'd be lost without her. But this wasn't the time to think about what would happen if Hallie decided to move on in a few months and Reese was left to tackle this beast alone.

"Well, I don't want to interrupt everyone's day, but I was hoping I could steal Sydney for a few hours if she's available." Mrs. King turned her attention to her daughter then. "Your father and I are going to visit my sisters, and we thought that since you haven't seen them since coming back, you'd like to join us."

Reese was still wrestling with keeping her desire in check, Sydney's ministrations on her back continuing in a way that was not at all helpful. But Rachel's words were a cold dose of reality that, needfully, brought her down from a boil to a slow simmer.

There was no way they were getting out of this quickly.

Sydney's fingers moved down to Reese's lower back, finding their way to the cutout in her dress, and in an instant, Reese was going higher, higher, higher.

"I'd love to Mom, bu—"

Reese ballooned with hope for the briefest moment before she deflated with a quick pop when Mrs. King said breezily, "Amazing. They'll be so happy to see you! And then maybe later this week we can all do dinner? Reese. Hallie. Anyone else in the Devereux family that I should invite?" Rachel asked, her implication clear when paired with a focused stare in Reese's direction.

And with that, the flames were fully doused. She'd been too off-kilter until now to notice that the vibes were definitely *off*.

Reese shut her mouth, teeth clenched as she swallowed quickly. Her instinct was to react, but she wanted the approval of Sydney's parents, she realized. So, instead of asking what Rachel King meant, she turned toward Sydney, slipping about a foot away so she could capture the hand that had been torturing her masterfully only moments before. "That sounds nice, Sydney. You can find me later?"

She didn't miss the confused stare that Sydney gave her, followed quickly by an appreciative smile. "Promise?"

Reese squeezed Sydney's hand at the same time she dropped a soft kiss on her cheek. "It's a date," she said when she leaned back, their stares catching in a way that sent electricity through her again.

Yeah, they were going to pick this up again later.

"Let's grab your father," Mrs. King said, cutting into the moment. "I think he's outside inspecting the shrubbery surrounding the inn."

Reese wasn't going to touch that one with a ten-foot pole.

Sydney threw Reese an apologetic look over her shoulder as she followed her mom out.

"Whew." Hallie said the word as more of a whoosh of air than anything else. She stretched her arms out against the counter, leaning over it to get closer to Reese. "How'd you get on Mrs. King's bad side so quickly?"

"You caught that, too?" Reese asked defeatedly.

Hallie picked up her tablet and scrolled through it absently. "I think the space satellites caught that."

"I appreciate that you don't pull any punches. It's really a rare trait." She could at least let Hallie enjoy having a little fun at her expense.

"How was the party at Casa Devereux? Canapés and Cristal abound?"

"There were also mini cinnamon rolls, but yeah, that's basically the gist."

"I cannot believe those made the approved menu," Hallie said, genuinely shocked.

Reese shrugged. "The father of the bride is a simple man who likes simple things."

"I like him already."

"I do, too," Reese admitted before adding, "If we could just keep Brynn's side of the family and get rid of mine, I think we'd really have something going."

"Tweedledee and Tweedledum not bringing the right energy to the family tree? Can't say I'm surprised."

Reese stilled, processing Hallie's words. "Are you talking about my dad and brother?" she asked, letting out a loud guffaw.

"I was never a Grant fan. He has a pompadour, for crying out loud!" When Hallie talked, she did it with her whole body, her arms swinging out in both directions. "Plus, I'll never forgive him for what he did to Sydney."

"That makes two of us," Reese agreed. Still, him ruining the best thing he'd likely ever have was only playing out to be Reese's gain in the end. She only wished that Sydney hadn't ever had to suffer through it.

"But we... like your mom? Just checking," Hallie finished quickly. "I want to make sure I know who to not let on the property."

"We do," Reese said with a fond smile that surprised her as she thought of her conversations with her mom over the last few weeks. "We've really reconnected this summer. I'm liking it a lot."

"A better relationship with your mom. A new girlfriend. A perfectly imperfect inn. Looks like it's all coming up Reese Devereux lately."

Reese smiled because nothing about Hallie's words were untrue, and it felt good to let the feeling wash over her. "You know, things have been going pretty well lately. Besides Grant's idiocy at every turn, it's been a pretty amazing summer."

"Oh, tell me, tell me." Hallie held out her hands, opening and closing them like a baby asking for candy.

"He's... even worse than I remember, if that's possible." It didn't feel fair to talk about Grant with Sydney, which was ironic considering he was the thing that had brought them together. But maybe it would be nice to have, while not completely unbiased, another person to bounce the situation off for perspective.

"He was wasted today. Like 'day-drinking kegger at the frat' wasted by noon."

Hallie scrunched up her face in disgust. "This was, in fact, his couple's shower, correct?"

"Ding, ding, ding." Reese ran a hand through her hair, trying to make sense of it herself. "His fiancée seems lovely, but it's like he's being dragged to the gallows. Is this how everyone feels about marriage? Like, why is he even getting married then?"

Hallie popped a grape in her mouth from a bowl she had nestled beneath the counter. She crunched on it thoughtfully. "The men-children, at least. But no, normal people don't feel that way."

"Yeah, I just... ugh. I don't even know why I'm thinking about this."

"Because you're being dragged through an awkward-as-hell summer with a couple that's on the verge of a quick divorce or a wildly unhappy marriage."

"That's pretty accurate," was what Reese settled on after she'd taken in Hallie's words. Because Hallie was absolutely right. She, and by extension Sydney, was party to something that was making her more uneasy by the day.

Hallie hopped down from her seat behind the desk. "It's a gift. Anyway, Candace called out today, so I'm about to go restock the rooms. Something about Greg's third eye being in an emotional affair."

Reese looked at Hallie, who was staring back at her. "Are you serious?"

"They invited me out to The Lobster Trap last night, so do with that what you will," Hallie answered, seemingly nonplussed.

Reese hadn't been to the local dive bar, The Lobster Trap, since she'd been twenty-one and briefly home for a summer in college. She doubted very much that it had changed in the last decade, and her face scrunched up reflexively.

But more importantly than remembering the patina of grime coating all the surfaces at the bar, she really needed to work on finding a balance with Hallie between being a good boss and being a pushover. But that was a conversation for another day.

"Let's go," Reese said, rapping her knuckles on the countertop. "We'll be done faster if we tag-team it."

Plus, it would give her something to focus on instead of the empty feeling that Sydney had left in her wake.

* * *

After the sixth lap, Reese was glad she'd taken Hallie up on the recommendation to use the pool after hours. The sun had just set, and Reese glided through the water with a practiced, albeit rusty, ease.

The pool was at the edge of the property, secluded by rows of hedges that created a privacy barrier between it and the large lawn next to the inn. Her master key card opened it even after hours, and the combination of setting sun and fairy lights created the perfect blend for relaxation. It was like Reese had stepped into her own little world, and even though the pool could use a little love and care, it was a gorgeous and heated addition to The Stone's Throw.

In high school, she'd loved swimming. Built for distance, she was almost unbeatable at the 500-meter freestyle. But swimming was something she'd never considered a professional pursuit, though she still made time in college and at her gym in San Francisco to do laps whenever she had a free hour.

Right now, she needed to do as many laps as her body could handle. For the last ten hours, she'd been straddling some sort of invisible line between exhausted and wired. After working with Hallie until about six p.m., she'd been hoping to hear from Sydney so they could pick up where they'd left off.

Sadly, all she'd received was a text that Sydney's visit with her family had taken on a life of its own, and without a car of her own, Sydney was at their mercy.

Which left Reese feeling... adrift. After grabbing dinner and returning to her room, with still no word, she'd tried to distract herself.

A book, which she'd kept losing her place in.

A movie, whose lead looked way too much like Sydney.

She'd even tried to do a crossword puzzle, but groaned in frustration and threw her pen onto the floor when a question about a certain formerly retired tennis player came up.

So instead, she focused on her stroke, on her exhale like a metronome guiding her along. Swimming used to be the one thing that allowed her mind to blank out, and it was devastating that not even her comfort activity could dampen her thoughts.

What had she done to deserve this? It wasn't like she'd gone looking for Sydney or had asked to be thrown into this sexually frustrated limbo where she was so keyed up and had nowhere to put her energy.

She paid her taxes. Donated to nonprofits. Stopped for pedestrians crossing the street—which was no small feat in a tourist town like this one.

So... why? Why did the fates seem intent on keeping the two of them from having more than five minutes alone together?

Hell, they'd even talked about what was happening between them. Like responsible adults!

This was all so... foreign to Reese. She'd never considered herself an especially sexual person. She was driven. Focused. Usually unaware of her baser instincts.

But now? Now, all she could think about was Sydney backing her up against the next flat surface they found and finishing what felt like a month in the making.

Maybe it was all the touching, she'd considered between laps four and five. The playing at something from the start that was deeper than where they'd truly been, like it had been priming Reese before she'd been fully aware of what was happening.

Which meant that as all the pieces were clicking together, her mind and her body in sync, she was *ready*.

Inhale.

Exhale.

Inhale.

Exhale.

When she came up for air, about to kick off the wall, a gorgeous vision stopped her in her tracks. Waves pushed outward while she found her footing against the pool bottom, and she sputtered air, trying to catch her breath.

Sydney stood at the edge of the steps, a small towel tied around a bright purple bikini. Heat pooled in Reese's center, her body right back to that anxious edge of anticipation and wanting, so much that it hurt.

"Hallie told me I could probably find you here," Sydney said as she dropped her towel at the edge of the pool. "Mind if I join you?"

Reese, first and foremost, wondered if she was hallucinating. That seemed like the most likely option for how Sydney was standing in front of her, toned legs disappearing into the water with each step closer to Reese.

"I tried texting you." Sydney was fully in the water now and slowly moving toward where Reese stood dumbfounded at the front of the single swimming lane on the far side of the pool.

Reese's brain was having trouble keeping up, and she struggled to find her words. "I, um... I left my phone upstairs."

Arms wrapped themselves leisurely around Reese's shoulders. Her whole body trembled with the contact.

Sydney frowned. "I texted you."

Reese groaned, deciding how much to admit. "And I was waiting for that text. So much so that it became a little bit of an issue."

"Oh, yeah?" Now Sydney's face was all smiles. She reached up and tucked a strand of wet hair behind Reese's ear. Sydney leaned forward then, her warm breath ghosting across Reese's ear. "Well, if it's any consolation, I was not the best guest with my family today. I was *very* distracted."

The words settled low in Reese's body. As she moved her legs together to relieve the friction, Sydney slipped her thigh between them. She extended her hands beyond Reese to the pool edge, pushing them both back until Reese was bracketed between the solidness behind her and Sydney's long frame.

It was excruciating in the best possible way, how their bodies joined together. Sydney's hips held but didn't push, like they had all the time in the world.

"Seems like you want to pick things up where we left off?" Reese breathed, overwhelmed by how many things there were to focus on.

The curve of Sydney's breasts, rising and falling with her own labored breathing. How Sydney's thigh brushed against her center with each small movement in the water. The way Sydney's fingers had magically found their way to the back of Reese's neck, massaging gentle circles to the point that Reese thought her head would fall back in ecstasy.

"Sydney?" Reese asked, a hint of uncertainty creeping into her voice when Sydney didn't immediately respond.

"You are so beautiful." Reese forced her eyes open, the deep green of Sydney's boring into her. The way Sydney said it, soft and reverent as her hold tightened against Reese, made her head swim.

"I want this," Reese said, her hands easing from Sydney's hips to the front of her bikini, fingers skimming where skin met fabric. She dipped beneath the band, just for a second, before scratching gently at the skin beneath her belly button. "God knows when we'll have another chance the way things are going."

"Yeah?" Sydney's voice, paired with how her eyes looked at Reese so softly, made the moment feel more intimate than she'd expected.

Earlier today, all she'd thought about was touching, tasting, exploring. Those base instincts that so often escaped her.

And now? At this moment? With the world outside forgotten, no one and nothing separating them?

What she wanted, more than anything, was to feel connected to Sydney, to experience this together.

"Yeah," Reese echoed back before inching forward to capture Sydney's lips.

Reese could feel the thrum of her own pulse hammering in her ears, the intensity ratcheting up when Sydney bit gently at her bottom lip before licking across it. At the same time, Sydney dragged her fingertips from Reese's shoulders down her sides.

"Sydney." She was breathless, needing Sydney to keep touching her. Anywhere. Everywhere.

It was all coming to a head. The anticipation and frustration and attraction and a million other feelings that were threading and weaving and threatening to burst free from Reese if she didn't get some type of release.

"I want to make sure that you still want this," Sydney said, nails lightly dragging up Reese's thighs. The touch caused her to instinctively open her hips wider, and Sydney slotted in between them effortlessly. "I've thought about this all day. Honestly, I've thought about this for the past month."

God, what planet were they on? That Sydney didn't think Reese was anything more than a puddle of want for Sydney to do with what *she* wanted.

Instead of answering, she found Sydney's hand and, enveloping it in her own, guided her to the waistband of her bikini before dipping beneath it.

She moaned as she pressed Sydney against her, Reese's effort only needed for a moment before Sydney's hand started working on its own, playing softly against Reese's folds. She traced a long, leisurely line up and then down, though she still didn't push forward.

"Please," she gasped when Sydney pushed in for a moment before retracting her fingers. It wasn't enough. She needed Sydney inside of her, and in turn, she needed to feel her in the same way.

Reese slipped her fingers into Sydney's bikini and instantly moving inward. Unable to go slower. She found what she was looking for almost immediately. Her thumb rubbed circles around Sydney's pulsing clit, and she eased a finger inside.

"Is this okay?" she asked, pausing to give Sydney time to adjust, her breath ragged against Sydney's cheek.

She waited what felt like excruciatingly long seconds before a soft moan escaped Sydney's mouth. And if that sound wasn't enough to make Reese's center tighten with want, quickly following it, Sydney bit down into Reese's shoulder as she pushed two fingers into Reese.

"Fuck," Reese breathed out, easing in a second finger of her own. "Please, don't stop."

Reese was already close, but she wanted more. She wanted whatever Sydney would give her.

She found Sydney's lips. This time, their kiss was messy and wanting and felt like a circuit competing with the electricity that it sparked inside of her.

Sydney guided them to a rhythm, and Reese keened into Sydney's mouth, pushing her hips in as she met with Sydney's already slick fingers.

She needed more friction.

She needed...

She *needed*.

"Harder," she begged into Sydney's mouth. "Please."

"My god, Reese. You feel so fucking good." Sydney's words

sounded exasperated, almost overwhelmed, as she pushed in harder, her other hand anchoring Reese's hips in place.

She loved how out of sorts Sydney was, her hips pushing erratically against the hand playing deftly against Reese's clit and fucking her senseless.

"Put your leg around me," Sydney practically growled.

A thrill went straight to Reese's clit with those words, and she was so, so fucking close to coming undone around Sydney's fingers. With Sydney's lips on her own. Sydney's body anchoring her to the moment.

"Sydney. Please. Please don't stop. I'm so close."

Sydney shifted out of their kiss to suck softly at Reese's neck, right at her pulse point. Against Reese's hot skin, she felt the words more than she heard them, Sydney's fingers pushing and working and taking her higher. "I want to feel you come around my fingers. Reese, I need it. Please."

The coil inside of her snapped, her back arching as Sydney continued to work her fingers against her, the gentle nips on her neck turning into soft kisses as her center pulsed, keeping Sydney's fingers inside of her.

And even though she felt wrung out and barely able to function, she didn't stop either. She couldn't, not until she elicited the same feeling in Sydney that she'd just experienced herself. She pushed her thumb harder against Sydney's clit until she felt Sydney clench around her, as Sydney burrowed her face against Reese's neck to dampen the moan she let out.

They stayed like that, with Sydney's face resting in the crook of Reese's neck, Reese leaning her forehead against Sydney, listening to their ragged breaths even out as the sky turned to darkness above them.

It was Sydney who spoke first, after she lifted her head and captured Reese's lips in a quick kiss. "Worth the wait?" she asked, her voice throaty but tired.

Reese considered the question, genuinely. "I think it would have been as good, no matter what."

"Just good?" Sydney asked, mock indignation in her voice as she scratched lightly at Reese's neck.

Reese lifted an eyebrow and pushed lightly against Sydney's shoulder. "You want an 'atta girl' after you've already made me come?"

Sydney drew her back in, a self-satisfied smile threatening to take over her whole face. "Maybe it's the competitor in me."

Laughing, Reese planted a light kiss on Sydney's lips. "I'm glad you're finding such healthy coping mechanisms."

Sydney played with a strand of Reese's hair, the water rippling around them as they continued to shift and touch—anything to hold on to the closeness of the moment.

"I emailed Sara. About the job offer," Sydney clarified, her fingers stopping at the shell of Reese's ear before she started to rub gentle circles against it. "Thank you, by the way."

"For what?" Reese asked, genuinely confused. She found Sydney's stare, her eyes still half lidded, like she was ready to crawl into bed.

Sydney leaned forward, and in a soft, electrifying moment of intimacy that warmed Reese from the inside out, she brushed their noses together. "For making me feel like it will all be okay."

"It *will* all be okay. I know you'll be amazing, and the only real question is whether you like it or not and want to accept their formal offer." Reese was sure the fans, the cameras, and the network would love Sydney. She wasn't a hard sell.

In spite of the nervousness that sluiced through her at the idea of Sydney moving on from Stoneport, from *her*, encouraging her had been the right thing to do. For both of them.

"I'm coming in there. Everyone better be decent," a voice called from beyond the hedges, and Reese heard the faint click of the gate opening.

Sydney burst into laughter, throaty and full as it echoed into the night. "My god. We cannot catch a break." She gave Reese another quick kiss and rolled her eyes before finding Reese's hand underneath the water.

Hallie rounded the corner, and both of them stood up a little straighter, not knowing who she was coming to find.

"Your mom's here."

Sydney moved to speak, but Hallie held her hand up before pointing at Reese. "*Your* mom. She said she texted you."

Truly, what had people done without cell phones? She'd been away from hers for an hour, and suddenly it was like everyone in the world needed her immediate attention.

But her irritation at their moment being interrupted was quickly replaced when she realized how strange it was, her mom showing up at the inn at almost ten o'clock at night.

Taking Sydney with her, she moved toward the pool steps, apprehension drawn across her features. "Is she okay?"

Hallie didn't speak immediately, her face inscrutable. "I'm honestly not sure, but I told her I'd try to find you. She said it was important."

Urgency propelled Reese forward. She moved quickly up the steps and put on the robe she'd brought down with her.

"Later?" she asked, shooting Sydney an apologetic look. Her focus had shifted in the blink of an eye, and all she could think about was getting to her mom, trying not to catastrophize about whatever was wrong.

"Definitely. Let me know if I can help with anything," Sydney said, no hesitation in her voice.

And with that, Reese was already sprinting toward the gate, wondering what other surprises this day could possibly have in store.

"I've left your father." The words hung heavy in the air, Reese struggling to make sense of them, even though they were about as clear as could be.

She'd taken her mom over to the sitting room off the lobby after she'd made sure that nothing was urgently wrong. Her mother had insisted she just wanted to talk, so being seated seemed like the best idea. Which was how she found herself on the sofa in the lounge area, her mom seated next to her. Goose bumps were already prickling her skin in the air-conditioning, but that was the least of her worries.

"Mom, what happened?" When she grabbed her hand, she realized it was shaking slightly. All it did was make Reese hold on more tightly.

And then, she waited.

Not that Reese needed an explanation on the why. More than anything, it was the *why now*.

Their divorce was long overdue, given everything Reese had seen this summer. But still, her mom hadn't hinted at anything like this. Not after he'd left her on her own with her cancer scare. Not when he abandoned her with the Fitzpatricks a few weeks ago. Not even when he did the least but expected the most credit, putting her mom in the impossible position of constantly navigating around Grant's absurd behavior at every turn.

Long seconds passed; then her mom let out a strangled titter before taking a deep breath. "Something in me just cracked today. I can't even explain it."

"Did you two have a fight?" Reese asked, trying to help her find a path toward explaining what had happened. Something she herself was desperately curious to understand.

"I don't think you could qualify it as that." God, she was making Reese work for it.

"Will you talk to me about what happened?" To her mom's credit, she looked a little shell-shocked by what she'd just done, which was why Reese was trying to approach the situation with kid gloves.

"We had..." Her mom stilled, trying to find the words. "I'd call it a difference of opinion regarding your brother."

"What about him?"

"I didn't want to get into it today, given that I was trying to keep the party on track, but you were right. It's more than just 'some mood.' He's the worst I've ever seen him, and I don't know what's causing it. Contrary to his flaws," she said, looking at Reese pointedly, "of which I am well aware, he's my son. The same way you are my daughter, whom I'd do anything in the world to help."

Her mom took a deep breath, and Reese stayed silent to give her the space to get her thoughts out. "After your brother left with one of his friends, I tried to talk to your father about it. About whether he knew what was causing Grant's behavior. He blew me off. Told me not to worry about it, that nothing was wrong."

The room was silent around them, and Reese reached out to grab her mom's hand.

"And I stood there thinking about how this man could watch his children struggle and not care. How he wanted to be willfully ignorant. I can take his indifference. Not that it's okay," she added, "but watching him with you this summer, and now with Grant, I cannot in good conscience stand by that man, regardless of the years we've had together."

"Mom." Reese's voice cracked with the weight of emotion, of how deeply, in that moment, she knew the love for both of her children ran.

"I was hoping I could stay at the inn for tonight, if that's okay." Her mom's voice was so hopeful that it made Reese want to move mountains to help her.

Reese's parents had been married for thirty-two years. Over half of her mom's life. They shared children. Shared a home.

Even if her mom's voice was surprisingly clear, Reese saw turmoil brewing behind her eyes. "I just didn't want to stay in that house alone tonight. Your father decided to go back to Boston, unsurprisingly. Actually, he told me that when I wouldn't drop the conversation about Grant."

Of course he'd left. She was pretty sure he lived in Boston these days, only spending occasional weekends at the Stoneport house to keep up appearances or host parties there. Nothing she'd seen this summer dissuaded her from that impression.

On top of the uncertainty and anger and sadness that were likely to ebb and flow in the coming days, Reese knew that her mom must be desperately lonely. And, in her time of need, she'd come to Reese for help.

So yeah. Reese was going to find a room for her to stay in tonight, even if none were available.

Seventeen

"THANK YOU," Reese said for about the dozenth time as she fluffed her pillow against the headboard. "This is only for tonight. I'll figure out a better plan tomorrow."

Sydney stood, hands on her hips, facing Reese from across the bed. "In what universe are you thanking me for sleeping in my bed? I feel like I should be the one thanking you."

Reese calling her thirty minutes ago and asking if she could sleep in Sydney's room tonight was, she had to guess, similar to how she'd feel if she won a Grand Slam tournament. Like the luckiest person in the world, to put it mildly.

While Reese was getting her own room ready for her mom, whose reasons for being at the inn were still unclear, Sydney had busied herself cleaning up errant dirty laundry and making her bed.

She hadn't even unpacked from her trip to Florida yet, and after taking a quick shower, she realized that she was dead on her feet. A hellish night of travel. A day with Reese's family. The rest of the day with *her* family. Committing to trying out the commentator position. The scene in the pool that was like something out of her fantasies.

And the truth that couldn't be dampened by her exhaustion

was that, in spite of her overwhelming desire to crawl into bed, she was so grateful for how the night was playing out. All she'd wanted to do after making Reese come undone around her fingers was for them to find somewhere soft and warm and horizontal to simply exist together, enjoying the post-sex languor brought on after a month of buildup and a day of interruptions.

"I am going to crawl into this bed now, and I can't promise I'll be awake for longer than a few minutes," Sydney said, already easing under the covers. The sheets were cool against her bare legs, and she sank immediately into the softness of the mattress.

Reese followed suit and slid in on her side. "I really appreciate this, Sydney."

"We're consenting adults who have been interrupted all day like we're teenagers trying to find a spot to hook up. We deserve this," Sydney said in a sleep-soaked voice, inching herself closer to the middle of the mattress.

"I know, but even your parents weren't able to stay here." Which was the truth, given that, when her parents had shown up earlier today, every room had been booked. And really, she loved her parents. But maybe having them twenty minutes away and staying with one of her aunts wasn't the worst thing in the world, given her mom's less-than-warm response to Reese earlier.

Which reminded her, even through her sleepy haze: "I'm sorry that my mom wasn't nicer to you. She's just really protective, and after the whole Grant thing, I don't think she thought she'd ever have to deal with a Devereux again."

Reese nodded and inched closer to Sydney, too, so that both of their heads were resting on their respective pillows, only a few inches of space separating their faces.

Sydney could feel the sleep pulling at her eyelids, keeping them closed for longer every time she shut them.

"I can see that she really loves you. And hopefully," Reese said, tugging Sydney's lower lip into her mouth before letting it go with a *pop*, "she'll come to see me the way you do."

"And how's that?" she asked, feeling like the conversation was happening in a dream when she felt Reese's arm drape across her hips, pulling their bodies closer together.

"Like someone you can count on."

Sydney didn't know if those words were real or imagined, but they stayed burrowed in her mind as she drifted off to sleep.

* * *

Sydney groaned as she felt the covers start to move and warmth drifted away from her.

Yesterday was starting to come back to her in foggy memories that were slowly piecing themselves together. Way too many parents. Unbelievably good sex.

She was still tired, but what she clung to was the knowledge that Reese was in bed with

her and she didn't want her to leave.

"Stay. It's too early," she said, extending her arm across Reese's hip.

At some point during the night, they'd shifted into Reese as the little spoon, her back pressed against Sydney, their legs tangled together.

Sydney inhaled against the pillow they'd ended up sharing, the scent of Reese's shampoo clinging to it, already making Sydney miss her.

"Please," she said, a little desperate this time. "Just five more minutes."

"I didn't think you'd notice," Reese said as she scooted back against Sydney. "You were sleeping like the dead."

"I was sleeping so *deeply,* thank you very much, because I was so comfortable. And then you tried to sneak out of here, and all that comfort was over." She ran her finger tips down Reese's arms, loving the small shudder it elicited.

Any barriers she had left were gone. Sydney had completely given herself over to what was happening between the two of them, and she desperately hoped that Reese felt the same. So it was more than just her own comfort at stake, when she'd asked Reese to lay back down.

Her mind raced as she tried to keep her breathing even against Reese's back. She needed to know if Reese felt the same way.

"I'd already told Hallie that I'd take the early shift this morning," Reese said, snuggling flush with Sydney.

The closeness kicked off a wave of arousal that finally settled in Sydney's center. The pulsing of her clit thrummed in tempo with her heartbeat, and she stifled a groan as Reese moved again, pushing into her.

"What time is it?" she said between gritted teeth, her hands tightening around Reese's torso.

It was instinctive, how her own hips began to push forward, searching desperately for friction to ease the pressure building inside of her.

"A little before seven," Reese said, Sydney loving the hitch in her voice when she began trailing her fingers down Reese's stomach, her T-shirt pushing upward so she had access to soft, warm skin.

"So does that mean we have time to have sex in bed like real adults?" Sydney chanced, stopping her fingers just above Reese's waistband and tapping lightly.

"Sydney," Reese breathed, her voice throaty and wanting.

Sydney lifted her hand an inch above Reese's stomach, no longer flush with her skin. "I want you to say you want it."

She didn't know why, but she needed to hear it. Needed to know that Reese was a wanting, uncontrolled mess in the same way that she was. That no matter how things between them had started, this thing between them was real.

Reese tipped her head back. When she got close to Sydney's ear, a raspy, "I want it," was all the invitation Sydney needed to hear before she slipped her fingers lower. At the same time, Reese reached her hand around to Sydney's ass, pulling them impossibly closer.

Sydney rolled her hips, Reese matching her beat for beat. And when Sydney touched between Reese's thighs, she was greeted with wetness that made her hips jerk erratically. She wanted to draw out Reese's pleasure, but she couldn't go slower. She rolled her hips, hard, at the same time she found Reese's clit and began to massage.

Reese let out a low moan at the same time she dug her fingertips into Sydney's ass and then scratched down as far as she could.

It was like a bomb had exploded in Sydney's body. She ground down against Reese, finding the friction she desperately needed from their closeness. Her fingers didn't stop, rubbing and toying and touching as she found a rhythm that made Reese's breathing grow ragged, her body getting tighter.

"Like that. Yes. Just like that, Sydney." It was the most beautiful sound Sydney had ever heard, the way Reese said her name when she was so close, so wanting and on the edge. She felt that sound in her own clit, pulsing with need, which only made her grind her hips harder.

"Can you come like this?" Reese asked, her voice strained, her back beginning to arch.

Normally she couldn't, not even close. But if Reese kept making those sounds, something between a cry and a moan, like her body was turning itself inside out, then Sydney didn't know what would happen.

And then she felt fingers find her own clit, insistent and methodical. She looked down to see Reese had snaked her arm backward, miraculously finding a way to slot it between them. She had started this because the idea of not touching Reese had felt impossible, but god, she hadn't realized how desperate she was when those fingers found her, soothing at the same time they electrified, the pressure inside of her mounting.

"Baby, you feel so fucking good." The endearment slipped out, and for a split second, as she felt Reese stiffen, she thought she'd done something wrong. Had moved too fast.

But then Reese's whole body bowed, and she let out what

Sydney could only describe as a strangled moan. Her body began to jerk, her hips jutting forward erratically, like she was trying to milk every single drop out of her orgasm, out of everything Sydney could give her.

And Sydney wanted to give her all of it. Every hitch of Reese's breath and jerk of her hips. Every sound of pleasure that Sydney could tease out of her. She wanted to be responsible for all of it.

That was the thought in her mind as she careened over the edge, her ragged breaths coming out against Reese's neck, her heartbeat running wild inside of her chest.

God, it was good with them. The best, if she was being honest, and the more she got of Reese, the more she wanted.

Slowly, like she wasn't sure she had control over all of her limbs, Reese scooted herself over to lie flat on her back. "If you keep doing that, you're never going to get rid of me," she said between uneven breaths, pushing stray auburn hairs from her forehead.

Sydney was enchanted. That was the only way to describe it, as she watched the rise and fall of Reese's chest. How her hair was a little disheveled from her shower last night, when she'd gone to bed without drying it. The way she'd do anything for her mom, even though that one had really ended up a boon for everyone involved.

Which was why it was so easy for her to say, even if Reese needed to get up soon to work, "I don't want to get rid of you at all."

* * *

Sydney had fallen back asleep after Reese left. When she finally emerged from her bedroom hours later, she wasn't expecting to see Hallie sitting on the sofa, staring absently at her phone.

"Surprised you're not out living your best life with your morning off." She picked up the coffee pot and poured an overly full cup of the steaming liquid, taking a few extra seconds to infuse her senses.

A jolt of caffeine and a few orgasms had her feeling better than she had in months—at least until she looked at Hallie again and clocked her vacant stare for the second time.

"You okay?" she asked, sitting down next to Hallie on the sofa. She tapped her foot against Hallie's leg when she didn't get an answer. "I'm going to get progressively more annoying, so please just know that."

Hallie shot her an annoyed look, which wasn't like her. At all. "Can't a woman lament in peace?"

"Not on my watch." If Hallie was struggling, Sydney wasn't going to leave her flapping in the wind.

"My parents closed on their house in Colorado."

"And you're having feelings about this?"

Hallie sighed and shifted her body so that she was sitting cross-legged. "It's all real now, you know? I think before I was deluding myself into thinking they were just on vacation or something."

"I'm sorry, Hal. I didn't know you were struggling with this." Sydney had dropped back into Stoneport and quickly picked up with her own dramas, leaving Hallie to completely fend for herself. The guilt hit her like a brick to the stomach, and she leaned back against the sofa with the weight of it.

"It's just, like, how much more settled can a family be than owning an inn in a charming coastal town? I never really planned for the possibility that they'd sell it or that my entire family would pick up and move to Colorado."

"Do you want to go to Colorado with them?"

"Not really. You know I'm not exactly an outdoor enthusiast," Hallie said with a self-deprecating smile.

Sydney ran her fingers along the back of the sofa to soothe herself. She'd hate it if Hallie moved to Colorado, but her best friend had never given Sydney an ounce of guilt over following her own dreams. "I'm sure there are other things to do there if you want to be close to your family."

"I think the problem is that I don't know what I want. I'm twenty-eight years old, and I feel like I have no idea where my life is going. My family moved away. I've never had a serious relationship. I'm staying on at this job, but what happens after that? You're going to leave Stoneport at some point, which means my social circle that's not confined to coworkers will be back to zero."

Those were all fair points, and the guilt made her stomach clench again. But still... "I really have no idea what I'm doing or where Stoneport fits into it. Not that me saying that is really helpful right now."

"I know, and it's okay that you don't know what you're doing. The point is that you're trying to figure it out. Trying new things. Putting yourself back out there. I feel like I don't know how to do that. What I feel like..." Hallie stilled, working to find the right words. "I feel like I'm just a side character in other people's lives. You know what I mean?"

Sydney nodded. "That's how I felt in Grant's life, when I found out about Brynn. But Hallie"—she grabbed her best friend's hand—"you are so much more than that. Smart and funny and lovable and truly, the best friend in the world. If you want to put yourself out there, I want to help you do that. If you want to take a few weeks and go visit Colorado, I'll be happy to pick up the slack with Reese."

Hallie lifted her eyebrow.

Sydney laughed. "Yeah, I can't say Reese would want to agree to that, given it would really be the blind leading the blind, but we'd manage. For you, I'd make it work. Because your happiness and life are just as important as anyone else's."

"She must think you're phenomenal in bed if you think she'd consider something like that," Hallie teased.

Sydney could feel a faint blush spread across her cheeks. "It's not like that."

"These walls are most definitely not as thick as they should be —you should really have Reese look into that—and judging by this morning, it most definitely sounded like that." Hallie, in a very Hallie fashion, aggressively waggled her eyebrows.

"I really like her, Hal." There was no point in lying about it to herself or her best friend.

"Well, if she adds another plus in the 'spend more time in Stoneport' column, then I am all for it!" Hallie said at the same time she slapped Sydney's leg.

"Yeah? You don't think it's weird that she's Grant's sister?" Sydney had mostly gotten over that little inconvenience, but with every step forward they took, it cropped up in her mind.

"It seems like you're the one who thinks it's weird," Hallie challenged.

"I try not to think about it, but this whole thing literally started because of him."

"He only gets the power you give him," Hallie said sagely. "Does she make you happy?"

Sydney nodded, a smile blooming across her face when she thought about how much she looked forward to seeing Reese. Talking to her. Getting lost in her touch. "Ecstatic."

"And does she treat you right?"

"Yeah, she does," Sydney said wistfully, thinking about how attentive and supportive Reese had been since they'd met. "Even from the start, when she agreed to go along with the fake dating to make Grant mad."

Hallie held her hands under her chin and batted her eyes at Sydney. "And look how far you've come. Is it serious?"

"I—" Sydney knew she was falling for Reese. Knew it in her bones, could hear it in her own voice when she said, "I want it to be."

"Man. Your mom's going to lose her mind."

Sydney groaned. "I know. She saw me at my worst, when I threw myself into tennis to get over what Grant had done. Getting over Grant himself didn't take much effort."

"Yeah, because he's a doofus. You were always too good for that nepo baby," Hallie said with conviction.

Now, it was Sydney's turn to lift her brows.

"They are not the same! Reese is hardworking and built her own life. Yeah, she's had the advantage of privilege, but she didn't spend her life riding her father's coattails."

"Wow, Hallie. Tell me how you really feel," Sydney said sardonically.

"It wasn't my place to tell you that I thought that you could do better than Grant. You seemed happy, and if you were happy, then I was going to be happy for you." Hallie flashed her a cheesy smile.

Sydney knew, in retrospect, how she'd gotten into this situation. "I liked that he didn't put pressure on me when my career needed to come first but also that I had a plan already lined up for what came after it."

Hallie fake-swooned. "How romantic."

Sydney pointedly ignored her comment, which Hallie had to see coming. "But this thing with Reese, it's like a live wire. I want her and I'm drawn to her and she makes me feel like a better version of myself. And it's still so new, but I want to talk to her about the decisions I'm making and to have her be on board with them. Is that crazy?" Sydney asked, genuinely wanting an answer.

Because she'd started feeling a little crazy the past few weeks.

"No crazier than your last month," Hallie batted back before her stare softened, probably because she saw the genuinely stricken look on Sydney's face. "Look, you were so focused on your career for so long, and that's okay. Now, if you want to focus on other things, that's okay, too."

"She encouraged me to accept the interview for the commentator position."

Sydney had told Hallie about it when she'd gotten the offer, though they hadn't gotten into what she'd been planning to do. Hell, when Sydney had told her, she hadn't *known* what she was going to do.

"Seems like she doesn't want you to have any regrets either."
Sydney cocked her head to the side. "Explain."

"I'm sure she doesn't want Stoneport to be the place you stay —even if it's with her—because you're too afraid to put yourself back out there."

Hallie stood up then and walked over to the coffeepot to pour another cup. "It seems like she has your best interests at heart, and I think that, whether she and Grant are related or not, –is what sets them apart. At least from where I stand."

"You know what, Hallie? I need to run an errand," Sydney said, popping into a standing position and bouncing in place.

Reese had been looking out for her every step of the way since they'd met, and now, she needed to do the same.

* * *

"I didn't know you were coming by today." Rachel King looked up from her newspaper, the reading glasses she'd only started wearing in the last few years perched low on the bridge of her nose.

It was a startling reminder to Sydney that her mom wouldn't always be around. That while Sydney was getting older, so were her parents.

Still, it didn't change why she was here. She wanted to make sure that she could share with them the best parts of the new life she was building.

The side door, which everyone used at Aunt Nancy's, opened directly into the kitchen, her older Cape Cod house filled with thirty years of memories.

Sydney sat down at the round kitchen table across from her mom. "Where's Aunt Nancy?"

She didn't ask about her father. She'd seen him upon arrival, wandering the yard and looking at the shrubbery. He'd always been a nature lover, so instead of getting caught up in his thoughts on the summer bloom on the sweet pepperbush outside, she'd given him a quick kiss and headed inside to find her mom.

"She's picking up Tess and Callie after their soccer game to bring them to hang out for the afternoon." Tess and Callie were Nancy's grandchildren, the daughters of Sydney's cousin, Steve, who was about seven years older than her.

"That'll be nice, spending time with your grandkids once removed."

"Is that what we're calling them?" her mom asked. She put down her newspaper and picked up a bundle of something that had been seated on the chair next to her, out of view. A crochet hook and yarn. Guess she'd been serious about the baby blankets.

"Mom," Sydney groaned. "I thought we'd left things in a really good place in Florida. Why were you so"—she scrunched up her nose reflexively—"hostile at the inn yesterday?"

She'd thought about bringing it up multiple times yesterday, when they'd been trekking across the greater Stoneport area to visit all of her aunts, but there had never been a good time.

Now, she was determined to get to the bottom of things. Especially after what had happened between her and Reese last night.

Fingers that had already dexterously started working across the blanket, looping stitches, stilled. Her mom peered up at her, brows drawn together. "I didn't realize that I was hostile."

"I'd already told you that I was dating Reese. You said you were happy for me. What changed?" Sydney pushed.

Looking at Reese and seeing anything other than an amazing woman was something Sydney couldn't understand. But this was her mother, and she wanted to make sense of her reaction.

"In my defense, Cade told Beth who told me that your cousin saw you at the Devereux house for a wedding-related party. For Grant. And I was happy that you seemed so happy. But then you left, and I kept thinking about it."

Sydney scooted her chair a little closer. "And what did you start thinking?"

"That I was concerned. You're my daughter, Sydney," her mom said, "and I know that you're an adult. I support you making your own decisions."

"But you can see how it doesn't feel that way when you treat the people I've made decisions about the way you did? That dig about Grant coming to dinner, too? Come on, Mom. Really?"

She saw a hint of embarrassment flash through her mom's eyes. "It wasn't my best moment, I'll give you that. We arrived at the inn, and I asked Hallie if you were around when I couldn't get ahold of you. I'd assumed you were sleeping given how late you'd gotten back."

Sydney could already see how it played out. Hallie had never been good at lying to her mom. Neither of them were. "And Hallie folded like a piece of paper?"

Her mom smiled ruefully. "Something like that."

"So I was out with Reese. That shouldn't be surprising to you?" Sydney was still trying to pick at the fraying edges of her mom's story, trying to understand where her true issue was stemming from.

"After you'd sat at the airport for about eight hours in the hopes of making it back here, only for me to find out that it was so you could go to another event at the Devereux house. For something related to Grant's wedding, I assume?" her mom asked, though it was clear she already knew the answer.

"I like her. *Her*. And while it's not the most amazing thing that she's the sister of my ex-boyfriend, it's not going to stop me. And honestly..." She took a quick, steadying breath. "This summer has really helped me make peace with the Grant situation."

"Is this some kind of exposure therapy?" her mom asked, half joking but with an underlying tone of seriousness.

Sydney considered the question. "Sort of? I mean, I caught him, and I walked out of our apartment. I stopped answering his calls. I sent him any of his stuff back in the mail. I still don't think he deserved a conversation after what he'd done, but I was left with all of these *questions*. I didn't have answers, and I didn't have anywhere to put all my frustration."

Sydney stretched out her arms, thinking about how it had been too many days since she'd held a tennis racket in her hands. "And for a while, it was fine. I had tennis to throw myself into. As many hours and workouts and matches as I could handle. But then I got injured..."

Her mom's hand encircled her own, and she felt like a child again, wanting so desperately to have her mom's comfort. Something she'd pushed away for the last year for fear that she'd crumble.

"I couldn't make it work anymore, but still, I kept trying. Working. Training. But it didn't matter," Sydney lamented. "And then my career just petered out. It was like I'd been running and running and running, only now, there was nowhere for me to go."

"You never told me any of this." Even though her mom had been there in the aftermath, Sydney hadn't wanted to talk about it. All she'd managed, all she'd had to say at the time, was that Grant had cheated and things were over.

Her mom had wanted her to talk about it at first. Had tried all the different tactics, actually. Giving Sydney space. Asking her very pointed questions. Encouraging her to speak to a professional, if she wasn't going to confide in her own mother. But Sydney had wanted to keep moving forward, to throw herself into tennis and forget what had happened.

Now, she was starting to see it a little better from her mom's perspective. Sydney had pushed things down. Bottled them up. Done everything to avoid the reality of her situation.

She could now see, with startling clarity, how that must have looked from the outside.

All so that a year later, when she popped up with Reese Devereux as her girlfriend, inserting herself into Grant's life, she looked... "I'm not crazy, I promise. I didn't know that Grant was going to be around so much when I came back into town."

"Reese didn't tell you her brother was getting married?"

"Ehh…" Sydney felt the heat flame her cheeks, caught in her mother's curious stare. "Our relationship is a little newer than we'd let people believe. We connected when I came back this summer, given that she was at the inn so much."

"Got it," her mom said, absorbing the information with a neutral look.

"I promise you, it doesn't change how I feel about her. I've felt more like myself this past month than I have in years. I understand now that I shut you out and that this all seems like it's out of left field, but I think you'd really like her. She's smart and driven and incredibly sweet to me. I'd like to think that she's exactly the type of person that you'd want your daughter to end up with."

And even if that was a loaded statement that exploded in Sydney's brain and made her feel a little lightheaded, she tamped down the idea. Whether this was going somewhere long-term, Reese was good for her right now, and she wanted to see where things would go. That was what she was focusing on. Not her overzealous desire to always have a multistep plan that stretched years into the future.

She'd much rather take a chance on happiness than settle, like she'd done before, on something she'd thought was a sure thing.

"You do really seem happy, Sydney. I was just trying to reconcile the situation, when confronted with Reese, as I tried to fill in the gaps from the last year. I wish I'd handled it differently."

Sydney smiled, warmth threading through her veins. "I really am happy. And I'd love for you to get to know Reese. I think you'll see where some of my happiness is coming from."

"I'd like that," her mom said, leaning forward and giving her a kiss on the forehead.

Shifting her focus, Sydney removed her hand and leaned back in her chair, her arm draped across the table. "Now what about you? What's going on with Florida?"

"What do you—"

"Mom, I was honest with you. I'd like the same thing in return."

Her mom gave her a surmising stare before something settled across her face. "Wow, your time in Stoneport really has done wonders."

"As I told you," Sydney said with a decisive nod, coupled with a smile. "Now, what's going on?"

"I don't think I'm a Florida person," her mom admitted. "It made sense when you were there."

"But I'm not right now."

"But you're not," her mom agreed, "and I think after two years, I'd feel more settled."

"You haven't gotten invested in the local flora of Florida?" Sydney joked.

That earned a smile from her mom. "This last year, with you so withdrawn..."

Guilt prickled across Sydney's skin, itchy and uncomfortable.

Her mom shook her head when she saw the anguish on Sydney's face. "I don't say that to make you feel badly. All I mean is that, with you so focused on tennis this last year and less willing to be open with me, I really did try to create a network. To integrate into the neighborhood and make it feel more like a home for myself."

"I'm sorry, Mom. I couldn't see that you were struggling through my own pain." Sydney had been single-minded since she'd broken up with Grant. On moving forward. On pushing past. On not letting Grant take one more thing from her.

And what had it gotten her? A whole lot of relationships she was just now beginning to mend, including the one with herself.

"It's okay, baby. And if we're being honest, I wanted to come to Stoneport to check on you, but I also wanted to be here. With my sisters. My family. This is my home, and it always will be, no matter where I live."

"I understand that feeling completely," Sydney said. As she bit back the emotion in her voice, tears started to pool behind her eyes.

Her mom wiped at her own eyes. "Well, I really didn't expect us to be having this conversation, but I'm really glad that we are."

"Me too, Mom. And if you and Dad want to move back to Stoneport, I want that for you. Truly."

"You bought that beautiful house because we loved it. You took so much thought and care to make sure that we felt at home there," her mom argued.

"It's a house. We'll sell it, and you can buy one here. I want you to be surrounded by the people that make you happy."

"Well, first and foremost, that's you."

Sydney had been thinking about it a lot, though she was trying not to rush into any decisions. Her parents in Stoneport was just another check in a column that was quickly overflowing with positives.

"And I'll be around, I promise." She gave her mom a slightly self-satisfied smile. "And regardless of where I live, if I'm dating Reese, I'll be around a lot."

"So you're saying I should be nicer to your girlfriend, then?"

Her grin spread wider across her face. "That's exactly what I'm saying."

"Well then," her mom said, matching Sydney's smile, "I guess we should get that dinner scheduled soon. Is humble pie on the menu?"

Sydney stood up and walked around to the back of her mom's chair before wrapping her long arms around her in a hug. "No promises, but I'll at least make sure they have crow."

Eighteen

REESE HAD STOPPED TRYING to make sense of the last two weeks. At this point, she was just going with it.

Which is how, on a casual Saturday, she found herself in the small dining room at the inn with Hallie, her mom, and Sydney's mom, Rachel.

"Do you think Sydney is having FOMO?" Hallie asked before shoveling a large bite of lobster roll, one of the inn's specialties, into her mouth.

"She probably wasn't until you just sent her a barrage of group photos," Reese said at the same time she kept an eye on the line of sight she had to the check-in desk.

But Hallie beat her to it, standing up and scurrying off when she noticed a guest heading to checkout.

Really, she'd never expected this would be where her life would end up. A healthy relationship with her mother, who still, two weeks later, hadn't relented and returned to her father. She and Hallie were better than ever at working in sync, and she was proud of herself for the rhythm they'd developed. But the dark horse of the month was Rachel King, who, after their first meeting, was like an entirely different person with her.

She had a sneaking suspicion that she had Sydney to thank for that, but an admission, even under duress, had not been forthcoming.

Her mom and Rachel were in a heated conversation about something insignificant that had happened in Stoneport more than twenty years ago, so she could easily slip her phone out of her pocket when she felt it vibrate.

SYDNEY KING - 2:15 P.M.

I feel like your mom shouldn't have bothered moving back home, given all the time she's spending at the inn

REESE DEVEREUX - 2:15 P.M.

Is this your way of saying you feel left out? I owe Hallie five bucks. I didn't think you'd admit it.

SYDNEY KING - 2:15 P.M.

I feel... like I'm in a parallel universe. All of you together, and I'm waiting in hair and makeup to do a dry run for tomorrow's start

Sydney had been gone since Wednesday, heading to the event early to prepare for her first time as a commentator. There was no doubt in Reese's mind that she'd kill it once the matches started, but she did understand how it all must feel a little absurd to someone who used to compete there as an athlete.

REESE DEVEREUX - 2:16 P.M.

You're going to be amazing, I have no doubt. How's it going?

They'd talked on the phone every night since Sydney had been gone, but her schedule was generally jam-packed with screen tests, meeting the other commentators, and going over the best practices for on-air behavior.

SYDNEY KING - 2:16 P.M.

They act like I don't know anything about
tennis! There was even a session on not
accidentally making sexual innuendos!

REESE DEVEREUX - 2:16 P.M.

???

Reese waited with bated breath for Sydney's response to come through, smiling down at her phone.

"Wonder who you're messaging?" her mom asked with a look on her face that said the statement was absurdly rhetorical. This was further amplified by how she didn't even give Reese a chance to respond, instead turning right back to Rachel to pick up their conversation.

In her wildest dreams, Reese had never considered that her mom would be making fun of her for having a lovesick smile on her face. For so many reasons. For one thing, Reese never thought they'd be around one another for long enough for her mom to see it. Not to mention how she never expected them to be close enough that her mom would feel comfortable doing it.

And, lastly, until Sydney, there'd never been a look like this to see. No silly smiles. No dopey grins. No losing herself in the memory of an especially soft morning or debauched night. Sometimes the other way around, too.

Reese couldn't get enough of it. Couldn't get enough of *Sydney*.

How she made her breath skitter and her knees wobble and her body pulse with need.

Over the last two weeks, things had only intensified. Reese hadn't returned to her own room. Her mom had vacated it about a week ago, insisting on returning to her home regardless of whether Reese's dad decided to show up there or not.

But after a week of going to bed and waking up in Sydney's arms, sleeping in a lonely bed was far from an attractive proposition.

Deep down, Reese still didn't know how this would all end. If Sydney did pick up the commentary job full-time, there'd be a lot of nights, entire weeks even, spent apart.

So with that thought, she told herself that it was okay to throw herself into the time they did have, that it was the practical thing to do.

She'd rather feel good in the immediacy and rip the Band-Aid off at some unknown later date than temper her emotions now to make the eventual comedown less intense.

Reese had become a wanton woman, and she had no problem acting the part.

Finally, she felt her phone vibrate again.

SYDNEY KING - 2:19 P.M.

Sorry, they had to explain to me that I should "warm up my voice" to prepare for talking for long periods of time

REESE DEVEREUX - 2:19 P.M.

Did you explain to them that you've been doing daily vocal exercises?

SYDNEY KING - 2:19 P.M.

I don't think that screaming your name while I come counts…

REESE DEVEREUX - 2:19 P.M.

But you do it over and over again…

Desire sluiced through Reese's veins, heady and potent as she typed the words. She could hear perfectly how Sydney said her name when they had sex. Sometimes it was breathy and wanting. Other times it was guttural and hedonistic.

But it was always hot. So, so hot.

And she couldn't get enough of it. Three days ago, she'd lain in bed with Sydney, and everything had felt so right.

The sex. The compatibility. The support.

All she wanted to do was wrap herself up in the way Sydney made her feel forever. Or at least for as long as she could.

SYDNEY KING - 2:20 P.M.

Bad. And unfair, considering I have to practice in a minute and my body is on fire. I probably look like a tomato.

REESE DEVEREUX - 2:20 P.M.

A cute tomato, undoubtedly.

SYDNEY KING - 2:20 P.M.

Takes one to know one. I'm sure you're not getting out of this unscathed.

Sydney really did have her number because Reese could feel her own flush, her pulse thrumming intently as she imagined— and missed—the sound of Sydney's voice.

SYDNEY KING - 2:21 P.M.

Send me a pic later?

REESE DEVEREUX - 2:21 P.M.

You just got a pic of all of us.

SYDNEY KING - 2:22 P.M.

You know that's not what I mean. No pressure, but I miss you. And you're teasing me and you know it, which I am not complaining about by the way.

SYDNEY KING - 2:22 P.M.

To be very clear: TEASE AWAY.

On top of Reese's own arousal, it felt good to feel wanted, to know that Sydney was missing her and thinking of her and wanted to *see* her. But it also made her nervous. She felt exposed at the idea of upping the ante on their text-based flirting.

But she could do it. She wanted to do it.

REESE DEVEREUX - 2:23 P.M.

> I will. It may have to be tomorrow because I
> have Brynn's bachelorette thing tonight.

Reese intentionally called it a 'thing' because the plan for this evening was fairly unorthodox, as far as modern bachelorette parties went.

SYDNEY KING - 2:23 P.M.

OH MY GOD HOW COULD I HAVE
FORGOTTEN!

Brynn, Reese had learned earlier this week, wanted to have a slumber party.

REESE DEVEREUX - 2:23 P.M.

> You're lucky that you were out of town
> because you were invited, too.

SYDNEY KING - 2:24 P.M.

And what a tragedy I can't attend. But i'm
sure you'll fill me in on everything. Promise?

SYDNEY KING - 2:24 P.M.

I've gotta run. Miss you <3

Feeling wholly unsatisfied that their conversation was over, Reese begrudgingly put her phone down and tuned back into the conversation.

They were discussing her mom's next steps, as far as divorce went.

Never a dull moment with this crowd.

"I've reached out to a few lawyers," Sharon was saying. "Tripp is still refusing to accept the reality of the situation."

Reese snorted, and both pairs of eyes turned toward her. At the same time, Hallie ambled back into the dining room and took her seat at the table.

"I mean, he's used to getting what he wants. I'm sure he's not going to make this easy if he doesn't want it."

"I'm really proud of your mom for sticking to her guns," Rachel said, casting a sympathetic but supportive look at Reese's mom. "Sometimes, standing up for ourselves is far harder than doing it for other people."

Well, hadn't those two just become thick as thieves these past few weeks. Still, Reese was glad her mom had someone outside of her normal social circle to provide unbiased support. A lot of the wives in Stoneport and Boston would find her mom's decision unimaginable.

"I'm proud of you, too, Mom," Reese said, and meant it.

Her mom blushed at all the attention, clearly wishing it would end. "Anyway, what time are you heading to Brynn's?"

The slumber party, which Reese was truly trying to get on board with, was at Brynn's apartment in Cambridge.

"I'm leaving at seven," she said, checking her watch. "I guess the good news is that I don't need to get all dolled up."

"Gonna wear your jammies there?" Hallie teased.

Reese groaned. "I'm trying to be a good sport about this, but I am not planning on spending the night. I think Brynn will understand."

"She's sweet," her mom cut in, adding, "maybe a little naive."

This time, Reese let out an indignant scoff. "Look, I don't disagree, but she's still going through with marrying Grant. I think we're moving beyond naivety and bordering on stu—"

"Reese," her mom chided, cutting her off.

"I like her," Reese defended her word choice, "but after Grant's show a few weeks ago at the couple's shower, you cannot tell me, honestly, that you aren't thinking the same thing."

The difficulty about tonight came, more than anything, from the fact that Brynn was still going through with the wedding. It was clear that Grant didn't prioritize her. That he didn't have much respect for her. And that, on top of it all, he could care less about her feelings.

A real catch, her brother was.

"I think we all know where I stand, so I'm going to stay out of this conversation," Rachel said, and laughter broke out, easing the tension of the moment.

"When do you head back to Florida?" Hallie asked, voicing a question that Reese herself had been wondering. Not that she minded Rachel being around; she'd been nothing but kind since their first run-in, and she'd provided a much-needed activity partner for Reese's mom.

Really, the big question was when she'd be coming back to pick up that mantle again. Reese loved her mom, but there were only so many hours in a day.

"We leave tomorrow, but I think we'll be back sooner than later."

"Great," Hallie beamed. "Then we can all do this together again when Sydney's back, too."

And, in spite of what a strange group they made, Reese found herself sincerely hoping that they would.

* * *

"So Jennifer just texted. She's not going to be able to make it." Brynn put down her phone, staring around the room. "I guess we can order dinner, then?"

Reese had been at Brynn's apartment for less than an hour, and the hits just kept coming.

Reese was one of four bridesmaids and had expected at least a little bit of a buffer tonight, provided by women who would be far closer to Brynn and able to provide the right type of excitement for her impending nuptials.

Reese didn't think she fit the bill on being that person for so many reasons.

Kate, Brynn's cousin, had let Brynn know a few hours ago that she'd been called into surgery near the end of her shift. She was a neurosurgery resident at Boston General, so Reese couldn't really hold that against her.

Too much, anyway.

And two other women was still a perfectly adequate number of people to let Reese slink into the background. They could joke and squeal and do whatever it was that Brynn wanted to do tonight.

Jennifer and Carrie were both Brynn's friends from undergrad, and with all of them around twenty-six, Brynn's age, she was banking on them to bring the enthusiasm.

Sadly, that wasn't to be the case.

Carrie had tapped out first, citing that her sister had an emergency, and Carrie was providing childcare.

Annoying, from Reese's perspective, but she couldn't really begrudge the woman. Probably.

So they'd been waiting on Jennifer, the last hope to diffuse Reese's responsibility toward hyping Brynn up about making, in Reese's mind, the most ill-advised decision of her young life.

Which was why Reese let out a long, quiet sigh when Jennifer's text came through. She reached for the open bottle of wine on the coffee table and topped off her glass.

Reese had stared down her father while he looked at her with hostility in his eyes. She'd dealt with board members who made decisions outside of any common decency and stared her down while they did it. She'd wrangled Grant, whose drunken spittle had flecked her outfit while he'd blamed her for everything going wrong in his life.

And yet all of that paled in comparison to handling Brynn in this moment, who didn't even realize that she should probably be upset.

In a way, it made things easier for Reese. If Brynn wasn't distressed, which was astounding in its own right, then Reese should follow her lead.

"What are you thinking about for dinner?" Reese asked,

standing up with her glass and walking over to a floor-to-ceiling bookshelf that covered one of the living room walls.

"Originally, I was going to have us all do a tasting menu at Nori Nori, but when I decided I wanted a more casual night, I figured that we could still order sushi."

Reese tried to hide how the pieces were clicking into place, and she pretended to study the titles of the books on the shelves. Nori Nori was probably the most sought-after reservation in Boston, unique because it was only two private rooms for a nine-course tasting menu for dinner.

She couldn't be sure, but for Brynn's college friends, at least, it seemed like maybe a slumber party had less of an allure than a reservation at the most exclusive restaurant in Boston.

Guilt hit her at the current state of Brynn's romantic and personal lives. And maybe, more than a little, she still felt badly about earlier today, when she'd been on the verge of being disparaging to Brynn.

Sure, she didn't understand her future sister-in-law, but that didn't mean that she was dumb. Or that she didn't know what decisions she was making.

Which was further evidenced by... "So you're into philosophy?" Reese asked as she finally focused on the titles before her. There were rows and rows of books by authors Reese had never heard of.

Brynn looked a little shy then, even younger when you added in her navy pajama set with pineapples repeated across the top and shorts. "I just finished my PhD in philosophy in the spring. Modern analytic philosophy, to be exact."

Reese's brows lifted, and she touched one of the spines. "So, I guess you and Grant have a lot to talk about then?"

Brynn laughed. "Well, most people don't want to talk about philosophy, so I can't exactly hold that against Grant either."

"So, what comes next?" Reese asked, changing the subject but keeping it high level. Trying to get into anything related to philosophy, she was quickly realizing, would be like bringing a knife to a gun fight. "Teaching?"

Brynn came to stand next to her at the bookshelf. "Still figuring that out."

Reese realized, as they stood shoulder to shoulder, that she had an opportunity here. She was already a glass of wine deep—not enough to be drunk, but her tongue was a little more loose, and she had questions that, for weeks, had been begging for answers. "So, tell me more about you. I think this is the first time we're really hanging out one-on-one."

"Well, I'm an only child."

Reese pointed at Brynn with the hand holding her wineglass. "Which I already knew."

"Hmm..." Brynn scrunched up her face in thought. "Well, we've already covered my academic pursuits."

Reese made a little 'aha' sound, like the idea was just coming to her. "Tell me about you and Grant. That is what we're here celebrating, after all."

"I can say that I never really saw Grant coming," Brynn said, her voice full of earnestness.

"What do you mean?" Reese asked casually.

"Studying philosophy, from the outside, looks a lot like having your head in the clouds. I wasn't looking for anyone. I finished undergrad and went right into my PhD program, which was pretty rigorous."

Judging by the number of books, Reese thought that 'rigorous' was painting too merciful of a picture. But then, that seemed to be Brynn's whole thing, understating everything about herself.

"How did you two meet?" For someone who'd spent their life making sense of the world, Brynn wasn't exactly forthcoming with information about her own place in it.

Brynn rubbed affectionately down the spine of one of the larger books. "There was a social event at a business club in

Boston. I went as my dad's guest, and I met Grant there. And he was so..."

Irritating? Grating? Frustrating?

"Charming," Brynn finished, and Reese just managed to hold back her surprise. But it made sense, given that Brynn had agreed to marry him.

"So you two started dating?" Reese knew she was treading into dangerous territory.

At this point, she didn't really believe that Brynn knew she was a party to infidelity, but Reese still wanted to know for sure. It would determine how the rest of the night went, at least on Reese's side.

"It was a little more casual than that at first, but I guess you could say that. He asked for my number, and then I didn't hear from him for a few weeks. One day, he reached out, asking to get drinks."

Romantic, Reese thought, making sure not to say the quiet part out loud.

"I was deep into my penultimate year of my program, so it really didn't matter to me one way or another."

"Had you dated before?" It would make sense, if Brynn had no basis of comparison, how Grant had snuck in through the side door and given her the impression that he was a stand-up guy.

"I had a boyfriend in undergrad, Gregory. He was my best friend."

Reese lifted her eyebrow, mostly eyeing her almost empty glass. "And what happened with Gregory?"

"Devon happened," Brynn said very matter-of-factly, her fingers dancing over to another book.

Maybe Brynn wasn't as naive as she seemed, if she skipped from Gregory straight to Devon. "So, you and Devon?"

Brynn shook her head. "No. Gregory *and* Devon. Gregory accepted that he was gay, and a lot of things started to make sense."

"Gotcha," Reese said, polishing off her drink. "Are you two still friends?"

Brynn nodded, smiling genuinely. "We are. He'll be at the wedding in September."

Yes, the wedding. That was still, against any sense Reese could make of things, pushing forward, full steam ahead.

"And it makes it really nice, having one of Grant's exes there, too. I'm just really glad everyone could stay friends."

Reese couldn't hide the side-eye that she gave Brynn, who luckily, didn't seem to notice.

They really needed to order dinner. The second glass of wine had gone straight to Reese's head, and she had all kinds of comments sloshing around in her brain that she had no right to ask.

"I wouldn't qualify Grant and Sydney as friends. She's my girlfriend, and he's my brother. That's about the extent of it." She felt the need to defend Sydney's honor in this moment, that she'd never willingly have stayed in Grant's life after what he'd done.

Did Brynn know?

The million-dollar question reared its head again.

"I'm glad you two found one another," Brynn said before a look crossed her face. She had almost said something, then stopped.

"Go ahead," Reese encouraged her.

Brynn pursed her lips. "I have to admit, after hearing how hard she took the breakup, it was a bit of a surprise to see her pop up in your life."

So Brynn was more observant than she let on. At least if it was about anything outside of her own relationship.

And she was implying, even if it was true—but not for the reasons she thought—that Sydney couldn't let go of the past.

Reese didn't like that.

And with that admission, it became clear that Brynn hadn't been aware that Grant and Sydney had still been together when she had met Grant.

Reese warred with how much to say, but her need to be honest was mounting. Neither of these women deserved to have Grant in their lives, and Brynn didn't have all the facts.

Still, she wanted to couch her language as much as possible, mostly for Brynn's sake. "I know that most people want to present the best version of themselves in a new relationship, but Grant didn't break up with Sydney. It was the other way around."

There, she'd set the record straight without divulging too much.

Brynn squinted, clear she was trying to make sense of this information. "You're saying that Sydney broke up with Grant. Why?"

Oh, the list was endless. Narcissism. Selfishness. Infidelity.

This is what it had all been building toward, which some part of Reese had known from the beginning. Could she pull the trigger and upend Brynn's world? Would it even matter?

Lots of women stayed with men even though they were cheaters.

And once Brynn found out, she may shoot the messenger. Metaphorically, of course.

But Reese didn't owe her brother anything, and she didn't want Brynn walking into her marriage blind. She should move forward, or not, with all the information available to her.

"He cheated on her," Reese said before she could talk herself out of it. It was strange, how saying the words felt so good and so awful at the same time. She was voicing the truth but knew that it came at the expense of a good person caught in the crossfire.

Brynn's face crumpled. "No. He said that long distance had gotten to be too much. And that even though Sydney wanted them to make it work, he was ready to settle down and get more serious, which wasn't possible with her career."

Reese pinched the bridge of her nose. In for a penny, in for a pound.

"I believe what Sydney's told me, Brynn. And maybe it was a fluke, but she caught him. *That* is why they broke up."

Brynn began to pace the room, back and forth in front of the coffee table adjacent to the bookshelves. Reese walked over to the sofa and sat down. She stared at Brynn, who looked like a video game character who had to turn around when she got to the edge of the screen.

"Why are you telling me this?" Brynn asked. She stopped and stood with her hands on her hips. The emotion in her voice wasn't anger or sadness, but genuine confusion as she tried to make sense of what Reese had just told her.

"I like you, Brynn," Reese said with a soft smile that didn't alleviate the tension radiating through her body. There was no stuffing the cat back in the bag, so she pressed on. "Let me be clear, I'm not doing this to hurt my brother, even though he and I don't have the best relationship. I'm doing this because I think that you deserve the truth, and I don't think that Sydney's name deserves to be disparaged. And I'm a big fan of having the facts in order to make decisions."

She could see Brynn thinking, slotting everything new that she'd just heard into place. "Grant didn't mention that he'd dated anyone else after Sydney before we met. I'm just having trouble fitting the pieces together."

Oh.

Oh no.

Sweet, honest-to-a-fault Brynn hadn't taken the last step in working out the logistics.

It was coming. Reese could *feel* it coming.

"So... Grant cheated on Sydney with someone, but for whatever reason, they didn't work out. And then he met me." Brynn's voice wasn't hopeful enough that Reese believed she was trying to find an alternate possibility to the truth she knew deep inside.

Reese squinted, her whole face tight. She didn't want to do this. She didn't want to do *this*.

The idea of giving someone the facts and watching the realization play out in real time were orders of magnitude apart, and it was something Reese herself hadn't understood until this moment.

"You said Sydney walked in on them? Did she know the woman?" Brynn ran a hand through her hair. A piece stuck out at an odd angle when she dropped her arms back to her hips. Reese would have laughed except she was on the verge of crying.

She needed to put an end to this. The feeling gripped her, overwhelming, like she'd crumple if she didn't get to the finish line soon.

"Brynn," she said, sitting up straighter and looking her in the eye. "It was you."

Nineteen

"YOU WERE A NATURAL," Gary, one of The Tennis Network's producers said, clapping her on the shoulder. "They loved you, I know it. The way you clearly articulated where Makarova was off her game, it built a story that fans could follow through the rest of the match. That's what tennis needs these days, especially as we work to attract newer fans."

Sydney removed her headset and hopped down from her chair. "She has a tendency to struggle against left-handers with single-handed backhands," she said, repeating essentially what she'd said during the match.

They'd just wrapped day one, a surprisingly difficult first-round match for the
current number four seed, Maria Makarova. The match had gone to three sets, with Makarova pulling off what should have been a much more resounding win.

Still, Sydney was pleased with the compliment. Gary had been in the producer's chair for a decade at this point, and his belief in her meant something as she ventured into this possible new career path.

"The production team is heading out to dinner. Care to join us?"

Sydney looked down at her watch. She'd gotten to the box at nine a.m., already having gone through hair and makeup, and it was just after six o'clock now.

"I could have a quick bite to eat." She wasn't talking to Reese until a few hours from now, so the timing should work. Because there was nothing that was going to stop her from laying eyes on Reese's beautiful face, not even the chance to rub elbows with the people who decided her fate.

"Hotel restaurant in an hour?" Gary asked, his tablet in hand as he jotted down notes at the same time.

"Sure." Sydney left the box then, making her way down to where the cars reserved to shuttle the commentators from the hotel to the venue were waiting. She was lucky to find one available during the crew's rush hour.

She'd take a quick shower, have dinner with her possible new coworkers, and then she'd be on to today's main event.

She smiled reflexively as the car made the quick trip back to the hotel. God, she was excited to talk to Reese.

SYDNEY KING - 6:06 P.M.

Heading to dinner with some of the production people and commentators.

REESE DEVEREUX - 6:06 P.M.

Aww, that's my baby. Making friends!

SYDNEY KING - 6:06 P.M.

Hardly. I'm just passing the time until I get to see you!

She felt the thrill of excitement that Reese elicited in her skitter through her body, especially at the pet name being used. Sydney was so gone, and she knew it.

The quick drive was passing her by, but all she could think about was taking these few minutes with Reese while she could get them.

SYDNEY KING - 6:07 P.M.

How did today go?

Yesterday, Reese had ended up staying with her mom at the Devereux house overnight, and today, she'd gone with her into the city to start meeting with a few divorce lawyers.

REESE DEVEREUX - 6:07 P.M.

The whole process seems brutal. Remind me
to never get divorced!

Sydney waited to respond, about to make a joke on a conversation about marriage, when she saw text bubbles pop up.

The moment lost, she tucked the thought away for a later time. Not the idea of them getting married, obviously. That would make her crazy. There was no reason for her to imagine what type of wedding she and Reese could have, though she'd always loved the idea of fall weddings. And the color palette would go perfectly with Reese's skin tone.

No. She didn't even know where Reese stood on the subject of marriage.

But still, Reese hadn't said that she never wanted to get married, just that she didn't want to get divorced.

Another thought to tuck away. For a later date. Much, much later unless she wanted to scare Reese all the way back to California.

Especially given their current topic of conversation. Nothing screamed 'romantic conversation about the future' like discussing your parents' impending divorce.

REESE DEVEREUX - 6:07 P.M.

We met with three lawyers for consultations.
We both liked Caroline Parker the best. The
other two were like sharks who smelled blood
in the water and just wanted their piece of the
chum.

SYDNEY KING - 6:08 P.M.

This is big. How do you feel?

REESE DEVEREUX - 6:08 P.M.

About being a child of divorce?

SYDNEY KING - 6:08 P.M.

No one gives you credit for how funny
you are.

This was good. Keep the mood light. It was obvious that Reese wanted to, and she was going to follow her lead.

REESE DEVEREUX - 6:08 P.M.

You're giving me credit right now.

Light flirting. Perfect.

She loved when Reese flirted with her. It was always witty and understated and made Sydney smile uncontrollably.

Still, she really did want to make sure that Reese was okay.

SYDNEY KING - 6:09 P.M.

I mean it. I'm trying to be sensitive to what
you're going through!

REESE DEVEREUX - 6:09 P.M.

Honestly, I'm thrilled. I know this isn't going to
be easy for my mom, but she's already done
the hardest part. And she has so much life to
live. I'm glad she's going to get to live it on her
terms.

REESE DEVEREUX - 6:09 P.M.

I feel like I'm getting a front row seat to the
implosion of my father's life. Is it wrong that I
don't feel badly about that?

SYDNEY KING - 6:10 P.M.

Absolutely not. He's reaping what he sowed. I,
personally, love some karmic justice.

REESE DEVEREUX - 6:10 P.M.

Perfect. Because if we don't both enjoy the misfortune of others (when they deserve it), I don't know how this could ever work.

Sydney only briefly considered not sending her next text.

SYDNEY KING - 6:10 P.M.

Good. Because I really, really want this to work.

REESE DEVEREUX - 6:10 P.M.

Me too. Okay, gotta run. We're already late to our dinner reservation. Talk later?

SYDNEY KING - 6:10 P.M.

Yes. Text me if your plans change.

As Sydney arrived at the hotel, with enough time to take a shower before meeting the crew for dinner, with a huge next step of her professional career looming before her, all she could think about was what Reese was doing and whether she was thinking of Sydney, too.

* * *

"Tell me everything. Don't leave a single bit out," Reese said as the video call connected, her soft face coming into view.

Sydney had just closed her hotel room door behind her. She threw her leftovers on the desk near the television and slid her shoes off. "There's not that much to tell."

Reese let out an adorably indignant huff that Sydney found downright charming. "I don't believe that for a second. You were back at a pro tournament. Around friends and foes alike. Working in a completely new role."

"What colorful commentary, babe. Maybe you should have been the one on screen?"

"Seriously, Sydney. I want to know," Reese said, her voice softening and cutting through all of Sydney's defenses.

Sydney plopped down in a chair next to the window, holding her phone a few feet away from her face. "Honestly, I've been so busy that I haven't really digested or processed a lot of it yet. And we're only on the first day of live matches, so I'm trying to temper making any judgments about the commentator aspect of it."

She had six more days of live commentary to provide, leading through the final matches happening on Sunday. It was unclear yet if she'd be tapped to commentate at the finals, but she had to be on standby through the weekend regardless.

Reese nodded along, her back resting against the headboard in Sydney's hotel room at The Stone's Throw. "That's fair. How do you *feel*, then? Take the big-brain thinking out of it."

"I feel..." Sydney sat with the question for a moment, tapping into her senses. "My body is tired. It's a whole different type of exhaustion to have to be 'on' for so long at a time. And I like getting dolled up as much as the next person, but hair and makeup is not a gentle process."

Reese laughed then, and Sydney loved how she slid a little farther down into the bed, burrowing into the covers they hadn't shared in far too long. "Okay, that all makes sense. Did it feel good to be back at a tournament?"

"I feel like you're gentle-parenting me," Sydney said lightly as she kicked her legs up on the coffee table, only a little embarrassed by the situation.

"Is it working?" Reese asked, flashing Sydney a grin.

"I miss you." Sydney said the words before she'd articulated them in her mind. "That's how I feel."

"I miss you, too." The way Reese said it made Sydney's insides go all mushy, and she wondered how she was still retaining her body's shape.

"And it's hard to fully experience something with that always in the back of my mind."

Hesitation was etched across Reese's face when she said, "Should we talk less? To give you more time to focus."

Sydney shook her head resolutely. "That's absolutely not what I want. I'm just being honest. I think I'm homesick... for Stoneport."

She saw how Reese's cheeks turned pink, and it looked like the phone shook gently, cradled in Reese's hands. "Stoneport misses you, too."

But she'd promised that she was going to give the commentary position a chance, at Reese's insistence even.

So she thought about the positives. It had felt good to be praised by Gary, considering she'd never done something like this before. And parts of it *were* fun. Analyzing the players from a few levels removed, instead of her mind and body adapting in real time, making what felt like a million decisions a second during a match.

But there was something lurking at the back of her mind, something that hadn't taken shape yet in a way that made sense to her.

So she did what she did best and decided to distract herself. "Have you heard anything from Brynn?"

Reese groaned, sinking into the bed even farther. "I haven't. When I left yesterday morning, she told me I'd given her a lot to think about."

"Her life, her choices, I guess." Though Sydney couldn't imagine being able to sit quietly with that information and do nothing, she didn't know what kind of mettle Brynn was really made of, when it came down to it.

"I'm sure if word gets back to Grant, I'll be the first to hear about it."

"And your mom?" Sydney asked. "Any update on that front?"

"I dropped her off at home a bit ago. She seems really clearheaded about the whole situation. I wonder if I'm waiting for her to hit a wall when all of this becomes real."

"Well, if she does, we'll be there for her," Sydney said, meaning it. Nothing mattered more to her than making sure Reese, and by extension, Sharon, felt supported.

"I know." Reese's smile, like she really did feel as supported as Sydney hoped she did, gave Sydney that feeling of connection she'd been experiencing more and more, like she could *feel* Reese from thousands of miles away.

"Have you been sleeping in my bedroom?" Sydney had slept alone for the last five nights, and she wondered how she'd managed to for so many years.

Especially when she thought about waking up in the mornings, Reese's hair fanned everywhere. Her first conscious breath in the morning always involved a tickle against her lips or her cheeks or her forehead, silky locks billowing out gently before landing again wherever they wanted.

And their bodies. Always in a different configuration but connected in some way. Sometimes, Sydney was the big spoon, and she'd wake up, arms wrapped tightly around Reese. When the roles were reversed, she'd wake up with Reese's head tucked against her back, one arm languidly tossed across Sydney's taller frame. Other days, she'd wake up on her back, Reese's body half on top of her, especially if they'd fallen asleep right after having sex.

Sydney loved it all. She'd never known how soothing it felt to have consistent, physical comfort, provided by someone who could send her heart fluttering and calm her racing nerves, in equal measures.

The idea that Reese missed her enough to sleep in what had become their bed over the last two weeks sent a whole new flutter of butterflies through her stomach.

"I am. Is that okay?" Reese sat up a little straighter, like she was moving to get off the bed.

Sydney cut in immediately, pitching forward, toward the phone in her hand. "Please stay."

"If you insist." Reese settled back onto her side of the bed, and Sydney let out a breath she didn't know she'd been holding.

"I thought it'd feel different," Sydney said as the silence stretched between them while Reese was getting comfortable again.

Reese was busy, punching behind her back at a god-awful pillow that she'd brought down from her own room, something that had made the trek from California with her. But her head straightened toward her phone again, and she looked at Sydney seriously. "What would?"

"I didn't miss playing as much as I expected," Sydney said. Saying it out loud hit her hard as she finally articulated the feeling that had been escaping her.

"That's good, right?" Reese asked, concern in her voice. Probably because of the shell-shocked look on Sydney's face.

Sydney sat with the feeling for a second before her lips broke into a wide smile. "It's great. I mean, two months ago, I thought that my life was over."

"And now?"

"And now, I feel like it's just beginning." Sydney stood up, a sudden surge of energy infusing her body. She walked over to the nightstand and put the phone down, adjusting it so that it faced outward into the room. "I'm going to get ready to get into bed, if that's okay?"

There was silence on the other end of the phone, and she looked back to find Reese blinking before she said, "Yep. Totally fine by me."

"Are you in for the night?" Sydney asked as she walked over to the dresser where she'd unpacked her clothes. She found a T-shirt and decided that was enough in the balmy summer heat, even with her air conditioner cranked up.

She'd cover herself in the comforter and extra blankets, knowing it would only be a poor facsimile to how Reese's body felt draped over her own.

"I am," Reese said, her voice sounding a little breathless. It made the nerves in Sydney's body start to vibrate.

This was what she wanted. What got her excited, these days.

All roads led back to Reese and what was happening between them. The push and pull. The ebb and flow.

For the first time today, having nothing to do with tennis, she felt her pulse accelerate. She loved it.

Sydney had brought her own wardrobe, pre-approved by the network, so she was still wearing her on-set outfit from earlier in the day. She started to undress, adrenaline coursing through her veins as she did.

Sydney removed her pants first, the air cold against her already flush skin. She got to work quickly on her shirt.

"I caught some of your commentary, by the way."

Reese's words stopped Sydney in her tracks, and she turned around fully, her fitted button-down about half unbuttoned.

She played with the button that was next in line, her fingers running along the smooth hardness. "And what did you think?"

"You were amazing," Reese said quickly, her breathing a little labored in a way that made Sydney pluck at the button harder but not keep going.

She rolled the button between her fingers, watching as Reese's eyes followed the motion. "No specific feedback?"

Reese gulped at the same time she edged farther down the bed. "What do you want to know?"

Sydney loved the idea of Reese watching her, of Sydney pushing things between them. Not that Reese was any slouch in the bedroom, but she tended to be a little more reserved, letting Sydney generally lead where things would go.

But right now, she wanted Reese to want her. To miss her with the same hollowness that Sydney felt in her own stomach. That type of feeling where the more she drank, the thirstier she became.

She wanted Reese to feel *that*.

She wanted to be the one to fill, to quench, to send Reese into oblivion.

And if she couldn't be there with her in person, this was the next best thing.

"I'll undo another button for each thing you tell me you like about our sex life." The way Reese, in frame, stilled for long seconds, made Sydney wonder if the screen was frozen.

"Okay," Reese finally said, the single word breathy and wanting.

Sydney felt the agreement in her center, her clit already starting to throb as Reese looked at her hungrily.

"So tell me," she said, toying with the button but not releasing it.

She was mesmerized by Reese's face in frame, how the phone wobbled unsteadily as she maneuvered it into a different position.

"I love when you tell me what you want. Whether it's to wrap my leg around you to get more friction or to pump into you harder. I never thought I'd like taking direction so much."

Sydney could feel the ghost of Reese's long fingers with her words, how they filled her so perfectly. Her center clenched, but there was nothing for her to wrap around, her body begging for release it couldn't find.

"Where's my button?" Reese asked, her deep brown eyes fixated on Sydney's fingers.

Sydney, as promised, flicked the button open, revealing another few inches of her lean stomach. She touched lightly against her own skin, hot and tight with need. "I was just thinking about exactly what you described. Got me a little distracted."

"It's all about focus, King." Reese lifted her eyebrow in a deliciously teasing way, and Sydney wished more than anything that she could touch Reese right now.

"You're so right," Sydney responded, the arousal clear in Reese's gaze as her focus dipped down to Sydney's exposed skin and the next button, which was preventing her from seeing more. "Two more buttons."

Reese didn't disappoint, and that made her all the more turned on.

"I love how responsive your body is. How you're always ready. How easy it is to make you shake or moan or pant." Sydney watched, transfixed, as Reese's fingers, which had been touching her lips, dipped out of the camera's view.

"Are you touching yourself?" Sydney rasped, her fingers deftly undoing the button and sliding farther down her own skin, stopping near the last button, which rested at the hem of her underwear.

"Yes," Reese gasped quietly, the air around Sydney electrifying.

Sydney moved quickly from where she stood over to the bed, where she lay on top of the sheet, comforter already folded down. She was on fire, and without any barrier, it was easier for her to spread her hips wide, legs splayed outward.

It was lewd and sexy and she loved the feeling of how her muscles pulled where her hips met her thighs, her body jerking forward in response as she tried to find friction, anything to grind against for relief.

"One more," Sydney panted, wishing desperately to touch her own clit right now, to ease a finger inside and fill some of the need building deep within.

"I love when you fuck me from behind."

That was all Sydney could handle, and she quickly undid her last button, fingers disappearing underneath her waistband.

Reese looked so good, lips parted and her face flushed, and Sydney could imagine how she worked into herself, still wishing desperately she could feel the wetness from Reese on her own fingers.

Her whole body ached as she rubbed at her own clit, already moving in insistent circles to get some relief.

She couldn't think, couldn't really speak. All she could do was feel, her hips bowing out impossibly wider as she eased two fingers inside, beginning to pump.

"Baby," she said, missing the sound of Reese's voice desperately. "Please."

Reese's own voice sounded strangled, her breathing starting to come out at erratic intervals. "How you reach your long arms around me, holding me tightly against you. I love how encompassing it feels. Like you're going to send me spinning but keep me anchored while you do."

Fuck, she wasn't going to last much longer. It had been days since she'd had an orgasm, and the need, coupled with Reese's strained voice had already pushed her close to the edge.

Sydney managed to keep her camera tilted at the right angle while still holding it, trying to take in as much of Reese as she could.

And like Reese knew what she wanted, what Sydney's own eyes were begging for, Reese switched the view so the camera rested atop the nightstand. Sydney could see Reese's profile, her neck arching against her pillow, hands invisible beneath her shorts.

But Sydney followed the rapid movement, and Reese bent one leg up, her foot flexing into the bed.

She let out a guttural sound when Reese's free hand moved upward and she started massaging her own breast, the nipple puckering visibly beneath her thin T-shirt.

Sydney's hips rocked against her fingers, and she took Reese in hungrily as Reese played with her nipple, Sydney thinking about how good it would feel in her mouth. The way it pillowed into a hard bud that Sydney loved to flick with her tongue, knowing exactly the little pleas it drew from Reese.

And then Sydney came. Hard.

"Fuck, baby, fuck," she said as she continued working into herself, imagining that Reese was there with her. "You feel so good," she groaned into the empty room, needing to draw every last ounce of pleasure from her own body, wanting Reese to know the power she held over Sydney.

"Sydney," Reese cried, the name on her lips as her whole body went rigid, fingertips digging into her own chest.

Sydney stared, transfixed, as she came down from her own orgasm, deep breaths punctuating the silence. Reese's body finally went limp, and it sent a few more pulses of desire to her own clit, the way Reese looked so utterly spent and deliciously debauched.

Sydney let out a long, drawn-out sigh as she moved her camera to a similar view that Reese saw, placed on the table next to her bed. "That was..."

"Amazing," Reese said breathlessly before she rolled on her side to face the camera. She rested a hand underneath her cheek and stared at Sydney, eyes mapping everything.

"*You're* amazing," Sydney corrected, waiting for her erratic heartbeat to come back down to normal.

"I've never done that before." The admission was quiet, Reese's stare softening as pink flushed her already heated cheeks.

"I guess we'll just have to chalk this up to another thing you're incredibly talented at. Did you like it?"

Reese nodded. "Yes, I liked it a lot. Not as good as having you here, but I needed this. I didn't realize how much until just now."

Sydney could feel her eyes growing heavy, sleep threatening to overtake her now that she was utterly spent. "I needed it, too, baby."

And it wasn't just the sex, even if that had been mind-blowing. She'd wanted to feel close to Reese, to feel connected with her in a way that she couldn't quite explain.

"Are you going to bed?" Reese asked, her own voice sounding sleep-soaked and utterly satisfied.

Sydney burrowed against her pillow and jutted her hand to the side, managing to capture enough of the comforter to pull it on top of herself. "Mhmm. Are you going to put me to bed?" Sydney teased sleepily.

The exhaustion hit her then. From the last almost week of preparations and the first day of live commentating. From how much she missed Reese, the energy it took to focus on anything else.

"Yeah, baby, I am." Sydney's eyes were closed, but she could hear Reese rustling around, finding her own comfort in the bed Sydney wished they could share tonight.

"I'm glad this is how my day is ending. You're such an amazing girlfriend," Sydney said, snuggling into a ball under the covers.

Before she drifted off to sleep, she managed to open her eyes one last time to see Reese's soft gaze watching her.

Twenty

REESE WAS WATCHING SYDNEY, who walked around the room they shared at The Stone's Throw, picking up errant pieces of clean laundry that at some point had been considered and rejected. Guess today was their lucky day.

Truly, the distraction was a welcome one for Reese, who was more than happy to avoid thinking about her own day.

"It was easy when I was a player," Sydney said, a hint of annoyance in her voice. "All I needed were match outfits and loungewear. Now, who knows who the executives may want me to have dinner with? And I can't schlep around when not working, since I'm no longer an *athlete*. And you know I hate—"

"Checking a bag." Reese leaned back against the headboard, watching the melee play out. "And you'll always be an athlete. You're just... non-practicing right now," she teased.

Sydney threw another shirt in her carry-on suitcase. "At least I don't have to fly in early this time."

After the first tournament in D.C., which Sydney had returned from a week and a half ago, she'd succeeded on two fronts. Which was no surprise to Reese.

For the tournament in Cleveland that she was leaving for tomorrow, the network didn't need her to go in early to prep, and since she'd been so well received by fans, she didn't have to fly in until midweek to handle the men's and women's quarter-finals and beyond.

It was clear that the network was just as enamored with Sydney as Reese was.

"It gives us extra time together," Reese said, trying to focus on the positives. Even if she felt like she'd just gotten Sydney back, she wasn't going to mention how she already missed her, even as she stood across the room.

Sydney stopped suddenly, whirling around to focus on Reese. "I'm sorry, babe. I'm being so inconsiderate right now. I know you're going to lunch with Stan in an hour. I'm sure you're thinking about that."

"Your colorful commentary is a nice distraction," Reese said, but still, her body tensed with Sydney's words.

Coming over to the bed, Sydney sat down in front of Reese. "I'm sure he just wants to welcome you to the family."

Reese lifted a dubious brow. "At least we're meeting in a public place."

"Hey," Sydney said, enveloping Reese's hand in Sydney's own. "We have no reason to think this has anything to do with Brynn. You told her almost a month ago, and no one, including Grant, has said anything."

Still, little prickles of apprehension skittered across Reese's skin. Stan Fitzpatrick was a jovial, affable man, but he was as shrewd as they came in the business world. It was even more astounding that he was both deeply respected and incredibly well liked in spite of being at the top of his game. Which meant that, Reese's own family melodrama aside, he was not a man that you wanted on your bad side.

"And I'll still be here tonight, so if it does go badly, which it won't, I'll be here to give you a cuddle and a kiss." When Sydney's voice melted from decisiveness into sweetness, it made Reese's stomach flip pleasantly, a feeling she was still trying to get used to.

She'd thought that after almost a month of sleeping together, the feeling would have abated, that she'd feel a little more in control of herself.

Only that wasn't the case.

Every morning, she woke up next to Sydney's softly snoring body, and she couldn't stop the smile that bloomed wild across her face.

Sydney King was objectively the perfect woman, but she was also so much more than that. She was always in Reese's corner, whether about Grant or her father or Reese's struggles to find her footing at the inn. She made Reese so turned on that she thought she'd combust with want. She was a little petulant when she was annoyed with something, which, insanely, Reese found incredibly endearing.

She was just... *perfect*.

And as Sydney readied herself for the next tournament, with only the US Open in early September, the week before the wedding, left for her commitments this season, there was no doubt in Reese's mind that they'd be extending her a full-time offer.

Sydney's social media following had grown by tens of thousands in the last few weeks, and her agent had been calling almost daily to check in on Sydney.

Reese herself felt stuck in a sort of limbo where she wanted to preserve the life they had while also warming herself up to the fact that that likely wouldn't be possible.

Hoping for the best and planning for the worst, as it were.

But even that wasn't a fair assessment. Because if Sydney did take the offer, it would be what was best for Sydney, even if it would complicate their relationship. And Reese had promised herself that she'd do everything she could to support Sydney's happiness.

Which... sucked, a little bit, but she didn't want to be the thing that held Sydney back. She'd promised herself that at the start of things between them.

And it was made all the more difficult when she looked at

Sydney, remembering why she was already dressed in a tennis skirt and a tank top, her tennis bag ready and waiting at the door. "What time are you meeting my mom?"

Sydney looked down at her watch. "I need to leave in a few minutes. She's meeting me at Manhaven."

"I'll walk out with you," Reese said, scooting her legs off the bed and standing up.

Reese's mom had officially retained her divorce attorney, and they'd started preparations for the divorce, first and foremost, serving her dad with the papers.

He'd reached out to Reese a number of times since then, about benign things and general check-ins which in and of itself was incredibly disconcerting. Her dad didn't care about what she had going on, so she had to assume it was some weird play to get information about her mom, which, of course, she had no plans of giving him.

She'd left his messages on unread and gone about her life, liking the thought that because her mom was making this decision, Reese, too, could effectively cut ties with him.

He and Grant could go on to build their dynasty together, and Brynn could ascend to the position of invisible hand that kept the Devereux men functioning.

"And you're sure you're okay playing babysitter to my mom?" Reese grabbed her phone off the night table, working to quell her nervousness.

Who got into tennis in their fifties? Why not swimming aerobics or a Scrabble league?

Sydney waved her off. "I love playing tennis. I'm really excited that your mom wants to start taking lessons. I've set her up with Brian to do some one-on-one sessions. They met on the Fourth of July, so he's not a total stranger to her."

Reese looked at Sydney dubiously. "I cannot deal with any broken bones right now."

Sydney laughed and stood up, too, before placing a quick kiss on Reese's nose. "Tennis is a lifetime sport. People of all ages play.

I promise, Brian knows your mom's skill level already, and she'll be in safe hands."

Picking up her keys, Reese let the trust that she'd come to feel where Sydney was concerned wash over her. "I know, babe. I'm sorry. I'm just stressed."

Sydney wrapped her arms loosely around Reese's waist and pulled her closer. "About your mom or about Stan?"

"Both. When did we become the most well-adjusted people in our families?" Reese lamented. "I feel like we've been chasing around parents all summer, working constantly to keep things from bubbling over."

Sydney laughed, and Reese sighed when Sydney nuzzled her face into Reese's neck. "The students have become the teachers," Sydney said before placing a soft kiss on Reese's pulse point.

Reese groaned. "Well, we definitely haven't gotten summer off."

* * *

Stan was already seated when Reese entered the Boston pub he'd selected for their meeting place.

He looked happy, as usual, so Reese tried to tamp down on the nervousness that made her legs shake as she walked across the pub and took her seat across from him.

"Reese," he said, waving her down into her seat. "I'm so glad you could make it."

"Thanks. Though I'm not exactly sure what you had in mind for today," Reese hedged, trying to get some visibility on the situation as soon as she could. She didn't like flying blind.

The topics were endless. Her parents' impending divorce. Grant's infidelity. The upcoming wedding. Something stupid her father had done, though she didn't know why she'd be involved in that. She hoped that she'd made it clear from their previous interactions that she had nothing to do with The Devereux Group, and she had every intention of keeping it that way.

Still, she smiled and picked up her menu, scanning the options. It was all standard bar food, the restaurant far more understated than anything her father would have chosen.

"I wanted us to catch up," Stan said evasively, though Reese couldn't figure out if that was intentional. It was a perfectly reasonable thing to say, and someone who wasn't on high alert wouldn't have been plussed by the answer.

"I saw Sydney on The Tennis Network a few weeks ago." He took a drink of the beer that had been delivered before she'd arrived.

Reese smiled, though her brows furrowed in slight confusion. She really, really hoped they weren't here to discuss Sydney—at least as she related to Brynn and Grant. "Yeah, she seems to be a natural, but who's surprised? She's actually heading out tomorrow to commentate at The Cleveland Open."

"Good for her," Stan beamed, genuinely meaning it. He was such an interesting man, and Reese couldn't help but get swept up in his enthusiasm.

"If she's happy, then so am I. But it's clear the network loves her." She was going to hold the party line of indisputable happiness for Sydney's next career, even if it picked painfully at something inside of her. Because she did want to discuss how proud of Sydney she was, always.

A waiter stopped by, and Reese ordered sparkling water and a salad. She had every intention of keeping her wits about her. Stan ordered another beer and a burger, sans cheese, because he'd told the waiter that he was "watching his figure."

Reese put her menu down to find Stan watching her, eyes inscrutable. "And how are you doing? How is the inn going?"

Well, wasn't that a loaded question. She'd been muddling through, though Hallie was still indispensable to her survival.

"A very different type of business than I previously managed," Reese admitted, wondering if Stan had ever felt like he'd gotten in over his head.

"The first one is always the hardest, but I have no doubt that it'll get easier."

"First one?" Reese asked before taking a sip of her water.

"If that's what you want. I'm not sure if The Stone's Throw Inn is the last stop for you, but if it's not, I thought it would be a good idea for us to connect. I'd love to know what you're considering in the future to see how I can avail myself to you if it's a good fit."

She almost spat out her water. In all the turns she'd considered their conversation taking, this wasn't one of them. She swallowed deeply and tried to ignore the burning in her nose.

But she'd be lying if it hadn't been something she'd been thinking about lately. The reality was, she was no good at managing an inn. Her interpersonal skills were less than up to snuff, and the reality was, when Sydney was available, she wanted to spend as much time with her as she could.

Hallie made some semblance of normalcy possible, but there was always a guest need or issue that cropped up in the middle of the already busy list of logistics and higher-level operations.

And Reese, more and more these days, felt a little bit like she was drowning.

Regardless of her excitement at the possibility Stan was opening up before her, she didn't think it was realistic. "As far as I know, you're also working with The Devereux Group. Don't you think that's a slight conflict of interest?"

Stan took a long sip of his beer before meeting her stare. "That deal's paused. I met with Tripp yesterday about it. We have some financial questions that need to be worked through. At best, I'd be able to pick it up early next year if their annual projections come to fruition. Longer if it takes the terms of the divorce to materialize."

So Stan did know about the divorce. She doubted that there was much that got past him.

His language was couched, but it was clear he had misgivings about going into business with The Devereux Group for a variety of reasons. And that, for all her dad's bravado about the success of the company, it wasn't doing as well as he let people believe.

"I am sorry to hear about your parents, by the way. It's never easy when things change."

"But sometimes it's for the best," Reese said, leaning forward. "From one businessperson to another, I'm surprised you didn't have their projections and earnings statements already. Earlier this summer, I was told that the deal would be closed by now. Seems like it all fell apart right at the end."

Which, Reese knew, could always happen. People got cold feet all the time in multimillion-dollar transactions, but she didn't take Stan for the type of man who didn't dot all his *i*'s and cross all his *t*'s well ahead of schedule.

She could see Stan considering how much to tell her, and as he placed his hands on the table, she waited to hear what decision he'd come to. "Between us, I waited longer than I initially would for some financial documents, as a courtesy to your father because our children were getting married. Regardless of that marriage, I won't enter into a deal without the necessary information—and that information making sense from a business standpoint. No matter how close to the finish line we are."

Reese leaned back in her chair, trying to hide her smile. "That makes sense, and I appreciate your candor."

"Brynn's spoken very highly of you," Stan said, and Reese's whole body snapped to alert. They couldn't be talking about the same Brynn, to whom Reese had broken the news to that her fiancé was a philanderer. And that she'd been an unknowing party to it.

But she wasn't going to bring that up to Stan, regardless of what he may know already.

"I haven't talked to her since the bachelorette party. How is she doing?" She was here if Brynn wanted to reach out, but she wasn't going to bring it up again, given that she'd already said her piece, and with the admission hanging between them, there wasn't a whole lot else for them to talk about.

"Thinking a lot about her future."

A look passed between them, but Reese held herself back from asking more. "Seems like there's a lot of that going around these days."

"All I want is for my daughter to be happy. She's so brilliant and focused, and she has this genuinely positive outlook on the world that her mother and I never want to see dampened."

"It is a rare quality," Reese agreed.

Maybe believing the world was a good place wasn't realistic, but that outlook only had consequences when other people abused it.

People like Grant.

And it rankled Reese all over again. That he walked through the world, using people up and spitting them out when they were no longer convenient for him.

"It is. So, whatever she decides to do, her mother and I will support her," Stan said pointedly.

"I'm glad she has you in her corner. And she always has me, too," Reese said, meaning it. "*If* I do decide to build a portfolio, the inn will be going through a lot of transition soon. I'm not sure it's the right vibe for a curious intellectual, but I'm always happy to find a place for Brynn there."

Stan smiled then, his eyes bright. "I started as a porter at a hotel I eventually went on to invest in for a majority share. Regardless of where Brynn ends up, a little more hands-on practical application in the world may not be a bad thing."

"Well, if she's interested, have her call me. I can't promise it will be glamorous, but it's an option."

"I'd appreciate that," Stan said as the waiter dropped off their lunches. Placing his napkin on his lap, Stan looked at her like they hadn't just run a conversational marathon. "Now, tell me all about you. I like to know who I may be getting into business with."

* * *

Reese's lunch with Stan had given her a lot to think about. Namely, if she did decide to expand her footprint in the hotel space, how would she make sure that The Stone's Throw was taken care of? She had no plans to leave Hallie, or anyone else who worked there, in a lurch. It was antithetical to who she was as a person, and she couldn't imagine doing something like that to Sydney on top of everyone else who'd be impacted.

Which was why, when she got back and found Hallie sitting at the front desk, eyes focused on the tablet in front of her, she decided to test the waters.

"Got a minute?" Reese asked. "In the office?"

Hallie looked up at her, confusion drawn across her features. "Sure. Is something wrong?"

"No, nothing's wrong. I just want to run something by you."

Reese walked past Hallie and into the small office, Hallie a few seconds behind her after she'd placed the 'Back in five minutes' sign on the check-in desk.

On her drive back from Boston, the idea had started to crystallize more clearly in her mind, but it all hinged on Hallie, which meant there was no reason to wait to discuss it.

Instead of sitting behind the desk, Reese sat across from it. Hallie squinted at the only open seat before sitting down.

"You're being weird."

"You don't mince words. I just had a really interesting lunch, and it got me thinking."

Hallie leaned forward in her chair, placing her forearms down on the desk. "With Stan? About Brynn?" Her eyes grew wide. "Oh no. Are you fleeing?"

"Why would I be fleeing?" Reese responded dryly.

"Sydney keeps me abreast," Hallie said matter-of-factly. "The cheating is out in the world, and you're the one who released it."

Reese shook her head. "No, Grant released it by *doing* it. I just passed along information that I thought she should know."

"That's a fair point, and I think you did the right thing."

"Your approval means the world to me, Hallie."

"So if it's not that, what do you want to talk about?" Hallie asked, looking around the room.

Reese wondered how Hallie felt about the inn, a place she'd known for her entire life. She loved it, obviously, but had she only stayed out of obligation when her parents sold it? Was it what *she* really wanted?

"I want to talk to you about what comes next. After your six-month commitment as part of the purchase." They were two months into that agreement, but it would be the end of the year before they knew it, and if Hallie wasn't planning on staying, Reese should be looking for someone pronto to learn the ropes and take it over.

She'd accepted that person was not going to be her, and that was best for everyone. If Sydney did accept the commentator role, this would give Reese more flexibility to make their relationship work.

"That's, like, four months away." Hallie looked around the room again, a little evasive.

"I know, but, to be completely honest, I don't think that long-term I'm the best person to run the inn," Reese admitted, waiting to see how Hallie would respond.

She was surprised when Hallie let out a barking laugh. "Wow, I'm glad you came to this conclusion. I absolutely agree."

"I'm not *that* bad," Reese protested, even though Hallie's assessment was fair.

Hallie smiled softly at Reese. "You're right. But I can tell you don't enjoy it. Hearing stories from people. Asking banal questions about their trip and their days. You don't even get excited when the checkouts all line up perfectly so there's always something to do but it's at peak efficiency."

Reese closed her mouth. Hallie had read her like a book. "You're right, I don't. But the thing is, I think that you do. And I'd be stupid if I didn't try to get you committed to staying on full-time."

There was that evasiveness again; Hallie wouldn't meet her

stare. "If we're being honest, I have been thinking about what comes next, too."

Reese smiled sympathetically, realizing that Hallie was really struggling. No matter what she said next, Reese wouldn't hold it against her. "Do you see the inn as part of your future?"

"I do love it here," Hallie said earnestly. "This has always been my home, and I enjoy all the parts of the job that I just mentioned. I just..."

Reese waited as Hallie formed the thoughts that maybe were materializing for the first time in the face of Reese's probing questions.

"I feel like a big part of my life is watching other people live theirs. Does that make sense?"

A hollowness opened up in Reese's chest as she considered what that would feel like, as an outsider always looking in. "It does."

"So I've been thinking about making some changes," she said seriously, eyes trained on Reese.

Reese, to herself, reaffirmed her commitment that she'd support Hallie no matter what. "Like what?"

"I need a better work-life balance. I need to date and hang out with friends and go spend a Saturday seeing where the day takes me. Do you know I haven't done that in years?"

"I didn't know that, but it makes a lot of sense," Reese said, having had firsthand access to all the hours that Hallie worked.

"The reality is, my family doesn't own this inn anymore. I'm an employee, and I want to start acting like it. That doesn't mean I don't care or that I won't still be an invaluable member of the team, but I need to stop letting this place be my life."

Reese winced, thinking of all the days she'd begged off from work because something had come up with her family. "I think that's fair. And I'm sorry if I did anything this summer to make it more difficult for you to separate yourself from the inn."

Hallie waved her off. "I'd do anything to help Sydney, and at the heart of it, covering for you was mostly for her." She smiled wryly. "Not that I don't like you, boss, but we aren't there yet."

"No offense taken," Reese said, appreciating the honesty. She could understand wanting to do anything she could to help Sydney. "So, it does sound like you are open to sticking around? Provided there are some changes? Or are you looking for a fresh start somewhere?"

Hallie was clearly giving the question serious thought; her lip was pulled between her teeth as she chewed on it. The moment was on the verge of becoming comically drawn out when Hallie let go of her lip with a *pop* and beamed a smile at Reese. "I want better health insurance."

"Absolutely," Reese batted back.

"And a raise."

"Seems only fair, given the work you do here." Hallie had only ever been paid a nominal salary, all things considered. Reese had always been planning on increasing that at the end of six months if Hallie stuck around.

She could see Hallie practically vibrating. "I want every other evening and weekend off."

"I would never impede a young woman from having a vibrant social life."

Hallie pursed her lips before asking, "Is there anything else I should be asking for? I assumed you're better at negotiation, but it doesn't exactly seem like it right now."

That made Reese laugh. "How about I put together a packet and you can consider it as a formal offer, once you have everything to look over?"

She wondered if Hallie would start running around like an excited puppy when Reese told her about the profit sharing, which would incentivize Hallie to help the inn succeed in a way that paid off for her, too.

Hallie interlaced her fingers on top of the desk and nodded solemnly. "I agree to the terms of reviewing the terms at a future date."

Reese laughed again, and she felt a lightness in her chest, at least professionally, that she hadn't felt in a long time. *This* was what she liked. Solving big problems. Designing structures that helped the machine keep plugging away.

And Hallie, it seemed, really did love the day-to-day of managing The Stone's Throw, so it was a perfect balance, the two of them.

"Have you mentioned this to Sydney yet?" Hallie asked.

Reese shook her head. "I have not. This is between us, and I take our professional relationship seriously."

She could already see the laughter bubbling up in Hallie, and she put her hand up to stop it.

"Regardless of the various states of undress that you've seen me in," she said, remembering a week ago when Reese, topless, had run into Hallie while she'd been sneaking to their shared kitchen area late at night to grab a glass of water.

Hallie smirked. "Hydration is so important. Especially after exercise."

Standing up, Reese ran her hands down her shirt to smooth any wrinkles. "Great, glad we sorted that out. I'll send you the offer when I have it ready."

She didn't mind that she could still feel Hallie's smirk as she exited the office. Instead of going to see if Sydney was back yet, she seated herself at the check-in desk to give Hallie a much-deserved break.

* * *

"Remind me why your flight is so disgustingly early tomorrow?" Reese asked as she brushed her teeth, her mouth filled with minty foam.

Sydney walked up behind her and wrapped her arms around Reese's torso. "I believe it's so we can spend an extra night together, but with your tone, I'm beginning to re-evaluate that decision."

Reese spat out her excess toothpaste, Sydney giving her just enough slack to lean forward and rinse her mouth out with water. "Booking it seemed like such a good idea at the time."

Sydney laughed lightly into Reese's hair. "Until the reality of waking up at four a.m. comes calling?"

Reese was going to drive Sydney to the airport, and they had to leave six hours from now. She wasn't looking forward to it. Because of the ungodly hour. Because she'd be separated from Sydney for another five days. Because it made that hole in her chest that felt empty when Sydney wasn't near flare up, and she could already feel it beginning to carve itself out.

She leaned her head back against Sydney's chest, loving how, at a few inches shorter, she nestled perfectly into the crook where Sydney's collarbone and neck met.

"We could just be hedonists," Sydney said, her fingers beginning to play across Reese's exposed stomach. "Quit our jobs. Travel the world."

"I thought you hated packing your suitcase," Reese said, her words coming out in an uneven rasp as Sydney's fingers scratched lightly, just below her bellybutton.

Sydney didn't miss a beat. "We'll get an RV then. Live life on the road."

Reese turned her face so she could see Sydney's eyes, alight and playful.

"I don't think we'd do well at that, but something tells me you already know that," Reese answered, savoring the feeling of closeness, Sydney's warm breath ghosting across her cheek.

She broke the moment to wrap her hand around one of Sydney's own and pull her over to the bed.

Reese had gotten back to the room first tonight, and she had already been in bed reading a book when Sydney had returned. With Sydney's arrival, she'd forced herself to take out her contacts and brush her teeth, but she wanted nothing more than to crawl back into the warmth and comfort of their shared space.

"How was dinner with Brian?" Reese asked sleepily, already snuggling in against Sydney's chest.

"Your mom tagged along for the actual dinner, but then Brian and I stayed longer to catch up."

Reese picked her head up to look at Sydney then. "My mother? Sharon Devereux?"

"Possibly soon-to-be Sharon Walcott again. She mentioned it at dinner tonight," Sydney said as she carded her fingers through Reese's hair.

Reese snuggled back down against Sydney. "Good for her."

"Yeah, I think she really liked the tennis lesson." Sydney quieted before adding, "I think she really liked Brian, too."

"I cannot lift my head again for the life of me, but it does deserve another look."

"I know, babe, but I'm just telling you what I saw. They were pretty cute together, I have to admit."

"Sydney King, you softy," Reese said. She tried to punch lightly at Sydney's arm, but she got distracted and ended up running her hands along smooth skin instead.

She felt Sydney melt into the touch, and they both stilled, the steady thrum of Sydney's heartbeat audible with Reese's ear so close to her chest.

"What are your thoughts on marriage?" Sydney asked, and Reese was jarred from the hazy comfort she'd been experiencing until a second ago.

"Like you and me getting married?"

Sydney groaned. "Not specifically, no. I just meant... we've been dating now for a few months, and I know we haven't really followed the usual steps—"

"Understatement," Reese cut in.

Sydney squeezed her a little tighter. "Anyway, it's something that people talk about when they're dating. Whether their future desires align. So I was just curious where you fall on the subject."

Reese felt her own heartbeat pick up, and she scrambled to work through her thoughts so that whatever she shared didn't make her sound insane. "Megan and I, I now realize, had a very practical relationship. We didn't talk about marriage because we were already running the business together, and to me, that had felt pretty serious."

She sighed when Sydney started running her fingers through Reese's hair again.

"So you haven't really thought about it?" Sydney asked, her voice soft and coaxing, like she'd give Reese all the time in the world to figure out her thoughts.

That made Reese want to give her an honest answer, to lay her cards on the table. "It's something I do want. I want to share my life with someone. I want to make that kind of commitment. I want to know that we're going through the world as a team, and that we're stronger because of it."

"I like that," Sydney said, and Reese could feel the smile on her lips as she kissed the top of her head.

"I don't think I'd ever thought about it like that because, well, you've seen my parents' relationship," she said vaguely, hoping that explained things.

"I get it, babe." Sydney kissed her head again, and Reese let the pleasant warmth at the simple, comforting gesture float through her.

"And you?" Reese asked, moving her hand to run her fingers along Sydney's arm, wanting to feel connected to her.

"I do. It's something I've always wanted. Kids, too," Sydney added, "but I know that's a bigger conversation."

"Well, it's not going to happen accidentally, so we'd have to talk about it eventually," Reese joked, realizing that the idea of having kids with Sydney didn't scare her. At all.

She wanted everything with Sydney, and her heart skipped a beat at the thought that was becoming more and more common.

"I need to think through the second one a little more, since it's not something I've fantasized about or had a plan for, but I am cautiously open to the idea," she settled on, hoping that was enough for Sydney for the moment.

Sydney scooted down farther on the bed so that she could look at Reese. "I think that's a really responsible way of handling this. I love that about you," she said before kissing Reese on the nose.

"I'm glad you asked me," Reese admitted before adding, "And that you're thinking about the future. I am, too."

Sydney pulled her closer, and as Reese went back to listening to the rise and fall of Sydney's chest, of the steady thrum of her heartbeat, she wondered how life could feel any better than this.

Twenty-One

SYDNEY WAS BACK at a Grand Slam tennis tournament, one of the four most well-respected tournaments in the world of tennis, and the only one that took place on US soil. A year ago, she'd have killed to be here. She *did* almost kill to be here— her own body, of course, with her unrelenting exercise regimen and single-minded focus on pushing her career as far as it could go.

Last year, she'd been here competing and had made it down to the final four women who vied for the honor of winning.

What a difference a year made.

Her attendance here wasn't at all in the way she'd planned for, but that didn't change the fact, as she walked through a more private path that wove throughout the large outdoor venue, that it felt so familiar. The smells and sounds and the still-scorching early September heat. That buzz of excitement, as close to a million people would attend one of the hundreds of matches; the event taking almost two full weeks to complete.

There were parts that were strange, though. Walking around without her tennis bag, for one. She missed the security it provided as she'd snug it tighter over her shoulder, her body perfectly attuned to walking with the extra weight on one side.

She'd been gone from Stoneport for a week, missing the moments when August rolled into September.

They were heading into the last weekend of the tournament, and Sydney had almost fulfilled her obligation with the network. A formal offer was likely coming any day now.

She'd been called into extra meetings with The Tennis Network's producers, who had a private section in the venue to run what was a fairly large broadcasting operation at an event of this scale.

She was walking back from one such meeting now, where they'd all but said that she needed to name her terms to come on board full-time.

And that felt *good*, in the simplest terms. To be so wanted, especially in a world to which she'd given so much.

But there was also a feeling, one that she hadn't been able to shake since arriving, that she was an outsider looking in on a life that didn't quite make sense to her anymore.

Her conversation with Brian a few weeks ago hadn't helped, bolstered by the fact that she'd been spending most of her days at the Manhaven Tennis Center with him, hopping in on group lessons and working with Jenna and a few other teenage players who trained there full-time.

And instead of basking in the sights and sounds and the frenetic 'anything could happen' energy, which she'd already seen play out across some of the dozens of courts during the tournament, all she could think about was how Reese was coming to town tomorrow morning, joining her for the last full weekend.

She'd moved through the venue and into a waiting car on autopilot, the network's hotel only a few minutes' drive away. When she was a player, she'd stayed in the city, but here, they wanted the commentators close to the action, especially with the unpredictability of game lengths.

Her tennis life and her personal life with Reese hadn't overlapped before, except as Sydney struggled to make herself go through her ritual of begrudgingly packing, Reese usually taking her to the airport and picking her up when she got home, regardless of the hour.

Sydney entered the hotel, already thinking about how good it was going to feel to lay eyes on Reese, to hold her in her arms.

One more night.

"Ms. King?" The concierge waved her over. Sydney was used to notes from fans or network-wide messages being left at the desk for her, but she was surprised when the concierge, a young woman with vibrant hair and an ear with studs running the length of it, pointed around the corner to the lounge area. "You have a guest waiting for you."

Sydney's pulse picked up, and she wondered—dared to hope, even—that Reese had decided to come in and surprise her a day early.

Her body, exhausted from a long day of commentary and signing autographs when spotted by fans, suddenly roared to life again, an excited energy flowing through her at the mere thought.

But as she rounded the corner, her mouth dropped open, and she tried to make sense of what she was seeing.

"Hey, Syd." Grant stood up from the wingback chair he was seated in, and he tucked his hands meekly in his pockets as he shifted his weight from his heels to the balls of his feet.

Nothing about this was right. *Nothing*. A wave of uneasiness rolled through her as she took Grant in.

He had a look of contrition on his face, like a schoolboy who'd been caught doing something wrong. Even still, there was a small, hopeful smile on his face, his eyes bright and taking her in, too.

The questions started to knock around her brain.

How did he know she was here?

Why was *he* here?

How quickly could she get him to go away? Ideally without causing a scene?

She shook her confusion away and stood up a little straighter, wishing she had her tennis bag to tighten protectively across her shoulder. It wasn't that she was scared of Grant, that had never been the case, but giving him a good *thwack* with the bag had been something she'd considered more than a few times over the last year.

"You're surprised to see me? A good surprise, I hope?" he asked, taking the smallest step forward but still affording her personal space.

"Why are you here?" He was getting married next weekend, which added an extra layer of insanity to him showing up here, now.

"Sit with me, please." He gestured to the chair adjacent to the one he'd been sitting in. "Five minutes. That's all I'm asking."

Sydney briefly wondered if he'd found God. Or if he was in some sort of twelve-step program that encouraged him to apologize for the things he'd done wrong. Except, Grant was perfectly capable of making bad decisions completely sober, so that one probably didn't track.

The sooner she got through this, the sooner she could send him on his way.

In over a year, they hadn't had an honest conversation. They'd never had a huge blowout after she'd discovered him cheating. She'd gone radio silent, intent on extricating him from every facet of her life and pretending, as much as she could, that he didn't exist.

While she'd never regret the insanity of the situation that had thrown her and Reese together, it hadn't exactly been her most mature decision. Nevertheless, it was a position she'd ended up in because she hadn't dealt with her grief and his betrayal.

So maybe this was a necessary step as she looked to move forward with Reese.

At least, that's what she told herself as she sat down in the chair, eyeing Grant warily as he did the same, albeit with that same sincere, soft focus that made her uncomfortable given how it was being levied in her direction after so long.

"It's really good to see you," he said, running a hand through his perfectly coiffed hair. Even in the balmy heat, Grant looked like a model.

As Sydney looked closer, though, she noticed faint dark circles under his eyes, and she glanced at where his nails were bitten down, a tell-tale sign that he was stressed. There were very few things that ever got Grant Devereux stressed, and they mainly had to do with his father.

"You've always known my tells," he said, stretching his fingers out if she wanted to get a clear look at them. She didn't.

Her brow rose instinctively. "Not as many as I should have."

Why was he here? Truly. She hadn't seen him in six weeks, since he'd drunkenly spilled champagne all over her.

And except where Brynn was concerned, she hadn't thought about him. With respect to the two of them and their past relationship, it had been even longer.

"I made a mistake, Sydney. I want to take full responsibility for that. I've never told you how sorry I am for everything that's happened. For everything that I did."

Shock coursed through her at the sincerity and humility on full display in his tone. It was like a Grant from the past, when he'd been sweet and doting and she'd felt like he was truly in her corner.

Sitting before her was the Grant who used to show up at her matches to surprise her, who always knew the right thing to say and do.

Sydney warred with the things he'd done and the person she'd thought she'd known battling to stay in focus in front of her, and she felt a little dizzy with the weight of the cognitive dissonance.

Finally, when she pulled her thoughts together, she gave him the only response she could. "I appreciate the apology."

He was always going to be Reese's brother. Which was the entire reason she was entertaining this conversation. They were never going to be friends, but she was building a future with Reese, and she didn't need the tethers of her past waiting to pull her apart at any second.

"I want us to be *us* again."

"That's not going to happen, Grant." Her rebuttal was swift and immediate as Reese's face flashed through her mind. And even if Reese wasn't a part of her life, she had enough self-respect to never let him back in.

"We were good together. And I'm not making excuses for anything I did, but it was a mistake. I'll spend every day of the rest of my life making it up to you, if you'll let me," he pleaded.

"You cheated on me, Grant," she said, a little wound that she'd thought had healed cracking open inside of her. "You broke my trust."

He dropped his head, voice pained when he said, "I know. It was a terrible mistake. Brynn was a mistake."

"The woman you're planning on marrying next week? Seems like you're really sending her mixed messages." She tried to hide the disgust that wanted to work its way across her features at the idea that Grant was laying himself at Sydney's feet, all while Brynn was planning their future together.

He ran his hands down his thighs and took a deep breath. "It's complicated."

"I think I can follow along."

"I did cheat, but Brynn was the only one. I promise." Debatable, but Sydney waited for him to continue. "I was trying to break it off with her, but The Devereux Group was gearing up to do business with Stan. So when you broke up with me and I admitted to my dad what had happened, he told me that I needed to see things with Brynn through. That this was an opportunity to secure our family's future. I'd just lost you, and I wasn't thinking straight." He ran a hand through his hair, and it seemed like he was almost talking to himself when he said, "This whole thing has gotten so out of control. I never wanted this."

Sydney didn't think she'd had any more disgust left, but she found some deep inside of her, and it welled up at the thought of what a terrible person Tripp Devereux truly was.

But Reese and Grant had been raised in the same home, and

they couldn't be more different. For any sympathy she felt toward Grant at living his life under his father's thumb, it was a decision he'd made, ultimately, and, worse than that, he'd been willing to leave as much collateral damage in his wake as necessary all to stay on Tripp's good side.

For what? A job? A flimsy at best legacy?

He truly was his father's son.

"Say the word, and the wedding is off. It's always been you, Sydney. Do you know how hard it's been this summer, watching you with Reese?" he lamented, genuine pain in his voice.

"Grant, that's—"

"We can move to Stoneport now. Start a family. Our plan doesn't need to change. We got together too young, and I made a mistake. But that doesn't change how I feel about you. How good we were together."

"I only ever thought our relationship was good because you showed me the side of yourself that you wanted me to see," Sydney bit back, losing her patience at his mawkishness.

She started to stand up, but Grant's hand captured her own. "Sydney, please. I'm begging you; we can make this work. I will do everything in my power to make this work. You were the best thing that ever happened to me, and I'd be an idiot to let you get away."

She hated how his hand felt, holding on to hers, her body revolting at everything about him. His cologne, the same one he'd always worn. His too-soft fingers, which had never known a day of real work. And his eyes, pleading with her but only seeing what he wanted to see in them.

It was the realization that she was nothing more than a prop to him that settled deep in her bones; she didn't think he had it in him to be the type of person who understood what it meant to truly love someone else.

The compromise.

The trust.

The want to truly exist as a team, whatever that brought.

The way she loved Reese.

Despite the love flowing through her body at the thought of Reese, her face painted a different picture as she looked at Grant. She could feel her features morph with disdain as she pulled her hand away.

"Don't touch me," she said and was grateful that he immediately let go. She took a step back. "I'm already gone, Grant. You just need to accept it."

She left the lobby before he could follow, her phone already out to call Reese.

* * *

Sydney awoke to knocking on her door, the sky still enveloped in darkness. She'd managed to fall asleep a few hours ago. After she'd called Reese and told her everything that had happened. After she'd taken a long, hot shower before falling into bed, intent on washing any traces of Grant and their conversation from her mind and her body.

It took her a few seconds to orient herself in the darkness, and she rubbed at her tired eyes, but once she heard the light knock again, she padded over to the door, willing away her apprehension.

Her conversation with Grant didn't feel real, and if she'd woken up a few hours from now, you could have probably convinced her that it was all a strange dream.

But it had happened, and she was letting the reality of that settle in her.

Still, she wasn't going to take any chances. She'd had overzealous fans in the past, though none she'd shared quite as personal of a relationship with. Unfortunately, that meant that she knew the rigamarole when there was the threat of fanaticism.

Her last point of order before falling asleep had been to call the front desk and give them Grant's description, asking that he be removed from the premises if he hadn't left already.

But when she stared through the peephole, her body instantly felt lighter. Reese's gorgeous face came into view through the fisheye lens the peephole created.

"You're here," Sydney said, the words rushing out of her in hushed surprise at the same time she threw open the door.

Reese was in her arms immediately, enveloping Sydney's senses. She breathed in Reese's scent, clean and floral, and all the anxiousness inside of her steadied.

"I'm only a few hours early." Reese stepped out of the hug but held Sydney's hand, which allowed Reese to pick up her weekend bag and usher them both inside. "I wanted to let you get some sleep. I know you have a big day today."

"You trump sleep, every time," Sydney said as she waited for Reese to put her bag down.

Reese looked like a dream in a soft, oversize button-down and a pair of tapered, navy-colored slacks. Sydney couldn't get enough as she took her in. The way Reese's full lips pillowed so delicately, pressed together. Even her worried brow made Sydney feel warm, knowing that it was concern about *her* causing the furrow.

"Are you okay?" Reese asked, taking Sydney in her arms. "I'm so, so sorry that Grant showed up here."

Sydney's stomach shifted uncomfortably at his name. "It's not your fault. I was a little shocked, too, but it was a conversation that was long overdue, I guess."

They'd gone over the high-level details on the phone. Sydney hadn't wanted there to be any confusion or miscommunication as to why she'd entertained the conversation with him, and there was no world in which she wasn't going to call Reese and tell her everything.

"He's such an ass," Reese said, which was a phrase Sydney had already heard at least a dozen times on the phone earlier tonight.

"I couldn't agree more." Sydney leaned forward and brushed a soft kiss across Reese's lips. "But I don't need to give any more of my energy to him, unless there's anything you want to discuss."

She shook the sleep from her mind when Reese stood up a

little straighter. Sydney immediately missed the softness from moments ago.

"What's wrong?" she asked, leaning back so she could look Reese in the eye.

"I was thinking on the way here... about Grant showing up, now."

"A last-ditch effort before he marries Brynn?" Sydney responded, her own words causing the uncomfortable churn that now bubbled up in her stomach whenever Grant was involved.

But if being forced to deal with him for the next fifty years was the cost of keeping Reese in her life, it was a price worth paying.

"I just wonder if Grant would have made the same decision, if the deal with Stan's company hadn't gotten pushed back. Maybe indefinitely shelved."

Sydney considered the idea. Grant had been childish to a fault this summer, but he'd never once publicly commented that he didn't want to go through with the wedding. "Have you talked to Stan any further?"

The week had been hellishly busy, so tonight had been the longest she and Reese had had to talk on the phone.

"We met twice this week. Once for lunch again, and once at his office in Boston," Reese said, rolling her shoulders uncomfortably, though Sydney was well aware of those two meetings. Reese had texted her about them, even if they hadn't fully debriefed on the details.

Still, Sydney didn't understand her distress. She ran hands she hoped were soothing down Reese's forearms, could feel the goose bumps pebbling on Reese's skin. "That's good, right? He's serious about doing business with you. Expanding your footprint. And judging by how your dad and Grant have been running things, there may be some inventory coming on the market soon," Sydney joked, even though it was very possibly the truth.

Truly, Sydney was thrilled for Reese. She'd seemed so alive the past few weeks, thinking about what an expansion could mean, running ideas by Sydney, and picking her brain endlessly on hotels.

What Sydney liked about them. What she disliked about them. What made her want to go back to a place again.

Sydney had laughed one night when, in their bedroom, Reese had stopped pacing at the foot of the bed before squaring Sydney with a look of pure decisiveness, a look that Sydney thought could command a stadium.

She'd been entirely turned on by how in control Reese seemed when she made a decision within a world where she excelled. Her excitement had been infectious.

"Privacy and predictability. That's what you care about. I'm talking to a literal celebrity about their hotel experience." And then, she'd lightly thwacked her palm on her forehead before adding, "I need to talk to Hallie about this. Maybe ask guests for some feedback."

Sydney had watched Reese run over to the desk near the door and pick up her notebook, furiously scribbling in it before Sydney had lulled Reese into bed, notepad still in hand, so that they could at least cuddle while her girlfriend plotted her plans for world domination.

In the here and now, with Reese looking surprisingly forlorn during what should be a happy reunion, Sydney led her over to the bed. "What's got you upset?"

"I *know* this isn't about me, but once I accept what a not-great guy my father is, he goes and does something else to blow his previous poor behavior out of the water."

Sydney was dealing with accepting the lengths that Grant would go through to obfuscate his selfishness, but she knew that it was something different to accept that your parent could do those things.

"And Grant's just as bad. I think he was willing to go through with this charade if it meant that he'd get to take over The Devereux Group, and now, with the investment on hold, he's that much further away from the keys to the castle, all while being saddled with a marriage that he clearly doesn't want. It's—"

"Diabolical," Sydney said, her head swimming with the reality of the situation. She agreed that Reese was probably spot-on, and it gave the already gross situation a whole extra layer of disgusting sludge to wade through as she tried to make sense of it.

Suddenly, all of her plotting and strategizing on the tennis court seemed like child's play compared to what Tripp Devereux had been up to this summer.

"I think I'm just reckoning with accepting the reality of the man I idolized growing up."

Sydney wrapped her arm around Reese's waist and pulled her close. "You can like the world someone lives in but not like how they move through it." And suddenly, it clicked into place for Sydney, where Reese's apprehension was likely stemming from. "Babe, you expanding the business doesn't mean that you're like your father. You are nothing like him."

"But would I have been? If he'd let me into his world, I mean? Is Grant no more than a product of what he was exposed to?"

Sydney made a gagging sound. "We are not going to start feeling badly for Grant. I'd do anything for you, but, in the eternal words of Mr. Meatloaf, I won't do that."

She loved the smile that broke across Reese's face, absorbed the softness of Reese's body as she leaned against Sydney's side. "You're right. You're always right."

Sydney was half humming, half speaking when she said, "Music to my ears."

Reese laughed then, and Sydney let out a sigh when Reese's hand came up to brush the hair near her temple, dancing her fingers along Sydney's ear and jaw and chin.

The air was still around them, and Sydney's breathing picked up at the way Reese was looking at her, like she, too, couldn't imagine a world that didn't have Sydney in it.

Using the hand resting at the bottom of Sydney's jaw, Reese pulled Sydney forward gently and placed a kiss on her lips. "I love you, you know. And I should have led with that when I walked in the door."

Butterflies exploded in Sydney's stomach, and she knew that her grin was taking up most of her face. "I love you, too. I was planning on telling you this weekend. Guess you beat me to the punch."

"You don't think it's too soon?" Reese asked, nervousness edging into her voice, her light breath tickling against Sydney's cheek. "I know this has been an insane summer, and I don't want you to feel like I'm putting more pressure on you with everything else going on in your life."

Sydney almost volleyed back some glib response, even with the weight of the moment, but she stopped herself. Reese deserved serious thought before Sydney answered, even though she already knew what was in her heart.

Because on paper, it seemed a little crazy. Impulsive, even.

They'd only been dating for two months, had only really gotten to know one another over the last three. And they'd been brought together by a strange, half-cocked circumstance born of Sydney having felt like her life had fallen down around her.

"You're making me nervous," Reese said, her eyes wide as they tracked the thoughts flashing across Sydney's face.

"Don't be nervous." Sydney laced their hands together to quell any apprehension that Reese was feeling. "I'm just thinking. I'm giving this question the seriousness that it deserves. Because I do love you. I'm so *in love* with you."

Sydney turned then so that she was facing Reese fully. She had her answer now. "I wake up with you, and I feel so soft and safe and like I could hide away in bed with you forever because it would be the best day, doing nothing but getting lost in how you make me feel. But then I think about everything else in our lives and how I want to know whatever is going on with you and how excited I am to tell you what's going on with me. And I just want to *be there* for you. To love and support you unconditionally. I loved what you said about marriage. About wanting to be part of a team. It's exactly how I feel when I'm with you. Like we're a team, and there's nothing that can stop us."

Sydney felt tears prickling behind her own eyes as she saw Reese's go glassy, too. She couldn't stop herself now. She didn't want to. "You changed my life this summer. You were willing to go along with my crazy idea, but you also kept me so grounded. You gave me the space to feel and learn and grow. You gave me the space to *love*. How could that love not be directed at the person who inspired all the other good things in me, too?"

"Sydney," Reese said, her voice choked with emotion, tears falling freely down her face. She brought her other hand up, holding Sydney like she was something precious, something to be treasured.

Sydney nuzzled her cheek into Reese's hand, her eyes fluttering closed when she said, "You changed my life, Reese. You're the reason for all the good things I have now, but you're the best thing, by far."

She immediately missed the warmth from Reese's hands, and her eyes sprang open to see where she was going. And that was a sight to behold, as Reese moved to stand between Sydney's legs before lowering herself to the ground. On her knees, she looked up at Sydney, her eyes filled with so much love that Sydney felt it pouring out of her and touching her as clearly as if Reese's hand had still been on her cheek.

"Lie back, Sydney," Reese said, full of conviction as she edged Sydney's legs apart to fit herself between her thighs.

The steady thrum of arousal that she always felt when Reese was close roared to life, and her muscles clenched instinctively as she lay back against the comforter.

She could already feel heat and wetness pooling in her center, and it only intensified when Reese scratched lightly up and down the tops of her thighs. Her hips jerked when nimble fingers came close to the edge of her underwear, but they moved away again, leaving fire in their wake.

"I say I love you, and you torture me," Sydney pushed out

between uneven breaths. Her clit ached to be touched, and when she pictured Reese's perfect mouth wrapping around it, she let out a harsh groan that cut against the silence.

"I promise it will be worth it." As Reese said those words, Sydney looked down to catch her stare, determined eyes looking at Sydney hungrily.

Sydney was a goner, and all she could do was lie back against the bed and let Reese do with her what she wanted.

When Reese hooked her fingers into Sydney's waistband and started pulling, she lifted her ass off the bed to make the process as smooth as possible, the air cold on her newly naked skin.

"You look so good," Reese said at the same time Sydney felt palms that sparked electricity through her, this time anchoring against Sydney's waist. "I've missed you. Tasting you. Kissing you. Making you come."

And then Sydney forgot how to breathe as Reese leaned forward to place light open-mouthed kisses along the inside of her thigh. She felt the touch through her whole body and wondered how much more she could take.

But it seemed like Reese was only getting started.

She hooked Sydney's leg, lifting it gracefully over her shoulder, allowing Sydney's hips to shift wider. And it was that feeling, of being so open and ready, that ratcheted up her desire. Her center was dripping, and she knew that Reese could see how much she wanted it.

How much she needed it. Needed Reese.

"You're so fucking gorgeous," Reese said, her own voice hoarse. She ran a finger along Sydney's slit. It wasn't nearly enough pressure, but Sydney jumped at the touch anyway.

"Baby," Sydney whined, her hips jutting upward, looking for any friction.

"I'm the only one who gets to touch you like this. Who gets to make you feel like this." The words came out against Sydney's thigh; Reese said them while peppering little bites against her skin.

She was going to explode. That's the only way this could go. Reese had never been possessive before, and Sydney loved it. She loved it so fucking much, and she knew that her wetness must have made it down to where Reese was kissing by now, coating her lips and tongue.

"You taste so good," Reese said, confirming Sydney's suspicion, her lips trailing closer and closer to where Sydney desperately needed them to be.

All she could do was ball her fists against the mattress, trying to hang on for dear life.

She let out something between a moan and a cry when Reese finally closed her lips around Sydney's clit. Reese sucked the aching nub between her lips, flicking it gently with her tongue.

Sydney arched off the bed, and her hands moved reflexively up to wrap her fingers in Reese's hair, holding on for dear life.

"Baby," she chanted as Reese found her rhythm, licking and sucking and threatening to explode Sydney's body into a million pieces with her tongue. The pressure mounted. She ground her hips to match the tempo Reese's tongue worked at, her breath harsh and wanton.

She couldn't describe the sound that she made when Reese slid two fingers inside, entering with ease. She was soaked, and she barely managed to say, "More," before Reese was sliding in a third.

Reese pumped methodically, her tongue never relenting against Sydney's clit.

And all Sydney could do was take it, her fingers digging into Reese's scalp, her hips jerking unevenly as Reese began to fuck her harder.

Her thighs ached, shaking with each thrust, each roll of Reese's tongue against her.

"I love you, Sydney."

And with that, the wave building inside of Sydney crested. She came, knowing that she was soaking Reese in her desire.

But Reese wasn't done, and she lapped at everything Sydney

gave her. She kept pumping. Kept sucking. She continued working Sydney, pulling every ounce of need out of her, thoroughly fucking her to the point that Sydney saw stars behind her eyes. Desire began to mingle with pain, her clit swollen and sensitive.

"Come here," Sydney growled, unable to stand the idea of not touching Reese, too. She slid her leg off of Reese. Her hands could just reach Reese's shoulders, and she pulled her upward.

Reese relented, her chest rising and falling heavily as she followed the guidance of Sydney's hands until they were both on the bed, their legs dangling off the edge.

Sydney could see the wetness coating Reese's lips, and she pulled her into a hungry kiss, tasting herself on Reese's mouth.

"I need you," Sydney said, her hands already unbuttoning Reese's pants. A sense of urgency propelled her forward, and nothing was going to stop her from getting lost in her girlfriend, in making her feel the same exhaustion and release that she'd just given Sydney.

Reese already looked as debauched as Sydney probably did, and she hadn't even come yet. Her hair was mussed, her eyes lidded, her lips pouty and still wet.

It made Sydney ache all over again, but she had more important things to think about.

Namely, making Reese scream her name until her voice was hoarse with it.

Reese whimpered when Sydney found her clit. Her entrance was dripping, and Sydney's fingers tried to find purchase amidst the wetness.

She rolled deftly, bracketing Reese between her legs, pinning her down on the bed.

"Yes," Reese moaned into the room as Sydney was able to find the right angle, slipping fingers inside and beginning to work into Reese.

Sydney leaned down and kissed Reese, their tongues dancing

as her fingers were enveloped in heat. It felt so fucking good. She wanted to do this forever.

"You feel so good. So fucking wet. Is this for me?" Sydney questioned. She started rubbing harder against Reese's clit, focused circles against the tight bud.

Reese's hips jerked upward, and she cried out, Sydney swallowing her moan with a kiss. Sydney met her arching, thrust for thrust, her hand in between them unrelenting.

It happened quickly, then, as Reese cried out into her mouth.

Her legs were shaking, hips jerking uncontrollably as Sydney worked her through her orgasm. "You're so good, baby. So good," Sydney whispered. She slowed her fingers down, softening her touch before sliding her fingers out completely.

Reese was breathing heavily, her stomach muscles clenching as little aftershocks worked their way through her body.

"Come up here." Sydney rolled off of Reese and moved up the bed, patting the place next to her.

There was no hesitation, and Reese quickly shifted into what had become Sydney's favorite position, with her head resting on her chest.

They lay quietly together, until their breathing returned to normal. Sydney ran her hands down Reese's arms, giving her soft kisses on top of her head.

"So maybe there really is a difference between sex and making love," Reese teased, scooting impossibly closer against Sydney's chest.

Sydney glanced at the clock on the nightside table. She had about two more hours before she needed to be up, and after that orgasm, sleep was threatening to overtake her quickly.

Still fully clothed, she could already note the change in Reese's breathing. She'd fallen asleep, and Sydney looked at her before placing another kiss, this time against her temple. "Whatever that was, I can't wait to do it again."

Twenty-Two

"ARE WE CRAZY FOR ATTENDING THIS?" Sydney asked as they made their way down the sidewalk to the Boston restaurant where Grant and Brynn's rehearsal dinner was being held.

Reese put her hand on Sydney's back as they maneuvered around a few tourists. "Tomorrow's going to be even weirder, so this is probably good to get us primed for dealing with it."

"I can't believe Brynn's going through with it," Sydney lamented as they reached the door, almost like she was personally disappointed that a twenty-six-year-old that she barely knew was making a poor decision.

Reese resisted telling Sydney that that exact feeling was a big part of what her thirties would involve.

"The good news is that she can always divorce him. It's not like she's saddled with his kid or something," Reese pointed out, Sydney holding the door for her to head inside.

Sydney groaned and followed her in. "Ugh, yeah. I hope that doesn't happen."

When they entered the restaurant, Reese stopped and turned to Sydney. "Though they would be Reese Jr. and Sydney Jr.'s cousin. Which would be nice for the kiddos," she teased, already expecting the look of judgment on her beautiful girlfriend's face.

She loved the indignant huff that Sydney let out. "You know that I am all about a feminine junior. And that I'm ecstatic that you're seriously considering kids at some point in the future."

"Then what's the problem?" Reese pushed. She loved riling Sydney up.

Sydney lowered her voice as a couple passed by them, very possibly heading to the same place they were going. "The problem is that I don't know that the world is ready for Grant Devereux V. He'd probably end up running for president and kicking off the downfall of the world as we know it."

"You make a compelling argument," Reese said before kissing Sydney squarely on the lips, loving the little zing it sent through her body.

"Ready to head in there?" Sydney asked, like she was readying herself for battle.

Though Reese had no idea what the vibe of tonight was going to be, she was on high alert, too. Her mother and father would be in the same room, a divorce looming between them. Tripp's likely negative feelings toward Stan for putting a pause on their business deal would be on full display. And then there was Grant, on the literal eve of his wedding, exactly one week after falling at Sydney's feet and begging for her to take him back.

She blanched. That one still made her a little sick to her stomach.

There was a private room in the back for the party, but Reese pulled Sydney aside, into an alcove that held the coat check during colder months.

Reese interlaced their hands and stepped back from Sydney, eyeing her from head to toe. "You look so beautiful. Have I told you that yet?"

The fact that she had Sydney on her arm as her date, as her *girlfriend*—for real—was what truly mattered.

Everything else was just background noise that they'd filter through as needed.

Sydney was dressed in a black, form-fitting dress that had little shapes cut out around the sides. Her long, lean muscles were on display, already making Reese a little crazy whenever she caught sight of them.

"You've only told me about a dozen times so far." Sydney counted off on her fingers. "When you saw me try it on at home. While I was getting ready. On the drive. When you had it hiked up around my waist before we left."

Heat rolled through Reese, remembering how only a few hours ago, she'd pinned Sydney against the bedroom wall and fucked her right there, needing to watch her come in a dress that her girlfriend had no business looking that good in.

They'd come back from the US Open on Monday, and since then, Reese's desire had been almost uncontrollable.

In the office at the inn. In the car when they'd been taking a drive. In the shower. In the pool again. Against the wall. She couldn't get enough.

Sydney had unlocked something inside of her, and it took all the resolve she had not to pull her into the empty coatroom and pick things up again.

"And what about you?" Sydney asked, taking her own leisurely journey up Reese's body until their eyes met. Heat bloomed on Reese's cheeks with the intensity of Sydney's stare.

Reese had opted for high-waisted pants and a fitted dress shirt that hugged her frame, much like the first event they'd attended together this summer.

It felt right, as things came full circle.

Tomorrow, the wedding would be over, and she could officially cut Grant out of her life. Her father, too.

Hand in hand, they walked back to the private room, large enough to hold well over a hundred guests.

"I didn't even think about having to sit with the wedding party," Reese said, leaning toward Sydney. She loved the visible shiver that worked through Sydney's body, her lips brushing softly against the shell of her ear.

"Let's get a drink before sitting down." Sydney led her over to the bar, a faint tinge on her cheeks.

Once they each had a drink in hand, they scoured the room to find Reese's mom. She was over near the center table, likely where they'd all be sitting. With Reese in the wedding party and as the sister of the groom, she doubted that Grant could find a passable reason they should be exiled to one of the far tables.

But wouldn't it have been nice.

They meandered around the throngs of people. It looked like most of the guests were already there, and Reese didn't recognize the majority of them. She knew from her mom that the Fitzpatricks had kept their invite side small, opting for close friends and family. Tripp, however, had probably invited everyone who had ever been in his Rolodex.

When they reached her mom, it was Sydney who spoke first. "Sharon, you look incredible," she said, letting out a low whistle.

It didn't bother Reese, mostly, but Sydney clocked the look immediately and flashed her a winsome smile.

"She looks gorgeous. It's just a statement of fact. And she brought you into this world, so I'd like to give credit where credit is due," Sydney said, wrapping her arm around Reese and pulling her close. Reese melted into her immediately.

Really, her mom did look incredible. She wore a knee-length red dress; her hair—the same color as Reese's but a little shorter—was perfectly styled and made her look downright youthful.

Reese leaned forward and kissed her cheek. "You do look beautiful, Mom."

Her mom leaned conspiratorially close, her eyes playful. "It's amazing how light dropping a couple hundred pounds of dead weight can make you feel."

"I'll cheers to that," Sydney said, lifting her glass to toast.

"Where's the happy couple?" Reese asked, and now, it was Sydney who shot her a side-eye as she tried to hold back a grimace.

Her mom and Sydney seemed to be on the same wavelength, a similar stare to the one Sydney had given her crossing her mom's features. "Reese," her mom chided, though it did nothing to deter her.

She wasn't going to put Sydney's private business on blast, nor would she do anything to stop the train of marital woe from barrelling toward the cliff, but this whole wedding was a farce.

The most adult promise she'd made herself was that she wasn't going to punch Grant in the face when she saw him.

He was welcome for that wedding gift.

Waiters began to mill around the room. The guests who hadn't sat down yet were finding their tables, and the time for Reese's petty banter was over.

"Let's take our seats," her mom said, ushering Reese into the spot next to her, Sydney on the other side of Reese.

Stan, Margie, and Brynn appeared at their table, and they sat down next to Sydney in that order.

"Great to see you," Stan called to Reese and Sydney, his voice booming in the still-chattery room.

Her father would be seated next to her mother, unless he wanted to stop the couple of honor from being seated together.

Honestly, Reese didn't know how that would go until it happened.

She did find out momentarily, though, as a glowering Grant and an even angrier-looking Tripp sat down in their assigned chairs.

Sydney leaned toward her, and Reese was grateful to have a reprieve from the awkwardness that permeated the table. "You aren't giving a speech, right?"

Reese quickly stifled her laughter by bringing her napkin to her face and pretending to cough. When she'd gotten herself under control, she turned back toward Sydney, whose hand had found its way to the top of her thigh. "You would have heard about that."

Waiters walked purposely around the tables in a well-timed

pattern, and salads were deposited so quickly it was like they'd materialized in front of each place setting.

After everyone had been served, the salads provided a nice distraction from the tension. Reese was seated at, by far, the quietest table. She glanced around the room, confirming her suspicions. The other guests seemed to be having a great time, so at least the insane amount of money that had gone into hosting the rehearsal dinner was well spent.

About ten minutes into the first course, a woman walked up to the table with a portable microphone and leaned down toward her father. She handed him the microphone, which explained who exactly had paid the insane amount of money in question.

"I'd like to give my speech soon, if that's okay," a voice to Tripp's left piped up. "I'm not the best public speaker, and waiting will only make me more nervous."

Almost all eyes at their table turned toward Brynn, varying degrees of curiosity on their faces. Grant shot a furtive look at Sydney, which Reese noticed that her girlfriend missed. Sydney, like the others, was staring at Brynn, her mouth open in surprise.

Reese's father was holding the microphone awkwardly, but he almost seemed relieved that he didn't have to kick off the speeches.

It was Stan then, who broke the silence. "I think that's a wonderful idea, Brynn. I'll start you off?" he asked, already standing up from his chair.

With the microphone secured in his beefy hands, making it almost look like a toy, he did the obligatory *tap tap tap*, and asked, "Is this thing on?"

"For what I paid, it better fucking be on," Reese heard her father mutter from where he was seated before downing the rest of his drink.

Sydney had caught it, too, and they shared a look, Reese wondering if she needed to brace for an impending storm.

The crowd quieted as a hundred pairs of eyes turned their

attention to the hulking man who had love in his heart and a tiny microphone in his hands.

"I'm Stan Fitzpatrick, the father of the bride. I'm going to wait to give any sort of speech, given that I'm likely to end up in tears and it'll really ruin the mood." There was a smattering of laughter, and Stan smiled good-naturedly.

Truly, Reese couldn't have liked this man more if she tried.

"I'd like to introduce my daughter, Brynn, who is the light of my and her mother's lives. Please give her your attention."

Brynn stood, more purposefully than Reese would have expected, accepting the microphone from Stan and giving him a kiss on the cheek.

"Hi, everyone." Brynn waved, which the crowd returned with varying degrees of enthusiasm.

"I don't know if I can sit through this," Reese said as she considered fully what was about to happen.

Sydney squeezed her leg as she quietly said, "It'll be okay," her voice only slightly managing to quell Reese's rising nerves.

The music had been turned off, and the room was silent except for the clanking of silverware on plates. A light shone directly on Brynn, who had moved over to stand next to a large wall.

Slowly, a projector screen descended from the ceiling. When it stopped, an image appeared in surprisingly high resolution. It was a photo of Grant and Brynn, arms wrapped around one another and smiling broadly at the camera. Another photo flashed by, of Grant and Brynn aboard a sailboat, Grant at the helm with Brynn helping Stan to raise the sail.

This was a nightmare. Brynn was going to make a fool of herself, waxing poetic about love and honor and supporting one another, all while Reese knew her brother's true colors. Her only consolation was that there were few people in the room privy to the information that she knew, and she hoped it stayed that way for Brynn's sake.

Could Reese die, though, of secondhand embarrassment?

Her skin was hot and itchy, and she wondered briefly if she was having some kind of allergic reaction. She looked down, expecting to see her skin mottled with hives, but she was presented with nothing more than a faint redness that looked far better than it felt.

The photos continued to play on a slow carousel when Brynn finally spoke. "Some of you may not know this, but earlier this year, I graduated with my PhD in modern analytic philosophy."

Stan was already out of his chair, clapping wildly. "Yeah, you did," he yelled toward her. "We're so proud of you, honey!"

That earned another laugh from the crowd, which Stan tried to calm by shushing them as he returned to his seat.

"Thanks, Dad." Brynn smiled broadly before continuing. "So what most people may not know about my area of study is that it's deeply focused on logic, which I can honestly say went completely out the window when Grant swept me off my feet."

Brynn flashed another affable smile, which earned her a few coos from the crowd.

Oh no. Was Reese going to vomit? She felt the bile rising in her throat, wondering if she should stand up and object to the wedding.

"You don't put an objection out during the rehearsal dinner," Sydney said in a low, fast rush of words that made Reese realize that she'd said, "I object," out loud, under her breath.

"I'd say there's never a good time to cause a scene, but better now than at the wedding itself," Reese responded through gritted teeth.

Reese moved to stand up, but Sydney held tight to her thigh. "Whatever happens, this is Brynn's life to live."

Still agitated but no longer struggling against Sydney's undeniably strong hand—she was really putting all those years of tennis to good use in this moment—Reese remained seated. Begrudgingly.

"But this summer," Brynn continued, "as my wedding loomed on the horizon and I planned for the happiest day of my life, I realized that I missed studying. Missed the research that goes into understanding something."

She took a step forward, closer to Grant, who was still about ten feet away. "So I decided to understand my future husband so that we could both have the best life possible."

Reese looked over at Sydney, who had a bit of a deer-in-the-headlights look in her eyes, and she wondered if Sydney was starting to come around to her way of thinking.

Painful didn't even begin to describe the feeling Reese experienced as Brynn looked at Grant with a moony gaze, and Grant gave her a tight-lipped smile in return, clearly not a part of the planning of his fiancée's speech.

"The basics." Brynn clicked something invisible to the guests, and a new photo slotted onto the screen. It was a photo of Grant on the golf course, hand covering his eyes post-swing as he watched his ball. "Are pretty simple. Grant. Age twenty-nine. Hobbies include golfing, sailing, and watching his beloved Red Sox."

That earned a loud cheer, as if that was a surprising revelation in the Boston area.

"But I wanted to know more."

Another picture flashed across the screen, this time a text message thread. "The great thing about Grant is that he's always predictable, especially in using the same password for everything, including his Tinder profile."

A deafening silence fell over the crowd before nervous murmurs broke out at various tables.

And Reese. Was. Riveted.

Sydney's hand was gripping into her thigh like it was a claw, but Reese couldn't feel the pain over the exhilaration of whatever was coming next.

"Grant would tell you—at least he tells the women he chats with and meets up with for casual sex—that he's a good guy." Brynn rolled her eyes exaggeratedly then, like a little kid doing a bit for attention.

Well, she had everyone's attention now.

Reese hadn't breathed in about the last minute, and when air rushed into her lungs unexpectedly, her eyes started to water. Sydney looked at her with concern, but Reese waved her away. The only way she was leaving right now was in a body bag.

"According to his profile, which mentions all the things I've already shared, he also goes on to say in his messages that he works a demanding job at the family company, which his father is running into the ground through a variety of poor decisions. And that if he were in charge, which he will be one day, they'd be the industry leader."

Reese looked over at her father, who'd gone from a deep red to a dangerous shade of fuschia that made Reese wonder if medical intervention was required.

"This approach appeals to women differently, but it includes a 40-percent success rate at earning him sympathy, as they think he's trying to help his family legacy endure."

Stan's large hands, which had so gently cradled the microphone only minutes ago, were now balled into dangerous fists that looked like they could smash rocks.

And Grant was... well, it was hard to describe what he looked like except that he looked like he was about to shit his pants. He pulled at his tie like it was choking him.

Brynn looked like she was having the time of her life, having pulled out a handheld laser pointer from somewhere, flashing the parts of the screen where she wanted guests to focus.

On the next slide, various bar charts broke down Grant's success with women on the app.

"I wanted to keep it simple, so I only used a sample size from this year, though he's had a profile since the age of twenty-two. Our boy was busy," Brynn added with an airy laugh before continuing on to say, "Within this year, he's matched with sixty-five women. Messaged forty-three of them. Gone on dates with a lucky dozen and, for the big reveal, and what we've all been waiting for..."

Brynn paused for effect, and it worked.

The whole room was absolutely silent until Reese's dad stood up and bellowed, "You stop this right now. I will not have you embarrassing my family at a party that we paid, for no less."

Of course. Because those would be Tripp Devereux's two biggest problems with what was playing out before them.

Not that Grant was an absolute coward of a human being or a serial philanderer, but that Brynn had had the audacity to bring it into the light.

Reese was positively gleeful, and as she chanced a glance at Sydney, she found they wore the same expression, shock mingled with awe at what Brynn was doing.

It was poetic, how Brynn turned toward Tripp and lifted the microphone back to her lips. "I'd like to be clear to all the guests here—and especially to the rest of the Devereux family—that I'm only embarrassing Grant. And you."

Tripp took a menacing step toward Brynn, and Stan moved far more deftly than she'd expected a man of his size could. He looked her dad dead in the eye. "Sit down, Tripp. You will let her speak, and you will not say another word about it."

"I'm not staying to listen to this," her father said with the strength of a newborn baby in the face of Stan's ire, and Reese thought she heard his voice crack. She didn't have much time to question it because, within seconds, he'd fled out the door and into another part of the restaurant.

"I thought this part might be a showstopper," Brynn said, glee radiating from her tone. "So anyway." She flashed the last slide onto the screen, which was blank. Slowly, she walked over to where Grant still sat, and she placed her hand on his shoulder. "The big reveal isn't how many women Grant's slept with this year because all you need to know is that it's more than one. But the great news, ladies, is that he's back on the market, and what a catch he is."

That was apparently Grant's last straw, as he stood up quickly and followed the escape route his father had also taken.

"With my presentation concluded, I anticipate there won't be any other speeches tonight, but the bar is open and the main course will be coming soon. I'd encourage everyone to stick around and have some fun on Tripp Devereux's dime, and if it wasn't clear already, there's no need to show up for the wedding tomorrow."

And with that, Brynn literally dropped her microphone on the ground and sat back down at the table.

"Holy shit," Reese said, unable to keep the words inside any longer. She'd gone through every emotion possible in the last seven minutes, and she now felt both wrung out and exhilarated, wondering what would happen next.

"I cannot believe you just did that," Sydney said from beside her, both of them clearly still processing what had just played out.

Brynn shrugged. "He shouldn't have lied to me. All I did was tell the truth."

"Understatement of the century." And when they locked stares across the table, for the first time, Reese was desperately curious to know what her almost sister-in-law would do next.

* * *

Sydney walked a half step ahead and pulled Reese along, Sydney slightly tipsy as she galavanted down the sidewalk. They'd decided to take a walk around the city, the early fall evening a little balmy but still refreshing.

"I cannot believe it," Sydney repeated, astonished.

Reese, too, was struggling to accept that the events of only a few hours ago were real. "Brynn went scorched earth."

Suddenly, Sydney stopped, her eyes going wide as she was clearly realizing something. "Didn't I tell you! Didn't I tell you that it was the quiet ones that you have to worry about!" And then, she did the most adorable little dance that made Reese want to throw out her arms and steady Sydney, given that she was wearing heels on cobblestone.

But her girlfriend was completely unaware, and Reese took a moment to enjoy the view. The way Sydney smiled, light and free and like she didn't have a care in the world.

Reese walked faster to match Sydney's stride, and they fell into step together.

They'd wandered over to a more residential neighborhood, beautiful brownstones stacked next to one another, but Reese missed the smell of the ocean, the sound of the waves crashing on the shore. It was hard to believe that she'd spent most of her adult life living in cities. Now, she felt more at home than anywhere else when she walked out onto the ground-floor patio of Sydney's room, starting her morning with the sun rising above the clouds and glittering across the expanse of water.

She sighed deeply, inhaling the warm air.

Sydney looked over at her, a curious look on her face. "A penny for your thoughts?"

"I was just thinking about how much I love Stoneport," she admitted as they continued walking.

"I feel the same way." Sydney had mentioned earlier this week that her parents were putting their house in Florida on the market. For Reese, that was amazing news, given that at least now, Sydney's time would only be split between two places.

Or two lifestyles, more accurately. One, where they got lost in small-town revelry defined by lazy mornings and everyone knowing their business. The other, where Sydney was jet-setting around the world, her star continuing to rise.

Reese hoped what they had together would be enough. That Sydney would look forward to coming back to Stoneport instead of resenting it. That the life that Reese had to offer her would continue to feel like enough.

And with that, she let out another quiet breath, steeling her resolve for whatever came next. "Have you given any thought to the contract?"

The official offer from The Tennis Network had come through this morning, by way of Sydney's agent, and as far as

Reese could tell, Sydney hadn't seriously looked at it. Then again, she had gone to MTC earlier to hit around with Brian, so it could be that she was running the offer by him.

Reese didn't want to be too pushy, but the reality was, she was dying to know.

Sydney kept walking, but her pace slowed down as they rounded a corner and headed back in the direction of where Reese's car was parked.

"I don't want my decision to change things between us," Sydney said quietly, their steps slowing to a crawl.

They stopped in front of a quaint rowhouse with the lights still on, some type of party going on inside.

"It won't. I promise," Reese responded, hoping she could live up to her words.

"I'm not taking the offer."

It's okay; we can do this, Reese was already telling herself as Sydney spoke, hoping to protect her heart.

But... what?

She met Sydney's stare then. Sydney's eyes were wide and unblinking, her lower lip pulled between her teeth. "I hope that's okay. That it doesn't have to change things between us. I certainly don't want it to."

Reese was trying to catch up at the same time that her heart was hammering in her chest, but she was struggling to make sense of things. "In what world would this change things between us?"

"You seemed like you really wanted me to consider the job. And I did, honestly, but it's not what I want. I want to be in Stoneport, and well, Brian's offered me a job at MTC, which will give me a much better schedule and work-life balance. Plus, I'd get to coach, which is something I've realized I love over the past couple of—"

Reese threw her arms around Sydney, her girlfriend absorbing the weight with surprising grace, holding on to her tight as they only took a small step back.

Of all the wrong things that Sydney could think!

Reese let out something between a groan and a laugh, and she felt like a million pounds of weight had lifted off of her chest. "I wanted to make sure you didn't feel held back, but I've always wanted you here. I needed it to be your decision, not mine." She pulled back so that she could put her hand on Sydney's cheek, cupping it gently. "The only changes that will come from this are good ones."

"Yeah?" Sydney asked, a smile starting to overtake her face that made Reese's heart stutter-stop.

Reese nodded. "I hated the idea of heading back to my house alone every night, missing you. Wondering what you're off in the world doing. Whether you were thinking about me too."

"Your house?" Sydney asked, lifting a curious eyebrow.

"Well... I'm not going to stay at the inn, considering I won't be managing it anymore. I don't think that really screams 'executive oversight' to Hallie if I'm in her space all the time. I was thinking of renting a little house on the coast, somewhere close by but that I could see myself staying for a little while."

Sydney nodded along, picking up when Reese stopped talking. "So I guess I'll live with my parents again..." She looked at Reese with the biggest, most innocent eyes, knowing exactly what she was doing.

Which meant that there was nothing for Reese to do but hold up her heart, mock offense written across her features. "Sydney King. Are you angling for an offer to move in? Out of wedlock and everything!"

Sydney shook her head. "No, I was angling for us to both move in with my parents. It's more dignified that way."

They laughed at the same time, and Reese pushed Sydney lightly, which didn't work as intended when Sydney pulled Reese against her chest, holding her close.

"You're mean. Toying with my emotions like this," Reese said, her breath ghosting across Sydney's exposed clavicle.

Reese didn't know if she'd ever been this happy, her future

unfolding in front of her like it had been meant to happen this way all along.

"I figure it's too soon to ask you to marry me, so I'll settle for us living together. At your place," Sydney amended, and Reese could feel the way Sydney's heartbeat picked up as she said the words. "I love you, Reese, and I don't need to go chasing something because everything I want is right here. I don't want to wait to start living the life that I already know that I want. With you."

When they finally pulled apart on the sidewalk, Reese feeling a little unsteady on her feet from the giddiness coursing through her, she realized that she had to amend her thinking already, thirty seconds later, because this was the happiest she'd ever been.

And she figured there would be a lot of happiest moments in her life overtaking one another in rapid succession, especially if Sydney was involved.

Epilogue

Three years later

SYDNEY, with a significant amount of effort, propped her feet up on the coffee table in front of the sofa. "I feel like a beached whale."

"You're beautiful," Reese batted back immediately, scooting in closer and trying to wrap her arm around Sydney.

Reese had just gotten home from meetings in Boston with Stan, and Sydney's parents had left about an hour ago after spending the day setting up the nursery—at their insistence.

"I want to hold *you*." Tears were already welling in Sydney's eyes for some unknown reason. There'd been a lot of that these days.

Maybe it was because she'd just thought about the nursery, decked out in shades of green with beautiful plants painted all over the wall, her dad's excited contribution to their future children's upbringing.

"Okay, baby. I'd like that." Humoring her, Reese inched under Sydney's arm, working to fit herself in between the back of the sofa and Sydney's stomach, which in the last few weeks had popped to a laughable size.

"Twins," Sydney said in a slightly disbelieving tone, like she'd done more times than she could remember in the last eight months.

Reese snuggled in closer and kissed the top of Sydney's belly. "Serena and Venus can hear you, you know."

Sydney would have laughed, but it was quite possible that she'd never get back into this exact position, and she was feeling more comfortable than she had all day. Showing Reese around the nursery had worn her out like she'd just run a marathon. "We really need to stop using those placeholder names or else they're going to stick. I cannot have our future children, who may or may not take an interest in tennis, being named after two of the greatest players who ever lived."

"May or may not?" Reese said dubiously. "I saw those tiny tennis rackets in their bedroom closet."

Sydney should have known that nothing would get by her wife. "The rackets were too cute not to buy, but I promise I'll do everything I can to let them follow their own paths." She sniffled.

More tears. Again!

It was just that, when Sydney thought about her life, about Reese and their twin daughters, who would likely be coming any day now, she felt overwhelmed. With love. With anxiety. With excitement.

Reese managed to give Sydney another kiss, this time on the bottom of her jaw, which was the only place that her wife could reasonably reach given the position she was wedged in. "I know you will."

The last three years of Sydney's life had felt like they'd gone by at blink-and-miss-it speed. Sydney had proposed six months into their official relationship, but she'd never been more certain of anything in her life. She hadn't wanted to wait to start living the life she wanted with Reese.

And once they'd been engaged, there was really no reason in

Sydney's mind to wait to get married. Even though Reese's new venture, The Stoneport Group, had been taking off. And they'd been considering buying a home.

Nothing was going to stop Sydney from making Reese her wife, to solidify her intentions of making Reese the happiest woman in the world.

Sydney had rented out all the rooms at The Stone's Throw, and they'd had a small, private ceremony that was exactly the right balance of raucously fun and intimately charming. Hallie had seen to that.

It was like, once Sydney had stopped pushing so hard to control her life, the pieces had all fallen into place better than she could have dreamt.

Which was how she found herself in this moment, snuggled up with her wife in a home they'd purchased together two years ago. They'd spent the first year of their marriage wrapped up in one another. In spite of that, they made time for Sydney's career as a trainer at MTC, and Reese, in partnership with Stan, had launched The Stoneport Group. Their expansion had happened about eighteen months ago, when Reese and Stan had purchased about half of the properties that became available when The Devereux Group folded.

Sydney wasn't going to lie, that had felt good. *Really* good.

So a year ago, when Reese had come to Sydney and told her that she was ready, seriously ready, for them to start a family, Sydney had started crying tears of happiness.

And when she'd gotten pregnant four months later, it seemed like she hadn't stopped crying since, constantly awash with emotions and endorphins for three now coursing through her.

"I just love you so much," Reese said, burying her face in Sydney's side. "You make me so happy. And I know that you'll make our daughters so happy, too."

"We can never tell them how we really got together," Sydney mused as she wiped her face. "I need them to think of us as infallibly honest."

"You mean how we helped one another through a difficult time and ended up finding true love?" Reese challenged her as she rubbed Sydney's stomach.

"I just don't want them to think it's okay to lie. Even for the right reason." Sydney had started thinking about all kinds of things lately. How she and Reese had met. The place Sydney had been in emotionally and the circumstances that led to she and Reese finding their way to one another.

She could feel Reese scooting around, working to prop herself up. When she was finally level with Sydney's face, she felt the soft, warm touch of Reese's fingers on her jaw. Reese traced soothing patterns against her skin before she leaned forward and pressed a kiss against Sydney's lips. "Honey, I promise you, we can cross that bridge when we get there. But the most important thing for me is that, regardless of how we ended up here, there's nothing about our love that's a lie."

The End.

About the Author

Monica McCallan was an enthusiastic fan of romance novels long before she began writing them. She currently lives in Massachusetts with her incredible wife and their dog.

A Quick Note

Thank you for reading The Love Lie!

As an independently published author, reviews on Amazon or Goodreads are greatly appreciated.

If you'd like to stay up-to-date on what I'm working on, you can find me on Instagram @monicamccallan

Made in the USA
Middletown, DE
11 February 2025

71114250R00230